Peter Tonkin was born in Northern Ireland, the eldest son of a Forces family, and was raised in the UK, Holland, Germany and the Persian Gulf. He is married and is the Head of English and Director of Post-16 Provision at the Wilderness School in Sevenoaks. He has written six previous novels, including four Richard Mariner adventures.

Praise for Peter Tonkin and his adventure-thrillers, THE COFFIN SHIP, THE FIRE SHIP, THE LEPER SHIP and THE BOMB SHIP (all available from Headline):

'A master of sea-going adventure. Enough taut suspense to satisfy any reader' Clive Cussler

'Good technical detail, plus an exciting climax, makes this entertaining reading' *Publishing News*

'Edge-of-the-seat terror on the high seas' *Daily Post*

'In the rattling good yarn mould, this story . . . never flags and has the virtue of being well written' *Yorkshire Evening Post*

'Riveting and action-packed adventure set in international locations' *Newcastle Evening Chronicle*

'A rattling good seafaring saga' *Bolton Evening News*

'Sea trip of super suspense' *Oxford Mail*

Also by Peter Tonkin

The Bomb Ship
The Leper Ship
The Fire Ship
The Coffin Ship
The Journal of Edwin Underhill
Killer

The Iceberg

Peter Tonkin

Copyright © 1994 Peter Tonkin

The right of Peter Tonkin to be identified as the Author of
the Work has been asserted by him in accordance with the
Copyright, Designs and Patents Act 1988.

First published in 1994
by HEADLINE BOOK PUBLISHING

First published in paperback in 1995
by HEADLINE BOOK PUBLISHING

A HEADLINE FEATURE paperback

10 9 8 7 6 5 4 3 2

All rights reserved. No part of this publication may be
reproduced, stored in a retrieval system, or transmitted,
in any form or by any means without the prior written
permission of the publisher, nor be otherwise circulated
in any form of binding or cover other than that in which
it is published and without a similar condition being
imposed on the subsequent purchaser.

All characters in this publication are fictitious
and any resemblance to real persons, living or dead,
is purely coincidental.

ISBN 0 7472 4638 6

Printed and bound in Great Britain by
Cox & Wyman Ltd, Reading, Berks

HEADLINE BOOK PUBLISHING
A division of Hodder Headline PLC
338 Euston Road
London NW1 3BH

For Cham, Guy and Mark
And in memory of Debbie Curran

ICEBERG: 'A detached portion of an Arctic glacier carried out to sea; a huge floating mass of ice, often rising to a great height above the water.'

First used 1820. *Oxford English Dictionary*

With sloping masts and dipping prow,
As who pursued with yell and blow
Still treads the shadow of his foe,
And forward bends his head,
The ship drove fast, loud roared the blast,
And southward aye we fled.

And now there came both mist and snow,
And it grew wondrous cold:
And ice, mast high, came floating by,
As green as emerald.

S. T. Coleridge, *The Rime of the Ancient Mariner*

PROLOGUE

Meltdown

CHERNOBYL, 1986

'On 3 and 4 May, the temperature reached its highest level yet: over 2,000° C . . . On 5 May [this caused] a second peak [of radioactive emissions] of over 8 MCi. On 6 May the emissions suddenly dropped . . . It may never be known what caused the sudden decline of emissions and temperature . . .' Viktor Haynes and Marko Bojkun, *The Chernobyl Disaster*, London 1988, pp. 22–3.

Chapter One

Major Bohdan Valentinov slid out of the sluice and into the bubbler pool beneath reactor Number Four, screaming at the top of his lungs. Only the pain in his throat made him aware of the fact; the roaring of the fire above him was so loud it drowned the sound he was making, even though the bellows of terror echoed in the mouthpiece and headpiece of his black rubber diving suit. The water he plunged down into appeared to be boiling fiercely and some atavistic part of his mind howled uncontrollably in expectation of an agonising death although his well-trained intelligence insisted he had nothing immediate to fear. Nothing much from the water, at any rate; relatively speaking. The liquid was, in spite of appearances, cold, and the feeling of it was quite welcome against his nerve-heated skin as it filtered through the wet suit he was wearing. This fact was noted only distantly, however, and then placed with the overwhelming sound in the back of his mind. The moment he found his footing and regained his nerve, Valentinov was in action.

The water came up to his barrel chest and the bubbles exploded fiercely in his armpits as he fought to stay erect and look around. Yevgeny Popov would be here with the first of the equipment soon and Valentinov had to have decided on the best place to put it by then. Time in here was going to be strictly limited, he knew. In the ten days – less one hour – since the first explosion, the core had only

3

become hotter and more dangerous. The first firemen, Valentinov's colleagues from the nearby town of Prypiat, had been in hospital for more than a week now and they weren't expected to live. The radiation, impossible to sense, able only to be understood on the red gauges of the dosimeters, would begin to kill him, too, in a very short time indeed. 'Imagine you are inside a microwave oven,' General Gogol had told him half an hour ago at the final briefing. 'Imagine that the power is turned up high and you are going to cook very quickly.'

It wasn't quite like that, Valentinov knew, but the image was clear and highly effective. He flashed his torch around, still overcome by the cataract of thought and sensation raining down upon him, and was so disorientated that he actually shone it up into his face to check that it was working properly because the beam seemed so weak and dim.

Then it struck him: the beam seemed dim because the tomb-like chamber was not in fact dark at all. It was glowing. The walls were glowing dully, but the roof was actually shining, like a huge red alien sun in one of the science fiction films Valentinov liked so much. The colour shaded from a dazzling near-white in the centre of the roof through vivid rings of ruby to heavy shadows, dark as dry blood, at the edges. It seemed to hang down, as though the white heart was already beginning to sag as the molten core above prepared to pour through unstoppably towards the centre of the earth. But a more careful look, squinting through streaming eyes, showed this to be an illusion caused by the light. The roof was flat and seemed sound enough for the time being. And as he realised this, so, in sharp contrast to the coolness of the water on his body, the heat upon his head and shoulders struck through the black rubber, and he realised that the arm which held the redundant torch out in front of him was beginning to steam.

Slowly, in slow motion, imagining himself to be like

some lost astronaut in *Solaris*, Valentinov began to move around, immersing himself in the boiling but cool, and highly radioactive water whenever the weight of the super-heated radioactive air became too much. At least the air he was breathing was pure, he thought, and then found himself wondering whether the alpha and beta rays he knew were mingling with the long light rays all around him could penetrate his air tanks and get into his lungs that way.

The chamber he was in, immediately below Number Three and the blazing core of Number Four itself, was the better part of one hundred and fifty metres long and more than seventy metres wide. It was full to a depth of nearly one and a half metres with fiercely bubbling water designed to purge heat and radioactivity from the gaseous emissions of the reactors. It was supplemented now by the residue of the millions of tons of water which had been poured on the fire during the last ten days, and no one really wanted to imagine what the result would be if the core dropped into it. Less than twenty metres above Valentinov's head, more than a thousand tons of blazing graphite was combined with one hundred and fifty tons of uranium currently boiling at about 2,000 degrees centigrade. If that broke through the glowing concrete, it would be met by 15,750 cubic metres of cold water. The result would make Hiroshima look like a firework. And it was going to happen later tonight.

There was almost no doubt about it; all General Gogol could hope for was that the bubbler pools at least could be pumped dry before the core broke free so that the body of the building stood a chance of containing the explosion – the much smaller explosion – as the core met cold concrete instead of cold water. What they really needed to do, had there been time, was to fill the chamber with sand from the floor of the nearby drainage pool to supplement the five thousand tons of boron carbide, lead, clay, limestone, and sand from the floor of the Prypiat River which had already been dropped on the blazing core from the air in a feeble attempt to cap it after the water had boiled off or drained away. But the best they would be able to manage by the look of things was to pump this water out down the deep channels they had just finished cutting and into that sand-bottomed drainage pool. It would take a couple of days to move this amount of water and they probably didn't have that long but, as General Gogol had observed, they now had the expertise, the equipment and the all-important drainage channels in place. It would have been a dereliction not to try.

A hand descended to beat against the back of Valentinov's shoulder and the major jumped with shock. He swung round and jumped again, so close was Popov's face plate. The captain was shouting and gesturing but all Valentinov could hear was the continuous thunder of the fire. Such a situation was not an uncommon one for fire fighters, so Popov and he immediately fell into an agreed system of signals which communicated as effectively as sign language between the deaf. Popov had brought the first great hose and wanted to know where to place its massive nozzle. A few metres down its length, squatting up in the opening of the sluice itself, was a light but powerful pump. This was set up and ready to go, but Popov wanted to know whether Valentinov wanted more than one hose per sluiceway. The major nodded and held up his fingers: at least two. He gestured: and another pair in that sluiceway there and another . . .

Popov nodded and began to move away. Valentinov thumped him on the shoulder and the young captain turned back. *I'm going to look over that way*, the major's gesture said. Popov nodded again and began to cross towards the sluiceway's tunnel opening. Valentinov watched him as he hoisted himself out and slid like a seal past the still engine of the pump mechanism. His eyes had adjusted to the light now and he could see almost as though he was outside in daylight. Once Popov emerged from the ruined reactor building, General Gogol would know that this part of the plan was working and he had agreed that the next part would be to dispatch a communications expert with a waterproof telephone on a long line so that Valentinov could make a report on what he could see. The long line was needed because they had discovered very early in the emergency that radio communications became all but impossible this near to a nuclear explosion. Valentinov had been impressed with what he had seen of Gogol, but even had this not been the case he would still have wanted to make a full and detailed report.

He began to cross the chamber, unconsciously letting his body slide below the surface of the water as he came closer to the white-hot section of the roof. At last only the very top of his head remained exposed to the roasting heat, and even then he kept dipping it under the water in order to stop his scalp from burning – or, as he imagined it, to stop his brain from boiling. The effect of this was completely disorientating; the water was bubbling fiercely and the gases exploding through the liquid all around him made it impossible to see, in the same way that the overwhelming noise made it impossible to hear. It was unlikely he would have noticed the first change in the circumstances, even had he had been able to do so. As things were, he stood no chance at all.

Captain Yevgeny Popov slid out of the outside end of the sluice and into the deep gully running like a dry river bed straight down to the distant glimmer of the shallow, sand-bottomed drainage pool. The air was cuttingly cold out here and he had no desire to linger. He ran up the roughly shaped clay steps and paused for an instant at ground level. Behind him the ruin of the reactor building reared darkly, capped with fire like a restless volcano. Before him lay thirty metres or so of debris-littered desert, beyond which he could see the figures of his colleagues, the experts from Moscow and the military. Out there somewhere was General Gogol awaiting a signal. He waved his torch slowly in the agreed signal and was relieved when the answer came so promptly. He turned, grabbed the next pump and heaved it up. The warmth of the sluice tunnel was almost a relief. Until he remembered where it was leading. He was one of the growing number of Ukrainians who were replacing the creed of communism with the burgeoning faith of Russian Orthodoxy and so he started to pray.

In the inner mouth, Popov set the second pump on the rough concrete floor beside the first and paused, looking across the seething subterranean lake to see if he could work out where the major was. He put all thoughts of hell firmly out of his mind, for the idea that he was damned was even more unnerving than the reality of the radiation. It was impossible to make out the black shape of the fire fighter's rubber-clad body or the long cylinders of his air tanks, and there was no way of working out which of the millions of bubbles came from his commanding officer's lungs. It struck the young captain quite suddenly that the light in this place was playing all sorts of tricks on him in any case, changing colours – there were no blues, violets, indigos or greens – and twisting distances. After a few moments of increasingly nervous inspection, however, Popov made out a determined movement in the centre of the chamber, almost exactly beneath the white heart of the glowing roof. The next section of the plan required Valentinov to be back here to greet the communications expert Lieutenant Mykola Drach, but it looked to Popov as though the major was going to be on the far side of the chamber. Popov decided that it would be best for him to remain here himself. He knew what to do next, and a moment or two's wait now would allow him to send Drach to Valentinov directly and save time in the long run. So he stayed where he was and squinted into the chamber as he waited.

Valéntinov was in another world, exactly like a character from the works of his beloved Stanislav Lem. He would never know whether the euphoria which overtook him then was a result of the near perfect conditions for brain-washing, or reaction to the stress and simple terror of the situation, or actual damage to the cells of his brain caused by the radioactive environment. He was floating quite con-tentedly and increasingly less actively through a dream world where the spectres of his loved ones were beginning to appear ever more powerfully. His wife and daughters were swimming like naiads beside him and he was distantly concerned about their lack of protective clothing until he realised they were all actually on holiday at the beach in Berdyansk anyway. And his parents were there too, although his mother had died many years ago. And there was Grandfather Anatoli waving to him; this did not seem strange in spite of the fact that he had only seen photo-graphs of Anatoli who had died at Stalingrad in 1942. Valentinov looked across to his wife who was performing the strong breaststroke he loved so much to see. 'Look, Katya,' he said, unaware of the rubber mouthpiece slurring his cheerful words, 'there's Grandfather Anatoli. He's a hero of Stalingrad; I've always wanted to meet him . . .'

And everything stopped, as though the whole of reality had been switched off like an electric light.

Popov saw. Not everything, but enough.

The core was just beginning to break through. It did not come, as expected, all at once. At first it came in tiny drops, spoonfuls, thimblefuls, falling like the blazing hail that Moses summoned down. The lethal drizzle was diffi-cult to see, for the refraction caused by the heat made each smoking fall look as if it was taking place behind layers of twisted glass; the water was bubbling, so that each tiny explosion of impact was hidden like a tree in a forest.

Until half a thimbleful of pure uranium, at 2,000 degrees C, hit Major Bohdan Valentinov square on the top of his head. It was hardly bigger than a raindrop, but where even the largest raindrop would have shattered against the rubber and run off the thick black curls of the major's hair, the uranium burned its way through the impediment with the celerity of a laser beam. Immediately beneath the dome of bone, which it penetrated in a nanosecond, lay the major's brain, and brain tissue is largely composed of water.

It so happened that Popov was actually looking at Valentinov when this happened. He saw the flash of brightness leave its twisting smoke trail hanging in the air as though it had always been there. He saw the water erupt and realised – though it took him a little while to do so – that the major had simply exploded, as though he had somehow swallowed a live grenade. Shock hit Popov, shock and a terrible recognition of how many tiny trails of smoke were hanging in the air. And what the tiny trails of smoke signified.

He turned to run away and crashed into the solid body of Lieutenant Drach with such force that they both fell backwards, sprawling down the tunnel of the sluice. Drach reacted violently – from his point of view he had just been attacked by an apparent madman. Popov's simple terror was enough to overcome the lieutenant's clumsy resistance however, and he managed to bundle the pair of them back along the sluice until they fell out into the chilly air. Then, long before the confused communications expert could even begin to work out what was going on, Popov had the handset and was screaming down it at the top of his lungs, 'We're too late, the core is coming through. It's coming through, I say!'

Chapter Two

General Valerii Gogol looked down at the handset and then up at the ruined reactor building as Lieutenant Fireman Popov's words continued to spill out into the still night air. It was fortunate no one was close enough to overhear. 'It's coming through, I say! Not all at once, a little at a time, as though it's raining uranium. Major Valentinov's dead. He just seemed to explode. I saw it. I think some uranium must have hit him. It's so hot it just . . .' There was the sound of retching.

The boy must have a weak stomach. Or perhaps he was fond of his commanding officer. The fire service was not like the army, after all; regard could replace regulations as long as the job got done. But then, Popov had been subjected to such a massive dose of radiation in that terrible, water-filled chamber that nausea was only to be—

The general pulled up the speculation abruptly, his mind veering away from contemplating the unthinkable.

They had meltdown; the core was coming through.

'That's it, the rest of you,' he called, hoping his voice sounded firm and decisive. 'Take a break. Get some hot tea. I won't want you back here for a while.' They looked at him blankly and he frowned in irritation. Power workers, fire fighters, advisers, experts, they were all under military command now. He didn't want them hesitating over obedience to his orders. 'Go!' he snapped, and they went. He could get them back within moments if he needed them, but at the moment he wanted time alone to think. Advice, discussion, plans of action, all that could come later – if they had time. Now he needed time to think. Alone.

He put the handset back to his ear, squinting to see across the stark, floodlit wasteland which lay between his position and the building. How cold the Bakelite of the instrument was! He shivered, abruptly remembering his father's stories of the Eastern Front in the war against Hitler. The telephone with its long wire, however, was more like something his grandfather would have used in the Great War of 1914–17, before getting caught up in the Glorious Revolution. Gogol smiled grimly, realising that his mind was running away from reality again. How numb his lips felt. 'Popov! Can you hear me?'

'Yes, General.'

'How long? Can you estimate how long we've got?'

'No. I'm sorry. I don't think there's any way to tell. Hours. Seconds. I've no idea at all.'

No, thought the general grimly. No one will have any real idea now. That's why he didn't need the director of the power station or any of the structural engineers here at the moment. He knew the plans as well as they did – almost as well, at any rate – and everything else was guesswork. No one had ever been in this situation before in the history of the world. No one could advise him how best to proceed when faced with the meltdown of a nuclear core. It could be coming through joints between the concrete slabs of the reactor vault floor or it could be melting through the hearts of the slabs themselves. The original explosion must have sent force downwards as well as upwards and it had had power enough to hurl a thousand-ton concrete-filled steel lid up into the air like a kopek flipped for a bet. The second explosion, when cold, damp air had hit 1,700 tons of graphite and 1,661 uranium fuel rods weighing more than 200 tons, all at nearly 700 degrees C, had been even bigger still. The uranium coming through into the bubbler chamber could be seeping through hairline cracks in the blast-damaged concrete reactor floor. If that was so, it might be some time before the cracks became wide enough to let out the whole core. It was all guesswork. Popov was right. They might have hours or they might have seconds. It was impossible to be sure.

What he could be sure of, however, was that nobody on the site of the Chernobyl Nuclear Power Station would see daylight tomorrow unless he came up with a miracle now. But he knew he could not act absolutely on his own – or on his own authority. Trailing the phone wire after him like the tail of a dejected dog, he walked into the makeshift hut he was using as a headquarters. The bank of communications instruments it contained looked nothing like a leftover from the Great War. He eyed the young communications officer who had leapt to attention as soon as he had entered and who now stood like a statue beside the humming equipment. 'Get me Moscow,' he said at last. 'I have to speak to the General Secretary.'

He saw the shock and hesitation in the young man's eyes. Who phoned Comrade Gorbachev at one o'clock in the morning, even under these circumstances? And *why*?

'And hurry up,' snapped the general. 'Time may be limited.'

The junior communications officer's name was Ivan Baranov and he spent the next fifteen minutes standing outside the communications hut, dying for a cigarette and trying not to look at the utterly sinister, quietly snarling, dully glowing ruin which towered overpoweringly a mere thirty metres away. Once connection had been made with the office of the General Secretary, Ivan had been summarily dismissed by the glowering general with a curt order against any mental speculation whatsoever. It did not occur to him that the general had no right to tell him what he could or could not think, and he obeyed.

Ivan had been stationed on the outskirts of Kiev since last autumn, under the command of Colonel Ryzhkov. It wasn't a long time, but it had been long enough to get to know a few people down here and get a girl friend. Her name was Larisa. She was a student with a slim body, hair like corn and freckles on the bridge of her nose. She had the ability to be deadly serious one second and utterly frivolous the next and Ivan quite enjoyed never knowing where he was with her. The first time they had made love – an occasion treasured in his memory – he had been convinced she was about to throw him out of her tiny apartment right up until the moment she had unbuttoned her blouse and revealed the fact that she had freckles in other places than her nose.

She was an active Komsomol member and had spent much of the last week, he knew, helping to dredge up the tons of sand from the bed of the River Prypiat, which the heroic pilots of General Antoshchkin's command had dropped onto the core from their helicopters as they passed mere metres above the billowing flames. Ivan knew the pilots would be lucky to survive and he hoped that none of the lethal radioactivity had seeped down to the river and infected Larisa and her friends. He ached to be able to slip out through the lines of civil guards surrounding the immediate area and go to see her in the worker's flat in Prypiat she was currently staying in. But things had tightened up a lot since General Gogol had arrived. Colonel Ryzhkov had been transformed into a martinet, there was a curfew and the risks of breaking it had escalated drastically during the last few days since the tanks had showed up. Quite what a squadron of state of the art battle tanks was doing supplementing a civil defence exercise, even in an emergency such as this, no one could make out. Someone had asked the colonel and received a pretty dusty answer. No one had dared ask the general, of course. But there they were, and there were their crews, obviously hand-picked to a man and looking extremely dangerous; and there was the fact that the tanks were clearly fully armed. Speculation was rife but very, very quiet. That was true of the soldiers in Ivan's unit at any rate. Ivan had mixed with more of the civilians than the other soldiers because he had worked so closely with the general and the general worked with them – up until now – but even Ivan had a limited view of how the nuclear power workers, the atomic experts and all the others were reacting to the presence of the tanks. Also speculatively, he assumed.

A footstep crunched on the hard ground behind him and he slammed to attention automatically. A tall man hurried past without giving him even a glance. The door into the hut opened and closed. A bar of yellow light fell across Ivan's face. As it did so, it revealed the profile of the stranger. Ivan Baranov frowned. He had never seen the strange man before and he thought he had seen everyone here, even the tank crews. Automatically, Ivan moved a little closer to the flimsy wall of the hut, but his keen ears could pick up little more than a low hum of urgent conversation. He took a step nearer, only to leap back as the door opened again.

'Wait,' said the general's voice, quite clearly. 'I can phone him from here, it will be quicker. In fact I can phone them both.'

The door closed.

Ivan stood at attention, just in case.

Colonel Ryzhkov appeared within moments and hurried into the hut only to reappear almost at once. 'What's going on, sir?' Ivan ventured.

'We're clearing the area. You wait here.'

'Yes, sir. What . . .'

Colonel Ryzhkov was gone. Very soon, Ivan heard the bustle of large numbers of people moving none too happily away. Then there was silence. He remained at attention, rigid, as though the iron control he was exercising over his body could extend to his terrified mind. He could feel sweat trickling down his neck although it was by no means warm out here. He had never felt so alone and exposed. He knew with absolute certainty that, with the exception of the general and the stranger – and presumably of the two fire fighters and his best friend Mykola Drach who were still over there at the mouth of the sluice – he was all alone in the Chernobyl Nuclear Power Station.

The lieutenant's nerve broke. He reached into his uniform pocket and pulled out a cigarette. The bitter black tobacco was just beginning to singe the long cardboard tube of the mouthpiece when the first distant scream made the soldier's hair stir. It was a long, drawn-out haunting scream of tortured agony, distant but powerful enough to pierce the dull, thunderous rumble of the fire. Ivan had done his stint in Afghanistan and he knew a lot of reasons for sounds like that and he hated them all. The scream came again, bringing to his mind all too vividly the picture of a mujehaddin fighter being crushed to death beneath the tracks of a tank.

A tank! That was it! They were bringing up a tank and the screaming was the sound its tracks were making on the concrete. His relief that the sound was not issuing from a human throat was so overwhelming that he forgot to wonder why General Gogol had ordered up a tank.

Ivan had hurled away the cardboard stub and was standing at attention once again when the tank pulled up beside him. He had always considered tanks clumsy vehicles, but as he watched this one coming up to park beside the communications hut, it was as though he was watching the sleekest Zil limousine being guided to the door of the General Secretary's dacha. There was no more screaming from its tracks and the rumble of its engine mingled with the noise of the fire so that it seemed to move silently. So precisely did the driver guide the massive vehicle that the lieutenant didn't even feel the need to move out of the way.

As soon as the tank stopped, its cover was lifted up and back to reveal the head and shoulders of its commander. Ivan gazed up, entranced, as the slim figure pulled itself out of the port and scrambled lithely down. Only then did Ivan realise that the tank commander was a woman. She gave him a glance and a curt nod in passing, then the silence returned.

The silence underpinned by that sinister, continuous thunder-rumble, as though an earthquake was erupting nearby. Now that he had leisure to stand and think about it, Ivan realised that the ground was, in fact, trembling. Had it been doing that for the last ten days and he'd simply never noticed? Or was the whole thing building up to some kind of climax?

No, he didn't want to think about that.

The door to the hut slammed open and General Gogol came out, with the stranger and the tank commander immediately behind him. The general stopped dead when he saw Ivan. 'What! Are you still here?'

'Yes, General. The Colonel said—'

'Never mind. Make yourself useful. Tell the people in the reactor building to get over here at once.' He handed Ivan the old-fashioned handset and waved him vaguely towards the hut. Ivan obeyed and got out of the way of the three busy officers. Oddly enough, even on so short an acquaintance, Ivan had no doubt that the stranger held military rank.

'Mykola! Can you hear me? It's Ivan! The general says you and the fire fighters must come back now. At once. Mykola?'

'I hear you, Ivan. Thank God. We're on our way.'

Ivan felt himself nodding, as though Mykola could see him. He was surprised to hear his friend referring to God. Things must be pretty bad over there. Then he thought that 'over there' was only thirty yards distant.

The three officers were poring over a large piece of paper which was spread over the front of the tank. At first glance, it looked as though they were consulting a map or battle plan, but the white paper was in fact an architect's drawing of the building. Ivan was still gripped by mild surprise that such a thing existed. He was one of those many who were extremely cynical about the manner in which even nuclear power stations were constructed.

The tank commander had a clear, decisive voice. 'The angle is perfect,' she was saying. 'My gunner should be able to pierce the chamber. Under the circumstances, any fallout from the shell will go unnoticed. So we just have to worry about how much of the building is actually destroyed.'

'Yes, indeed,' answered Gogol. 'There is a risk but it's well worth taking.' He paused. '*Any* risk is worth taking. We have no option now. If we can drain it, we stand a chance of keeping some kind of control. If it goes into the bubbler pool as things stand, there's no way to calculate what the damage will be.'

'Not that we'll be in any position to care,' the commander observed drily.

'Let's move,' said the stranger, and there was no doubting the fact that he was in command. 'You say you can do it. We know it must be done. We know there is no alternative and no time. That's all there is to it. No matter what the risks may be, we can't make things any worse. So let's do it.'

The commander scrambled up into her tank like a cat going up a tree and the others turned away. Ivan went cold. Mykola and the fire fighters were still over there! He swung round, his mouth open to remind his seniors, but as he did so, he saw two figures scurrying across the debris-littered wasteland towards them. He stepped forward towards his friend, crossing the line into the forbidden area without thought. 'Mykola, are you all right?'

Drach fell into his best friend's arms and let Lieutenant Popov fall. Popov sprawled onto the ground and Ivan looked around for help. The stranger and the general stepped forward side by side and lifted the fainting fireman between them. No sooner had they done so than the turret of the tank whined into mechanical motion.

'Get behind the hut!' yelled the stranger, and the five of them hurried off. It was a short, stumbling run to get their chilled and shaking bodies behind the flimsy structure. Ivan made it without too much trouble because Mykola could at least run. The senior officers had more trouble because Popov had not regained consciousness, and his dead weight was obviously unwieldy. As soon as they were behind the building they all crouched down, their backs to the clapboard wall, and General Gogol yelled, 'Shut your eyes! *Now!*'

They had scarcely made it before the flat report of the tank's gun told them that the commander had fired her shell as ordered.

There was a flash like summer lightning, which dazzled even those who had clenched their eyes shut. Immediately the thunder of the fire intensified, became overwhelming, grew as loud out here as it had seemed to the firemen inside the bubbler chamber. Popov stirred and whimpered. The stranger clutched him sympathetically. Ivan moved, as if to get up and go to look at what was happening, but Mykola held him back. Nobody could hold back General Gogol from going to see what the result of his desperate plan was. He extricated himself from the tangle of limbs and staggered to his left, having wisdom enough at least to come out behind the tank itself.

What Valerii Gogol saw was this. The side wall of the reactor building had been pierced by the tank's shell. A perfectly round hole had been created in the concrete wall, and out of this came a tongue of intense, dazzling blue fire as though a moon rocket was blasting off sideways through the building. Even as he watched, feeling the backs of his eyeballs being destroyed by what they saw, the tongue of blue intensified into white, and a huge arc of white liquid sprang out as though the reactor building had been stabbed to the heart and was going to bleed to death.

The white arc of liquid fell like a molten Niagara into the wide trench they had dug for the water from the bubbler pool and began to thunder down towards the sand-bottomed drainage lake. With the bright curve of it imprinted on the backs of his streaming eyeballs, Gogol staggered back to crouch behind the flimsy structure of the communications hut once again. The thunder of the burning core began to diminish, only to be replaced by a different, hissing thunder, further away.

After a length of time he was never able to measure, Gogol blinked some of the brightness out of his eyes and opened them, to perceive a world clouded in white as though a billion spiders had been busily spinning webs over everything. The sight was enough to start Gogol choking as though the webs were smothering him; it was only when the coughing really began to shake him that the general realised that the spiders' webs were real. They were mist. No, not mist. Steam. Water vapour at the very least. And he knew where it had come from.

He staggered to the tank and beat against the side of it until the commander thrust her head up out of her trap door. 'Take me down to the drainage pond,' he yelled. The commander's head disappeared, and the tank's motor fired up.

Like Ivan Baranov and the majority of professional Russian soldiers of his generation, Gogol had seen active service in Afghanistan. He had served in strategy and intelligence, but he still knew how to ride a tank. He climbed onto the back of this one and rode it down to the outwash of the channel whose mouth lay under the sluice of the bubbler pool beneath the core of reactor Number Four. The banks of the pond were swathed in thick, foul-smelling fog which had a nasty way of reflecting the tank's battery of headlights. Gogol was no fool; he knew it was almost certain death to breathe the radiation-laden water vapour, but truth to tell, he didn't really care. He had to know whether or not the plan had worked. That was the most important thing, certainly more important than the life of one general officer.

He climbed down as soon as the tank stopped and staggered forward to the bank of the drainage pool. He used his hands to beat aside the clouds of steam which still billowed around him as though he was in the hot room of a Turkish bath. The edge of the water came as something of a surprise. He had expected vegetation – rushes, sedge. There was nothing. One moment he was on land, the next he was surrounded by water. No sooner had he registered the fact than his feet slipped out from beneath him and he found himself sitting down up to his waist in warm liquid. The water vapour thinned sufficiently for him to see that the water was unnaturally clear. In the light from the tank, he was able to make out the occasional water-borne detail: perch, exploded and half poached, hanging upside down as though they had been savaged by miniature sharks; a duck, with all its feathers gone, caught in the act of taking off and boiled.

Dazed and dying, the general slopped himself over onto all fours and looked straight down. No; more than looked. Stared.

On all fours like a dog, General Gogol gazed straight down through the limpid water of the drainage pond which had been cleared, almost distilled, by the process of boiling. The headlights from the tank glimmered off the still surface of the water and he found himself looking down through two feet of liquid onto a fathomless sheet of black ice. There was no mistake. The bed of the drainage pool was clear and crystalline, apparently frozen down to the depths of the earth. He could almost see his reflection in the dark heart of it.

His palms and knees seemed to catch fire abruptly and his face had the oddest sensation, as though he was staring down into a furnace, and he realised that the strange obsidian crystal beneath the shallow water was not ice after all.

It was glass.

Convergence

ARCTIC OCEAN, 1986

And as the smart ship grew
In stature, grace, and hue,
In shadowy silent distance grew the Iceberg too.

Alien they seemed to be:
No mortal eye could see
The intimate welding of their future history . . .

Thomas Hardy, *The Convergence of the Twain*

Chapter Three

Captain Alexeii Borodin looked past the ghostly outline of his reflection up along the streaming, rust-red weather deck of the *Leonid Brezhnev* towards the steel-grey convergence of the Arctic Ocean and the Polar overcast dead ahead. He felt the forward movement of his command lose the sedate steadiness which had characterised it during the last few hours, as she began to nose out of the coastal ice and into the open sea. On the starboard quarter to his right, the massive icebreaker *Novgorod* was already speeding away round the curve of the Kolskiy Poluostrov coast down towards the White Sea, her lights jewel bright against the smoke-grey background, until the fleeting squall drew its dull curtain across the scene and the ship disappeared behind it.

'I've got a lot of static, but I can just make out that *Novgorod* says "Goodbye and good luck", Captain,' announced the radio operator, popping his head out of the shack like a badger from its set.

'What's his hurry?' Borodin grumbled, more to himself than to anyone else on the bridge.

'He's going to open up the approaches to Archangel. I thought you knew, Comrade Captain,' answered political officer Fydor Sholokov.

Borodin looked across at the big bull of a Georgian. With his stubble hair and walrus moustache, Sholokov clearly, if unfashionably, modelled himself on the late

Comrade Stalin. Not much imagination there, thought the captain. He had a literal mind, too. A perfect Party man. A dinosaur.

'There's more to it than that,' Borodin persisted. 'Think about it. He's been treating us as though we have the plague since we pulled out of Murmansk behind him. "Don't come to slow ahead until I tell you, *Brezhnev*. Sail the course I signal to you, *Brezhnev*. Don't get too close to my lily-white stern, *Brezhnev*." '

'Did he actually say that? Lily-white stern?' Sholokov was really offended. Borodin felt a stirring of affection. Then he felt sick as *Leonid Brezhnev* pulled free of the long white line of the coastal ice and slid down the back of the first big dark sea. Even though the freighter was on the edge of the winter ice she still rode the black water uneasily. Borodin was surprised to find the sea so lively, though the squalls were vicious and clearly the outrunners of an easterly storm. He had overseen enough of the loading in Murmansk to know that the cargo could not have been better stowed but still he found the manner his command was riding the swell a little disquieting. It was as though the ship had sentience and a will of her own; as though she was scared. As though she would rather be turning round and going back home.

'Sail due north,' he said to the helmsman. 'Come to three-quarters ahead and keep an eye out for ice.'

She was on her own now, like a young son left suddenly to his own devices by an overbearing parent. Borodin had not enjoyed being bullied by the captain of the *Novgorod* during the hours the pair of them had bashed a channel out through the Barents Sea. But now that the massive icebreaker was gone, he suddenly felt almost lonely. Especially as he knew exactly why the pristine, state of the art icebreaker had wanted the battered old freighter to stay well clear of her skirts. It wasn't just a social matter; someone had told the icebreaker's captain what the freighter's cargo was.

'I'm going below,' Borodin said to the political officer. 'I want to check through the orders and the manifest again. Then I'm going to inspect the cargo before the weather deteriorates any further. Do you want to come?'

'Of course. It is my duty.'

'Good. Comrade First Officer Bulgakov, you are on watch and in charge. We will head due north until I personally order a change of course. Is that clear?'

'Yes, Captain.' Tatiana Bulgakov was a modern woman; no 'Comrade Captain' for her. Modern and massively competent. She would be a captain herself within five years – as long as the current surge towards modernism continued to flow through the Soviet Union. If not, she would marry some fortunate mariner and make as impressive a mother and matriarch as she would have made a master and commander.

Borodin put the lieutenant out of his mind and crossed to the starboard bridge-wing door. If there was going to be a storm, he might as well get a breath of fresh air now, he thought, and stepped out into the bitter cold. He paused on the bridge wing for an instant, his eyes slitted against the wind as he watched the outrunners of the current rain squall which had swallowed *Novgorod* on her way east and south towards Archangel. He waited until he felt the first icy drops shatter against his face, then he crossed to the forward rail and looked down at the weather deck again. *Leonid Brezhnev* was 20,000 tons of Gdansk manufacture. She was old and battered but sturdy. He had a grudging affection for her and it was good to be back aboard after a winter in Murmansk. He still enjoyed looking at her for the simple pleasure of doing so, like a lover out with his girl for the first time in a while. The battering wind arrived, gusting strongly from the north-east, after its sister the rain. In the chill which suddenly descended then, Borodin noticed a strange thing: part of the wet metal deck seemed to be steaming. It was probably some kind of illusion. Or maybe it was a freak of the conditions. But, right far forward, just this side of the steps up to the forepeak, near the hatch into the Number One hold, the decking seemed to give off a wisp or two of steam.

Then the wind whipped it away, and in any case the captain's thoughts were interrupted by the arrival of the political officer who did not share his love for open air and Arctic rain squalls. Borodin turned away and thought no more about it. He had more important considerations.

Like his orders. And the manifest of his cargo.

Neither of which he liked.

Borodin's cabin was only marginally warmer than the bridge wing so it was a blessing that the samovar he insisted should always be there was bubbling merrily and was able to supply two glasses of thick, dark, scalding tea. They cradled the heavy green vessels in their cupped hands, letting welcome warmth seep into their thick, calloused fingers, then sipped the first serving down before climbing out of their clumsy wet-weather gear. Sholokov hung the streaming black rubberised jackets as neatly as possible on the back of the captain's door as Borodin beat his arms across his chest and puffed with the cold. 'Another glass, please,' he ordered, then crossed to his desk and pulled out the ship's papers. Orders and manifest were on top of the pile, ready to be consulted first. By the time Sholokov turned from the samovar with the two little glasses looking faintly ridiculous in his great bear-like hands, Borodin had spread the documents on his desk top.

'I hate being first out,' confided the captain. 'You always get the worst of it.'

'Somebody has to do it,' sympathised the political officer, his voice guarded and a little distant. 'And orders are orders.'

Borodin glanced up. Perhaps he had gone too far; Sholokov and he had made two voyages together and he thought he knew the man well enough to risk expressing a little disquiet. Maybe not. It was difficult to tell with political officers. Everyone else aboard owed their first allegiance to the ship. Sholokov's first allegiance was to Dzerzhinsky Street, via the Port Authority political section perhaps, but there was no question about it. He worked for the KGB, not the merchant marine.

'I'm not questioning the orders, Fydor, I'm simply expressing a lack of satisfaction with our luck.'

'Luck does not enter into it, Comrade Captain. We serve as we are required to serve and are fortunate to be able to do so.'

A Party slogan for every situation; that's how you get to be a political officer, mused Borodin wryly. Sholokov registered the quizzical look in the captain's clouded blue eyes and had the grace to look just a little sheepish as he wiped drops of condensation from the ends of his walrus moustache.

'Well, in that case, our luck is almost overpowering on this occasion, Comrade Political Officer. We are being required to serve almost beyond the call of duty – could we ever admit such a degenerate idea. You have studied the manifest?'

'In the Port Authority office, before loading began.'

That gave Borodin pause. Most political officers would have quietly arranged another posting faced with that knowledge.

But Sholokov was still speaking. 'And, like yourself, I oversaw some of the loading.' He took a deep breath and leaned forward, his big hands spread on the desk. 'It is the most dangerous cargo I have ever come across but, quite frankly, Alexeii, you were the best man in Murmansk to deal with it. I would not have allowed it on any other vessel. I would not have accompanied it aboard any other vessel.'

Borodin looked down at the broad peasant hands spread across his manifests. He saw the thick yellow nails and the thick black hair across their backs. He noticed the stark contrast the dark curls made with the white paper and, indeed, with the dead white skin, but he did so almost unconsciously. Between the powerful, stubby fingers, like stray curls from the hairy backs, the black ink of the manifest showed the figure 50.

That was the dynamite, Borodin knew. Fifty tons of dynamite, much of it beginning to sweat clear drops of deadly nitroglycerine, none of it safe enough for use any more, all of it destined for the disposal sites off the remote islands of Novaya Zemlya more than a thousand kilometres north-east of their current position. A thousand kilometres across the black waters of the storm-lashed, ice-bound Barents Sea.

All sorts of rubbish, from ancient ammunition to the nuclear reactors of decommissioned submarines, tended to find its way to the seaports along the north coast of the continent. In the summer they were sent north for disposal in small, relatively safe loads. But the movement of the dangerous rubbish did not cease during the winter although its shipment did. Along the great rail networks all through the dark months came rivers of waste from all over the Soviet Union. Rivers flowing northwards, dammed at their outlet by the shore ice along the southern edges of the six seas lying between the continent and the Arctic Ocean. There was no knowing what might pile up in the dockside warehouses of Leningrad, Archangel and Murmansk during the long black winters, and the first ship out in the spring often got the worst of it to take up and dump off the barren coasts of Novaya Zemlya.

Leonid Brezhnev's cargo was almost entirely composed of such waste. In cases, crates, containers of all sorts, she was carrying a range of ammunition designed for use in everything from Kalashnikov rifles to MiG fighters, shells from tanks and Koni class frigates. Not just shells from the Konis, either; decommissioned warheads from their

SA-N–4 missiles. There were dozens of torpedo warheads and two decommissioned propulsion units from Victor class submarines. And there was the dynamite – commercial explosive. Nobody at Murmansk seemed to know how old it was or where it had come from. There was general agreement, however, that it was in a highly dangerous state and needed to be moved carefully and immediately.

And there were the crates stowed in the forward hold. The paperwork on their contents was vague but the order for their disposal was quite clear. Given what he knew about the rest of the cargo, these crates hardly warranted a second thought from the less than happy captain; but there was something about them which just didn't feel right. Perhaps it was the fact that the crates were so innocent, so obviously innocuous in among all the other lethal stuff. Perhaps it was the fact that there had been nearly a hundred tons of dynamite in the warehouse at Murmansk and he had had to leave half of it behind in order to get the mysterious crates aboard.

'Let's start in the forward hold,' he said.

One of the few positive things about their situation was that they had no deck cargo. That at least was forbidden. The two men walked out onto the deck and paused. Borodin looked up at the sky. It was, if anything, darker. That meant the storm was going to be a bad one; it wasn't as if it was even noon yet and already the day seemed to be drawing towards dusk. The sky and the sea were the same leaden colour and only the vicious white horses coming towards *Leonid Brezhnev* like a millrace on the skirts of the next north-easterly squall made any real differentiation between them. The air around the ship was still at the moment but the squall would beat them to the forecastle head, especially as Borodin had ordered the helm over to the north-east on the way down here, so they were heading directly up towards it.

The two men went down the broad red deck at a run, but they were still drenched by the time they got the hatch open. The lighting in the hold was elderly but reliable – like the ship herself. Borodin was a fine captain and was fortunate in his chief and engineers. Spares were few and far between of course, but the crew cheerfully spent much time making good and mending so that effectively she might have been refitted seven years ago when she had been renamed in celebration of Brezhnev's receipt of the Lenin Prize for Literature.

The yellow brightness revealed piles of crates slotted together like a three-dimensional jigsaw puzzle to within a metre and a half of the deck itself. Borodin jumped down onto the crates and, crouching uncomfortably, began to walk across them, pausing every now and then to check the way they fitted together. Sholokov leaped down behind him and performed the same simple checks along the other side of the hold. It was awkward, potentially dangerous work made worse by the cold, the wet and the roaring of the squall which caused the ship to pitch and heave in an increasingly frenetic manner. 'I'm glad I'm not standing on top of the dynamite in this weather,' called Borodin. The political officer grunted. He agreed, but failed to see the wry humour of the captain's observation.

'Any idea what we *are* standing on top of?'

'No, Captain. No idea at all.'

'You saw the paperwork in Murmansk?'

'Of course.'

'So did I. What there was of it. No decipherable description of the contents.'

'That's correct.'

'No original point of shipment.'

'Transshipped through Minsk and Belomorsk.'

'Not much help. Anything on the crates themselves?'

'Nothing—'

The full power of the squall hit. The ship seemed to stop

like a car hitting a brick wall. Both men staggered towards the bow across crates which suddenly did not seem so stable after all. Borodin fell sprawling onto the patch of wet woodwork beneath the streaming hatch. Sholokov managed to remain on his feet, dancing all hunched over like an ape performing ballet. He looked quite ridiculous and Borodin, though winded, still managed to laugh.

The wheezing laugh choked into horrified silence almost at once as Sholokov's dance was brought to an abrupt halt by the collapse of the crate he was moving over. It was not a partial collapse, the yielding of one or two boards to his bear-like weight. The whole crate simply opened beneath him like a trap door and gulped him down. One moment he was hopping and the next he was buried to his armpits in the box's contents. The two men were no more than five metres apart and the accident brought their faces level so that it seemed to Borodin that they were suddenly very close together indeed. He saw the shock on Sholokov's face. The widening of his eyes, the gape of the wide mouth revealing yellow teeth and steel fillings. The sudden absolute pallor of the skin.

The ship heaved again. The boxes shifted. The political officer screamed.

Borodin was up at once and stumbling across the rest-less wooden crates. Less than three steps brought him over to the side of the man he suddenly realised he regarded as a friend. He looked down. Sholokov was in what looked like a perfectly square hole filled with rough lumps of black, silver-speckled crystal. The depth of the hole was impossible to tell – more than two metres, or Sholokov's legs would hardly have fitted. The ship heaved. The crystal shifted. Sholokov screamed again, and slid a little downwards. Borodin realised the glass-like rocks were at once crushing and engulfing his political officer. Much more movement and it would be as though the sinister cargo had simply eaten the man. 'Can you breathe, Fydor?' he asked.

Sholokov shook his head, eyes bulging, mouth gaping. He looked like a fish out of water.

'I'm going to take your arms and try to pull you free.' Borodin suited the words with the action, but there was no chance of freeing Sholokov's massive body from the grasp of the crystalline quicksand. As he heaved, Borodin looked around for something that might help. There was nothing.

'I'll have to get some help down here. Hang on.'

He was just about to release Fydor's hands when another battering ram of wind made the ship pitch once again. The political officer's agonised grasp came close to crushing his captain's hands and they remained there, face to face, like children in a playground testing each other's grip. Sholokov's tongue came past the yellow line of his teeth. His nose began to bleed, a black worm of liquid oozing down into the hair of his ridiculous walrus moustache. Borodin realised that Fydor had not screamed since their grips had locked. And he realised that he was crying because he knew he was not going to save this man.

The ship's movement eased and Borodin tore his hands free. There was a phone at the top of the ladder, where the steel rungs met the hatch cover. He ran towards it, oblivious of the fact that he was hitting his head against the unforgiving metal just above. His knees actually gave as he reached the hatch and he knelt there as though he was praying, as indeed he might have been. He ripped the ancient handset off the rest and rammed it against his ear.

It sounded as though he was sitting beneath a waterfall.

'Bridge?'

The static on the line was like a deafening tropical downpour. He could hear nothing else. Except, like an approaching locomotive, the howling of the next squall.

'Bridge!'

Too late.

The ship's head dipped. Dived. The wooden floor beneath Borodin shifted forwards, heaving slightly, reflecting the roll of the waves outside. There was a clear, crisp, cracking sound like the snapping of dry branches, then a choking sound, soft as a whisper.

There was a sobbing sound, which Borodin realised he was making himself.

There came the most sinister hissing of cold crystal surfaces rubbing against each other; nothing solid was impeding their movement any more.

When Borodin turned back, Sholokov had vanished and the only evidence of his existence was the fact that the black glass in the broken crate, displaced by the bulk of his body, had geysered up to spew out over the boards around it like rough-hewn ice cubes carelessly dropped.

Chapter Four

The storm came out of the east hard on the heels of the final squall and, much against his will and wishes, Borodin was forced to batten down the hatches and leave Sholokov's body where it was. Any regrets he felt – and they were many and bitter – were soon outweighed by the situation *Leonid Brezhnev* found herself in. The freighter was less than a day out of Murmansk when the full force of the storm hit. She had made ten knots due north for a couple of hours after leaving the coastal ice and then come to a north-westerly heading, designed to take her across the thousand kilometres to Novaya Zemlya in about one hundred hours' further sailing. Even with the force of the storm pushing so powerfully against her, she should have made the passage within a week.

At Borodin's order, the crew first tried running directly into the teeth of the storm and for the rest of the day after Sholokov's death they plunged doggedly north-east along a rough heading of 60 degrees. It was hard work for all aboard as the wind slowly intensified through gale to severe gale and storm force. The watch officers had to be ready for any flaw in the wind, prepared to meet any of the cunning side draughts the evil pressure system enjoyed throwing at them. A couple of degrees to port or starboard seemed to give the storm the purchase it needed to push them wildly off course when it returned to the north-east – as it always did in the end. They also had to keep a weather eye out for ice as the storm centre was perfectly placed to break up the edge of the winter pack and send all sorts of danger down upon them. The chief and his engineers had done a lot of work on the radar while the ship was laid up in Murmansk and it had been functioning perfectly. This was no longer the case, however, and the radio was producing nothing but static. The watch officers were literally living up to their title, watching for dangers which the safety equipment could no longer see.

The deck officers were equally busy. They had to make sure that the lethal cargo was safe against the increasingly wild motion of the ship. This required constant and diligent attention. No system of ropes and stays could hope to keep the restless cargo safely in place as the ship was hurled up and down and from side to side. Every line and support had to be checked and re-checked at least once during each watch; everyone aboard was all too well aware that if the cargo of decommissioned ammunition in Number Two hold behaved like the cargo immediately forward of it, then the whole ship would be blown to pieces.

The engineers had to ensure that the labouring engine continued to deliver sufficient power to keep them moving along the captain's dictated course, in spite of the wilful imperatives of the wind. They also had to guarantee that the auxiliaries were all ready to fulfil their functions immediately and faultlessly, from the temperamental central heating system to the centrifugal falls of the lifeboats, which it looked as if they might need to use at any moment.

Nobody aboard got any sleep and precious few got any rest.

Borodin was so tired that he could not stop his eyes from streaming. It seemed that he had been crying almost continuously since Fydor Sholokov's death, though in all truth he had been too busy to do much mourning. He had remained on the bridge throughout all the watches, not as a gesture of mistrust in his officers but because he knew that the next mistake, the next piece of bad luck, was going to be their last. He sat in the watchkeeper's chair, comatose with increasing exhaustion and almost uncontrollable nausea. It was not until after midnight, twenty-four hours out of Murmansk and little more than a hundred kilometres along their course, that he suddenly began to wonder whether he had picked up some kind of infection.

He hoped not. He had seen how incredibly rapidly a virulent bug could go round the closed society of a ship at sea, and with what devastating effect. But he was certainly not well. He had eaten almost nothing and normally would have been ravenous, yet the importunities of the unusually excellent cook had been turned away. Even the promise of his favourite mixed vegetable borscht and bitoks had failed to rouse him.

'Are you well?' Tatiana Bulgakov had asked – he had refused the food during her second watch. 'Borscht is exactly what you need. It is hot and bracing. It will give you strength and energy.'

He had shaken his head like a pettish infant and she had shrugged and returned to her duty. She was first lieutenant after all, not babushka here.

Through the night watches, he had found it more and more difficult to contain the sickness demanding so insistently to be released from his heaving stomach, and at four, just when the watch was changing, he had found himself hurrying down to the latrine as the little food inside him, forbidden egress one way, demanded it the other way. After the first convulsion, he found that he suffered uncontrollable bouts of diarrhoea every couple of hours and, although he said nothing – and his crew naturally respected his icy solitude – he found the strain of each attack increasingly enervating.

At eight o'clock next morning he called a meeting of his senior officers while he still had the strength to conduct it.

'The storm is growing stronger,' he began, 'but I seem to be growing weaker. There is no doubt I have contracted an illness of some kind. I do not think it could be food poisoning, but if it is, it cannot be from anything aboard I have eaten, as I have eaten nothing since we sailed. It could be from my samovar, I suppose. That would be difficult to check, however. The only other person who drank from it was Sholokov. It may be an infection. How do the rest of you feel?'

None of them admitted to being in the best of health, but to his jaundiced eye they all seemed fit enough. With one major exception.

'Like you, Captain, I fear I may have contracted some kind of infection,' admitted the chief engineer. He certainly looked pallid and ill. He had dark rings under his streaming eyes and lines of strain running down from the corners of his mouth to the scraggy skin of his neck. 'And at least one of my junior engineers seems to have contracted the same thing. I'm afraid we will find it difficult to run the engine room as efficiently as—'

He broke off abruptly and half rose, obviously fighting to control the contents of his rebellious stomach. His lined face was dead white in the grey light of the stormy dawn. A big sea hurled the freighter's head to starboard and a vicious gust made her roll to the first red band on the gauge of the clinometer.

The captain's intercom buzzed and he lifted the handset. It was impossible to make out what the watch officer on the bridge wanted, so he sent Tatiana Bulgakov up to see what the problem was and dismissed the rest of them.

He was in the latrine when she returned and he was so concerned to hear what she had to report that he hurried out into his cabin without even flushing.

'The radio officer has managed to get some intermittent traffic past the static,' she reported. 'Apparently things are pretty bad up ahead. There's a lot of ice and a lot of very bad weather between us and Novaya Zemlya, both heading our way about as quickly as we're heading up towards them. The ship isn't riding all that well. The cargo will have to be watched even more closely if we're to continue on the current heading. And the watch officer says he feels too sick to continue his duty and asks to be relieved so that he can go to bed at once. What are your orders, Captain?'

Borodin stood, swaying, like a boxer about to hit the canvas. There was just too much for him to come to terms with. Through the nauseated haze, only one course of action seemed to make any sense at all.

'Come about. One hundred and eighty degrees,' he said. 'Reverse course completely. We'll run before the storm until things get sorted out one way or another.'

First Officer Bulgakov nodded once, decisively, in agreement. 'Come to two forty and run before the storm until I receive further orders. Yes, Captain,' she said, and was gone.

Borodin remained swaying where he was for a moment or two after she had gone, trying to remember what he had been doing before she came in. Then he remembered, and returned to the latrine. When he got there, he stood for several moments looking down into the bowl, his long face folded into a frown of deep concern. Rough squares of toilet paper were floating in what seemed to be a puddle of watery blood.

What in the name of God was going on here? he wondered. He staggered across to the washbasin and stood for a moment, the only clear thought in his head that if this was some kind of infection he had better wash his hands very carefully.

Above the metal basin was a mirror and, for the first time since they had left Murmansk, Borodin found himself looking at his own reflection. It came as a stunning surprise. His skin was white and lined. There were black rings below his bloodshot, streaming eyes. At the corners of his mouth and nose there were lines of pale, crusted sores. The vomit had left an iron taste in his mouth which seemed to be clinging to his teeth and he sucked at them speculatively, then spread his lips in a slow grimace, careful lest he split the sores open. His teeth were edged in blood from his gums.

He looked at himself. He knew what this meant. He knew what this meant and it was important.

The ship heeled and rolled as she began to come round. He lost his grip on the basin and staggered. He made it to his bunk and collapsed. His mind would be clearer after some sleep, he thought. He would work out what to do about everything after he had had some sleep.

Tatiana Bulgakov was an excellent first officer, dedicated, able and decisive. But the next few days proved far beyond her capacity. With the captain increasingly feverish, and the chief and a growing number of engineers, deck officers and crew going the same way, she found herself run to the edge of utter exhaustion. In common with the majority of Western ships, *Leonid Brezhnev* relied upon the first officer to act as medic for routine problems and a Pan Medic call for emergencies. But the radio wasn't working and the radio officer could find nothing wrong with it. Unable to summon aid, she had to intersperse increasingly long watches with ever more frenetic sick calls. There was no real question of controlling the ship – she certainly stood no chance of getting back into Murmansk – and she was content to keep running with the storm, trying to maintain some kind of idea where they were. Her measurements and calculations became increasingly approximate as her exhaustion grew deeper and, in the constant scurrying overcast, any sight of sun or stars remained impossible. The navigating equipment was no more reliable than the radio and all too soon they were effectively lost in the vast eastern approaches to the terrible Denmark Strait.

The current beneath the weary hull was moving sluggishly south, and the heading on the compass read 240 magnetic unvaryingly, but the storm and the circumstances were playing tricks. Degree by degree the wind moved round to the south, though it moderated not a jot. By dawn on the third day, *Leonid Brezhnev*'s course was coming up to the better part of 330 degrees and nobody aboard knew a thing about it. And even if they had, they would hardly have had the power to do anything much about it.

Captain Borodin awoke on the morning of the fourth day since his sickness – the fifth since they left Murmansk – with his head a little clearer. Tatiana Bulgakov's careful ministrations had filled him with warming, heartening borscht; increasingly his system had accepted the bracing liquid which was at once nourishing food and drink. She was, in fact, sitting next to his bed gently taking his pulse when his clouded blue eyes flickered open.

'What time is it?' he asked.

'Eight.' Her thick blonde eyebrows arched in surprise that he should be awake and apparently so alert. 'I'm just going to watch.'

'You look dreadful.' He was still too groggy for tact.

'You should see yourself.' So was she.

Her information sank in and he struggled to sit up. 'Your watch doesn't start at eight,' he accused.

'Does now. Has done for two days. Eight to four, morning and night.'

A whole series of questions clamoured. He didn't know which one to ask first, but the logical one came out first. 'Where are we?'

'Somewhere in the Denmark Strait.'

'How are we heading?'

'As per your last order. Two hundred and forty degrees magnetic.'

'How long have I been out?'

'Four days.'

His eyes flickered with the shock. 'Weather?'

'No change. North-easterly storm running down behind us.'

He licked his lips. They felt swollen, simian, edged with crusted craters. He took a shuddering breath.

She put his hand down and he lifted it off the blanket and looked at it as if it belonged to someone else entirely. There were blisters on it and he knew exactly what that meant. He raised it and ran the fingers across his scalp, closing them into a loose fist. When he lowered his hand he found he was shaking. His fist was full of black hairs and he had felt no pain as he pulled them out by the roots.

'Get out the dosimeters,' he said.

'I have,' she answered. 'I did it yesterday when I saw the pattern in the sickness. But they don't work properly.'

'What do you mean?'

'They're all stuck on maximum. That's all they read.'

'All of them?'

'All of them.'

'No variation?'

'None.'

'No matter where on the ship you are?'

'I haven't been everywhere, but pretty much. I think they're broken.'

'All four of them.' He remembered that somewhere recently he had heard of something like this happening. Now where . . . Ah, yes. At Chernobyl. The firemen at Chernobyl had thought their dosimeters were broken because they were all stuck on maximum. Chernobyl was still fresh in his memory, though in common with the rest of Russia he had very little idea of how serious the incident had actually proved. It had been only six weeks since the explosion.

'All four. I *hope* they're broken.'

They looked at each other, two blue eyes and two brown ones. All weeping. He noticed that she, too, had sores at the corners of her lips. He knew then with a kind of numb certainty that the dosimeters were not broken at all. 'How do you feel?' he asked softly.

'Tired. Sick.'

He nodded.

'What are we going to do?' she asked softly.

'I could be wrong,' he answered, 'but I think we're going to die.'

He had to be carried up to the bridge, but once he was there he found he was quite comfortable in the watchkeeper's chair. The spasms of diarrhoea had calmed during his long sleep and he had time to review their situation and talk to the few crew who were still fit and functioning, before the first spasm overtook him. When he returned, weaker but doggedly determined, there was time to begin to make some kind of plan.

The continuing savagery of the storm made it impossible for them to dump the cargo overboard, even had they the individual or collective strength to do so. They hadn't even got the strength to control the ship, really. Certainly it was far beyond the bounds of practical possibility to reverse course again and run back towards home. But he could not bring himself to view the prospect of continuing to run along their present course with any degree of satisfaction. At this rate, according to his calculations based on Tatiana's scribbled notes in the log, they would simply be spewed out into the North Atlantic somewhere to the west and south of Iceland. From the look of things, they would be past Cape Farewell before the weather moderated. For a nightmare moment he envisaged them ending up marooned with their lethal cargo somewhere on the eastern seaboard of the United States. But then, he thought grimly, if they did have radiation poisoning from leakage in their cargo, the United States was the best place they could possibly be. The only place where they stood a chance of immediate survival. But that was a hopeless fantasy. They would do far better to look for some shelter.

'Come north,' he ordered. 'Go to three hundred and forty degrees. We'll try for Spitsbergen.'

The helmsman obediently swung the helm, further and further over. His gaze was fixed on the binnacle and his open Uzbek face gathered into a frown of concern as the printed card sat immobile. For the first time in ninety-six hours, the heading was changed. And the act revealed that the compass wasn't working either.

They were utterly lost by then. Blind, deaf, dumb and dying. Hundreds of kilometres north of where they thought they were, hundreds of kilometres further west. Had the radar been working, it would have shown the coastal ice, perhaps the coast, towards which they were heading. Had the radio been working, the frustrated radio officer would have been able to talk to his colleagues at the nearest land-based radio station in Scoresby Sound, Greenland, which was slightly south and west of them, not very distant at all.

Since changing course at the captain's last conscious order to gather the wind beneath their skirts, they had been forced to maintain a steady ten knots to keep steerageway. But the wind and current had pushed them westwards, latterly north-westwards, at more than twelve knots and they had covered in excess of eighteen hundred kilometres. During that time they had come south of Bear Island and west of Spitsbergen. They had passed north of Jan Mayen Island yesterday and now, did they but know it, the forbidding wastes of King Frederick VIII Land on the north-west of Greenland, with its mountainous ice-capped cliffs and towering glacier outthrusts, was all that awaited them, a little more than twelve hours' sailing dead ahead.

It was a mark of the damage done to the ship's normally reliable equipment by the radiation leaking from the forward hold that something as massive as Greenland could remain so utterly invisible.

Captain Borodin continued unknowingly north-westwards, believing he was going one hundred and twenty degrees further to the south, pushing forward much more rapidly than he imagined possible. Had he been well and alert, things would have been very different, but of course he was neither. Had Tatiana Bulgakov been more experienced and less exhausted, she might have seen the danger. Had Sholokov not been consumed by the deadly cargo, he might have pulled the captain up and changed the heading or the orders to the engine room.

But because no one knew what the strange black glass actually was, where it had come from or what it could do, none of these things happened.

Leonid Brezhnev, laden with hundreds of tons of explosives and the result of General Gogol's wild attempt to avoid a meltdown at Chernobyl, was heading for disaster at what in calm conditions would have been full speed ahead.

Borodin held on until mid-afternoon, but it was obvious that his strength was all but gone by the time Tatiana's first eight to four watch was over. Although fast sickening herself, she had him taken to bed then checked on the sick. At six she grabbed an hour's sleep and at seven she forced herself to eat something. By eight she was back on the bridge, relieving the exhausted third officer who could at least sleep without having to worry about the sick crew. She slumped in the watchkeeper's chair, feeling the food in her stomach begin to rise in revolt. She tasted iron whenever she swallowed and knew her gums were beginning to bleed like everyone else's. She gritted her teeth and the sound that the roots of her molars made moving loosely in the gums beneath her cheekbones and ears was more than she could stand. She clutched her right fist to her trembling lips and fled.

The helmsman peered through the driving rain but he could see no distance ahead at all. He couldn't even see the length of the weather deck. The noise of the storm drowned out everything else, even the sound of surf against cliffs. The set of the sea was coming in from behind them so that there was little enough to tell the sensitive fingers on the wheel that the ship was entering a deep, cliff-bound bay. There was no one in the forecastle head and the radar was utterly blind.

So, in the end, no one aboard appreciated what happened at all.

The bay had a wide mouth and a deep, deep floor. In fact it was a wide sweep of cliff-walled shore only made into a bay by the inexorable thrust of the glacier debouching out into the stormy sea.

The glacier was more than twenty miles across and it was this fact that had allowed it to push such a massive tongue of ice out for so many miles into the northernmost waters of the Denmark Strait. It had propelled itself, millimetre by millimetre, out into the water for millennia and now it was ripe to break free. The stormy conditions had cleared away the protective shield of shore ice that it normally wore, and the blind ship was running swiftly into the groin that the glacier made with the mountainous wall of the shore. Under normal circumstances, the outthrust of the ice would have broken off in smaller pieces, cracked laterally across as it was. But the *Leonid Brezhnev* negated all that. Millions of years of painstaking physical geography were nullified in the instant of its contact.

The coastline lay at an angle along an axis from south-east to north-west. The glacier protruded at right angles, like an arrow from a bow, aiming up towards the Pole. Of all the cracks that ran across it, the greatest was parallel to the coastal cliffs at the very point the ice oozed out of the timeless rock.

It was exactly here, at half past eight that stormy evening early in June 1988, that the ship *Leonid Brezhnev*, laden with hundreds of tons of explosives and carrying just enough sweating dynamite to act as the perfect impact detonator – as well as nearly a hundred tons of rough glass impregnated with the core of the Chernobyl nuclear reactor – struck at full speed ahead.

She was not as strong as she had been. Her sides were growing thin and her lateral bulkheads weak. Her bow rode up into the fissure by the shore, a valley nearly a hundred metres high and some kilometres in length but only a couple of metres wide. At once the pressure of the ice stopped the forward movement of the forecastle, but the rest of the ship, and everything it was carrying, continued at thirteen knots. The ammunition smashed through onto the glass from Chernobyl and the warheads came through on top of that. The reactors from the decommissioned submarines came through onto the warheads and brought the crates of sweating dynamite along with them. In a process as logical as a theorem by Pythagoras, the length of the ship concertinaed as the thin, rusty sides tried unavailingly to absorb the impact. The last and heaviest units that she had been carrying broke free as the engines, complete with their massive, old-fashioned boilers, blasted through on top of the sweating dynamite.

It took less than a minute for *Leonid Brezhnev* to tear herself to pieces but that was like an eternity compared with the instantaneous totality of the devastating explosion which followed the impact of the boilers on the dynamite. There was no way to calculate the force unleashed by the hell's brew of explosives which suddenly found themselves on top of each other and all going up at once. How many cities it would have destroyed, how many small countries it might have devastated, how many states, republics or counties it might have laid waste cannot be counted.

But it did have enough force to crack the antediluvian tongue of ice. It had sufficient power to send that crack snaking along the valley from side to side of the glacier. It had exactly the impact needed to launch into the Arctic Ocean the largest iceberg that had ever been seen there.

The power of the storm took the iceberg at once and as it could not push the monster westwards, drove it north. With debris from *Leonid Brezhnev* and her cargo blasted deep into her flank like shot embedded in the side of an elephant, the iceberg crashed up into the pack ice at the top of the world.

Through that first brief summer she drifted, undiscovered by mankind, away into the Angara Basin north of Spitsbergen, and in the sudden autumn froze in place like an alp adrift in the midst of the slowly spinning continent of ice. Through that first winter she stood, three hundred metres of her reaching up into the sky, nearly nine hundred metres of her reaching down into the black depths which are so cold that only the weight of the ice above keeps them liquid. Through summers and winters the berg drifted round the Pole. It took her one complete year to grate across the Harris Ridge, but once she had done so she moved more quickly. By the time she wintered in the Beaufort Sea, there was a community thriving around her: on the deep reaches beneath the surface, she had grown weeds as though she was made of rock, and shrimp and krill came to feed on the weed. Cod came to feed on the shrimp, and seal to feed on the cod. As the summer released her to drift past Prince Patrick Island, so the Arctic birds also came to feed on the cod, and foxes came to feed on the birds and polar bears to feed on the foxes and the seals. But no man saw her. Not then. Not the next summer when she drifted majestically past the wildernesses of Ellesmere Island and back at last towards her birthplace. And now so many years had passed that no one remembered the good ship *Leonid Brezhnev*, and even the memory of Chernobyl was beginning to fade.

Just as a storm had condemned her to spend five years in the frozen wastes of the far north, so it was a storm which released her. She had never pushed deeply into the pack, but had instead inhabited the edges, following a narrow track along the top of the world where the waters were deep enough to accommodate her massive depth. The slow, unstoppable grinding against ridges and outcrops had shaped her into a long teardrop fifteen kilometres wide and one hundred in length. The bulk of her lay beneath the water but an outcrop, three hundred metres high and eight kilometres wide, stood along the first fifty kilometres of her length. A hook of ice stood out from her side, however, spoiling the symmetry of her shape, and causing her to spin slowly as she moved.

The storm came down from the north in the very middle of that summer and caught the berg as she hesitated at the mouth of the Greenland Sea. For the first time since her violent birth, she moved south. Spinning slowly, she followed the deep-water channels down through the summer-shattered pack ice past Jan Mayen and into the Denmark Strait. Spinning slowly, she followed the dictates of the current and sailed south in the gathering autumn towards Cape Farewell. For the first time since the lookouts of *Leonid Brezhnev* had seen too little of her too late, men looked upon her. From planes and boats, even from the shore, they looked in wonder. But they saw nothing of her true potential for good or bad. Not these men. Not yet.

By the time winter closed in across the Davis Strait, she was drifting north again, but this time ice and a maze of islands stood between her and the Pole. North she ran, however, until the sea froze solid enough to stop her up in Baffin Bay on the edge of the North Water.

Spring released her into the grip of a new current which pulled her, like a great bird migrating out of season, south.

And men and women came to her at last. Men and women who understood what a wonder she really was.

Colin Ross the glaciologist came with his wife Kate, a glacio-biologist, to study the unique environment she created simply by existing. Robin Mariner came with her ship *Atropos* to effect urgent repairs. Richard Mariner came in the sister ship *Clotho* to find Robin. He found her and they took their ships home.

And then he came back.

Manhattan
THE DAVIS STRAIT, NOW

I'll take Manhattan,
The Bronx and Staten
Island too . . .

Lorenz Hart (slightly adapted)

Chapter Five

Deep-sea research vessel *Antelope*'s Bell UH–1H Iroquois helicopter skimmed along the surface of the restless sea like a lost dragonfly. Steel-grey waves reached hungrily for its sleek little fuselage and tumbled back roaring in thunderous frustration. The spray they spat up fell thickly on the windscreen and the wipers had a hard job keeping it clear. The storm wind had calmed temporarily between squalls, but there was still very little time to make the transfer. The apparently frail little craft was nose down, tail up, dashing wildly through the murk above the Davis Strait.

Richard Mariner, sitting in the left-hand seat, squinted through the roiling overcast dead ahead, but his eyes were defeated by the low cloud and the spray.

'Can you see it yet?' called Colin Ross from just behind, the stentorian bellow of his voice all but lost in the clatter of rotors and the thunder of great waters.

'Not a sign.'

'It never ceases to amaze me that something that big can be so hard to see at times.'

'It's there,' supplied the pilot, his eyes busy on the instruments. 'Dead ahead. Couple of miles.' An incoming radio signal crackled in his headphones and he stopped talking to his passengers for a moment. He stopped talking to them; he did not stop thinking about them.

The pilot, Sam Jenkins, was an old hand and by no

means easily impressed and yet the two men he was carrying seemed head and shoulders above the common run of passengers, even the sort of passengers who needed to be ferried between deep-sea research vessels and ice islands in the furthest reaches of the North Atlantic.

Head and shoulders above the rest both literally and figuratively. Both were unusually tall men. Richard Mariner stood well over six feet four in his stockinged feet and Colin Ross topped him by an inch or two. Neither man stooped, as is common with extremely tall people; instead they both walked with an upright vigour and went about all physical activities as though they were twenty years younger than they actually were. The pilot didn't know either man intimately enough to be certain of their ages, but both were public figures and it was general knowledge that they were at the late forties-early fifties line.

As far as the pilot was aware, each of his passengers was an outstanding man in his field. Colin Ross was a world-class scientist. He and his wife Kate had been on the short-list for a Nobel Prize a year or so ago for their ground-breaking work on glaciation and the Arctic environment. There was nothing the pair of them did not know about ice and the way it behaved in large masses on land or – as in this case – at sea. Or, for that matter, about any lichen, moss, plant, animal, fish or mammal associated with it.

Richard Mariner was a different kettle of fish. He was the last of the independent shipping men in Britain. He owned and ran Heritage Mariner, a company which had dominated the shipping world since the fifties. He owned and ran a fleet of supertankers transporting oil between the Gulf and Europe, out to the Far East, in to the States. He owned and ran the two great nuclear waste transporters *Atropos* and *Clotho* which carried waste product for safe reprocessing between North America and Europe – and, the talk was, his were the only such ships which would be allowed to pick up the incredibly lucrative Russian nuclear disposal market too. Heritage Mariner were also into leisure boating and were responsible for the *Katapult* series of multihulls – the Rolls-Royce of the boating world. And because he was a sailor as much as a pilot, the man at the controls knew that Heritage Mariner had a sub-section perhaps more famous than the mother company, an offshoot which was Richard Mariner's personal creation and ultimate achievement. This was Crewfinders, the most famous and efficient crew-finding agency in the world. A legendary organisation whose unmatched reputation was based upon their promise to replace any crew member on any ship anywhere in the world within forty-eight hours. The pilot wondered whether they dealt with marine helicopter men. He must remember to ask; he wouldn't mind going on the Crewfinders books himself if they would have him. He wouldn't mind working for Richard Mariner at all, in fact, and he was a notoriously hard man to please.

'Message received. Out,' he said. Just as he did so, the first gust of the next squall hit the helicopter and the little Huey dived closer to the hungry waves. The pilot turned the dive into a swoop and the turned-up nose came up into the stormy air again, frustrating the waves anew.

'They say they're just about to push the button over there,' the pilot yelled to Richard Mariner as soon as he had the helicopter steady.

'We'd better hurry then.'

'What?' yelled Colin Ross, for the brief conversation had been lost beneath the battering of the squally wind.

'They're just about to detonate the explosives,' yelled Richard in reply.

'Hell. I want to see that!'

'I've told Sam here to hurry.'

Son of a bitch, thought the pilot, he knows my name!

The instant the thought entered Sam's head, the full squall hit and, as it did so, the wind which accompanied it snatched away the overcast ahead and the first of the ice cliffs towered above them, tall, sheer and startlingly close.

'There it is!' yelled Richard. It was some months since he had last seen it and he was stunned anew by the scale of the thing. It was incredible that something this big could exist up here. It was as though the incalculable weight of it should have unbalanced the world.

Colin had been living on it for nearly a year now, on and off. He was more blasé.

From sea level, the wall of blue-grey ice rose through three hundred metres sheer. It stretched away on either hand as though determined to join Canada and Greenland. The Bell helicopter was so low that no one aboard could guess what lay beyond the crest of the cliff, but both of the passengers had been on the ice and they knew well enough. The wind roared over the high edge of it, pulling great streamers of spray off its crests. The crystalline cliffs ahead of them streamed with a deluge of rain, spray and meltwater. The helicopter dipped and swooped again.

'Over or round?' asked the pilot.

'Over!' ordered Richard.

The Huey climbed vertiginously, as though it was an express elevator. The cliff face seemed to plunge in and down at once, falling towards them like a great wave breaking. The illusion was compounded by the spray which foamed over them in the wind. Foamed towards them, overwhelmed them and was gone in a flash as they broke through into the higher reaches.

The strength of the wind keeping the overcast at bay allowed them a brief glance along the length of the iceberg – nearly fifty kilometres of it above water – before the helicopter pirouetted and dived west across the narrow southernmost section towards the south-western corner where the explosive charges had been laid. On their left hand, the cliffs which they had just passed stood in a long, curving line at an angle to the rest of the berg. They came in towards the central axis as though trying to form a point. Beyond the centre, however, the cliffs of the south-western section curved out into a hook, which over the last months had dragged the berg westward one kilometre for every kilometre south it had drifted, spinning it slowly on its axis. This was not easily achieved; the length of the berg under the water was more than one hundred kilometres, and forcing it to spin required forces which were almost incalculable.

As things stood, the monster berg, the ice island, largest of its kind ever seen in these waters, was just about to enter the Western Ocean shipping lanes. Unless something was done, it would cross them slowly and unpredictably, drifting south-westwards, spinning lethargically and presenting a massive danger. What it would do as it grated across the Newfoundland Banks defied calculation. What it would do if it drifted onto the eastern seaboard of the United States and ground down the edge of the continental shelf from Boston to Barbados went beyond imagining.

But, as the two tall men in the Huey knew, if the iceberg had an almost unlimited potential for destruction, it had an equal potential for good. By their rough calculation they were looking at about one and a half billion metric tonnes of water. All of it fresh. All ice cold.

So, before the US authorities called upon the full power of the armed forces to destroy it, these two extraordinary men were going to try and make some use of it – if they could manage to control, and ultimately direct, its movement. And they had sold their idea to the United Nations so that they had some backing and a little financial support, for the moment, if things went well.

The radio crackled into life again and Sam switched over to RECEIVE.

Below the helicopter, the southern section of the iceberg wheeled, the massive hook of ice seemingly trying to catch at Baffin Island, as though the distant land was some kind of fish. Abruptly, black figures came into view, scurrying across the milky surface below, and as soon as the eye discerned the existence of life down there, so it immediately discovered the geometric shapes of tents and even huts, and the rude beginnings of roads. There was an encampment on the berg and it was manned.

'*Five!*' relayed the pilot, the volume of his voice more than was needed just to overcome the noise.

'We won't be down in time, Sam. Keep clear!' called Richard.

'*Four!*' The helicopter danced obediently eastwards, but remained hanging high enough on the wind for the men aboard to see what was going on.

'Can we get round for a close look . . .'

'*THREE!*'

'. . . after the detonation?' bellowed Colin Ross. This was his baby, after all. He was in charge on the ice.

'Good idea. Sam . . .'

'*TWO!*'

'. . . get us in under the cliff there as soon as it blows.'

'*SURE! ONE!*'

The helicopter swung back, tail up, to give the three men aboard a grandstand view as Sam yelled '*ZERO!*' and in majestic series a line of explosions erupted across the base of the ice hook as though a stick of bombs had been dropped there. The burgeoning thunder of the explosions overwhelmed even the engine noise. The power of the blast made the little craft dance back in a way that even the squall wind could not enforce. A wall of ice dust and fragments hurled high into the lightening air, then thinned, billowed, became a cloud which joined the others scurrying southwards to rain on Newfoundland. The helicopter darted in behind it to overlook the destruction the explosions had wrought.

At first it seemed that nothing much was happening. Twelve craters in a curving line lay open to the stormy sky. The ice dust in them seethed and bubbled like some kind of volcanic activity. On one side of the line, the bulk of the berg with its little village stood firm; on the other, the massive hook of ice kept up its unwelcome pressure against the water, turning the southward pressure of the wind into a westward drift for the ice.

'Nothing doing!' yelled Sam.

'Give it time,' said Colin Ross, his voice quiet but carried to the others by its desperate tone. 'It has to work. We calculated everything so carefully.'

'Back to the drawing board, Colin!' said Richard. Then, 'NO! Look. Something's happening after all!'

The furthest crater was suddenly joined to the distant shoreline by a crack. It stretched for the better part of a kilometre. A crack a metre wide. No, ten metres wide, twenty, no . . . Distantly, a massive wall of spray rose up as though some huge surf had thrown itself against the ice cliffs. And the crack extended itself magically to the second crater and then to the third.

'There she goes!' exulted Colin but his voice was lost beneath the noise. It was as though the greatest tree in all the world was slowly toppling down and the sound it made was amplified a million times. The fissure, widening to a valley even as they watched, sprang from crater to crater beneath them. And the ice beyond the line was in slow, terrifying motion. Calving off from the mass of the big berg, another, made up only of the ice hook, was tearing itself away. Such was the power of the forces at work here that both of the bergs seemed to be in contrary motion. The main one seemed to be striking directly southwards, with the current and the wind, newly liberated and gathering way. The hook as it fell free spun westwards and, impelled by the force of its birth, seemed to be riding northward over the stormy, slate-grey waters.

But then the three men in the helicopter, almost stationary in the sky above this enormous process, saw other forces begin to come into play. The power of the explosion so carefully, and accurately, calculated by Colin and Kate Ross had lanced deep into the iceberg to ensure that not only was that portion of the ice above the water amputated, but a corresponding section beneath the water broke loose too.

The new berg, free of its mother, began to come to terms with its changed situation. Still spinning, it began to topple until it fell on its side in the ocean with an eruption of white water like the greatest of whales spouting.

That was the last the three in the helicopter saw at that stage, for Colin Ross, his excitement out of control, was pounding on Richard's shoulder and yelling, 'Down! Let's go down!'

At first, Richard thought the glaciologist wanted to go immediately to the camp atop the ice cliff, but no. Colin meant straight down and right now. Sam got the message fast enough and the Huey dropped like a stone thrown carelessly over the edge of the new cliffs. At first they could only see the sea ahead, which heaved and foamed as though a hurricane was passing, in the wake of the tumbling calf berg. The water foamed like molten lead and spewed up great pieces of ice to bob between the two greater pieces – debris from the explosion. Richard felt a fleeting worry for any wildlife in this immediate area of the ocean, but then he remembered how careful Colin and Kate had been to ensure that none of the creatures they spent so much time studying were anywhere near enough to be injured.

Then his thoughts moved on, as the helicopter itself moved round to show its occupants the result of all this destruction. The new cliffs were like galleries of blue-green glass. Shattered out of the heart of the ice, they had had no time to weather during the moments since their explosive birth. The rain had stopped now and the last of the runoff spread itself thinly down the new cliffs and froze into place so they seemed to be composed of massive panes of glass, almost like gigantic gemstones in the crystal beauty of their planes and surfaces. Had the sun been shining on them, Sam, Colin and Richard would probably have been blinded. As things stood, they looked, awestruck, into the very depths of the berg. It was as though they could see deep into the antediluvian soul of it, as though they could see back in time to the snows of a thousand years BC which had fallen on Greenland when it had still been a green land and had given slow birth to the monster before them. The crystalline past faded slowly, imperceptibly, into blue-green shadows which in turn became a velvet darkness calling like the spaces between the stars.

But only the longest of inspections would have allowed the spectators to plumb those depths. Now there was only the opportunity to register the dazzling surfaces and to see that this new, beautiful range of cliffs swept inwards along a line which brought them to a sharp edge against the first set so that, three hundred metres high from waterline to topmost gallery, with a bit of a rake from forecastle to forefoot, the iceberg had a pair of proper bows like a ship.

Even before the helicopter's skids kissed the ice, Colin was wrestling himself out of his seat strap and hooking his mitten-covered right hand round the door release. Richard was a little slower. He thanked Sam for the flight and advised the pilot to grab himself a hot drink from the camp; they would be returning to *Antelope* in half an hour or so, weather permitting.

When Richard leaped down onto the berg, he found his big colleague had waited for him. Side by side, crouching under the idling rotor blades, they dashed across the ice towards the makeshift encampment. As they ran, they splashed through the last of the puddles left by the rain before they were absorbed into the massive bulk of the berg beneath them. The ice was cold enough to freeze water and big enough to dictate its own microclimate, especially under calm conditions, but both men knew it was only a matter of time before it began to melt.

'She even rides differently,' called Colin the second they were clear. They paused for an instant and stood erect, testing the ice with the soles of their feet. Richard had been a seafarer since boyhood, a ship's captain for more than twenty years, but he would be damned if he could feel any movement in the ice at all. He might just as well have been standing on the pavement outside Heritage House in London. 'Good,' he said amiably, infected by the other's enthusiasm.

Then they were off again, running side by side towards the huts, and abruptly there was a figure from the huts running out to greet them.

This was Colin's wife and colleague Kate. Kate Ross stood tall and reed-thin, by no means dwarfed by her husband's massive size – or overcome by his ebullient enthusiasm; if anything, she seemed more excited than he, for she threw her arms round him and gave him the most unscientific hug and kiss. Were it not for their stature, they could have been Eskimos embracing, with their bulky sealskin leggings and hooded jackets of Caribou hide. But Inuit are a small-boned people and it would have taken several of them to fill Colin's clothing and a couple to fill Kate's.

'She's riding differently! Can you feel it?' she asked the instant they broke apart.

'Yes! I was just saying to Richard here . . .'

'I think we've got it right this time. Paul and his engineers are checking the new cliffs now but it *feels* right.'

The two glaciologists hurried off without a further word, leaving Richard to follow more slowly. Their excitement was perfectly understandable, he mused as he walked carefully over the treacherous surface. This was the climax of many months of calculation, experiment and planning. It represented the opening of a doorway to them; a doorway into an Aladdin's cave of possibilities, through which he had promised to accompany them.

Abruptly, Richard turned left. The camp and the waiting helicopter were now both behind him and only the cliffs, old and new, lay ahead. As the last squall fled away south ahead of him, he strode purposefully down the berg. Even if his sailor's feet were not attuned to the movement of the massive vessel beneath them, there was a vantage point relatively close at hand where his eyes would soon tell him what the soles of his feet would not.

The ice ahead seemed in fact to slope upwards as the edges of it closed together, giving the impression of a massive forecastle head. And it was onto this that Richard strode, marvelling as he did so at the manner in which the horizons fell away. Only as he reached the point which his observation from the helicopter had warned him was very much like the near overhang at the prow of a cruiser did his purposeful stride begin to slow. The new form of the ice was so much like the bow of a ship that it was all too easy to forget that this was not safe steel beneath his feet.

He looked down. The ice, weathered white here but containing the hint of a blue glow within, came to a sharp point a couple of metres further forward. Beneath that point, the two cliff edges met in a sheer cutwater three hundred metres high. Reaching back on either hand, the cliffs formed a carefully calculated forecastle big enough, they all prayed, to give the long, narrow iceberg a ship-like form regular enough to allow them to guide it along something approximating to a straight line. If they had managed that, then they were all in business.

Richard stood rapt, thinking about the business they were in and how they had come to be in it at all. The Rosses had come onto the ice because a berg this big in these waters was a once in a lifetime experience. The Antarctic calved bergs as big as Belgium – the largest on record was 335 kilometres long and 100 kilometres wide, twenty times the size of this one in surface area alone. But something this size in these waters was rare, to put it mildly. The Rosses saw it as a floating laboratory where they could carry out research impossible anywhere else. And they saw it as a unique chance to try and fulfil a dream long held by themselves and countless others: a chance to supply a worthwhile amount of fresh water to the drought-stricken coasts of Africa. It was a dream they had shared with many people over the years, and not just with academics like themselves. They had caught the interest of some senior officers of the United Nations for whom they did some of their scientific work. The Americans had been supportive too, for the experiment promised to rid them of a nasty and costly danger to the eastern seaboard. Various rich sheikhs and sultans were interested, for it had long been a dream cherished in the Gulf that icebergs could be pulled into the heart of the desert; pulling an iceberg even to Africa was something they would therefore be happy to support. And the Third World was interested, for the Rosses promised to bring some relief from the terrible droughts in Africa.

All that interest had firmed up into Paul Chan and his small team, the good offices of the nearby deep-sea research vessel *Antelope*, and the promise of more help. More political path-smoothing. More money. But only if the iceberg could be controlled. Controlling the movement of something this big was going to be nearly impossible, but at least an iceberg of this size would still be there when the African coast hove into view.

Richard had first come across the berg when one of his ships had been marooned upon its shores six months earlier. While trying to rescue the ship, her crew and his wife Robin who had been in command, Richard had met the Rosses and had become infected with their dreams. They had the idea of moving the berg. He had the power. Literally. He had a fleet of supertankers currently under-employed. They calculated that if they could make the berg begin to drift in what approximated to a straight line then six of his supertankers could control the drift – affect the course and speed just enough to make a difference. Icebergs had been sighted as far south as Bermuda before now; they just wanted this one to end up a little further west and south, that was all.

There were those who said it couldn't be done; of course there were. There were those who said it would be impossible to get the berg across the equator, and many who said that if they wanted to tug ice around the southern hemisphere, they should start with the big tabular bergs off the Ross Ice Shelf in Antarctica.

But the fact was that this berg was big enough to make the scheme look feasible. It was here. It was available. Together with the work of the Rosses, it had generated enough interest at a sufficiently high level to make dreams border on reality and words upon action. They had the backing. They had the will. They had an agreement with the United Nations that if Colin said this step was passed, the UN would charter six of Richard's tankers. It was the promise of this deal which had brought him a quarter of the way round the world during the last few days, from London via Reykjavik and Julianehab to the deck of *Antelope* where Colin Ross had come to meet him. Richard was a humanitarian but he was also a businessman. He would have swum up the Amazon to meet a man who had the power to charter six of his supertankers, all at once.

Everything depended upon whether this explosion had in fact given the berg a set of bows which would steady her and allow her to follow a simple straight line.

Deep in thought, Richard moved forward once again, his eyes at last busy beyond the edge of the ice. The point on which he stood afforded him an unrivalled view across the grey reaches of the south Davis Strait, along the course which they all prayed the berg would be following soon. Tall grey seas were rolling southward in majestic series, pulling at the departing skirts of the autumnal squall as they sailed away into the distance. It seemed to him then that he could see the whole of the North Atlantic at this point, from Baffin on his right hand to Greenland on his left, the one a brown-black line on the western horizon and the other a white glow far away to the east. But this was fanciful nonsense. All he could see was a couple of hundred square kilometres of rough water and the back end of some dirty storm clouds. A new wind patted him on the back and wrapped its chilly self round him, smelling of old ice and Arctic air. It was cold and would get colder, he thought, and the rain was gone for now, too. The berg would stop melting for a while, above the waterline at least, and that, too, was good.

He stood, lost in his thoughts, as the storm continued to clear in the distance and some blue sky began to peep through the overcast. Then, in the last of the distant shadow · under the heavy clouds, something caught Richard's eagle eye. Far away towards the phantom glow of Greenland, a light shone out green and eye-wateringly bright. It was *Antelope*, the better part of thirty miles away.

'Richard!'

Colin's excited cry called Richard back to himself. 'Yes?' He turned and found the big glaciologist pounding up the slope towards him, waving a pale paper flimsy.

'Look at this,' called Colin. 'It's come through more quickly than I could have hoped. Look at this and then we'll go back to the hut for confirmation. Kate's getting the next read-out now.'

Richard obligingly looked at the paper. A frown gathered on his high forehead as he concentrated, then it cleared and he smiled. 'You're right. Let's go talk to Kate.'

It was warm in the hut and Kate had taken off her outdoor clothing. Richard was poignantly reminded of his own wife Robin by the way in which the marine biologist's hair tumbled in a thoughtless golden profusion; but there was nothing of Robin's steady grey gaze in the green gleam of Kate's eyes. 'It's just coming through now,' she said. 'And it's looking very good indeed. Here.'

On the table in front of her lay a chart of the Davis Strait. Marked across its wide blue surface was a series of points. They were increasingly dense but it was possible to see that they were joined by a line which corkscrewed in a south-westerly direction.

Colin and Kate had been plotting the progress of the berg for more than a year now and the denser series of points showed the regular readings obtained on a twelve-hourly basis since the full station had been set up less than three months ago. And in all that time, the berg had been literally going round in circles.

But not now.

Richard had lent the scientists a satnav system from one of his ships against this very moment. The first flimsy Colin had brought up to Richard on the forecastle head was the test printout from the equipment. Kate was now receiving the first official confirmation of their exact location on the surface of the globe as read by a low-orbit satellite somewhere not too far above. She took the reading across to the chart and plotted it. She drew a line up to the previous mark and straightened. Then she turned to the men, her face alight, the whole of her slim body vibrant with excitement. 'Look!' she whispered. And they did.

For the first time since the readings started, the iceberg was moving in a straight line.

A straight line heading due south.

A beam of sunlight came in through the window and surrounded the map with a glory.

And Sam came in through the door with an empty coffee mug in his hand yelling, 'Your men have fallen over the cliff! The edge of the ice collapsed and I think all three of them are gone.'

Chapter Six

Disaster struck Dr Paul Chan, medical doctor, scientist, explosives expert, jack of all trades and United Nations worker, with a sound like a rifle shot. Later he rather fancifully thought that perhaps it had been the sound of Death's scythe hitting the ice. But he never really got it out of his head that it all began with a rifle shot.

There was no overhang and the new ice cliff had seemed to be absolutely safe, which was why the engineering team had chosen this particular spot to check their handiwork in the first place. The cliff was sheer. At first glance it looked disturbingly like a wall of green glass but there were fissures and even a small gallery or two and the way down looked easy – another good reason for checking here. Even so, Paul had insisted on full safety gear, including hard hats, and he had been careful to anchor the ropes securely at the top before he and the others went over.

They each had a rope of their own and were spread along the whole section of this face. The other two had gone first, with Paul checking the anchorage of their lines. Then he had caught up an ice axe from the equipment box beside the anchorage point of his own rope and gone over himself. He had half-expected to be abseiling down a massive slope of glass, which was why he had brought the ice axe, but the cracks and ledges he had seen from the top in fact made his descent easy. It wasn't even climbing, really. He found himself turning side on to the crystal cliff and walking down an overlapping series of ledges like a complicated staircase. Even in his bulky bright orange survival suit with its built-in Mae West, it was easy. A glance down showed that the others were doing very much the same thing. It was a brief glance down, however, for Paul was all too aware that nothing lay below them but the freezing depths of the North Atlantic; one slip would mean a swim, something he didn't fancy, even in this outfit. It was a brief glance also because he wasn't here to admire the view. He was here to check the state of the newly exposed ice.

Blowing the ice hook off the front of the berg was only the beginning, really. They had to make sure, as far as was possible, that the new cliffs were going to stand the pressure of being the bow of a ship one hundred kilometres long. The weathered cliffs on the other side were obviously up to the job; they had been standing up to the full force of the sea for however many years the berg had been afloat. These new cliffs might not be so strong. They might be backed by hollows, perhaps even caves, which would weaken them fatally. The ice itself might be weak here, soft, grainy, ready to collapse or wash away. It could be full of ground moraine caught up from whatever valley it had come from – dark soil which would soak up sunlight and quicken melting. In removing the ice hook, they could have exposed any number of fatal weaknesses which might still put the whole project at risk. They could, simply, have done more harm than good, no matter how carefully they had studied the ice, made their calculations, laid their charges and prayed.

The first impressions he got were that they had been lucky, that their prayers had been answered. That was good. He was not a particularly superstitious man, but there was something about the atmosphere on the iceberg which had him always expecting disaster. It was a feeling he knew; he had experienced it in many forms, but never quite like this. When he had worked for the UN in Somalia, he had felt just such a sensation across his shoulder blades and down his spine. He had felt it there most strongly and most memorably. In Mogadishu the feeling had originated with the sight of ten-year-olds armed to the teeth with automatic weapons and looking for someone to kill. He had felt it in most of his travels with the World Health Organisation across the war-torn, drought-stricken hopeless wastes of Africa but there had always been a reason for it, something to put his finger on – like a child carrying a Kalashnikov. But here there was nothing. The Rosses were pleasant, easy to get along with, and not at all in the common run of research scientists. The other two men in the team assigned by the United Nations to this project with him seemed pleasant enough and quietly efficient too. His own area of expertise was Africa and he had felt like a fish out of water during the ten days he had been on the ice, but even so, he should not have been jumping at shadows and waking in cold sweats at night for no apparent reason.

'What's it look like, Dave?' he called down to the man below.

'Looks like ice, Paul.'

David Brodski was a New Yorker like Paul, but he maintained a world-weary, cynical outlook on life which he blamed on his boyhood in the Bronx. Paul had yet to get an unbarbed, clear or direct answer out of him but he was amusing enough and good to have around. The pair of them had had a spirited discussion about whether it was worth climbing into full survival gear just to take a quick look over the side of the berg. Paul had won, but Dave was still smarting a little.

'Alan?' Paul yelled to the member of the team furthest down the cliff face.

'Looks good. I think we've been lucky here.'

It was then that Paul heard Death crack his scythe on the ice and their luck ran out.

The sound Paul heard was the noise made by the section of

cliff edge above the three of them breaking free. From the edge itself, inland for about two metres along a line the better part of twenty metres, the cliff sprang into motion. It cracked along a sloping fault which gave it a roughly triangular section and allowed it to slide almost sedately down onto the heads of the men below, breaking into chunks of varying sizes as it came. By the grace of God, Paul had anchored his line more than three metres back from the edge, so, unlike the others, he did not fall at once.

He looked up at the sound. It was so sharp and clear. 'Now who could be shooting up there?' he thought.

Then it was as though his eyesight and hearing were failing both at the same time. Everything he could see jumped out of focus and a deep throbbing which could only be the onset of deafness filled his head. Where there had been glassy green was now unfocused white, as though cataracts were closing down over his eyes. The throbbing burst out of the confines of his head and beat upon his ribs from within his chest. The simple stairway on which he had been standing threw him off and the world went mad around him.

'AVALANCHE!' he screamed but the cry was lost in the wild roaring. As he fell free, still screaming helplessly, he saw Dave falling, anchored still to an ice boulder which was falling with him; and Alan being swept into the white heart of the avalanche.

Then he went under himself.

Once in his youth on a holiday in California, down the coast from Big Sur, Paul had come off his surfboard on the crest of a huge breaker. The wave, more than five metres of it, curled over him as he fell and crushed him under as it broke. It had turned an expensive board to matchsticks and had come dangerously close to doing the same to him. Paul had never forgotten the wild, terrifying power of the water and the way it had whirled him about like an atom, powerless, helpless.

This was worse. The rope danced and jerked and he wished it would part as the iceberg seemed to break over his head like that wave had done. But the water here was rock-solid, sharp-edged and heavy. It bashed and shattered. Rock against rock, boulder against boulder, all of it against him: wrists, elbows, knees, shins, shoulders, ribs, back and front. He thanked God for his safety helmet, and the instant he did so it was gone. The full power of the avalanche closed round him like a giant, freezing fist. He was sure he could feel his bones breaking in the fearsome grip of it. Then everything went black.

Richard reached the cliff edge first and did some damage to his knees as he crashed down on them, skidding forward to the edge. There was a rope anchored here and another away to his left, but he could tell that the rope there was broken. There should have been one in between by the look of things, but there was no sign of it. He held on to the bright braided nylon and craned over the edge as the other three came rushing up. All he could see was an impenetrable cloud of mist and spray which roared up into his face. It was unexpected and wildly disorientating, as was the thunderous noise which told of a massive battle being fought between water and ice somewhere invisibly below. He was a fisherman, however, and his fingers read the rope as well as they could read a fly line; he knew there was a body on the end of it. A live body, by the feel of it. 'There's someone down there on the end of this rope,' he called into the freezing fog and the deafening thunder.

'That's Paul's rope,' came Kate's reply indistinctly, seemingly from some distance.

'No such luck with the other two,' observed Colin grimly. His voice was suddenly clearer. Richard looked back over his shoulder to see the loom of Colin's great body through the thinning vapour.

The mist fell away then and Richard was able to follow

the orange thread of the rope down and down until at last it was connected to the bulk of an inert body hanging helplessly against the sheer cliff face.

'Quick! Pull him up!' called Sam as he scrabbled to a slippery halt beside them. The other three hesitated, looking at each other.

'Just a second,' temporised Richard. 'We don't know how badly he's hurt.'

'He'll be dead for sure if you don't hurry,' insisted the helicopter pilot.

'I know—'

'Richard's right,' Kate interrupted. 'It's no use rushing if we put him more at risk. I'm going down to him. I can check that it's safe to move him, it'll only take a moment. I'll get my bag.'

'She's a doctor,' Colin explained to Sam who was looking after the determined woman with wonder on his face.

While they waited, Richard kept an eye on Paul's inert body and Colin prowled the very edge, searching in the surf below for any sign of the other two. There was nothing to be seen but grey waves, white foam and a restless jumble of ice. The big glaciologist's lips tightened in a grimace of frustrated anger at his inability to help the missing men.

Kate was back after a few moments carrying her bag and another length of nylon rope. It was taken for granted she would go; she was the best qualified, though her doctorate was in biology, not medicine. She was the expedition medic. She was also the lightest and perhaps the weakest. The men could lower and lift her easily and relatively safely. She could not do the same for either of them.

She tied the rope round her waist and looped it round the handle of her medical bag.

'Keep an eye on Paul's line, would you please, Sam?' asked Richard, picking himself up.

By the time the pilot was crouching over the orange rope, the two other men were standing side by side, ready to lower Kate over the edge. No words were exchanged between them, but they worked with a mechanical precision – a perfect team. It was hardly surprising that Colin and Kate should have this facility, but Sam was struck by the ease and efficiency with which Richard Mariner fitted in. When all the knots were tied and tested, and Kate was ready to go, Richard stooped and handed her the little ice axe from the equipment box at their feet. 'You may need to cut yourself a foothold,' he said.

The slim figure of the doctor backed over the edge and began to walk carefully down, with the men paying out the rope as she went. There was quite a slope, but because a whole section had fallen away, the cliff did not become vertical until she was quite near the unconscious man. It was hard work keeping her footing, for the surface of the ice was flat, featureless, slick and slippery. After her first fall, she learned to twist her body so that her shoulder hit first, not her forehead. Richard could well be right; she might indeed need to cut herself a foothold or two.

Like her husband, she was coldly furious that fate should have robbed her of two, possibly three, important colleagues just at the moment of apparent triumph. Typically, she was less concerned about herself and the danger she was going into than about the wellbeing of the victims and the potential damage to Colin's plans. What effect would this accident have on the still sceptical men at the United Nations? They were already voicing some concern about the potential cost. Chartering Richard Mariner's ships would not be cheap, even though he was offering a special rate, and there were no others on offer. Would this accident give the doubters the excuse they needed to pull out? Would this be the end of their research, their plans, the iceberg itself? She was not a sentimental person, but she had formed some attachment to this great timeless piece of ice during the year she had spent camping on it and the thought of having the US Navy blow it out of the water was not a pleasant one for her.

Still, let come what would come. She would worry about imponderables later. For now she had a hurt man to check on. She hung beside Paul's body for a moment, working out the best way to start tending him. It would be even harder than she had feared. The first move would have to be to get over him somehow. By stretching her legs apart until the insides of her thighs smarted, she could just straddle him and this is what she did, placing her feet on either side of his knees and leaning in against the pendulum pull of the rope to check his head and thorax. If he had broken legs or a broken spine at pelvis level, there was little she could do, but she would check these later. Her prime concern was to discover whether he had a broken skull, neck, or shattered ribs which would do him fatal damage when he was moved.

It was hard to be sure, especially through the bulky cold weather gear, but careful exploration revealed the pulse was steady and strong. As soon as she was sure he was alive, she injected the strongest dose of painkiller she dared, straight into the pulse in his throat – the only bare skin she could get at other than that on his face. At once he seemed to relax into an even deeper sleep. Only then did she continue her manual exploration which within the next few moments revealed a dislocated shoulder and a nasty gash on his scalp. There were swellings and bruises aplenty, but these seemed to be the only serious damage. Relief welled up in her. She leaned back and yelled up, 'He's OK from the waist up. I'm just going to check his legs!'

Here the luck seemed to have run out. As soon as she began to run her hands down his right thigh, she knew they were in trouble. Even through the bright survival suit he was wearing she could feel the thigh bone moving. She froze at once, all too aware of the possibility of sharp splinters of bone cutting into the huge arteries or veins of the thigh. Hell! she thought. They shouldn't even try to move him without some kind of splint to keep this mess steady. She checked the left leg. That seemed fine. Could she bandage his legs together and use the good thigh as a temporary makeshift support? Yes, if push came to shove, but she would be far happier if she could put something else on the other side as well.

She looked up towards the hard line made by the cliff edge and the sky. Because of the slope, neither of the men holding the rope was visible. She could call up and send one of them to get her a splint of some kind, she thought. Colin would be quicker.

As she hesitated, Paul began to come round. His first sign of returning consciousness was a deep groan of agony.

Kate looked around with gathering concern. They had better be quick about this. She didn't want an agonised patient thrashing about like a drowning man, doing himself heaven knew what damage. She opened her mouth to call up to Colin.

And just as she did so, something strange caught her eye.

In the ice beside Paul's lolling head, some debris was buried. The ice all around was deep, green, crystal clear, with nothing but silvery air bubbles like fish suspended within it. But just beyond Paul's head there was something else. It looked like a plank of wood. It wasn't very big, scarcely a metre long and maybe fifteen centimetres wide, but it was planed and square. It was battered and burned, but looked as though it had been painted. It was man-made.

It was exactly what she needed. With no further thought, she pulled the ice axe into her hand and started to chop the plank free.

Five minutes later she was able to worry the wood out of the ice, her eyes busy to see whether there was any more debris deeper in the cliff. Five minutes after she had decided there was nothing else and this miraculous piece of wood must have been dropped by a passing gull – a very big gull – she had it strapped in place. Paul was definitely coming to now, in spite of the drug she had injected, and it was imperative they get him up.

She swung back and pulled in her breath to call out, only to have her cry drowned out by Sam's astonished yell of, 'There's somebody down there! Look! In the water! There's somebody down there *alive!*'

Dave Brodski hated taking orders. Even when someone told him to do something self-evidently sensible, like putting on a survival suit before climbing down an ice cliff three hundred metres above the freezing ocean, he still gave them a hard time. This time the order had saved his life. So far.

He had not been as quick-witted as Paul. He hadn't heard any sound and he hadn't looked up to see the ice coming down on his head. It had come as an absolute surprise to him to find that he was suddenly falling. It had come as a stunning revelation to discover that about a million tons of ice were falling with him and that his safety line was securely anchored to the biggest lump among the whole collapsing mess. He actually saw it sailing past him, the rope still secure, then it simply jerked him firmly after it, deeper into the heart of the falling ice. He got a clear if momentary idea of what it must have felt like to be the captain of the *Titanic*. Then he hit the water and the last of the ice came down on top of him. His hard hat remained in place for long enough to save his skull from being shattered and he was swept down into a stunning maelstrom of foam, ice and water. The cold knocked the breath from his body and a blessedly small ice boulder knocked him senseless.

His life preserver inflated automatically and in an instant the fat, air-filled Mae West was pulling him to the surface where he floated for a while, still unconscious, hidden among the varyingly massive blocks of ice. How many minutes passed before he came to his senses he would never know. Perhaps fifteen, but no more than that, for the survival suit could only have kept him alive for twenty or so under these conditions. It was the pain which woke him: not the pain from battered limbs and bruised bones, but the growing agony of having the vital warmth leeched out of his limbs and organs. This was no restful numbness tempting the weary survivor into a deadly slumber. He felt as though every joint in his body was expanding from within, as though he was on some terrible, invisible rack and ready to explode. He screamed and the sound he made echoed so strangely that his eyes sprang open – though he had not really been aware that they were closed.

He looked around in wonder, as close to being awed as his sardonic soul could come. 'Now I know what it feels like to be the olive in a Martini,' he thought. All around him were lumps of ice, from cubes to boulders, bobbing in the grey water. The waves rolled under him, lifting and turning him, sucking him in towards the foot of the ice cliff he had just fallen down. Such was the scale of the thing that he gasped. Water went into his lungs. He choked, puked, started coughing and fighting for his life. The first thing he did was panic. He thrashed around and screamed but it soon dawned on him that no one could hear or see him down here among the ice. So he calmed down and started to think.

His paroxysm of futile splashing and arm-waving had one benefit, however. It wrapped the bright orange safety harness round his numb hand. He looked at the bobbing strand for an instant and then he thought, 'Perhaps this thing is still anchored.' The vision of an ice boulder seemingly half as big as a house with his rope safely anchored to it crossed his mind. If he could pull himself across to it, he thought, he might just be able to pull himself up on it too.

Doggedly, with the will power only ever granted to those at death's door, he began to pull the rope in, hand over hand. The action was dangerously repetitious, however, and not even the agony in his joints could keep his mind active so that after a moment or two he began to slow down without meaning to and by the time he reached his goal he was too far gone to do anything other than hang there and wonder what it was he had planned to do next.

In the final analysis it was Alan who saved him.

Alan had been the unluckiest one of all. The first big ice block had hit him on the side of the head and killed him at once. His rope had held firm for just long enough to let the succeeding boulders smash into his head and face, splitting skin and bone like a Halloween pumpkin, before it had parted, dropping him into the thickest section of the ice fall. By the time he had reached the black depths of the ocean, there was hardly a bone in his body left unbroken. His survival suit was torn and bloodied, hanging in rags around him. His Mae West was punctured in several places but the gas bottle and the automatic release still worked.

Dave, hanging comatose against the edge of the ice block, was suddenly confronted by the ruined corpse of his friend which burst out of the water beside him as though still fighting to survive. For a moment they remained there, frozen, face to face. Alan's broken visage with its burst eyes bulging and its shattered jaw flapping seemed to be screaming, and indeed the sound of gas escaping from the ruptured Mae West would have drowned out a banshee. Dave was transfixed by the gruesome power of it. His dying body was flooded with the greatest dose of adrenaline it had ever experienced. He gave a shriek of naked terror and fought his way frantically up onto the rocking ice floe. Behind him, Alan, as though satisfied with a job well done, toppled forward to lie face down, hiding the horror his head had become. The last of the gas whispered out of his wrecked Mae West and he sank into blessed oblivion.

They pulled up Kate and Paul with all the despatch safety would allow. As he relieved Sam at the top of Paul Chan's line, Richard rapped to the pilot, 'Fire up the Huey. We'll have to go down after the other one in that.'

Sam nodded numbly and ran. What sort of people were these? he wondered. Did they ever get lost and confused? Did they ever hesitate or stop in the face of a crisis, uncertain what to do?

He hit the side door of the helicopter and swarmed aboard.

The man had said to fire her up and Sam wasn't hesitating either.

As soon as Kate came over the edge she was running over towards Richard who was pulling her patient up. As she reached him, Paul's body came in over the edge and she was there on her knees, her hands as busy as her eyes, making as sure as possible that the groaning man was brought onto the ice with no further damage. Only when she was satisfied, in that moment of leisure before Colin came panting up with a stretcher from the emergency hut, did she look down towards the sea where the miracle of another figure lay spread out on the largest ice floe like a bright orange star fish.

'We'll both have to go in the helicopter,' Colin was saying as they put Paul onto the stretcher and began to hurry him towards the biggest hut.

Richard had already gone, pulling the nylon rope from round his body, preparing to use it as a lifeline to the second survivor. Kate's green eyes followed him as he ran across the ice.

'I know,' she said. 'But be careful. Remember your hand.'

He booted the door open and then caught it on his

shoulder as it rebounded. 'I will,' he promised.

He swung the head end of the stretcher onto the nearest bed and paused only until she had placed the foot end safely in place. 'Got to run,' he said.

'I'll be fine.'

'Good.'

He was gone.

Kate took a deep breath, counted to ten, kicked the door shut with more force than was absolutely necessary, turned the heating up full and began to take Paul's clothes off. As she finished undoing the first zip on the survival suit, she heard the helicopter clatter up into the air.

'I'll go down onto the ice,' Richard was yelling. 'You lower me.'

'I can do that but I don't think I can pull you back up.' Colin held up his left arm. He stripped off mitten and glove to reveal a hand that was all too obviously plastic. 'It will hold while I lower but I wouldn't trust it to pull you up. Kate was about the limit.'

'OK. You get me down and then secure the rope in here. Sam, can you lift us up and carry us up to the top of the berg?'

'You'll have to be careful to tie the right knots.'

'I haven't had to pass elementary seamanship in a long while but I'll manage.'

'Look,' persisted Colin, 'I can go down. You're strong enough to pull me up, I'm sure.'

'Too risky, Colin. That outfit wouldn't be much help if you went into the water. At least I'm in one of *Antelope*'s survival suits.'

The big glaciologist nodded in reluctant agreement.

'Nearly there,' called Sam.

As the helicopter danced down the last few metres to hover above the marooned man, Richard knotted one end of the rope round his waist. Colin belayed the other end to a seat foot and pulled at it until the whole fuselage shook. 'Right!' he yelled.

Richard opened the sliding door in the Huey's side and looked out into the battering waterfall of air beneath the rotors. The floe was a couple of metres below him with the body spread across about half of it. It lay quite still, giving no indication at all whether or not the survivor had heard the helicopter or was in any condition to react even if he had done so. Richard's ice-blue eyes narrowed for a moment as he took stock. Whichever one of the men it was, he was hanging on to the anchorage point Paul had driven into the ice before it fell from the cliff top. How on earth could it have remained secure through all this?

If it was Alan, then he was simply holding on to the rope as a safe handhold. If it was Dave, then he could well still be tied to it. Richard turned to yell at Colin but even as he did so, his big companion shoved a wicked looking knife out towards him. Richard grinned wolfishly, put the icy blade between his teeth and jumped.

He hit the slippery surface of the ice jarringly hard and felt his knees twist in agonised protest. He pitched forward, as he had calculated – and hoped – he would, to sprawl across the body of the man he had come to rescue and share his handhold. He saw at once that it was Dave Brodski. Dave seemed to be unconscious. That was hardly surprising. He had been in the water for the better part of twenty-five minutes. He would be lucky to pull through.

Richard knelt up on his protesting knees and sawed at the rope by the anchorage point. The knife was sharp. Half a dozen desperate pulls and the orange fibres parted. Richard pulled as much slack towards himself as possible and hitched Dave's line to his own. Then he turned into the savage, numbing blast of the helicopter's down draught and gestured to Colin.

At once the Huey began to lift and he just had time to pull himself to his feet before he was lifted gently into the air. Less than a metre below him, his lolling head level with Richard's aching knees, Dave Brodski followed suit.

Dangling there, one hand on the rope reaching up above his head and the other on the rope down below, fighting to breathe against the constriction of the rope round him, Richard had an even better view of the Davis Strait than he had enjoyed from the front of the iceberg. And he had some leisure to enjoy it, though it was an incongruous position for sightseeing. The great bow-formed cliffs seemed to be driving southwards now and the calming waves held enough of the last squall to look like a bow wave foaming at its counter. Beyond the dazzling, deadly beauty of the ice, the end of a bright afternoon was drawing out into the long evening of early autumn in high latitudes.

His mind was racing. He was going over the things he needed to do at once before he left to return to *Antelope* tonight, and London tomorrow. And he was already drawing his plans – or, more accurately, firming up plans already drawn – to liberate six supertankers and get them here before winter set in.

He wasn't sure precisely when, but sometime this afternoon he had become convinced that Colin Ross's plan would work. That they really were going to take this thing to Africa.

Kate looked up as they carried Dave into the big hut. Paul was lying on the stretcher clad only in his Calvin Kleins and she was putting the finishing touches to a proper bandage on his thigh. 'It's not as bad as I'd feared,' she said, 'but I think he'd better go back to *Antelope* with you, Richard. If Dave has to go too it'll be a bit crowded, though.'

'We'll manage,' said Richard. 'First order of business is to see how he is.'

As a first officer, Richard had done his stint as acting medical officer on several ships, but his knowledge had only been basic then and was rusty now to say the least. Kate went to work and there was nothing further for him to do on the medical front.

He made some coffee and went into a close huddle with Colin. By the time she had finished, they had ironed out all the details that needed to be addressed at the moment. The three of them, with a fascinated Sam in tow, went to consult the satnav. Still in a straight line. Still due south.

'She's sailing like a ship now,' observed Richard. 'Perhaps we should give her a name.'

'She may already have one,' said Kate. 'I found a plank of wood in that ice cliff. God alone knows where it came from but it was heaven sent to use as a splint. It has a name written on it.'

'What? Where is it? Let's have a look,' said Colin, speaking for them all.

They went back into the big hut and she found the painted plank where she had kicked it under Paul's bunk.

'There you are,' she said, holding it out for them to see. 'It's part of a name. It's Russian. I'm a bit rusty, but I think it says Leonid.'

'Leonid?' asked Richard, frowning down at the strange piece of wood.

The Russian characters were painted in black on wood which had once been painted white. Both coats of paint were scorched and blistered now. Just looking at it made Richard feel uncomfortable, as though there was something supernatural at work here.

'Yes,' answered Kate. 'My Russian's rusty, as I said, but the word is familiar because it's part of such a well known name: Leonid Brezhnev. The late Chairman of the Soviet Party. Yes. I'm sure it says Leonid.'

Richard frowned. 'Well, I suppose in these post-*glasnost* days we could give her a Russian name, but—'

'Leonid Shmeonid,' rasped a weary Bronx voice behind them. 'This mother nearly killed two New York boys this

87

afternoon and I guess that gives us some say in the matter.'

They all turned round to see Dave Brodski leaning up on one elbow. He was dressed only in pyjama pants and his battered face and barrel torso were covered in so many scrapes, scratches, welts, blotches and bruises that it looked as though he had just lost a long, hard boxing match with the likes of Muhammad Ali.

Kate was still holding the mysterious plank of wood. She used it to point at the battered man. 'Well, what do you think we ought to call it, then?' she demanded.

'Hell, it's obvious, lady. What you got here is a boat made out of ice that's the size of an island. So you should call it after the most famous island in the world. You got to call it "Manhattan".'

Chapter Seven

The boardroom at Heritage House doubled as the dining room and was available to anyone who worked in the building and their guests between twelve and two. At two thirty in the afternoon, exactly a week after Richard had stepped down from the Huey onto the iceberg, the air in the boardroom was still redolent of gourmet luncheon, in spite of the discreet efforts of the extractor fans to push all such odours out into Leadenhall Street.

The atmosphere was not as relaxing as the sweet-smelling air.

The room was panelled in oak said to have been rescued from one of Nelson's Trafalgar fleet, and on the lovingly tended wood hung a series of naval prints. At one end of the room stood a glass case containing a detailed model of *Prometheus II*, the flagship of the Heritage Mariner fleet. She was a supertanker, a quarter of a million tonner, currently making her way back from the Gulf with a cargo of oil; a situation which everyone in the room knew to be increasingly rare. At the other end, in pride of place under the windows looking out across the busy London street, a pair of smaller glass cases contained models of *Katapult*, the elegant multihull which represented Heritage Mariner's unexpectedly successful move into the world of leisure boating, and of *Atropos*, the nuclear waste transporter, currently working between Canada and Europe, moving the byproducts of nuclear power and weaponry as safely as it was possible to do. Her sister, *Clotho*, was even now in dry dock at Harland and Wolff's, having her bow section replaced and strengthened after an accident-filled and deadly dangerous summer.

Four members of Heritage Mariner's executive board sat silently round the table while the fifth, Richard himself, stood. Richard was unexpectedly feeling isolated, almost threatened; on trial. It was a feeling he knew well enough – he had spent part of the summer in litigation, with the future of the company at stake – but it was a novel feeling in his own boardroom.

His ice-blue eyes swept round the table again as he re-ordered his thoughts and prepared to begin his argument again. Robin was on his side. She had met Colin and Kate. She shared the dream. Her steady grey gaze met his and she gave him a tiny smile of support and a minuscule nod which made her gold curls glint like guineas in the strong September sunshine.

Her father, Sir William, sitting at her side, was not so convinced. Still tired looking and gaunt after heart surgery and the insertion of a pacemaker, he was ready to vote for a period of conservative retrenchment. That was under-standable. His heart attack had been the climax of the worst couple of weeks any of them had ever experienced. He was still convalescent and only the importance of this meeting had called him down from Cold Fell, his great house in Cumbria where he spent almost all his time now.

Beside Bill sat Helen DuFour. The calm, pragmatic Provençal chief executive was not convinced either. She shared most things with Sir William and she shared his opinion now. They had been lucky to survive the summer, personally and financially. The court case had come too close to ruining them, and still might do so if things went badly at the American bar. The cost of keeping lawyers in New York was crippling. So was the cost of insuring the ten hulls they owned, but the fact that it was the insurers who were fixing and refitting *Clotho* proved how worthwhile the crippling expenses really were. They had just survived some extremely bad publicity and they were all too well aware that they had made some dangerous enemies in the media. They had been on the wrong end of terrorist action, one of the reasons their insurance premiums were so high, and looked likely to remain a target as long as they continued to handle nuclear byproducts. All in all, it looked as though there was a hard winter coming, especially as the promised upturn in several important economies was failing to materialise. This was not the time for harebrained experimental schemes.

And at the far end of the table, with the secretary quietly behind his shoulder waiting to continue with the minutes of the meeting, sat the least convinced board member of all. Charles – never Charlie – Lee's eyes were long, dark and narrow, as befitted a man who had cut his teeth in the frantic markets of Hong Kong, but his face had none of the roundness of common Chinese ancestry. On the contrary, it was fine and thin with high, sharp cheekbones and a broad, domed forehead. When he spoke, his inevitably quiet voice coupled an American twang with an English drawl in a manner which whispered of an extremely broad education.

They had been lucky to get him, for he was a very high flyer indeed and a man of awesome business acumen. He had come to them for a whole series of reasons reaching – inevitably, given his background – back into the mists of time. He claimed Manchu blood. His face and form supported that claim. He was the only son of one of the founding families of Hong Kong. The generations before him had amassed and lost great fortunes. His father, starting with next to nothing after the war, had done much to re-establish those fortunes without moving the basis of his business out of the sight of Kowloon harbour. This was apt enough, for he had been a shipping man.

Although he had little education himself, Charles's father had realised its importance and had invested much of his new fortune in educating his only offspring. After education at Winchester, Johns Hopkins and the London School of Economics, Charles had returned to spend the eighties extending the family business. But, like many men of his generation in Hong Kong, he had fallen foul of the Chinese government. His name had been mentioned by several student leaders caught in Tiananmen Square and the new mandarins in Beijing suddenly realised what an effort he and some others had been making to win over the next generation of Chinese officialdom, the generation that would be ruling Hong Kong when the colony returned to Chinese control in 1997. It had not occurred to the Chinese government until then that anyone could be so arrogant as to foment unrest, infect young minds, finance nascent political parties, all in an attempt to control the government itself and the power of a money market that they had hoped to control themselves. It came as a shock. It was seen as an outrage. It had so nearly worked, too. Consequently, it had been borne forcefully upon him that as soon as Hong Kong became Chinese again, Charles Lee and his company would cease to exist. So he had come west to work, to wait and to watch.

He was even more careful than Sir William, the man whose executive power he had assumed. It was paper power in Charles's case but none the less real for that, and the Hong Kong Chinese executive knew this very well. All the stock of the company was held in this room. Originally it had been held by Sir William's family, by himself, his wife and his two daughters. Lady Heritage's portion had gone in equal shares to Rowena and Robin on her death, but some of Rowena's had gone to Richard on their marriage and he had held on to it during their stormy relationship and during the years of estrangement which followed her death. Now he held some of Robin's too, for he had married the little sister ten years ago and his second marriage had been everything the first had not.

Only Sir William held more stock in the business; only he wielded more power when push came to shove. But the family had agreed that the company could only survive if the power of ownership deferred to the power of senior company executives such as Helen and Charles. Richard had never seen this as any constraint. Until now.

'Look,' he began again, 'it's a once in a lifetime chance. We have the interest, the political and financial backing ready to go. It looks as though it can be done and there are suddenly a lot of people all over the world who want to see it done. If it is done, then a whole new door opens. If anyone proves that pulling an iceberg to a desert and delivering fresh water to drought-stricken areas is actually feasible then we suddenly have a whole new industry, a new *shipping* industry. It'll be like oil transport in the seventies, the sky will be the limit, and if we get in now we'll be holding all the chips. You must see that.'

Charles Lee shook his head. 'I see us committing more than half of our entire fleet to one venture which has incalculable risks and uncertain rewards. I see winter closing in while you try to move this thing through the North Atlantic. I see you arriving off the Gulf of Mexico at the height of the hurricane season. I see you pulling a lump of ice across the equator into high summer where it will be very hot indeed and watching it all just melt away. I see problems of contract, payment and command structures. I see problems rearranging tanker schedules at this end and I see no final destination at the other end. I see no one in their right mind at the United Nations actually wanting to get involved with this when they have properly assessed the financial and political risks and dangers. But most of all I see no one in their right mind offering us any insurance cover whatsoever and without that, this is a dead issue.'

'We can't just stand still and catch our breath,' Richard

shot back. 'We compete or we die, and we've got to keep looking for new markets. The oil market's collapsed. The leisure market will take off when the recovery does. *If* the recovery does. The waste disposal market's dead slow to stop. *Atropos* is fully employed but it's a blessing *Clotho*'s in dry dock, because we couldn't make much use of her until the British government make up their minds about Thorp and Sellafield and the whole question of reprocessing. The whole question of fast breeder nuclear reactors. The whole nuclear question itself, come to that. The only possible area of expansion is Russia. How's that coming, Helen?'

'Slowly. The government in Moscow's still in trouble. The republics are dragging their feet. They don't want fast breeder reactors either, not after Chernobyl and Tomsk Seven. And of course the whole point of reprocessing like British Nuclear Fuel propose at Thorp is that you extract the elements needed in fast breeders. And to make matters worse, the Russians don't really want to part with the nuclear weapons Yeltsin and Bush agreed must be decommissioned. Some republics even see their nuclear arsenals and expertise as their only short-term chance of earning foreign currency. And the really dangerous stuff, the stuff they don't want and only an outfit like ours could handle properly, still doesn't come our way because they just shove it onto container ships and dump it on Novaya Zemlya – though of course they swear they don't do that any more and the Americans would probably cut off all their aid if there was any real proof. All in all, it's slow, hard work. And you know the Russians. One minute you've got a contract, the next . . .' She gave one of her expressive Gallic shrugs.

Richard sprang into the attack. 'So, retrenchment isn't as risk-free as you seem to think, Charles. That iceberg may well represent a real chance. A genuine business deal. With a responsible, reasonable, reliable, rich client. Look at it. Look at what happens in Africa when the drought sets in. Look at Somalia! Don't you think the UN and the US and all the other countries and organisations trying to police the world realise how much cheaper it would be to avert a war instead of trying to contain one? And this is a real chance to do just that. Sure there are risks. Yes, there will be problems, dangers even. One man is dead already, God help us. More might die. Yes. But think of the benefits if it all works. For the world as a whole! For us!'

Charles shifted in his chair. His brown-black eyes swept round the table, reading the expressions there. 'Two for and two against,' he said and four heads nodded. 'I have the casting vote then, and I vote to put it to a full board. If you can persuade the duly appointed representatives of our bankers and most of all our *insurers*—'

The phone rang and the secretary quickly crossed to answer it. Silence settled on the long room, a silence emphasised by the quiet of the footsteps and the conversations in the street outside. Like the centre of Belfast, the centre of London was ringed with steel against the IRA now and there was little traffic allowed.

The secretary turned, her hand automatically covering the mouthpiece of the phone so that their deliberations remained private. 'It's the secretariat upstairs,' she said quietly. 'A fax has just arrived for Captain Richard Mariner. They'll bring it down when it's finished printing out.'

'What is it? Any idea?' asked Richard.

'Yes, sir. According to the title page, it's the draft contract for the hire of six supertankers and it's apparently being sent directly from the office of the Secretary-General of the United Nations in New York.'

Chapter Eight

Ann Cable ran across her suite in the Mawanga Hilton, tearing off her clothes as she went. The buttons of her bush jacket ripped free of the buttonholes and those of her shirt burst loose to rattle against the wall. She paused only to get rid of her desert boots and rip her shorts down, then she was in motion again, heading towards the bathroom and the blessed promise of the shower.

The air conditioning in the whole hotel was down again, so even with the big fan turning up above her head, the air was as thick and hot as boiling oil. Although the shutters were closed against the afternoon sun, it glowed round their edges as though each one was a grill full on. There was no relief from the blistering heat, inside or out. She threw a sock across the room and it landed in an explosion of coarse red dust.

As she strode past the long mirror, she glanced automatically across at it, catching a glimpse of herself in a bar of sunlight, every curve and hollow of her covered in that same red dust as though she had first-degree burns. The whole of her long body felt as though it was infested with crawling things – things which scuttled restlessly over her olive skin and nested in her groin and under her arms, biting her mercilessly there. She tore her flimsy brassiere away and supported herself against the frame of the open door as she hopped on one leg to rid herself of her dust-caked white cotton pants. The tile of the bathroom floor was cool beneath her hot feet but this only served to emphasise the agonised discomfort of the rest of her.

She was actually groaning with expectation as she entered the tall cubicle, her need too great to allow her to bother with minor details like closing the shower door. Her concentration as she used both hands to turn on the cold tap was that of an addict injecting a drug and her gasp of relief as the first cold spray hit her upper chest was hoarse and guttural. She swept her hands up over her ribs and cradled her breasts in cool pools cupped in her palms until her nipples tensed with the cold. For an instant more she stood beneath the numbing blast, then she turned, mouth open and eyes closed, to let it pound against the back of her neck and slide like grains of ice across the breadth of her shoulders and down the length of her spine. She arched her long back ecstatically until the needles of cold beat through her thick, dark hair. But even this was not enough. She turned again, reaching up to pull the shower's handset off the wall, then she ran the freezing power of the water quickly down her body until she could aim it directly up between her legs until coolness at last began to come. And with it came her self-control. Her left hand flew out and smashed against the tap, bloodying her knuckles as she turned the water off.

Then she was on her knees in the disappearing pools of water, swearing out loud, sobbing with anger and frustration, almost all of it aimed at herself and her Western, white-skinned weakness.

She had become so wildly over-heated out in the bush, interviewing local tribesmen and women who were dying in their thousands because of the drought. During the last few, unforgivably self-indulgent moments she had used enough water to keep a village baby alive for a month.

She sat back on the cool porcelain and slid across the shower stall until she could curl up in the corner with her back against the tiled wall, and while she waited for the prickly heat to return, she sucked her bleeding knuckles and she thought. She thought about this place where she was trapped, watching a tragedy and waiting for a war.

The state of Mau lay between Guinea and Gabon, north of Zaire on the west coat of Africa. At the back ends of the Bights of Biafra and Benin in the Gulf of Guinea as they had featured in her old school atlas in the days when Africa had seemed a romantic place to her. Now it looked very different. Now a country like Mau, a city like Mawanga just looked like the crippled, dangerous offspring of uncaring, abusive parents. Just like so many other states on the west coast; like so many in Africa as a whole.

Mau had been formed – malformed from the very beginning – by volcanic activity soon after the birth of the continent which would one day become Africa. At some time far back in pre-history, the rocky plains which would become this dark continent split. One block of land was thrust up while the one beside it fell. For hundreds of kilometres in from what would one day become the west coast, a tectonic cliff thrust up. As the years passed into centuries and millennia and the continents drifted apart, so the water of the young Atlantic came to the foot of the cliff and then withdrew to run north/south at right angles to it.

At the top of the cliff grew a thick, lush jungle which swept northwards down the back of an incline into the forests of what would later become Guinea and the mountains of Cameroon. This jungle was supported by the weight of the rain which was carried in the moist winds that moved along the northern edge of the equator and was made to fall by the sudden upthrust of the cliff. But the jungle itself could not contain the rain and so a river was born which ran, in common with its brothers the Shangha, Ubangi and Zaire, south and west. Over the cliff edge came the great River Mau to thunder down two hundred metres sheer. At the foot of the cliff, the lie of the land turned the flow of water due west at once to run along the foot of the escarpment until it was gulped in by the greedy ocean more than five hundred kilometres distant. But the great flow of the Mau brought all sorts of silt and detritus and this formed a delta over the years, thrusting the coast away from the cliff foot into a flat alluvial plain. No matter how wide the plain became, it seemed the flow of the river was always enough to keep the centre of it clear so that a pair of sandy horns thrust out, like the tusks of the lowland elephants which wandered the green thorn country at the foot of the cliffs. But in fact there was more to it than that. The power of that first tectonic heave had been such that it had split the continental shelf. Although the plain and the sheltering harbour horns reached out, the bottom of Mawanga Bay reached down nearly a thousand metres and not even the mighty River Mau could fill it.

The N'Kuru tribe lived on the plain by the river at the escarpment foot from the dawn of the age of man. They were a tall people, who soon learned to organise themselves into loose confederations of villages and to keep, and trade, the cattle of the grasslands. They hunted little, mostly to protect their villages and half-wild cattle from the marauding herds of elephant and antelope, and the lions and cheetahs which roamed and hunted on the green pastures with their outcrops of baobab trees and thorn scrub. The N'Kuru took great delight in the bones and antlers, the skins, teeth and ivory their expeditions brought back home. Their hunting weapon was the long spear. When they made war they used intricately carved clubs fanged with lions' claws, and the ox-hide shield. It was rare that they warred among themselves, for they had other enemies close by.

In the jungle at the top of the great escarpment lived the secretive, mysterious Kyogas. They were slighter, darker. They were not farmers at all, only hunters and explorers, ranging widely through the forests to the north. Their weapons were those of men who need to kill at a distance or at a great height: the bow and arrow. They tipped their arrows with poison prepared by wise women who passed the secret down from generation to generation. Inevitably they began to climb down the great cliffs in the darkness to enjoy the easy, rewarding hunting of the N'Kuru cattle on the plain. They found the N'Kuru women pleasing and would sometimes steal them, too; but no N'Kuru woman was ever told the secret of the poison. If forced to trade, a pastime they tended to look down upon, the Kyogas would part grudgingly with ornaments made of bright copper. But they would never say where the yellow metal came from. For centuries, a lazy rivalry festered, erupting occasionally into warfare as the farmers and traders of the plain were roused by some mighty warlord to defend themselves against the savage, witch-driven hunters of the high jungle.

Such a warlord was the great Mwanga who ruled from the coastal village which was later to bear his name in the year when the first Arab trading dhow came nosing down the coast. The Arab traders had spent the better part of a century exploring the length of this coast, watch by watch, from Tunis. On the far side of the continent, in a world undreamed of by the N'Kuru or even by the most intrepid Kyoga explorer, the sons of Sinbad had struck out into the magic vastness of the Indian Ocean, borne upon the wings of the monsoon. Here there were only winds like the harmattan blowing up and down the coast, and the sea to the west was forbidding and tall. No one who had ventured out upon it had ever returned, so now the capains crept along, never out of sight of the land, camping ashore each night. The Arab traders came seeking rare wood, spices, ivory and slaves. The N'Kuru were glad to trade; it was a profession they had followed since the dawn of time and they were proud of their commercial abilities. They had traded long in all the goods of interest to the strange, light-skinned men. In all except one. The Arabs added to their education in a single, important regard. Even Mwanga himself had only considered killing his enemies; he had never thought to sell them.

But the Arab craft were small, suited only to the shallow coastal waters, and the way from Tangier was long. The Arabs never took many slaves, though the dark seed was sown. The villages, especially those along the coast, began to stockpile goods they knew the traders would want. Mwanga, a practical man, quickly understood that the strongest of his farmer subjects should be made into a warrior class whose task would be to fetch ivory, antlers, pelts and hides, and the fairest, most saleable of the sons and daughters made by the marauding Kyoga on the kidnapped N'Kuru girls.

The English captain John Smith came to the thriving village of Mawanga in the year Europeans called 1560 when the son of Mwanga's son's son was a very elderly king. The strange white creature in his boat as big as the great hut of the warriors wanted everything that the Arab traders did but in unimaginably greater quantities. Fortunately he was not too interested in the quality of the goods, and the N'Kuru soon understood – though they could hardly credit the fact – that the white skins were quite content to take even ugly little full-blooded Kyoga men and women.

During the next three centuries, Mawanga grew from a village to a trading port and to a town – almost a city. The English drove the Arabs out and built a stone fort to the seaward side of the village which was designed to protect the anchorage. The fort was a good idea but it was rarely adequately manned and the Arabs took it back with ease whenever they found the energy. As did the English, come to that. The relationship between the northern traders and the natives varied from co-operative peace to outright war.

The fort was sacked and the garrison slaughtered on more than one occasion, but the stone walls remained and the traders came back again and again. Mwanga's dynasty became dissolute and greedy. The white skins and the Arabs connived at its overthrow and replaced it with a series of their own chosen men. Peace came, and a kind of prosperity. Mwanga the great leader passed into shadowy legend. At last only the name remained as the name of the town itself.

A new breed of white skin arrived; men and a few women who were not content to stay on the coast but wished to explore and map and describe what they found. They followed the River Mau up to the great falls and beyond. Sometimes they found a N'Kuru spear, sometimes a Kyoga arrow. And, like the traders, they continued to come. As did the missionaries who set up their churches first and then their schools. They taught about a white-skinned god who loved the world so much that he allowed himself to be nailed to a tree to save it. The N'Kuru, exposed to this first, were far too proud to be influenced by a man who preferred to die rather than to kill. They liked the idea of nailing people to trees, however, and did it to several missionaries. But still they came. The Kyoga reacted differently to religion. Perhaps the missionaries were less arrogant with them, for they had seen what the N'Kuru had done to several of their martyred number and it was common knowledge that the hag-ridden devil worshippers in their jungles atop the mighty ridge were twenty times as deadly. In fact the Kyoga were intelligent and interested. The school did well, though the church never really took hold. And for once the natives seemed resistant to the diseases of civilisation while the missionaries contracted ailments without number which were usually fatal.

The relationship between the N'Kuru and the Kyoga remained the same as it had been before the pale-skinned

Arabs and the white-skinned Europeans began to interfere but then, as the twentieth century began to loom, it worsened. And the reason was rubber.

In spite of the persistence of the English slave traders over the years, Mau never fell into the British sphere of influence. Instead it became an outcrop of those territories owned absolutely by the Emperor Leopold. He offered great tracts of the verdant country to his hangers-on at court, but none had the wish or the will to be farmers, even by proxy. One or two settlers arrived in long wagons pulled by oxen modelled on the successful design favoured by the Dutch further south. The N'Kuru wisely slaughtered them and blamed it on the Kyoga. And then, as it had been in the forests around the Congo, rubber was discovered in the jungle atop the escarpment where the Kyoga continued to live. Leopold's men were quick to understand the contempt with which the N'Kuru viewed their smaller, darker neighbours, and so the rubber growers gave the tall ex-farmers guns, whips and, most importantly, heavy, sharp pangas, and they made them overseers.

This was the darkest hour in all the history of the Kyoga. Their jungle villages were overrun and their people placed in a new and savage bondage. Quotas were dictated in far Brussels by businessmen with no knowledge or understanding of how impossible it would be to fulfil them. Made arrogant by distance and ignorance, they demanded that their local representatives force their workers to greater efforts. The local men, deaf to the protests of the last, sickly missionaries, began to threaten the N'Kuru: if the local tribes were not up to the job, they would import outsiders who were – they had no end of experienced overseers on the black banks of the Congo. The N'Kuru and the Kyoga could work side by side in the jungle. Such threats spurred the N'Kuru to frenzies of cruelty – cruelty imported, like slavery, by the pale skins. For every man, woman and child of the Kyoga nation, a quota was set. At the end of each quota period, the white latex each had collected was weighed and measured. The first failure to meet the quota cost a finger. The second cost a hand. The third a foot. The fourth an eye. The fifth – and there were blessedly few – a testicle or a breast. The missionaries tried to help by searing closed the wounds and bringing the sufferers back to working fitness as quickly as they could. By the time a couple of million men were being slaughtered on the fields of Flanders, a similar number were being disfigured and destroyed in the anonymous western African jungles to supply the white-skin armies with the ton upon ton of rubber they needed to keep the killing going: men and women and children; arms and legs and eyes.

In that strange combination of exhaustion and euphoria which followed the end of the Great War, the voices of the missionary societies were at last listened to and it was decided that more humane ways could be found to gather rubber, and the N'Kuru were ordered to stop disfiguring their charges. But because they had tried to help, and so had seemed to condone, the missionaries had lost the good will of the Kyoga. Their churches were burned and the last few of them slaughtered. But the Kyoga had learned about white-skin education – the most important lesson of all although it availed them little in the face of their N'Kuru overseers.

Only after the likes of Joseph Conrad and Roger Casement had been up the river to the Leopold Falls and then up into the jungle beyond did the European world begin to learn of the atrocities their representatives had caused, and the injunction was rigidly enforced. In any case, the rubber market was easing and there were other areas which could supply it. So the jungle was left to the crippled Kyogas and attention was turned once more to the N'Kuru's plains. Farmers arrived, fresh-faced and hopeful, ready to colonise the vast pasture lands. This time they arrived in large numbers, in motorised caravans armed to the teeth with the kind of weapons which can only be perfected in a war. The N'Kuru watched their farmland being split among white skins and their grazing land surrender to the plough. They watched fences chop the bush into ugly, pointless squares, and they saw the elephant chopped down like trees because they too failed to understand the fences. The bottom fell out of the ivory market because of the massive over-supply. The lordly, arrogant herdsmen became mere farm hands employed to cultivate land which had been theirs for all time. Men who had never deigned to bow their heads were forced to bend their backs or starve. Princes were paid pennies for their pride.

Mawanga, however, prospered. As the farms began to flourish, so their produce had to be shipped. The port, deep beyond measuring but sheltered by those welcoming harbour horns, was filled with an increasing bustle of shipping as tobacco, meat and grain went out and a range of new fertilisers and supplies came in. White hunters arrived, expecting to clear the plains of game for the farmers but instead they rediscovered the escarpment. Jungle safaris were arranged and tourists arrived expecting to be able to shoot antelope, elephant, wildebeest and lion on the plains one day and mountain gorillas up the escarpment on the next. The N'Kuru, understandably uncertain of these developments, were soon characterised as sullen and lazy. The Kyoga, discovered anew in the jungle, were immediately recognised as excellent bushmen, mighty hunters and natural askaris. A few intrepid film directors arrived from Hollywood. The yodelling cries of Tarzan echoed from the high edge of the escarpment. Some Hollywood stars arrived. Conrad Hilton thought he'd better put up a hotel. With a keen eye for a good location, the Hilton Organisation raised their tall hotel on the northern inland outskirts of the town, where the lower coastal slopes of the tectonic cliff overlooked the city and the harbour from a safe, exclusive distance. Where the air was cooler and sweeter. It was a suburb which soon attracted many others who could afford to leave the hot, malodorous bustle of the busy port. Mawanga grew and grew.

And then, just as the political sky to the north began to darken once again, somebody discovered copper, cobalt and uranium upcountry. Heavy industry arrived and engineering plant passed through Mawanga and up the Mau to the Leopold Falls. A powerful funicular railway was built to move equipment, ore and metal up and down the tectonic cliff. The mines were all on Kyoga land. The Kyoga were recognised as hard workers, bright and trustworthy. They took responsibility. In return they were given education. With that they earned money and, most precious of all, power. The N'Kuru were treated as sullen children and their resentment simmered towards boiling point.

The Second World War, when it came, touched the country of Mau hardly at all. It was physically removed from large theatres of conflict and all that was noticed was that the demands for supplies were more strident and the European managers fewer. The Kyoga took over. They were the educated class, the businessmen with the proud history as hunters. The N'Kuru continued to grub in the red dirt of their land, ordered to grow unsuitable crops by inefficient farmers required to meet more and more impossible targets. At least they didn't lop off hands and feet this time. The Kyoga watched and waited.

The resentment of the N'Kuru nation overflowed soon after the end of the war. A new wave of settlers, sent out as soon as they were demobbed, settled into areas hitherto considered unfarmable and began to fight the land in their efforts to produce coffee, cocoa, groundnuts and cotton. The N'Kuru's patience ran out. In camps and what was left of the old villages, young men began to band together in the night carving again the old war clubs and arming them with lions' claws.

When the farmers and their families began to be found

clawed to death by lions in their beds, it took very little time for the local government to realise what was going on. Neither the white skins with their hearts in Europe nor the Kyoga government ministers could control the uprising. They called to Europe for help and Europe sent troops in. Within six months of the first death, there was a dirty little bush war going on. No obvious leader emerged from the ranks of the N'Kuru Lion fighters, and the reason for this soon became obvious. The liberation army was receiving advice on the best way to organise themselves – in little cadres, each member of which knew only his immediate associates. It was a format which the intelligence officers with the European troops recognised all too well. Communist advisers had arrived in the ranks of the N'Kuru secret army.

The men in Brussels shook their heads. It was nearly 1960. The English Prime Minister Harold Macmillan had observed that a wind of change was blowing over Africa. A gust of that wind arrived in Mau. The point of colonisation was to make money. As soon as the army of occupation required to control the communist-inspired insurgents began to cost more than the country was earning for its imperial overlords, it was granted independence. Power was simply handed to the Kyoga politicians who had been running their own puppet parliament since the end of the war. The white-skin Governor shook the small-boned, black-skinned hand of the new Premier and Mau was on its own. The European civil servants left. Many of the farmers on the plains, who had been hanging on only because of the protection afforded by the European army, left with them. Up in the highlands, the mines remained viable and to begin with it looked as if there were enough foreign businesses interested in supporting the economy – enough European banks willing to offer loans – to enable Mau to stand on its own feet. But the guerrilla war went on. The army and the police force conscripted from the

Kyoga youth, trained and paid through foreign loans, swung into brutal action. They had no trouble with the communist-style organisation of the N'Kuru Lions; they assumed all N'Kuru were communist terrorists and took it from there. They had no trouble with white-skin sensitivities in questioning suspects; they remembered how their grandparents had been forced to collect rubber and applied the same techniques. A brief and bloody war swept over the farmlands. When it was over, the leaders of the Lions were in hiding in Angola and neighbouring Congo Libre. Their power was destroyed. But so was half the country's economic base. The army was victorious. But it was incredibly expensive and had no further reason to exist. It soon became obvious that Mau was not such a good investment as had been thought in the white-skin market places. Companies began to pull out. The copper mines closed. Banks began to ask that loans be repaid. The Maui franc crashed on the international money market. Inflation hit one thousand per cent. The economy collapsed.

From under the wreckage rose a giant whose simple mission was to save his people. All of his people. In the days when Mwanga had been a man, not a city, an N'Kuru girl had been kidnapped by a Kyoga man – one of thousands. Their mingled blood ran through the generations and down the centuries to flow in the veins of Dr Julius Karanga. Educated first at a mission school in the bush and then with a scholarship at the Sorbonne in Paris, he had been subject by chance to the French method of colonisation and had been not only well educated but also fully trained in the practicalities of government. He understood the systems which had to be put in place. He knew that Mau needed not armies and secret police but law, justice. And that meant courts. Schools. Hospitals. A social structure. He had the vision to see that his country could only afford these things if she produced the goods to pay for them. And she would only produce the goods if she was united and well governed. He saw that the first step was to bring the people together, *his* people together, and allow them to choose a government they trusted.

Invited home from his work as a political commentator in Paris, he accepted the post of President only on condition that it was a temporary appointment, to be confirmed or cancelled by due process of democracy. He made it his first mission to explain democracy to a people who had known only supposedly benign dictatorship. He toured the country, talking to the elders in the villages and townships. He described how his vision of democratic government would work. He began to ask for men to come forward and present themselves as being worthy of government office. Kyoga men came and then, at last, N'Kuru men. This was the early sixties. Women, largely uneducated, still worked on the land. He took the men, fired them with his vision and began to try and organise elections. As his year of office ran out, he held his precious elections. They were violent but ultimately successful in their immediate aim. A government was formed and he was recognised as its head.

Companies began to return with the new stability. Banks. The World Bank. As if to add a divine blessing to the process, diamonds were discovered in the Kyoga lands, then, right up near the border to the north, reserves of coal and oil. Slowly, painstakingly, over one decade and then another, this great leader began to unify and restore his country. The high jungle was carefully cleared to allow access to the mineral wealth of the outback. But it was not wilfully destroyed and the habitats of the gorillas and the jungle leopards were preserved. The farms on the plains were organised into communes, for the French-educated leader was not too proud to see that some of what the communists had instilled into the N'Kuru freedom fighters was wise and practical. The communes held their land on condition that they, too, would protect the dwindling populations of antelope, wildebeest, rhino and elephant; on condition that they were careful with the pesticides and chemical fertilisers they used on the land, that they chose their crops with care and did not over-farm the soil. The grasslands had been over-farmed, however, and badly so. The farmers found their work painfully difficult and became increasingly grudging about protecting species they saw only as vermin which put their livelihoods at risk. A trade grew up in ivory and rhino-horn poaching as some N'Kuru came close to starving. Rumours began to circulate that the N'Kuru Lions were getting ready to return.

Julius Karanga's reaction to this was typical. He set in motion his greatest project so far: the great Mau dam and irrigation project. He gathered all the power and prestige he had and poured it unstintingly into the project which would make the N'Kuru farmlands bloom again. By early 1985 it was ready to go. The elder statesman was invited by the dam-building consortium to lay the first stone – the dam was destined to bear his name – and he accepted. On 16 July, he stood high on the southern bank of the river and declaimed to the world, 'I lay the first stone of the Dr Julius Karanga Dam here before you today in the land of my N'Kuru ancestors. In the fullness of time I shall stand on the land of my Kyoga ancestors and lay the last stone so that we can bring back life and prosperity to all of our country! I tell you, my people, the future has never looked so bright.'

These were the last words he was ever to speak, for the bomb wrapped round the body of a young N'Kuru freedom fighter standing nearby exploded at that moment and twenty people nearest to her, including the Premier and many of his closest colleagues, died at once. The N'Kuru Lions were back.

In the political turmoil which followed the outrage, twenty years of Karanga's work fell apart overnight. The new government, Kyoga men, began an undeclared war on the N'Kuru. The Lions reacted in kind. Terrorism came to Mawanga with a vengeance. The great plains became no-go for anyone associated with the powers that be – the army, the police, the commune organisers. The crops died. The land dried. The red soil began to blow away. Five carefully planted terrorist bombs closed the coal mines and set the oilwell on fire. Only the diamond mine remained in production, for security there had always been tight.

The people began to starve. Desperate, the government begged aid from its neighbours. The Congo Libran government which had sheltered the Lions sent cattle to supplement the N'Kuru herds but the cattle were infected with rinderpest and the plague wiped out all the herds. Shipments of food began to turn up desultorily: meat from Europe which had already been refused by Russia because it was contaminated; grain from the United States which had been sprayed with illegal chemicals; free milk powder for the children, which did not contain the nutriments they actually required to develop properly. The usual. But there were other demands on the aid agencies much more urgent than Mau's seemed to be. For twenty years, the country had stood as a symbol of everything positive in African independence. It was difficult for the rest of the world to come to terms with the speed and the scale of the disaster overtaking the once prosperous state. And, just as divine power had chosen to give to those who had by adding oil and diamonds to the security brought by Julius Karanga, so the same power chose to take even from those who had not, and the great drought came. The grassland became a bowl of red dust. The black soil of the escarpment became cracked and dry as the jungle withered. The mighty River Mau dried to a stinking trickle which oozed a full half-mile away from the place where Karanga had died, where the first stone of his dam had been laid. All that kept the harbour of Mawanga open was the depth of its tectonic floor;

the river itself could hardly make it to the sea.

The drought was in its third year now and the world was just beginning to wake up to it. Because Julius Karanga had achieved so much so independently in the sixties and seventies and because his cabinet had been wiped out with him, the United Nations had few contacts in Mau, and so even that organisation, so widely experienced in the causes and results of disaster, was only just beginning to wake up to it. And there was much to wake up to here. The whole N'Kuru nation on the move. The better part of five million people seemingly mere weeks away from death as the last of the food and water trickled away. The desperate Kyoga government on the verge of collapse, relying on the increasingly uncontrollable army to keep an impossible situation under control. A number of general officers building well-armed, dangerous power bases, ready to grasp control. The Lions set to 'liberate' the country by any method, no matter how brutal, and at any price, no matter how high. The neighbouring states quietly massing their own armies along the frontiers, all set to snap it up, for Mawanga was the best harbour on the western coast, and that alone would make invasion worthwhile.

It was going to be Somalia and Rwanda all over again and at the moment, it seemed, the only person in the world who could see it coming was sitting naked in a shower in the Mawanga Hilton, crying because she had just taken a shower.

South

THE LABRADOR SEA

Perched on my city office-stool
I watched in envy while a cool
And lucky carter handled ice . . .
And I was wandering in a trice
Far from the grey and grimy heat
Of that intolerable street
O'er sapphire berg and emerald floe
Beneath the still cold ruby glow
Of everlasting Polar night . . .

W. W. Gibson, *The Ice Cart*

Chapter Nine

Richard Mariner stepped out of the elevator onto the 38th floor of the United Nations building in New York and followed a secretary called Veronica down the corridor towards the offices of the Secretary-General, dripping onto the carpet as he went. 'As you know,' Veronica continued, 'the Secretary-General is in Oxford at the moment, preparing to address the Union,' she was a Girton girl herself, he had discovered, 'and so you will be seeing the Executive Assistant first before talking to the Club.'

His head was whirling. He was soaking, storm-battered, airsick, jet-lagged and exhausted. Most of this was going over his head and he hoped to God he would soon be talking to someone who made more sense.

'The Executive Assistant is waiting for you in the Chef de Cabinet's office,' she explained brightly. The introduction of another language, even when it was simply a job title, just added to his confusion. He was going to have to pull himself together as a matter of urgency here. He had the contract for the hire of his supertankers in his briefcase and, although the detail was a matter for lawyers, he was going to have to be clear about exactly what he was committing his company, ships and crews to.

Veronica stopped and he nearly collided with her. She opened a dark panelled door and ushered him in. 'Captain Mariner,' she announced, and left, closing the door behind her.

The office was large and comfortably furnished. There were two people waiting in it and both of them rose as he entered. There was a window along one wall with a beautiful view over the river and the city beyond. As he entered, the wide picture was lit by a distant fork of lightning which seemed to illuminate every single raindrop. The thunder, like the storm-force wind, was kept at bay by the double glazing. All he really noticed was the jug of coffee steaming fragrantly on the Chef de Cabinet's desk. A quiet, melodious voice, deepened by an invisible but clearly audible smile, said, 'Coffee first and introductions later, I think. Please sit down, Captain Mariner, and tell me, how do you like it?'

Richard collapsed into a deep, deeply comfortable armchair. 'Black, no sugar, please,' he answered.

Immediately, a long hand, the colour of *café au lait* half covered by a red and gold silk garment of some kind, placed a brimming cup of black liquid in his hand. He looked up thankfully into a pair of breathtaking almond eyes the colour of the coffee in his cup, and he nearly spilt it.

'No, Captain, sit where you are and drink your coffee,' said that laughing, musical voice and, having poured herself a cup as well, Dr Indira Dyal, Executive Assistant to the Secretary-General of the United Nations, sat in an armchair at his side. 'Mr Aziz prefers his in the Turkish style, you will observe,' Dr Dyal continued as the slight man behind the desk raised a tiny cup to his lips.

Mohammed Aziz, Chef de Cabinet to the Secretary-General, nodded to Richard as he sipped, the eyes behind his pebble glasses crinkling to show that he, too, was indulgently amused by the situation.

The coffee hit Richard's system like an antidepressant drug. After the first few sips of the heavenly liquid, his head began to clear and his horizons to expand. He began to appreciate the fine furnishings of Mr Aziz's office. He registered the view from the wide window, though from this angle it consisted mainly of the tops of skyscrapers, the bottoms of storm clouds and wild sheets of teeming rain hurled hither and yon by the wind. Storm force ten at the very least, he thought, and not for the first time that day. Another couple of sips and he felt able to turn to face his hostess; the possibility of reasoned communication seemed not too remote after all.

Dr Dyal sat, her back ramrod straight, perched on the very edge of the chair beside him. Her tall body was swathed in a sari of red and gold silk so bright it seemed to glow. Part of it fell across her head to cover her hair, but the material was so fine that it did little to conceal the black locks, streaked with silver and drawn severely back into a bun. She wore little make-up and needed none. The huge almond eyes, fringed with extravagant lashes under delicate black brows, emphasised the aquiline fineness of her nose; the patrician curve of her nostrils seemed at odds with the vivid fullness of her lips. Before accepting her post with the United Nations, Indira Dyal had enjoyed the reputation of being the most beautiful politician on the Indian subcontinent. Or anywhere else, for that matter, thought Richard.

The same could not quite be said for Mohammed Aziz, the Moroccan Chef de Cabinet. He was an outstanding, world-class politician whose acumen and knowledge, especially about Africa, were legendary; but he looked very much as if he should have been selling camels in the kasbah at Marrakesh. Except for the glasses and the suit, he was very much the sort of wiry, woolly-haired, gap-toothed, wise-eyed street Arab on whom the commerce of the whole Middle East had turned since the dawn of time.

'Are you with us, Captain Mariner?' he asked as Richard emptied his cup.

'I do apologise, Mr Aziz, Dr Dyal,' said Richard. 'The flight was dreadful and very late indeed. And getting a cab

119

out from Kennedy in the rain . . .' He shrugged.

'You should have got the helicopter.'

'It's been grounded until the storm moderates.'

'Ah. Of course.'

Lightning pounced down outside the window again, seemingly dangerously near.

'Still,' said Dr Dyal, 'you are here now, Captain, and under the circumstances, you seem to have performed a miracle to be so precisely on time.'

'I am extremely keen to do business with you,' he answered drily.

Dyal and Aziz exchanged a long glance which was by no means disapproving. 'Good,' said Dr Dyal. 'And I am pleased that we seem to be putting all our cards on the table. I like straight talking and so, I know, does Mr Aziz.'

'The draft contract seems quite satisfactory to you?' the Moroccan probed gently.

'In general, yes indeed. You have offered a standard open-ended charter at competitive but realistic rates. We supply six ships and three crews. You supply three crews and the personnel on the ice itself. Working with the people on the ice under the command of Dr Colin Ross, we are contracted to secure the iceberg in the manner we deem most practical and guide it at a speed we find most feasible along a course which we decide but which we must refer to you in case we need political clearance of any kind, to a destination on the west coast of equatorial Africa to be designated by yourselves. Once there, we are to make it safe by whatever manner we deem best and assist, if possible, in the bringing ashore of either ice or water. You are prepared to take overall responsibility for fuelling, provisioning and insuring the enterprise. All we have to do is get our ships to the iceberg, get the iceberg to wherever you decide, and help whoever may be waiting there to get it ashore and use it.'

'That about sums it up,' said Aziz.

Dr Dyal nodded in agreement. There was the slightest of smiles lifting the corners of her lips; she was impressed with the accuracy of Richard's breakdown of the contract, especially as it had been delivered from memory.

'You are aware that it is more than a hundred kilometres long.'

'We have Dr Ross's detailed report,' answered Aziz.

'Fifteen kilometres wide.'

'Yes.'

'And that it is currently about nine hundred metres deep.'

'As I say, we have the report . . .'

'Well, I cannot accept the contract without saying that I personally feel there is nowhere on the African coast where you will be able to get it ashore. Or even *near* the shore. Not near enough to do any good, anyway.'

This time it was Dr Dyal who spoke, and her voice had lost that laugh. 'No, Captain Mariner,' she said seriously, 'there I must disagree with you. We have a feasibility study which suggests that there is just one place where we could get something that large into a position where it could do some good. And it so happens that this place needs it the most at the moment.' She rose, and Richard automatically rose with her.

'Now that we have finished our coffee and our preliminary chat, I'm sure you'd like to freshen up,' she said. 'And then I'd like you to meet the Mau Club.'

Richard shook the water off his hands then thought again, cupped them, filled them with water and dashed the glorious coolness up into his face, running his hands up over his forehead and back into his hair. He straightened and looked at himself in the mirror. Five minutes and he would be back on mainline. He stooped and filled his hands again.

He knew about the Congo Club in the sixties, that group

of men in the United Nations who had overseen their involvement, in the terrible trouble there. He hadn't realised they still had clubs thirty years later. Perhaps the name had been dusted off for the occasion.

But Mau! Why hadn't he thought of Mau? Because the harbour at Mawanga had been more or less closed since that terrible business of the assassination of Julius Karanga nearly ten years ago. God in heaven, he thought, feeling old, *nearly ten years ago*. It seemed like yesterday.

Lost in thought, he scrubbed his cheeks dry and reached into his jacket pocket for a comb. He dismissed the memory of Dr Karanga's death and turned his mind to the practicalities. The harbour at Mawanga had no bottom. It was an abyssal valley between seven and ten miles wide from memory – an old one if he was thinking in miles – contained between two horns of sandy silt. It would need some engineering work – maybe some serious engineering work – but if anywhere was feasible, Mawanga was. And, he suddenly realised, pausing in his combing to grin as he did so, if he was going to Mawanga, then he wouldn't have to cross the equator. That thought somehow added considerably to his confidence about this enterprise. Yes, Mau was the most practical place to take the iceberg Manhattan to.

But why did they want it there so badly?

The Mau Club sat round the big oval table in the Secretary-General's conference room further along the 38th floor. Dr Dyal and Mr Aziz occupied the head of the table, clearly Chair and Deputy. Richard sat opposite them at the foot, the guest of honour perhaps. The rest of the Club sat down the sides between them, four figures, two a side. Dr Gunther Sepulchre, the Belgian 'expert' on the area, was just finishing his analysis of the historical background.

'So, since the assassination, the country has effectively been in turmoil. All Dr Karanga's outstanding political, social and economic work has come undone and anarchy looms. Without water, the country will have slipped into civil war by next summer, I am certain. And if that happens, unless we become directly involved, there will be an invasion. Mawanga is too rich a prize for several other nearby states to resist.'

Dr Dyal nodded once, decisively. 'Thank you, Dr Sepulchre. Most succinct. General Cord?'

General Warren Cord, US Army (Rtd), familiar from television and documentary footage of his part in Desert Storm and a dozen lesser peacekeeping campaigns, ran his broad hand over the white stubble of his regulation crew cut. 'Well, Dr Dyal,' he drawled, 'I'd have to agree with Dr Sepulchre's breakdown of the current status. There are a lot of folks out there who want to get at Mawanga. It's the best harbour on the west coast. Not only that. It's got the remains of all the infrastructure you would expect from what used to be a major business centre. Wouldn't take all that much to get it up and running. Back to being – what did they used to call it? – the Cape Town of the north. And I suspect Professor Kroll here will bear me out when I say that outside South Africa, Mau has the potential to be about the richest country in Africa. I'm speaking about the mineral deposits, of course, but I would also reckon the grassland to be worth a great deal if it can be farmed again. Yeah. Unless we take tight hold on this one really quickly it'll make Somalia and Rwanda look like a picnic.'

'Can you be more specific, General?'

'You want comparisons? Material estimates? Comparisons – worse than ten Somalias, worse than ten Bosnias. Cost you almost as much as World War Two, especially if the Angolans or the Congolese come in. Not a lot we could do to stop them either, unless we started sending major air cover – that open country's just heaven sent for battle tanks and they got plenty there. Especially just across the border in Congo Libre. More than ever since the Russian republics started selling off their equipment to the highest bidder. Men and materiel – now, let me see. Not counting aircraft carriers, you'd need—'

'No, thank you, General, I think you've made the picture clear enough for the time being. Professor Kroll.'

Professor Inga Kroll looked more like a dumpy hausfrau than an economics genius. Which was one of the reasons she was working here instead of at the Bundesbank in Bonn. But she sounded every bit as authoritative as General Cord.

'Yes,' she said. 'The general is correct. In Mawanga the banking systems and the Bourse are still in place. It would be very easy to bring the country back on line financially. And when one considers that it was largely the work of the terrorist groups like the Lions which stopped the production of the mineral and agricultural wealth needed to support such powerful financial dealing, then you will see that whoever can either enlist or negate these people has the opportunity to reawaken the country financially very quickly indeed. You are familiar with the story of Sleeping Beauty? Yes? Mau just needs a handsome prince to kiss her and she will awake. And we are not the only people to be aware of this, I think. It is as the general says. There are people who understand economics all over Africa these days.'

'And people who understand strategy,' broke in the final speaker as though she could no longer contain herself. Alone among the Club members she was not content to sit and talk. No sooner was she speaking than she had torn herself up out of her seat and was pacing round the table, every lithe movement speaking of impatience and frustration. 'You've got to *move* people. It's all to win or all to lose and you have no time to sit around speechifying. Warren's right: those borders in the bush were drawn by old guys in Brussels with pencils on paper. There's nothing *there* but the grasslands and maybe a couple of baobab trees and maybe an acacia or a thorn or two and that's not going to stop a squadron of battle tanks. And if you get tanks onto the farmland then the irrigation system will be shot to hell and even if the rains come back it'll take the better part of a decade to get the farms and communes up and running again. I mean, it's all still *there*, every ditch and channel. You've seen the reports from Bob Gardiner of UNHCR and the others who've actually been out in the bush to look for themselves. Even after all these years, the whole system is there even if the river isn't any more. But it's old and it needs work or it will all turn into dust like the rest of Mau is doing. And it needs more than the World Health people or Oxfam, for Christ's sake. It needs something major and it needs it now. It's my field of specialisation and you know I know what I'm talking about or I wouldn't be in your Club. But you've only got a few months, or maybe only a few weeks. Then it'll all be gone and you'll have a political and environmental disaster on your hands. And you'll be stuck in there just like the general says. The peacekeeping force you'll have to send to get things back under control will cost you an arm and a leg – and I've got Kyoga blood, remember, so I know what I'm talking about – and *then* you'll need a permanent police force there to keep everyone from each other's throats like you've got for the rest of recorded time in Bosnia and Somalia and God knows where else, *and* in the meantime, quite apart from your *men* and *materiel* – with or without aircraft carriers – you're going to have to feed five million N'Kuru in the bush and another two and a half million Kyoga in the cities and up on the escarpment, in the mines, the police and the army. *If* you can get their guns away from them, of course, and stop them slaughtering your aid workers and stealing all the supplies for their own people!'

'We know that, Ms—'

'I *know* you know it, Dr Dyal, which is why it's so frustrating that we're still talking about it instead of doing something about it!'

'But we are doing something about it. As of now. That's

why I have brought Captain Mariner to speak to us today.'

Richard's dazed condition was threatening to return, but this time it was nothing to do with jet lag or airsickness. The passionate words of the tall, willowy, mahogany-skinned woman had opened his eyes to the dazzling prospect of what the United Nations was actually proposing to do. The irrigation system that Julius Karanga had planned to fill from the Karanga Dam was *still in place*. He was to try and get the iceberg into the harbour at Mawanga and then get enough of that one point five billion tons of water up the Mau River to fill the irrigation ditches.

He found himself on his feet, leaning forward across the table with his face surprisingly close to that of the vividly impatient girl who had just finished speaking. Her eyes were long and sloping – cat's eyes as bright as copper. Her nose was long and spread generously at its end. Her lips were full and wide and sculpted like a model's. He was so close to her he could smell her perfume, something light and exotic that he did not recognise. They were so close that he could smell the musk of her body beneath the perfume and the faintest scent of cloves upon her breath.

'Emily,' Dr Dyal was saying, distantly. 'Emily—'

'Sit *down*, please, Miss Karanga,' Aziz cut in more forcefully, 'and let the captain explain how he proposes to finish your father's final project.'

Chapter Ten

Two days later, just as it was coming up to midnight local time, Richard, red-eyed, stood in the tiny cabin of the pilot's launch as she pounded out of Galveston Bay into the Roadsteads where *Titan* had just finished discharging. He was swaying with exhaustion but his individual movements were lost in the general motion as the tiny craft jumped and butted through the waves. There was a southerly gale blowing and the hurricane warnings were out already further to the south. Though the weather was by no means as bad as it had been in New York, it was still a foul night.

The tiny cabin was hot and claustrophobic, crowded as it was with crew, pilot and two passengers, each of whom had brought two big suitcases along, and all the doors, windows and portholes closed against the wind, rain and spray. At the back of the cabin was a shelf with a hotplate which ran off the launch's battery; it had just enough power to keep a pot of thick black coffee on the simmer and its bitter odour filled the air, adding to the uncomfortable atmosphere.

Dead ahead, the supertanker sat moored to an SMB, all lit up like a palace in expectation of their arrival. Her lights seemed to dance wildly up and down as the little vessel pitched and tossed until she came into the wind shadow of the great superstructure, extended to a considerable distance because she was riding so high.

As soon as she did so, the launch's motion moderated. The thunder of wind and spray fell back sufficiently for conversation to be possible. 'She's a hell of a ship,' shouted the pilot. Richard was too exhausted to reply.

'He's glad you like it,' called back Emily Karanga drily. 'He owns it.'

With no further ado, the pilot launch raced up to the towering side of the vessel and tied up at the foot of the accommodation ladder. The two men and the woman leaped over the restless little gap more or less nimbly. Their cases were swung across behind them. Richard picked up his and the pilot mutely offered to carry Emily Karanga's. She mutely declined and hefted them up herself and began to climb aboard, so the pilot followed her up the steps covertly appreciating, every step of the way, the shape of her bottom and the manner in which it filled the seat of her black leather trousers.

At the top of the ladder they stepped up onto the deck and back into the power of the wind. An officer was waiting to meet them there with three general purpose seamen ready to take the bags. This time independence would have been sheer bravado so Emily relinquished her bags at the same time as Richard did and the little group ran up across the rainswept deck towards the high white brightness of the bridgehouse.

Emily had never been aboard a supertanker before and right from the moment that the big metal door was slammed behind her to shut out the stormy wind, she was struck by the quiet – the near silence, in fact, emphasised by the distant throbbing grumble she would come to recognise as the generators. She looked around as they waited for the lift to arrive, very much struck by the clean, functional lines of everything. And the size. In the pilot's cutter she had been awed by the sheer size of the hull. At the top of the companionway she had been struck by the length and breadth of the deck she was stepping onto and by the scale of the pipes, conduits and deck equipment she could see. The bridgehouse looked to be about the same size as her apartment block from the outside and now that she was inside, it seemed like a huge plush hotel. Except that there was no luxury apparent, there was only linoleum on the floor and the walls were covered in cold white paint instead of wallpaper. So, not a hotel then; more like a hospital. She shivered. The lift came. Richard, the pilot and she got in. The officer and the seamen waited for the next car.

As they had been silent in the pilot's boat for the most part, and silent since they came aboard, so they remained silent in the lift. It powered up to the bridge and the doors opened automatically. The two men stepped out and Emily followed because she didn't know what else to do. She found herself in a long corridor which stretched away on either hand to end in a heavy door closed tight against the storm. The walls behind her were of painted wood or metal, but the wall in front of her, from the waist up, was glass. There were doors in it across on the right and left, standing open. But she could see what lay behind them by simply looking straight ahead. She knew it was the ship's bridge but it was nothing like she had expected it to be. It was more like something out of a science fiction movie, all flashing lights and glowing screens. And it was so big. And so empty.

She jumped a little and hurried forward to join her two companions who had been moving forward as she had been standing staring. The three of them entered, to be greeted by one of the three people in charge of the massive, spacious bridge. The man who rose to greet them was tall and white-haired. He wore an overall but he carried himself with authority and although they were all on first-name terms, Richard and the pilot treated him with such respect that it was obvious to Emily who he was even before Richard turned courteously to say, 'And this is Emily

Karanga. Emily Karanga, meet Captain Tavistock. He's in command at the moment but will be going ashore with the pilot after he's handed over to me.'

The captain smiled and shook her hand warmly. 'I'm in command,' he said, 'but here's the officer who's really in charge. First Officer Sally Bell.'

A second figure in white overalls looked up from a book in which she had been writing and flashed her a wide smile. 'How're you?' she said.

Emily smiled back, 'Exhausted, thanks.'

The first officer's smile became a grin. Then her face became serious as she crossed to the captain, the pilot and the owner.

'We've clearance to leave at once, as you know,' said Richard. 'I'll drop the pair of you in due course, but the first order of business is to get under way.'

Emily watched the female officer cross to stand by the third boiler-suited occupant of the bridge. She spoke quietly to him and then spoke quietly into a microphone beside him. Emily looked more closely, her interest caught. The man was holding a tiny steering wheel – what did they call it? The helm? It was smaller than the steering wheel on her car, for heaven's sake.

The first officer lifted a walkie-talkie radio and spoke into it. At once it hissed in reply and an indecipherable answer exploded noisily into the quiet air.

Sally Bell looked up at the three men standing silently observing her routine. 'Casting off now,' she said.

'Right,' said the pilot. 'I have her. Slow ahead, if you please, and come to a heading of . . .'

Emily heard nothing more. Suddenly gripped by an excitement which was almost childish in its intensity, she crossed to the window and looked out. The lights of Galveston, so bright, so close, were trembling and beginning to swing away. The ship was moving. *They were off.*

Ultimately it was Richard's own decision to go from New

York straight on down to *Titan*. *Titan* was the first of the supertankers which it was proposed to lease to the United Nations and he had decided to make her his flagship, as though he was an admiral in command of a fleet. From the moment he had agreed the contract, he had effectively been working for the UN, and he had no doubt that even if the lawyers changed small details of the agreement, the project – now officially named Manhattan after the iceberg itself – would proceed full steam ahead. *Titan* would be his headquarters until he delivered Manhattan to Mawanga and it seemed to him that no matter what else he had to organise between now and then, he could do it best from here. The great ship had a communications centre which would enable him to communicate fully and easily with Heritage House and almost as fully by radio and telephone with the United Nations building, or anywhere else in the world for that matter. For the next few days he would be making his way back up the coast of the United States and he proposed to collect anything or anyone else he needed on the way.

Apart from her availability, *Titan* had three other advantages. Captain Tavistock was due for some furlough dirtside, so Richard would be able to assume command with a minimum of fuss. She had a good helicopter. This was important because now that he was on the ship and heading up towards his rendezvous with Manhattan, he had a week to arrange everything; maybe ten days before the tow got under way. If he *had* to be anywhere else physically during the next five days, then he could helicopter ashore to the nearest airport and catch a flight from there. And the third advantage lay in the fact that if he was forced to leave the ship for any reason, Sally Bell had the papers to assume command. She should have been captain of her own ship already, but there were simply no berths available and so she was, perforce, content to sit and wait. But he had no intention of leaving the ship unless he was forced to. He planned to bring people to him as he made best possible time to the rendezvous.

Before the tow got under way, they would all be there, on the ships or on the ice, summoned from all over the world if necessary. Men and women from any walk of life whose expertise could be of use to him in the execution of this project. Money was no object, practically speaking, and his power was absolute – and awesomely effective. He would call and they would come: onto *Titan*, onto Manhattan, into the offices on the 38th floor of the United Nations building, wherever they were required to be by him. Some were in place, like Colin, Kate and Emily. Some were on their way already. Some had no idea as yet that they belonged to his team, but they would find out during the next few days.

As nobody else was going to do so, Richard sat in the watchkeeper's chair then dreamily watched the lights of Galveston disappearing into the murk. No, not a team, he thought to himself, contentedly, just on the edge of sleep, a Club. A United Nations Club. Like the famous Congo Club of the sixties. Like the Mau Club from which it was an offshoot. Richard's Club.

The Manhattan Club.

'No,' said Charles Lee, his voice distant but all too distinct over the radio link. 'It's simply not possible, Richard. We cannot let them have *Hero* or *Dido* for this project.'

'But we're contracted to supply six supertankers, Charles. We can't control the movement of one hundred kilometres of ice with less than six.'

'I see that, Richard. I have read the schedule which the Secretary-General's office sent with the contracts. All I am saying is that it is simply impossible for us to let you . . . . let *them* have these two hulls.'

The ether between the two men went silent for a moment and Richard sat, lost in thought, deep in the grip of bitter frustration. It was eight o'clock next morning local time. The day beyond the windows was bright and clear, scrubbed clean by the storm last night. The pilot and Captain Tavistock had departed in the early hours and *Titan* had been making twenty knots under his command since then while he grabbed six hours' sleep. Sally Bell had given over her watch to the second officer, grabbed four hours' sleep herself and now stood behind the helmsman while the second officer handed over to the third.

Richard was able to see this activity through the open door of the radio shack while he considered his response to the executive chairman of his own company. He had not missed the way in which Charles had calculatedly linked Richard with *them*, as though he had traitorously joined the other side.

He leaned across and swung the door shut. 'What are we talking about here, Charles? The United Nations aren't our enemies. They're just trying to get a job of work done. We're trying to help because it makes good sense in a bad market. I thought we had all this agreed.'

'We do, Richard. I apologise if I led you to think anything different. I am not saying I am disinclined to send *Hero* and *Dido*. I am just saying it will be impossible in the time. Physically impossible. *Hero* is due to dock in Nagasaki in three days' time. It will take her at least another day to turn around even if she can discharge at once. *Dido* is in the Malacca Strait, also bound for Japan. Even at optimum speed, she will take more than a week to get there, say ten days including discharge and turnaround. And even then, they are on the wrong side of the world. If we started them from Nagasaki *now* they would still have to cross the Pacific and come through the Panama Canal and that has to take anywhere between three weeks and a month, depending on weather. It puts them outside the time frame altogether. I'm sorry, but you must see that.'

Richard pursed his lips and sighed. 'Yes, you're right, Charles. I'm sorry. I do see that all too clearly. So. All we can offer of the current fleet are *Titan, Niobe* which is discharging at Mobile tomorrow, *Achilles* which is currently in Georgetown, Guyana . . .'

'But which will be turned around tonight.'

'Right, good. And *Ajax* at Stavanger.'

'That's correct.' Charles Lee's voice picked up a little more warmth. Richard had no doubt that the Hong Kong Chinese businessman basically disapproved of all this gallivanting around the world, and Richard was bitterly inclined to agree with him. Because he had not been in the office since the executive board meeting more than a week ago, he had effectively lost track of his ships and so had promised two hulls which he simply could not deliver. It was galling to say the least. But the fact that he had such a firm grasp of the disposition of the rest of the Heritage Mariner tanker fleet had obviously gone some way towards mollifying Charles, hence the thaw in his chilly tone.

Hence, in fact, rather more than that. 'Richard, are you still there?' came the distant voice.

'Yes. I was thinking.'

'Of course. But Helen, Sir William and I have had more time to think than you have and we may have come up with something.'

'Yes?'

'We think we can get you *Kraken* and *Psyche*.'

'What? But they're in mothballs off Piraeus. Have been for five years and more.'

'Quite so. But the situation is this. We understand from the Lloyds agent there that the hulls are still sound. It would take less than a week, we believe, to test and certify the engines if the last report on them is accurate. If it is not or if there is a major breakdown then that will be a different matter of course but in the meantime it seems possible to proceed. And there are several advantages to this course of action.'

Richard could see them all too clearly and his heart raced as Charles went carefully through what he and Helen had discussed.

The two ships had been purchased by Heritage Mariner in the balmy days of the early eighties when their business had been booming. They had got them at a knock-down price and when the oil shipping market had collapsed, they had mothballed them. It would have been uneconomic to sell them, incurring a massive loss, and moored off Piraeus as they were, they remained at least tax deductible. A paper loss. Heritage Mariner would probably never bring them back into commission. It would cost them too much to update their certificates of seaworthiness, to bring their engines up to scratch and to get them certified. The independent shipping company would find it crippling even to insure them, let alone crew them. But none of these would be particular obstacles to the United Nations. In fact they were insisting on doing the latter in any case. The contract stated that the UN had to supply three crews and all of the insurance cover.

And, of course, much of Charles's disquiet with the original contract rested upon the fact that Heritage Mariner would be required to commit such a high percentage of its fleet, which effectively represented the total collateral of the company. So this would satisfy everyone, if it could be pulled off in time.

'What time scale are we actually talking about here, Charles?' Richard asked, when his colleague's measured tones fell into echoing silence and only the airways whispered between them.

'Helen and I estimate that, all things being equal, we can bring the ships into commission within the week. Neither we nor Sir William can see any reason why the United Nations could not assemble a standard crew for each within that time. Crewfinders alone could probably find two crews within that time, I suspect. And then, according to Sir William, it would be quite possible to sail the ships from Piraeus to the Davis Strait within ten days or so. So, effectively, we feel if we receive an immediate.go-ahead, we can get these two ships to you before the end of the month.'

'That's wonderful, Charles, if you can pull it off. Proceed at once, if you please, and I'll check with the Mau Club at the UN as soon as the secretariat opens this morning. Now, I've been thinking about *our* crews. It seems to me that no matter what other experts I need, I shall have to have an engineer of real genius to keep our propulsion units up to scratch and a world-class navigator to tell us which way to go.'

'You seem to be a little modest, Richard. You are the most experienced captain we currently employ. Your knowledge of navigation, certainly, is unparalleled . . .'

'Thank you, Charles, but no. I know my own limitations. I'm an all-rounder and we need specialists here. Bob Stark is the best engineer we've got. He knows all about every propulsion system we are likely to be using from the big diesel four-strokes we'll have to deal with if we do get *Kraken* and *Psyche* to the RB211 turbines we have on the more modern ships. We really will need him if we're going to stand a realistic chance of putting six different propulsion systems into one effective unit. And, of course, he's currently master of *Achilles* so he'll be coming up from Georgetown in any case.'

'Yes, I see. I had considered none of this . . .'

'That's only to be expected, Charles. It's not your field.'

'Nor is navigation, you are just about to say.'

'Yup. Look. I've given this a lot of thought, and I will need to talk it through with several people yet, but it seems to me that the berg, Manhattan, is so big that it will effectively always be drifting in the grip of the major ocean currents. Even six supertankers would have a job to come up with enough power to move it against one of the major currents so I reckon what we're looking at is guiding it across the currents, shifting it from one current to another where they meet, and trying to hurry it up a bit while it's in the grip of the current. Do you see?'

'Dimly. It is not my area . . .'

'Quite. But if I'm right, the consequences are enormous. We'll have to pull the thing south for a little, then east, then south-west, then south again before going hard east. But within that broad course, I'm going to need a navigator who can read the sky and sea like the back of his hand; who can place us on the surface of the earth more accurately than the satnav system, who can feel the optimum for us, night and day, for a month and more. I need John Higgins.'

'He's on *Prometheus*.'

'I know. But we have other captains who can take even *Prometheus* between Kharg and Europoort with no trouble at all. He's the best qualified captain for the job I have in mind. And there's a bonus. Our medic Paul Chan is in hospital with a shattered thigh. If John comes then so will Asha his wife and she's the best doctor in the Heritage Mariner fleet.'

'Very well. Then it looks as though I shall be replacing Captain Higgins with Captain Welland from *Ajax*. I hope Captain Welland will not mind exchanging the icy weather in the north for the opposite extremes on the Gulf run.'

'You know he'll jump at it!'

'I do. He will. And that means that your friends – your Club do you call them? – just have to get their third captain and crew out to Stavanger. I think we can give *Ajax*'s complement a choice of alternative berths or paid leave until this contract expires. And that will be everything tied up tight from this end.'

'Charles, I never thought I'd hear you say that!'

'Well, Richard, I must admit to being quite surprised myself.'

After his talk with Charles Lee, Richard found that he was too wound up to sit still. He left the radio shack and crossed the bridge, then he was out through the bridge-wing door and thundering down the external companion-way. His energy felt boundless and his confidence infinite.

The morning spread out around him, bright and beautiful; he could hardly contain himself. He had spent so much of the summer locked in deep despair that he had forgotten it was possible to feel like this. Every cloud which had darkened his horizon in May, June and July was gone. Heritage Mariner was back on track; Bill, Robin and he were out of the woods in all sorts of ways. He was engaged on a project where he carried the power of responsibility but little of its weight. A project which allowed him to surround himself with many of the men and women he most admired among his wide circle of friends and colleagues. A project of great benefit to the world in general and to a country for which he felt a particular affection. A project which required him to try and complete work begun by a man who had been a hero of his youth, and in doing so would benefit his own company. A project which would require every ounce of seamanship and leadership within him, but which at the same time filled him with joyful anticipation and simple excitement. This is what it must be like, he supposed, to be in an Olympic final. To captain the England cricket team for the Ashes series.

He looked at his watch: just coming up for nine. Would breakfast be cleared away yet? he wondered.

An hour later, he was back in the radio shack, full of bacon and eggs and a little calmer. This time Emily Karanga was with him. He was talking to the Mau Club – or, at least, to Indira Dyal. She had informed him that the first official contacts with the Maui government had been made and a team of as yet unnamed Maui government representatives and experts would be on its way soon. That was the news which Emily particularly wanted to hear and Indira agreed to give her more details the moment they came to hand. And of course Emily would also be informed of the names of the other members of the UN team going with her to Mau as soon as they had been finalised.

Indira provisionally approved the recommissioning of *Kraken* and *Psyche* and noted that the third crew would be going aboard *Ajax* at Stavanger. She listened with patient lack of understanding to Richard's theories about using the ocean currents. At last she broke in, 'Captain Mariner, I must admit to being left breathless by the speed at which you have caused things to happen. I have never seen a project shape up so quickly or so promisingly. But I have a meeting in five minutes. Is there anything at all that we in the Mau Club can do at this stage? Any little problems you cannot see a way round yourself?'

And, almost without realising it had ever been on his mind, he answered, 'Rope.'

'Rope?'

'Yes. It's been niggling away in the back of my mind. I know that whatever we use, the pressure of the actual tow will cause the ice to melt at the anchorage points. I suppose we'll just have to work something out to overcome that when we see what we are actually dealing with, but what I *can't* quite see is what kind of rope, cable or line is actually going to be strong enough to tow something weighing a billion and a half tons.'

'I'll hand you over to General Cord, I think. I know that rope isn't a strategic consideration, but he's the man most likely to be able to help, I think.'

Emily had gone by the time General Cord came through. There was nothing much for her to do until they began drawing detailed plans for their arrival in Mawanga, though the plans would have to be drawn as early as possible because they would have to be negotiated with the Maui government and might well need time-consuming preparations on the ground. She would be here to draw up the preliminaries with Richard for the run up the coast. She had been educated and trained as a civil engineer and she was the person most perfectly placed to go through the detailed structural plans of Mawanga harbour as soon as they arrived via the UN and the fax. She was the person selected by the Mau team as being the one best qualified to check the irrigation system, too; it had been with this sort of task in mind that her father had overseen her education in the first place. So, as soon as the drawings came, the plans would be laid then she would be off via New York to Mawanga and to the irrigation ditches in the veldt – if they were still there as Robert Gardiner had reported forty-eight hours ago.

'NASA,' echoed Richard, the tone of his voice betraying his astonishment.

'Sure,' said General Cord, surprised that Richard was surprised. 'They've done a lot of work in that field. It was NASA who first put out the contract for this unbreakable rope, as far as I know, and I guess they'll still be the best place to start. I don't know whether they've gone much beyond the parallel molecule carbon monofibre they've been using for their suits, but if they have, then I'll find out. But it seems to me that if you get large bundles of carbon monofibre and then wind them round each other, you should end up with the kind of rope you're looking for. Maximum strength, minimum weight, minimum stretch. I mean, your standard braided nylon probably won't be long enough and will stretch to hell and gone if you're going to use any sort of *length* of the stuff . . .'

'Yes. That seems likely to me too. It's been a bit of a worry. Of course we won't be trying to pull over a billion tons dead weight. It'll be moving under its own power anyway, influenced by the currents, the winds, the spin of the earth, but we'll have to overcome some almost incalculable inertias, especially if we want to turn it.'

'Kinda like a fisherman trying to land a ten-pound steelhead on a line with five-pound breaking strain.'

'Yes, that's right. I'm afraid we'll go well beyond the capacity of normal ships' ropes, so I really do want the strongest available.'

'OK. I'll see what I can do. On the other hand, though,

having a known breaking strain might be all to the good. This pulling business can go both ways remember. You don't ever want to find that that thing is pulling *you* and there ain't no way to break free . . .'

'Manhattan is drifting down the Labrador Current at the moment. Making about four knots in a straight line roughly south.' Richard was on the phone in the radio shack. It was mid-afternoon now and Sally Bell was holding her own watch as *Titan* pounded through the dark brown outwash of the still swollen Mississippi River. Even out here it was hard to hold course because of the power of the river's current. The big tanker kept drifting away to starboard, behaving in exactly the way Richard hoped the iceberg would. 'My ships will try to get that speed up to ten knots by the time we hit the Gulf Stream, then we'll swing east with the Stream – and with the westerly winds behind us – and run it as fast as we can southwards across the main flow until we can pick up the Canaries current on the western edge of Biscay. The Canaries current will take us down to the Canary Islands themselves. It'll be a long haul but at least the water will be relatively cold.'

'An important consideration, I should think.'

'Yes. Now, at the Canaries we'll have to move under our own steam for a bit, but if we're lucky we can pull Manhattan south fairly quickly – I'm hoping for an average of about eight to ten knots – and hitch our final ride on the Guinea current which will deliver us to the very doorstep. What do you think, John?'

John Higgins' voice was very distant indeed – it was being relayed via Heritage House from the bridge of *Prometheus* off Kharg Island in the Gulf. 'You'll have to give me some time to think about it, Richard. It sounds feasible, though. My God! Does it ever! Look. I've got to go now. I'll be seeing you as soon as possible. I'm getting *Niobe*, I understand.'

'That's right.'

'Well, I hope it doesn't end in tears . . .'

Richard hung up with a wry smile. It was an old joke. A reference to the ship's name and a line from *Hamlet*. Richard pulled himself to his feet, muttering it to himself in his very best Laurence Olivier, lines which, all things considered, were surprisingly apt for the matter in hand:

'A little month; or ere the shoes were old
With which she followed my poor father's body
Like Niobe, all tears . . .'

He had no real idea that he was saying Hamlet's bitter words aloud, for he was too caught up in the coincidence that, if the plan went ahead, then a little month was just about all they would have before the iceberg reduced itself to tears and ran away.

Sally Bell watched him go. She could hardly believe her ears. His half of the conversation with Captain Higgins had shown an impressive enough knowledge of the oceans, especially as she knew he was looking only at the chart of the Atlantic Ocean's major currents which he carried in his memory, but that he should come out spouting *Hamlet* was simply too much! It was no wonder he was a legend, she thought; all this and Shakespeare too.

Sally – and, indeed, everyone aboard – was a good deal less in charity with Richard when he sat down to complete his final outgoing phone call of the first day. His own mood had darkened with the gathering of exhaustion once again. Even his massive energy could not really be renewed by six hours' sleep after four days without even seeing a bed. He was soaking wet, as were they all, for the weather had worsened again during the afternoon and the rain had been sheeting down by teatime. Which had not prevented him from calling a lifeboat drill at seven o'clock, just as everyone was sitting down to dinner.

'Hello, darling,' he said, the deep gravelly sound of his voice betraying his exhaustion. 'Sorry to be getting through so late. Twins off to bed all right?'

And Robin Mariner, who had been waiting for this call, relaxed into the big sofa and rested her golden head on the soft cushions behind. She was concentrating on the distant rumble of his words so hard that even the organ-pure tones of Lucia Popp singing the Queen of the Night's aria from *The Magic Flute* faded into nothingness, and the still grey eyes went out of focus as her mind represented in vivid detail what he was doing as he spoke to her. The French windows, open to the veranda for the last time this year, the gentle slope of the lawn down to the wall at the end of the garden, and the breathtaking view across the Channel from this, the next high shoulder of South Down to the west of Beachy Head, were all as nothing to her. She would have traded it all at once, traded even the great house Ashenden itself, to be there, in that tiny, cramped radio room, hungry and wet, exhausted and unpopular; and with him, with him, with him.

Chapter Eleven

Richard stood on the sternmost section of *Titan* with the binoculars clamped under his frowning brows. The lower cliffs of Manhattan's rough-hewn bow glimmered dully in the late afternoon overcast, which was a mercy. In the time he had been away, the iceberg melt rate had grown slightly and the skim of water even over the tall vertical surfaces added to the intensity with which they caught and reflected every candlepower of light. Colin and he had talked at length already about the advisability of spraying those parts with the fastest melt rate with some kind of protective coating, but they couldn't come up with a coating which was easy to apply, strong enough to do the job, and simple to get rid of at the far end. Even the expanded polystyrene that disposable cups were made of would be impossible to get rid of if they used it, and might leave an environmental legacy of the worst sort – a plastic cup fifty kilometres long which was non biodegradable. But there was time enough to worry about that later.

He was jerked out of his thoughts by a sudden ripple of brightness along a line exactly level with his gaze. Brightness which came from deep within the ice. The strange light was lost immediately in a blinding mixture of ice dust and spray which billowed out into the stillness of the calm afternoon. A series of flat, dull reports reached Richard's ears as the clouds began to thin and settle. The cliff face immediately above the line of the explosion began to move.

With the slow majesty of an avalanche, it lost definition as the cliff face shattered into boulders, then settled down into the sea.

'Looks good,' said Richard to the man standing beside him.

'Yes,' answered Major Tom Snell of the Royal Engineers, seconded to NATO and the UN.

Tom Snell was a solid bull of a man with broad shoulders and a thick waist. He had a square, pugnacious face with overhanging brows, a straight, short nose, a downcurving mouth emphasised by a clipped military moustache and a square, protruding jaw. He wasn't too happy to be here and he was not a man to hide his feelings. But orders were orders and he and his engineers had been pulled out of their posting in Norway to come and oversee the placing and maintenance of the tow lines. He might have said more than the flat monosyllable, but further conversation became impossible as the thunder of the falling ice overwhelmed them.

Richard refocused his binoculars up on the top of the cliff where the distant figures of Colin and Kate looked down at the results of the engineers' work.

The avalanche slowed and the thunder receded. For once, Tom Snell initiated the conversation. 'We'll need to go over for a closer look now.'

'I'll come.'

'There's no need.'

'I'll come anyway. Helicopter or inflatable?'

'Whatever you think, sir.'

'Inflatable. We'll have to get used to nipping back and forth so we might as well start now. Unless you want to clear off ledges big enough to allow the helicopter a landing site.'

'No. That would take more time than we have available,' said the square soldier, but his eyes lingered wistfully on the bright side of the Westland Sea King as they passed it.

Tom Snell did not like boats or boating.

It took them longer than expected to reach the berg, although Richard had had the foresight to equip the crew of the big inflatable with long boathooks. Snell's explosives had brought down a lot of ice and getting through the mess of floating boulders took persistence and time. The noise was unexpected. The ice boulders made quite a racket as they bobbed and clashed, rumbled and rolled, settling down individually and collectively, as though coming slowly to terms with the new situation. There was a very real danger of some of the larger, unstable pieces rolling over and swamping the rubber craft, so Richard who had the helm took things slowly and very carefully indeed.

As they passed through the ice field which the engineers had created, the noise being made by the berg itself began to reach them. Bits and pieces were still falling off the cliff, and they were careful to stay clear until the man-made avalanche had stopped falling into the sea. But even when the thunder of falling boulders had ceased, a pervasive sound still came from the massive piece of ice with unexpected intensity. Water flowed everywhere, its voice varying from a tinkle to a roar, as though somewhere deep within the berg there were massive waterfalls. And as water settled downwards over the surfaces and through the depths, so air rose up, its tones echoing the water's, from the bubbling whisper of a breeze to the distant thunder of gales magically entombed.

Richard remembered none of this noise from his previous visit, but then he had been high up on the ice cliffs. Perhaps things were quieter up there. He hoped so, or no one at the ice camp was going to get any sleep at all during the next month or so.

He let the inflatable bump gently along the sheer, crystalline coast of the iceberg until he found a good place for them all to climb up. Leaving one man to guard the big rubber craft, he followed the rest of them up onto the ice.

It was wet and slippery, running not only with meltwater but with salt spray from the explosion and avalanche. Scrambling up a shallow slope behind the others, Richard almost collided with the line of men who stood looking across the gallery the explosives had created.

It was obviously going to be impossible to tie the tow ropes to the top of the cliffs. That had never been a realistic option; too much expensive rope would have been required and the angle of pull would have been so steep as to have negated half of the ships' power. They had known for some time that tow ropes would have to be anchored in galleries blown into the ice cliffs like this one at a level a little higher than the little poop deck behind the bridge-house, where the mighty capstans sat. None of the tankers involved in the tow had strengthened sterns, so the capstans would have to be treated with great respect and the application of power from the engines which would bring pressure and stress upon the equipment via the unbreakable rope and the all but immovable inertia of the berg itself would have to be very carefully calculated indeed. But Bob Stark would be here with *Achilles* tomorrow and they would be able to discuss that then. In the meantime, Tom Snell had created the first gallery by blowing away a section of the cliff. He had been fortunate to find a ledge here big enough to work on. From the back of the ledge he had drilled into the cliff and laid a series of charges designed to send a flat edge of explosive power into the ice, creating a level area half the size of a football pitch with a safe overhang above it. And so he had.

Richard joined the group of engineers and seamen admiring the major's work, then he helped them clear the level anchorage area of any last bits and pieces of smashed ice. By the time they lost the light, the work was complete and the first anchorage point was clear.

'That's excellent,' said Richard, his voice raised to reach Snell over the tinkling of nearby water and the more distant rumbling of the floes. 'I think we've earned our supper tonight.'

Tom Snell gave a nod of agreement, then his usually grim face split into a wide grin. 'Yes, Captain,' he said. 'Yes, I think we have.'

The dinner was excellent but, as all meals were for Richard, a working one. He could rely on Sally Bell to run the ship for him – they weren't going anywhere or doing much in seafaring terms at the minute in any case – while he kept in touch with what was taking place on the ice. He needed to review what had happened today and begin to plan the detail of what would happen tomorrow. So dinner was a meeting of all the available members of the Manhattan Club.

'It's excellent work to have the first anchorage area clear so quickly,' rumbled Colin Ross. 'You've hardly been here twenty-four hours.'

'We'll have the next one done by this time tomorrow,' promised Snell. No crossed fingers or touch wood for him. 'Then we'll go down and look at the far end.'

'*Achilles* will be here tomorrow,' said Richard. 'I'll keep Bob Stark here and start talking propulsion and associated matters. His first officer will take you down to the far end, Tom, and you can look at things there. Colin, is there any dry ice down there?'

'Yes. As you'd expect, given the size of the section above the water here, there's a bit above the water there as a kind of counterweight or balance. The whole of Manhattan is the same shape as *Titan* here, except that it's mostly submerged, floating at a slight angle, and facing backwards. That means the bridgehouse is above the water at this end and a kind of forecastle is above the water at the far end. It's not all that big but it is level and clear. And not even a hundred metres high – you may be able to anchor your lines straight to it.'

'That would be very convenient.'

'Then all you have to worry about is where you're going to anchor *Kraken* and *Psyche* when they arrive in ten days,' observed Kate.

'Halfway along, of course,' said Tom, frowning, not too sure about the number of women who seemed to hold senior positions in this enterprise.

Kate nodded. 'That'll be at the far end of the section above the water level. Again, most convenient. But we haven't done much exploring in that area, have we, Colin? Maybe I'd better take a look down there tomorrow.'

Sally Bell leaned forward. 'You could do some reconnaissance in the Westland first. Map some likely looking areas from the air and then maybe go back on foot if it isn't too inaccessible.'

'Good idea,' nodded Richard. 'We don't need the Westland for a while. More boating for you tomorrow, I'm afraid, Tom.'

A steward appeared at Richard's elbow, holding a portable phone. 'A call for you, Captain.'

Richard took the phone. 'Yes?'

'John Higgins here, Richard.'

'John. Where are you? You sound very clear.'

'I've just arrived on *Niobe*. We're proceeding full ahead and are passing off Newfoundland three days behind you.'

Richard's bright blue eyes gleamed with excitement as they swept round the small group at the table. He didn't ask how John had managed to catch up with *Niobe* so quickly or in such a place; Crewfinders would have seen to all that. They could get anyone anywhere in the world with almost magical efficiency. 'So Bob arrives with *Achilles* tomorrow and I can expect you two days after,' he said, as much to himself as to the man on the far end of the telephone link.

'What about *Ajax*?'

'Fully crewed and on her way. Left Stavanger five days ago.'

'Phew! That's going it some! Any news of who's in command?'

'Not yet. One of the United Nations EGD crews.'

'EGD?'

'An old term Emily Karanga told me about last week before she went dirtside to New York. Equal Geographical Distribution. It means people who get given the job to fill a quota, not because they're any good.'

'Is that likely?'

'Used to happen more in the old days than it does now, I'm sure.'

Richard caught Tom Snell's gaze and the officer gave a slight world-weary shake of his head.

'Just so long as they can do their job,' said John.

'Just so long as they take good care of my boat!' said Richard.

'Too right. Look, just before I sign off, I've been told to expect two deliveries tomorrow. Professor Yves Maille, the marine biologist. I'm bringing him up to join the Club, I understand. He's the man who knows almost as much about warm water as Dr Ross knows about cold. And I'm to expect the rope. Is it really from NASA?'

'Yes it is, John. It's not really rope, it's non-breakable, monocellular carbon-graphite fibre woven into a cable.'

'Ah. Right.' The dazed wonderment in John's voice was clearly audible. 'I'll be bringing that up too, then. OK?'

'OK, John. Over and out.' Richard put the portable phone down on the starched linen of the table cloth. 'So,' he said, '*Achilles* will be here in three days, together with Professor Yves Maille and the rope. Which will, of course, give us yet another interesting conundrum.'

'What's that?' asked Tom Snell.

'How do you cut a length off something that's supposed to be unbreakable?'

The unbreakability of the rope was something which exercised the minds of Richard and Bob Stark the next afternoon.

Richard was there by the helipad to welcome his old friend aboard. The last time they had seen each other was at John Higgins' wedding and that had been nearly three years ago when Robin had been pregnant with the twins. Even then Richard had been struck by how little the American chief engineer had aged over the long years of their acquaintance. And now he was struck anew by the physical power and dynamism of the newly-promoted captain of *Achilles*. With his film star good looks, his Ivy League background, and his New England Four Hundred family you would have expected to find him following his father's footsteps into politics. Or at least his uncle's into the US Navy. But no. A love of marine engines and some vagaries of maritime chance had brought Bob to Heritage Mariner and he had always seemed content to remain, working his way up slowly but surely from third engineer to captain.

He looked at Richard almost quizzically as they shook hands. Then he looked at the iceberg. His blond eyebrows met his rich, straw-coloured head of hair and his dark blue eyes held an expression of incredulity. His wide mouth, over an impossibly wide jaw, turned up at one sculpted corner and he shook his head in mild disbelief. 'You really think we're going to be able to move that thing?' he asked.

'Yes,' said Richard decisively. 'We have the power. We have the rope. All we need to do is think it through.'

Half an hour later they were in conclave in Richard's day room while Bob's ship *Achilles* sailed off under command of its first officer to take Tom Snell and his men to the far end of the berg. Bob looked down at the diagrams on the desk. Then, sweeping the cow's lick of blond hair out of his eyes, he said, 'Even if it's unbreakable, there has to be a little give in it because it's woven into cable. Each individual fibre may have no elasticity whatsoever but when you wind them round each other they will stretch a little, even if it's only while the whole thing tightens up. And I guess that's all to the good because a little give will work to our advantage, give us some leeway.' He grinned. 'Cut us some slack.'

'OK,' temporised Richard, 'but we've still got trouble at both ends.'

'Damn right. The way I see it is this. Once you're anchored to the ice, that's it unless the anchorage points fail – which is a possibility we can look at in a minute. But the point is, if things go wrong, the cable isn't the weak link in the chain any more. It won't snap before damage to the ship occurs. So what would come next?'

'Capstans.'

'Right. Now each pair of capstans is motorised. So. The capstan post could be cut off or it could be pulled out of its mountings. With or without its motor.'

Bob paused there while Richard revisited one of his more recent nightmares. Beheading the capstan would be bad enough, but pulling it bodily out of the poop deck like a rotten tooth was something he didn't want to think about. And yet even that was preferable to the alternative.

'Or, of course,' he said to Bob, his voice rusty as though he had been shouting a lot recently, 'we could simply pull the whole back end off the boat.'

'Yup,' said Bob, 'we could certainly do that.'

The pair of them sat in silence for a moment, considering imponderables like if the poop did break away, how much of the stern would go with it. Whether the hull would remain watertight under those circumstances. Whether the engine would continue to function.

The impact of such a catastrophe was incalculable. It was one of those things you had to live through in order to get a proper hold on it. Like the separation of a supertanker. Richard had come through that by the skin of his teeth, standing on the deck of the first *Prometheus* in the

English Channel in a storm while she broke in two beneath him. All the foresight in the world could not have prepared him for the actuality of that. The same was true of pulling the back end off your boat.

'We also have the facility,' said Richard, 'of running a line back from the forecastle head.'

'So as well as being able to pull off the back end, you could pull off the front end too. You've started living dangerously in your old age, Richard!'

'Is it feasible? Would it help?'

'In theory it wouldn't help the actual tow. I mean, if you've got one unbreakable rope, why would you need two of them? Would it ease the strain on the hull? Probably not at this end. As I understand it, we plan to guide the thing and maybe get its mean speed up to five knots faster than its normal rate of drift, which should take it across the surface of the earth at about ten knots. Right?'

'Right. We would have to move at five knots faster than the current in any case, just to give the ships steerageway. Any slower than that and we're just drifting, really.'

'OK. I see that. So, what we need to do is apply propulsion to make it move faster until you have steerageway for your vessels, then force at some points to vary its course – you can't expect actually to *turn* it at all. Obviously the lead vessels and the rear vessels will have to do steering as well as propulsion while the middle vessels will just do propulsion. Therefore . . .'

The talk suddenly took an extremely technical turn.

Niobe hove into view thirty-six hours later and John Higgins came aboard at once. He and Richard shook hands a little formally. Although they were close friends – Richard had been John's best man – they had seen little of each other during the last couple of years, except for a taxing few days they had spent together in court fighting a case which threatened to cripple Heritage Mariner and destroy

Richard and his family financially for generations to come. 'Asha will be over later,' said John. 'I thought you'd want to get the business bits over first. I told Yves Maille to wait too. He's full of ideas and wants to discuss them, but we won't really be coming into his area of expertise until we swing her round into the Gulf Stream. I say, though, that's a bloody big bit of ice you've got there!'

Richard smiled down at the dapper, decisive man he had first met nearly fifteen years ago. Physically, John had changed little since that time. Five feet ten of restless energy, he only seemed slight when close beside Richard's six feet four inch frame. He had filled out perhaps, but there was no fat on his body; and if he carried himself a little stiffly these days, that was less to do with the passage of years than with a terrorist bullet in the ribs five years ago in the Gulf. The character was different, however. The happy-go-lucky third officer of *Prometheus* that Richard had first met had matured into a solid, reliable, senior captain who wore the weight of command easily and well. And the gifted navigator who had religiously taken noon and night-time sights with a series of beautiful old sextants had matured into a navigator of real genius, someone who they could rely upon to do even more for them than the dazzling array of navigation aids they had at their disposal.

They rode up in the lift towards Richard's day room locked in conversation. John was all for starting the final preparations for departure at once: *Ajax* was expected soon, though Richard knew nothing about her captain and crew other than the simple complement lists sent to him by the Mau Club in the UN building. Yes, agreed John, they would meet her captain and his men before putting them in place beside *Achilles* and getting under way, but even so, that was no reason for delay . . .

John had not come empty-handed, so the ride up in the lift was cramped as well as animated. As soon as they entered the day room, John unburdened himself of the largest of his gifts. 'Yves Maille will explain the details of these himself later, but I thought you'd want a look at them.'

'They' were a series of charts covering the whole of the proposed voyage, starting with the chart of the Davis Strait where they were currently, then following across the North Atlantic to the west coast of Ireland and down to Biscay, then on down the west coast of Africa to the Canaries. There was one chart for the sea area surrounding the Canary Islands themselves. Then another series took them into the Gulf of Guinea past the Bight of Benin and the Bight of Biafra into Mawanga itself.

Every chart was covered with drawings and notes which Richard, dazedly, began to recognise as the most incredibly detailed information about the currents they were hoping to follow. Mean flow speeds – at what depth if there was variation. Water temperatures – a careful gradation of colour to show which figure referred to what depth. Notes about possible variations. Offshoots, counter-currents, associated climatic conditions – whether and how they would be affected by them. Prevailing surface winds – force and temperature at surface level.

'This stuff is really only the beginning,' said John. 'The professor is going to go through it all and expand it at the first overall briefing we convene. Then he's going to update it daily and give us really detailed forecasts of all the conditions we will be sailing into from a thousand metres up in the air to a thousand metres down in the ocean. He's drifted across the Atlantic in a submersible just following the Gulf Stream so he literally knows it like the back of his hand, and of course the series of programmes he did for the World Wildlife Fund which were on TV last year were all filmed on the coral reefs off the Guinea coast so he knows our destination perfectly too. I really cannot believe how much he knows about the ocean. It's mind-numbing.'

'He'll get on with Kate Ross like a house on fire,' prophesied Richard.

'I wouldn't be at all surprised. Now, here's your next present.'

He laid it almost reverently on the desktop beside Yves Maille's charts. It was half a metre of black cable about the thickness of a strong man's forearm.

Richard picked it up. It was icy cold. Like glass. 'Is this it?'

'Some of it. The main cable's a couple of metres thick. This is the lighter line. And it goes right down to the thickness of string. Apparently they make it as thin as thread but that's too dangerous for general use. As you can see, though, it's just a bundle of threads all wrapped into a cable shape then held in place by this woven skin. It's incredible. But you've got to be careful of it. As I say, it's dangerous. Especially the thinner stuff.'

'How?'

'Well, for a start, it's damn near unbreakable. They've given us these things like pipe benders to cut it with. You clamp one round it and move a handle. It's as though you're trying to put a screw-thread on the outside of the cable but in fact the handle activates a laser beam which is all that can get through it. Apparently the beam gets between the molecules and breaks the magnetic link or some such. But the point is that scissors, knives, axes, oxyacetylene equipment are all useless. Even on the string. And what you've got to remember is that the thinner it gets, the sharper it gets. I read somewhere about someone training soldiers to use single fibres as a weapon. Use a thread of it like a garotte and you can take somebody's head off, no trouble at all. And that's what I'm building up to. Two of my men tried a tug of war with the thinnest string. Big blokes. Wrapped it round their hands and pulled against each other. They thought it would break. It was no thicker than a shoelace. But it didn't break. It cut their fingers off instead. I've got it all under lock and key now.'

Richard looked at the cable and felt a slight shiver. It

gleamed slightly, as though slugs had been crawling all over it.

'Have you worked out how you're going to anchor it in the ice yet?' asked John.

'Yes, I think so. I'm going to loop the end of the cable nearest the ice and then run two other lengths of cable through. That will give us four cable ends on the ice. And a spread of four anchorage points. What Tom Snell has done so far is to level the anchorage areas and then bore down into the ice four holes in carefully calculated positions at carefully calculated angles. Each hole is about five metres across and ten metres deep and they slope so that their bottoms are towards the ship while their tops are away from the ship. We'll fill each hole with quick drying concrete and embed the actual anchorage points in that so there is no direct pressure on the ice from the anchorage. That way we hope to keep the pressure-melting to a minimum. We'll have teams watching at each anchorage point in any case, certainly to begin with. In theory if even three of the anchorages fail, the fourth should be enough to maintain the tow while we get the others back into commission.'

'But having four should give you a fail-safe spread.'

'Like having four engines on an aeroplane.'

Dinner that night was close to being a social affair. Colin and Kate again came down off the ice – a five-minute hop in the Westland made it very easy to exchange visits. John had brought not only the rope from New York but also a Bell helicopter destined for *Achilles'* deck – it had been agreed as part of the overall equipping of the project that there should be one helicopter for each pair of ships. Bob Stark was still aboard *Titan*; he would go back to his own command with the new helicopter tomorrow, for *Ajax* was due within the next twenty-four hours and Richard intended to get under way within the next thirty-six. They would meet *Kraken* and *Psyche* in the Atlantic and get up to full speed then. Manhattan was drifting south with the Labrador Current so quickly now that she would be in the grip of the Gulf Stream within four days at the outside and Richard wanted to have her under some kind of control before then if he possibly could. So for the first and probably the last time they were all together at this table. John and his doctor wife Asha, Professor Yves Maille, Bob Stark, Richard, Sally Bell. Tom Snell and his men were still down on *Achilles*, putting the final touches to the anchorage areas at the stern of the tow. The Bell would bring them back tomorrow.

In the meantime, Kate, Asha and Sally were surrounded by witty, charming, highly attractive men, who for once were not talking exclusively about the tow. Asha had eyes for no one but her John, really, and Kate and Colin drifted in and out of an impenetrable conversation about phytoplankton and microclimates. Sally, on the other hand, found herself torn. Captain Mariner was so tall and distinguished with just those wings of silver sweeping back above his ears to emphasise the jet-black hair which in turn seemed to bring out to perfection his ice-blue eyes. But Professor Maille was also worthy of attention, all Gallic charm, the most irresistible accent, and old-world courtesy. But it was Bob Stark she finally plumped for – the wide grin, the boyish cow's lick of thick blond hair, the square jut of his jaw and the dreamy depths of his eyes.

It was a very great pity indeed, she thought glumly, that she would be separated from this gorgeous man by one hundred kilometres of ice.

They dispersed to their posts at the end of the meal. Colin and Kate were dropped up onto the ice then the Westland took John and Asha Higgins and Professor Maille back to *Niobe*. Richard went off to do some late checking and phoning and Sally drifted into the officers' lounge with Bob Stark and a big cup of coffee. She was due on watch duty soon and had nothing to do in the meantime. They chatted idly, like old friends. She told him about her childhood in Ulster and her education in Belfast. 'You should talk to old Higgins,' he informed her. 'He's got a lot of Irish in his background. Father's family, mostly. He's a Manxman, though.' And he told her of his own Ivy League background, his youth and education in New England, his father the senator and his uncle the US Navy admiral. But he spoke of these things naturally and thoughtlessly with no desire to impress her with his family wealth or social standing.

At midnight they went up onto the bridge together and he sat in the watchkeeper's chair on the left side of the bridge while she dismissed the third officer to bed and signed on as watchkeeper.

He crossed his legs and his trousers slid up to reveal a glimpse of calf. 'Good God,' she said, straightening. 'Is that a bullet wound?'

'Yup, sure is. Got it in an honest to God shoot-out, too.'

'Gunfight at the OK Corral?'

'Fighting terrorists on an oil platform called Fate. Though I was actually shot on the deck of *Prometheus*.'

'That's where Captain Higgins got shot too, isn't it?'

'And Asha nursed him back to health. They've been playing doctors and nurses ever since.'

Sally shook her head. 'Boy, do you all lead exciting lives.'

'We all. You're one of us now. Part of the team.'

'In the Club at any rate.'

'So your life should get a bit more exciting soon too.'

'*Och!*' she said, her Belfast background surfacing in the sound of disbelief.

Just then the warning light in the radio shack lit up.

'Incoming,' observed Bob cheerfully.

'I'll get it,' said Sally and crossed to the little room. She picked up the microphone and flipped the channel open.

'*Titan*, are you receiving me, over?'

'This is *Titan*, receiving you strength ten, over.'

'*Titan*, this is *Ajax*, over. Message for Captain Mariner.'

'Hold on, *Ajax*, I'm buzzing him now. Captain, it's Sally here. I have an incoming for you from *Ajax*. Yes, right . . . Hello, *Ajax*, the Captain's coming up at once. May I have your current position and ETA at our position?'

'Four hundred kilometres west of Julianehab. We will be with you by dawn, over.'

'Thank you very much, *Ajax*, handing you over to Captain Mariner now . . .'

Richard went in as Sally came out. He put on the headphones, switched off the open channel and swung the door closed, but he was speaking at once so Sally and Bob heard his first words quite clearly.

'Ah. Captain Borodin. Welcome to the Davis Strait . . .'

Sixteen hours later, everything was in place. *Ajax* had joined *Achilles* and their lines were secured to Tom Snell's anchorage places. *Titan* and *Niobe* were also in place and secured to the ice. Richard was standing at the capstans on *Titan*'s poop watching narrow-eyed along the sag of that strange, black almost crystalline rope which stretched back behind them, seeming to grasp the ice with an unnerving, four-fingered hand. The afternoon was dull and overcast. There was a storm due to break out of Hudson Bay later tonight or tomorrow. It was time to be gone.

Richard raised his walkie-talkie to his lips. All of them had agreed on channel four as the general hailing frequency and all of the key players in this scene had their walkie-talkies close at hand, open on channel four. Up on the ice, the radio shack behind Colin Ross's base was receiving and retransmitting channel four so that it could be heard by Bob Stark and Katya Borodin as clearly as by Sally Bell on *Titan*'s bridge and John Higgins on *Niobe* nearby.

Richard's stomach was knotted with tension. He knew

he was standing on the edge of the unknown. No one had ever tried to move anything this big before. No one in the history of the world had tried to take a piece of ice one hundred kilometres long and deliver it to a point eleven thousand kilometres away as the crow flies. He had thought about this moment, what he would say, how it would sound. He was not a self-publicist, but he knew that he had a reputation and that what he said now would add to it – or go a long way towards destroying it. He had planned a little speech. He had wondered about something as derivative as 'one small step', or as bland as 'slow ahead all', but now as he stood there on this grey, blustery afternoon looking up at the bow-shaped cliff of ice towering above him, the wind gusted five hundred metres up and blew a combination of ice dust and spray off Manhattan in two long, white horns. Because his blood was full of adrenaline and he would very much, just at that moment, have liked to be in another place or in another time, he was taken back to his childhood and the days – the only days in all his life – when he had wanted to be something other than a sailor. To the days when his first great hero on the television would turn at the end of *Rawhide* and say the same thing every week.

It fitted with how he felt, what they were doing and how the iceberg looked just at that moment with the white horns butting at the sky. For the first time in more than forty years he said the words Gil Favor used to say to Rowdy Yates, loud and clear, for better or worse, whether his listeners understood them or not. 'Head them up,' he said. 'Move them out.'

He felt the whole of his great vessel begin to throb and he walked swiftly back to the after rail. He stood sideways on so he could look back towards the ice, forward towards the second officer's team on the capstans, down towards the foaming water.

'*Slow* ahead!'

The water was foaming up under the counter down there as though they were sitting atop an underwater volcano. The black rope had lost its sag and the thin talon quivered as it clawed at the ice. He could see the figures of Snell's team moving about there apprehensively, checking the anchorage points with one eye on the rope in case it parted after all and cut back to chop them to pieces.

'*Slow* ahead!' he said again. The mountain of foam behind the ship seemed to grow and a low humming started. It was the tension in the rope and the sound dried his mouth out. He could hear his heart beating. This wasn't going to work.

The humming grew in intensity and was joined by a low groaning. He concentrated all his imagination on the soles of his feet: the last time he had heard a noise like that, *Prometheus* had been breaking in two beneath him and his feet had been the first part of him to realise something was wrong. Would they warn him if the poop was about to come free? If they did, would he have a chance to get back onto the main deck before he was snatched away with everything aft of the capstan? No. No chance. If it all went now, he was dead.

Thank God he had told Robin he loved her last night and asked her to give the twins a special hug.

The whole ship was quivering now. Like a greyhound in a trap ready for the off but restrained. There was a thudding thumping from below. Or was it just his heart again?

The cable sagged.

Infinitesimally. Almost indiscernibly.

But it sagged.

Richard took a deep, shuddering breath.

'Are we still at slow ahead, Sally?'

'Slow ahead and due south, Captain.' There was strain in her voice too, but her words lit a spark of hope in his breast. For if the ship was at slow ahead then the cable could only sag if—

'*Richard!*' Colin's voice through channel four so loud it made him jump. 'Richard, she's moving. Manhattan's moving!'

Then John came through over the top of him, yelling, 'My God! Richard! My God!' And behind John's awed tones was the sound of wild cheering. Abruptly, the sound exploded out of the radio and into the air immediately around him. Every throat on *Titan* was yelling in jubilation.

Richard found himself pounding on the after rail and grinning like an idiot. He wanted to yell himself. To cheer with the rest and to dance and sing. He had never in his heart of hearts really believed they could pull this off. Even the seemingly unquestioning faith of the Mau Club and the Manhattan Club had seemed unrealistic and faintly unreal. Yet here they were. And here was Manhattan. And they were pulling and it was following. It was impossible but it was true.

'We are moving at slow ahead, *Achilles*. Are you moving?'

'Son of a bitch, Richard. Son of a bitch.'

Richard took that as an affirmative.

'*Ajax?*'

'All lines secure. Proceeding as ordered, Captain. But this "Head them up and move them out", this I do not understand.'

'I'll explain it to you some time, Captain Borodin. In the meantime, slow ahead all. Come to five knots if you please. Our heading is due south.'

Chapter Twelve

Ann Cable rode down in the lift and bustled across the busy foyer of the Mawanga Hilton. She felt tired but full of a febrile energy, full of words and writing. She hesitated on the great doormat, just out of range of the infra-red beam which tripped the automatic doors. She took a last, lingering deep breath of the air-conditioned atmosphere and then, holding it in her lungs, she moved forward. The doors hissed open and she flinched. Even in the shade of the building's wide porch, the atmosphere rolled over her like a wave of hot oil. The temperature was in the mid-thirties already and the humidity was in the nineties. She had taken less than three steps, hadn't even reached the boiling brightness of direct sunshine, before her body was drenched in perspiration and she breathed cool air out and hot, humid air in. She felt the energy begin to leak away at once, ruthlessly sucked out of her like the sweat. She summoned reserves she didn't know she possessed and ran down the steps towards Robert Gardiner's jeep.

Even through the lenses of her dark glasses, the sun nearly blinded her. She wore a battered hat and headscarf and she could feel the weight of it on the crown of her head. She burned her hand on the door handle as she climbed into the vehicle. It was only nine o'clock in the morning, for God's sake!

'Has this thing got air conditioning?' she asked.

Robert laughed, his deep booming chuckle drowning

out the whine of the starter. 'You can open the windows,' he told her as the engine caught. 'But be careful of the dust.'

As he drove out to the airport, she swung round in her seat and watched him. His skin was incredibly dark, gleaming like polished ebony. His face was broad – broad forehead, lined from temple to temple, broad cheeks with long, narrow eyes above and broad flat nose below. Broad mouth, perfectly sculpted, with lips the colour of aubergine. Broad, square, absolute chin. Almost no neck, the great cannonball head sitting straight on the broad shoulders and great square chest above a powerful, elephantine barrel of a belly. The limbs complemented that massive torso, giving Robert the physical impact of an Olympic-standard weightlifter. In this heat, a man of his size ought to have been sweating profusely but, apart from the oiled gleam of his skin, there was no evidence that he felt hot at all. In fact, as her first breath inside the jeep informed her, he smelt faintly of cologne and nothing more.

Unlike herself. Since her semi-hysterical shower more than a week ago she had used water for drinking only, wherever possible. She bathed with a flannel which was little more than damp and flushed the toilet only when it became difficult to breathe in the bathroom. Her hair was a dusty mess of oil and she daily thanked God that she had had it cut so much shorter than usual before she came out here. Even so, she felt filthy, itchy and smelly. And exhausted. She rested her head on the back of the seat and closed her eyes as they sped through the all too familiar shantytown outskirts of the city.

In the seventies, when it had looked as though there would be a booming travel industry here, the road from the city to the airport had been a well-constructed highway with six lanes in each direction. The massive, impressive thoroughfare seemed out of place now, and it stood in increasing need of maintenance, as though the government tacitly admitted that the tourists would never come after all.

The airport, too, was over-grandiose; the result of plans and dreams which had died. They drove past the terminal building which stood semi-derelict, the home of a number of refugees who had come here from the dust bowls upcountry and remained, as though too weak to go on into the city itself.

'There are an increasing number of them, in spite of the aid camps and the roadblocks outside the city,' observed Robert. 'I don't know how they're getting through, but I'm afraid there will be more. It's a bad sign, the beginning of the end.'

'It can get worse. You know that.'

'I know; that wasn't what I meant. What I meant was that once this sort of thing gets rolling, it follows an inevitable course. There's no way back. It's like a law of nature. You know about *Fahrenheit 451*?'

'The science fiction novel? I guess so, why?'

'Not so much the novel as the title. Four hundred and fifty-one degrees Fahrenheit is the burning point of paper. That's why Bradbury chose it for a novel about burning books. But it's the physics I'm interested in. The inevitability. At 450 degrees paper doesn't burn. At 451 degrees it does and there's nothing you can do about it.'

'And you say we're reaching ignition point here?'

'I'm going to show you. Upcountry, in the heartland. And it won't be pleasant if the reports are true.'

He braked suddenly and the long green vehicle screeched to a halt outside a corrugated iron and clapboard hangar. There was a perky-looking little single-engined Cessna parked outside with a mechanic sitting beside it in the shade of a wing. He got up as Robert and Ann climbed out of the vehicle. 'Ready to go?' asked Robert in fluent Kyogi. The mechanic nodded, smiled and saluted. He saluted with his right hand which was holding an automatic weapon. Robert saw the direction of Ann's gaze. 'Not standard UN issue,' he admitted, 'but if we didn't have them, we wouldn't have this plane for long either. There's no safe UN compound here. Yet. Though as soon as the police realise what's going on they'll move in and clear the refugees out. Set up more roadblocks, just as they have been doing all week.'

They climbed in and, as he went through the pre-flight, she thought about this extraordinary man and what he had just said to her. Robert Gardiner had started out as a schoolteacher in his native Guyana but he had spent the long vacations working for Save the Children and had proved himself such an able organiser and administrator that he had been employed full-time by the organisation. During the succeeding years he had moved from organisation to organisation, retaining links with each one he passed through. He still had contacts with Save the Children, and with UNICEF, with the World Health Organisation and with the World Food Programme. But he was now a field man for the United Nations High Commission for Refugees, specialising in identifying the next likely trouble spots where refugees would result. Specialising in finding the potential flashpoints and trying to put them out.

Which was what he had been talking about earlier. Here they were in a situation already too familiar to him, to her, to anyone who cared to look around the world. A country which had hidden its tribal divisions beneath a veneer of good government, where increasing wealth and national hope was suddenly confronted with anarchy, poverty and despair. A country once strong enough to stand alone, now in danger of falling victim to rapacious neighbours; where millions, desperate and hopeless, were on the verge of becoming the playthings of civil and cross-border warfare. And it was here. Now. The whole situation was simmering on the edge of explosion. How it would come and where was impossible to tell. When would it come? Soon. A day. A week. A month at most. The UN could see it coming, warned by Robert Gardiner and their other representatives on the ground, and there was apparently much bustling in New York as they tried to find some way of slowing down the inevitable slide to costly conflict. But no one quite knew what they were up to and when relief would arrive.

The UN were not the only people involved. There were all too many people who could see immense gains to be had out of anarchy in Mau. And they were out there too. For every Robert Gardiner there were others with much more sinister motives plotting to undo his work.

It was 450 degrees Fahrenheit now, today. And someone was trying to turn the temperature up.

She had come across some rumours last week but hadn't really understood their full significance. She knew the rough history of the country, knew more detail than most Westerners because she researched her assignments so thoroughly, but it was only a couple of evenings ago when she had been talking to Robert about her interviews that the full significance had emerged.

The plane rumbled down the runway and swooped up into the air. She looked across at Robert but he was still deep in conversation with the control tower. She closed her eyes. In her mind's eye she could see the first woman she had interviewed as clearly as if she had been sitting on the engine cowling just beyond the Cessna's windshield. She had looked so old. Far too old to be cradling such a little baby, sitting wrapped in rags by a dead acacia by the side of a country road.

Ann had come out in the long-based jeep Cherokee with a guide duly licensed and recommended by the hotel. They had taken a hotel waiter with a supply of food and drink. It had been almost a picnic; an orientation trip, nothing more. At first.

Commissioned by an uneasy alliance of the publishing house who published her best-selling books and an independent TV producer who wanted a combination of grit and glamour, she had agreed to do a special documentary on Mau. Offered a research assistant, she had defiantly decided to do the groundwork herself and had flown out alone, only to realise when it was a little too late just how alone she really was. It was ten days until her film crew were due. She had that time to find her feet and get the outline of the programme clear in her head. She had phoned some of the names on the list of contacts the TV people had given her and had been invited to several garden parties and a literary evening. That was not what she wanted at all so she had approached the hotel manager and he had been more helpful. He had found her the jeep and the driver, at least.

They had driven out of town heading due east along the main highway. She realised now that they must have passed the airport buildings and she had never even noticed the refugees squatting within them. She knew now that she had chosen the last day before the police roadblocks went up – and suspected that her activities might have contributed to their existence. Had she tried to leave the city alone now, today, she would have been quietly but firmly turned back.

When she saw the figures, the long lines of figures walking wearily down the road, she had assumed they were women from the farms nearby come to trade in the city's markets. She had taken a photograph or two. Like a tourist. This was not her area of expertise; she had made her reputation writing books about the environment further north and the dangers facing those who worked around the shores of the Atlantic – and those who worked in frail ships upon it. This was her first exposure to Africa and she was only just beginning to realise how much she still had to learn.

Then she had come to the first person who did not fit the simple, safe picture presented by the tall figures walking slowly westward with huge bundles on their heads: a withered old crone sitting with a tiny child. It was a scene familiar from countless reports in the press and on television. The woman and child were clearly at the end of their strength. The shock of recognition literally knocked the wind out of Ann's body.

She had asked her guide, a Kyoga called Saul, to stop and she had climbed down with her tape recorder. Then, on closer inspection, she put the little machine in her pocket and went back for her water bottle. First the skeletal child and then the gaunt woman wet their lips. Their eyes, the only liquid things about them, came back to life a little. She reached for her tape recorder again. 'I want to speak to her, Saul, can you translate for me?'

'I am a Kyoga, lady. This is N'Kuru woman.'

'Can you understand what she says?'

'I can speak little N'Kuru.'

The servant from the hotel had climbed out by this point. He was hardly more than a boy but he said diffidently, 'I am N'Kuru, madam. I can understand her.'

Saul climbed back into the jeep, leaving her with the boy and the woman. 'How did she get here?'

'She say she walk.'

'Alone? Where is her family?'

'The lions took her husband and her brothers. The dust took all the rest.'

Ann rocked back on her heels at that, thinking of some kind of massacre by wild animals. It had not occurred to her that lions might have a capital L. Robert had pointed it out when she played the tape to him later.

'What about her daughter? The baby's mother?'

'It is her child.'

Ann looked deeply into that gaunt, lined face. A kind of horror swept over her.

'How old is she?'

This took a little computation, a comparison of events and dates, but at last the boy looked up at her. 'The woman say she is seventeen.'

They had put the N'Kuru woman in the back of the jeep and, much against Saul's inclination, driven her straight back into Mawanga to the City Hospital. There, rather dazed staff relieved the angry white-skinned woman of the dying bush native and put her and her child in a room well away from the city folk who understood such things as health insurance and the proper ways of becoming ill.

Ann had been standing, lost and deflated in the reception, with the woman gone and Saul nowhere to be seen, suddenly vividly aware that she didn't even have enough money on her for a cab back to the hotel, when a square stranger with incredibly black skin had walked up to her and grinned.

'I wouldn't have believed it if I hadn't seen it with my own eyes,' he said. 'I thought matron was going to have apoplexy. Don't you know that this is the most exclusive private hospital in downtown Mawanga?'

'I'm just beginning to find out how little I do know,' she answered ruefully. 'My name is Ann Cable and I don't even know how I'm going to get back to my hotel.'

The grin darkened. 'A dangerous admission to make here or anywhere,' he warned. 'A dangerous predicament, even for a good samaritan. But this time you're lucky. My name is Robert Gardiner. I work for the United Nations High Commission for Refugees. I've read your books. I'll take you back to your hotel.'

'I don't want to go back to my hotel. I want to go and find out what's really going on out there.'

'If you're really serious about it, I can show you that, too.'

'Let's go then.'

'It's been quite a week for you,' Robert said as the Cessna

settled into level flight, the great cliff fell back into a thunderous purple shadow on the left and the bush began to unroll before them.

'Tell me about it. I feel like I've been re-educated the hard way.'

'I fear your education is just beginning, my dear. You've been at the edge of things so far. We're going into the heart of it now. On the roads, at the aid stations and the camps I've taken you to visit, there have been only the survivors. Victims, yes; but the lucky ones, relatively speaking. I am concerned that we may soon be seeing people who have been much less lucky.'

'You're telling me it's going to be dangerous? Or just disgusting?'

'Both. But very dangerous.'

'Then why are you bringing me?'

'Because I want you to see. I desperately need someone influential to see what is going on. Someone with some influence.'

'But surely you have influence, Robert.'

'With the wrong people. I write my reports and they get considered and precious little gets done. Oh, I know they've set up the Mau Club now and they say they're trying to move this iceberg but I ask you! What sort of a response is that to a situation like this? It's a joke! Laughable! No. I need someone with influence where it counts: in the media.'

'But I won't even have a film crew here for another three days!'

'That may be time enough. We'll meet my contact, have a sniff around, see if there's any truth in what he's saying and get back to Mawanga tomorrow. One day to get a bit of a safari set up and your film crew and you could have decent footage by the weekend. Just in time for the Sunday papers. It's worth the risk. If there is something going on out here, something even worse than the drought, something which is driving the N'Kuru off their land, maybe we'll find out about it. You could really blow the lid off this. Like John Pilger did in Cambodia. Like Kate Adie in the Gulf. Get things moving with a vengeance.'

'Is that true, what you said? That the United Nations is trying to send an iceberg here?'

'Nothing official yet. It's so laughable they probably daren't admit it. But yes. That's what I've been told. They've hired some ships – tugs, I suppose – and they're trying to bring an iceberg here as an answer to the drought.'

It wasn't only empty desert down below. The outlines of the communal farms and the sharp grids of the irrigation system showed where cultivation had been tried, and would be again, but there were no men there over great swathes of dry red land, and here the animals had returned. At first there were thinly dotted groups of zebra and wildebeest, grazing on the ruins of whatever crops had been left unattended and whatever greenery had sprung up in damp hollows of the untended ground, but as they roared further and further into the bush, the neat cultivation began to falter and the sad regimentation of the failed farms began to break down as the indigenous vegetation reasserted itself. Then came a circle of huts with a thorn wall and a stockade. 'N'Kuru village,' said Robert. His first words in some time. They went low and circled. It was deserted.

After another half an hour, there was a kind of patchy green covering to the ground. Not grass, but some kind of plant. The regular pattern of the irrigation ditches, far behind, was replaced here by the organic, root-like patterns of dry water courses. But where the rule-straight, man-made channels had simply been marks across the desert, here the wandering branches carried vegetation which gave some faint promise of water underground. Tall palms appeared, singly and in clumps, thorn scrub, umbrella acacias and baobabs. And, as the vegetation increased, so did the animal life. The zebra were in herds here, as were the wildebeest. In the shade of some of the bigger clumps stood kudu and impala in small family groups. Enough wildlife to support some lean lions. Robert obediently circled the first somnolent pride they found while Ann took photographs.

It was not until they were close to the eastern border that they saw the first gleam of surface water. 'Here we are,' said Robert and the Cessna began to settle. 'That thicker forest up ahead is the beginning of a forest which stretches into Congo Libre. This is the wildest country Mau has except for some of the jungle up on the ridge in the high country and it has always supported a fair number of wild N'Kuru – those of the tribe who wanted nothing to do even with Julius Karanga. It's always been dangerous out here. It's where the N'Kuru Lions made their base before they were destroyed and sent away to Angola and Congo Libre to lick their wounds and learn about communism. Ironic really, that the least civilised part of the country should be the most self-sufficient now. But to be fair, it had help.'

The vegetation – it was thick thorn bush, with increasing forest cover – fell back to reveal a wide, shallow lake. The Cessna went down near the water only to bank away sharply as flamingoes exploded into the air. Ann's heart skipped at their beauty. This was the Africa she had dreamed of. 'That's proper bush down there,' said Robert, sounding almost proud. 'Impala, sassaby, kudu, hippos, crocodiles, elephants, the lot. In Mau they call it the out-back and this is all that's left of it.' As if to prove his words a family of waterbuck flew from the water's edge to the shel-ter of the trees, away from the sound of the engine.

The Cessna skipped across the trees and a flat landing strip abruptly opened out beneath them. At the far end were some huts, outside which a battered Land Rover was sitting.

'The lake is the heart of it and it doesn't compare with the Masai Mara or any of the others, but this was going to be Mau's great gift to conservation.'

The wheels touched the red earth of the runway.

'Welcome to the Dr Julius Karanga Game Reserve.'

He throttled back.

'There's somebody there,' she almost shouted.

'I know. He's come to meet us.'

'How does he know we're here? You didn't use the radio.'

'He heard the engine. It's an uncommon sound out here, nowadays.'

The man who was waiting for them was a slight white man who wore a wide-brimmed bush hat turned up at one side and the uniform of bush shirt and shorts, long socks and desert boots which went with it. He wore a double holster like a cowboy, with two businesslike handguns protruding convenient to his hands. He had been carrying a powerful-looking rifle under his right arm and it was not until he recognised Robert that he hefted it up and slid it through the Land Rover's window. Then he was striding towards them, hand held out.

'Welcome, Robert. Glad you could come.'

'This is Harry Parkinson. Harry, Ann Cable the journalist.'

His palm was dry, like snakeskin; his grip of handshake brief and crushing.

His 'How d'you do?' was very English indeed. His face was deeply tanned and lined, the wrinkles round his eyes deep and pale-floored; the nose red and webbed with veins. The pale eyes were given brightness by the contrast and the clipped moustache given depth and whiteness. His teeth were yellow and false, too big for his thin-lipped mouth.

'We're hoping to bring her film crew out here later in the week.' Robert's tone of voice changed as he spoke and Ann suddenly realised that some unspoken message had passed between the men. They turned and crossed towards the Land Rover. 'You have a problem with that?'

'I don't know, Robert. Miss Cable, would you mind sitting in the back? Just climb aboard.'

The two men lingered outside the battered vehicle as she settled herself onto the cracked and dusty leather of the long bench seat. It was hotter out here than it had been in Mawanga, but the heat was dry and less oppressive. Her mind was aching to wander away into the romance of the jungle but her ears were too well aware of the hurried conversation going on between the men.

'I think we ought to get the Cessna fuelled up and rolled over by the hut out of harm's way.'

'OK, Harry. If you think so. Any reason why old Chobe can't do it as usual?'

'Chobe's gone.'

'Gone?'

'Vanished. Disappeared. Last night, after I talked to you. Well, he may have gone earlier but I didn't know about it until I came down here to warn him to look out for you today.'

During this speech, the Englishman's voice faded. The pair of them were moving away. Ann glanced out and saw them walking purposefully towards the nearest hut. Their voices faded until they were swallowed by the bush sounds which filled the wavering air, sounds she had dreamed of hearing throughout her youth. They had filled her limitless dreams fostered on the fantasies of Tarzan and *Mogambo*, of the Hollywood movies on which her father had worked before he died.

And now she was hearing them for real, every well-remembered nameless film-soundtrack chirrup, whistle, cough, song and snarl. It was midday and hot; there was nothing hunting now, she knew, just the bustle of the bush going about its business. Then, loud enough to make her jump, came a whinny and the blowing sound of a horse seeking attention. Her eyes sprang open – she hadn't realised they were closed.

At the end of the makeshift landing field, where the cleared grass came closest to the trees, was a substantial fence. Over this, for all the world like a pet pony in a field, a zebra had pushed its head. She opened the door and climbed to the ground. The zebra watched her as she walked towards it. She had only seen zebra in pictures and zoos. What struck her about it most forcibly was the fact that it was not black and white. The red dust from the plains had coloured it so that it was striped red and umber – no, not striped, shadowed. Almost dappled. She bent and pulled up a handful of grass, offering it. The delicate nostrils flared. The velvet lips parted to reveal strong yellow teeth.

'Come on then, my beauty,' she purred, moving slowly forward.

But then the men behind her started up a wheezing, clanking old hand pump and the zebra's brown eyes widened with surprise and fear. Its long head jerked back over the fence and it galloped away. Immediately, a whole section of the grassland was in motion too and she realised that what had seemed to be a dusty, dappled field had been a grazing herd. Entranced, she stood and watched. They only moved a couple of hundred metres then they stopped and began to feed again. The dust of their movement billowed and settled, adding to their russet camouflage. The panorama before her seemed slowly to widen as she looked around, taking it all in. In the far distance away to her left, the thunderous line of the tectonic cliff folded into a series of tawny hills which she knew were in fact across the border in the neighbouring state of Congo Libre. Then, from the feet of the hills, as tawny as they were, as though the whole landscape was the flank of a lion, stretched the grassland where the zebra were feeding. On the right, however, the grass became thorn scrub and the tall bushes soon became the trees she knew were gathered round the lake they had flown across.

How she ached to climb the fence and explore. But she knew how foolish such an act would be. All she knew about her current environment was what she had read in the works of Rider Haggard, Edgar Rice Burroughs, Hemingway, Robert Ruark, James S. Rand and Wilbur Smith. However accurate these men had been in their portrayals of Africa, she knew that reading about it was never the same as being out in it. So she stood and strained her eyes, hoping, praying, to see the most coveted prize of all, the tall, lean, long-legged, high-shouldered, wide-eared tuskers of the African plains. She had seen Indian elephants in circuses and zoos, and the squat, square, reliable pachyderms had made her ache to see their great wild African cousins.

The clatter made by the men putting the pump away called her back to herself and by the time they returned to the Land Rover she was sitting back on the seat in the rear. 'Where first?' she asked.

'My place, I think,' said Harry. As he drove, he talked, giving her an unsolicited interview which she would have found even more interesting if he had not kept looking back over his shoulder at her while he hurled the Land Rover along the red dirt tracks at what seemed like breakneck speed.

'I've been here since the eighties. Helped to set the place up, you see. Stayed on to keep an eye on things even though it's all gone to rack and ruin. Just a game warden really, but I'm responsible for the better part of ten thousand square miles of assorted desert, bush and scrub. Everywhere south and east to the Blood River, which is the closest we have to a border with Congo Libre, and everywhere north to the escarpment. It's not all game reserve, of course. A lot of N'Kuru farmland, a couple of towns – real towns with buildings – and half a dozen villages. The N'Kuru Lion lands. The N'Kuru tribal homeland. Almost a magic place. Incredibly important in their religion. I and my askaris are the only law there is, really. Parkinson's Law, we call it. Prime Minister Mumboto seems happy enough to let me look after things. He doesn't want that bastard General of Police Nimrod Chala and his Kyoga sadists down here pillaging and looting. Nor Major General Moses M'Diid, the acting President's brother, with his tank regiment either for that matter. Though both of them would give anything to get their hands on it. If the farmland N'Kuru are on the move because of the drought, the only chance the government have of keeping the lid on things is if the bush N'Kuru stay on their homeland here. Which is why I told Robert I was worried. Something's up. Something not very nice. And that is why you're here, Miss Cable. Robert says you can get some publicity drummed up. International observers, press corps, stuff like that.'

'When you say "keep the lid on things", what do you think will happen if the lid comes off?'

'Civil war, plain and simple. Kyoga against N'Kuru with clubs and stones in the countryside until the Lions call in their friends from Congo Libre; and the army versus the police in the city, Moses M'Diid versus Nimrod Chala. The same as is happening in Rwanda and Somalia, the Vietnam of Africa. The Bosnia of the Dark Continent.'

'And the United Nations in the middle of it,' began Robert.

'The same as Kigali, Mogadishu and Sarajevo,' completed Harry grimly.

'And all the others,' added Ann, beginning to understand their desperation, and to feel all too keenly how inadequately she could answer their cry for help. She couldn't get the lid off a jelly jar, let alone off this.

If Harry Parkinson wore a pair of guns like a cowboy, his

long, low, wooden headquarters building was like a ranch house on the Kansas plains. There was a picket fence round it with an empty guard hut and a wide, five-barred gate. 'It's electrified now,' Harry told her as Robert opened the gate, let them roll through and then closed it behind them. 'Looks like old-fashioned crap but it's state of the art. I had it done when the Lions came back, but oddly enough they've never bothered me. Or my men. It's the poachers we have to worry about. The ones that come over the Blood River after the tuskers and the rhinos.'

'Why is it called the Blood River?'

'Not as grim as it sounds. About the only place in this neck of the woods which isn't. Right, Robert? No, it was called that because of the mud. It used to run red because of the red soil. When it ran. It's just a dry valley now and little commandos from the Congo Libre army pop across it in the dead of night to come after our ivory and rhino horn. Bastards.'

They pulled up in a storm of red dust and the three piled out together and went up the three long wooden steps onto the veranda.

'A-TEN-*SHUN*!' bellowed Harry as they entered through the door into what was obviously the main operations room. But nobody was there to obey his order. The big radio stood switched on but unmanned. The chair and tables all around the big room were scattered with open magazines and burdened with half-consumed cups of coffee. Cushions still bore the imprints of bodies. But there was nobody there at all. The three new arrivals stood, frozen by the strangeness of the room. The door swung behind them as though there was a wind but there was no wind.

A tiny lizard scuttled up the wall and through the ceiling boards.

'Now this is bloody odd,' said Harry Parkinson. Unconsciously, he eased his pistols in their holsters and Ann noted that she could see not the pearl handles of Colt revolvers she had half expected but the square, moulded, composite grips of modern, state of the art automatic handguns. She felt reassured, somehow.

'SHOP!' bellowed Harry.

Absolute silence by way of reply.

'There are, what, five rooms upstairs?' asked Robert.

'This room and kitchen down here. My quarters upstairs – lounge, dining room, two bedrooms and bathroom.'

'We'd better have a look.'

'You wait here. I'll look.'

He was gone, out through the still open door.

'Most likely a panic call over the radio,' said Robert cheerfully. 'Poachers or something like that. The askaris are supposed to leave someone to report if they get called out. They can't always find a volunteer to wait behind. They're all very keen.'

A floorboard above their heads creaked. A tiny cloud of dust filtered down through the still hot air. The lizard scuttled out, saw them and froze.

'It's more than that and you know it. What you were saying about the lid coming off. Do you think it has?'

He looked down at her. Their eyes met. Suddenly she was angry. At the situation. At her fear. At herself. At him. 'Look,' she said, 'I know I'm naive. I know I'm out of my depth. But I'm not some subnormal infant, and I'm good at my job. Tell me the truth, for God's sake. Stop trying to mother me!'

'I don't know,' he said, apparently capitulating. 'Harry and his askaris are a great team. Thirteen men. One mind. They need it sometimes, I can tell you. Ten thousand square miles and they're the only law. I've never known them all to go off like this before. Only something very big indeed would have made them vanish without even a message.'

'The same sort of thing as would have made Chobe at the landing strip desert his post as well?'

'I guess so, but he went last night. They went today. While Harry was picking us up.'

Harry reappeared framed in the doorway. 'Nothing,' he said. 'Not a hide or a hair. They took the lorry, though. Easy enough to track. Let's go.'

Robert frowned. 'Maybe I should take Miss Cable back.'

'If they've gone near the airstrip, ask me again. If not, you walk. Your choice. I'm going after my men.'

Ann had opened her mouth to protest at Robert's suggestion but Harry's answer suited her. 'I'm going with Mr Parkinson,' she said. 'I just need to use the john first.'

'Can you shoot?' asked Robert five minutes later. They were in motion as he asked the question, following Harry to the Land Rover.

'Shoot what?' she asked as she followed, thinking he was perhaps asking about marksmanship or hunting.

'This,' he said, pointing to the rifle in its clip above the windshield.

'What at?' she asked, settling into the back seat.

'At anyone who looks as though he's coming after you,' said Harry and he fired up the engine.

It took a moment for her to realise he had said 'any*one*' and for the first time since the shower she went cold all over.

This time it was Harry who swung down to let them out of the gate. He checked in the guard hut and looked at the red dirt of the road.

'Thought so,' he said when he climbed back in. 'They've gone up to the villages.'

He drove on, relatively slowly, talking again as he went. But this time he did not keep glancing back over his shoulder as he spoke.

'All my askaris are N'Kuru. When I came here I was told the N'Kuru were lazy, arrogant and bolshie and the Kyoga

183

were intelligent, trustworthy, hard-working chaps. That's not been my experience at all. Quite the reverse, in fact. I'm much happier working with the N'Kuru, especially out here on their land.

'There are three N'Kuru villages between here and the Blood River. They've remained more or less unchanged for several reasons. Firstly, they are the last viable villages able to provide for themselves in the old, traditional ways. Secondly, they were preserved as part of the game reserve. Finally, they bear a cultural importance to the N'Kuru people. The Heart of the Homeland, or some such. The N'Kuru phrase is impossible to translate exactly.'

'And you think something has happened there to call your men away so suddenly?'

'It's the only reason I can think of to account for what they seem to have done. They are highly trained and absolutely reliable, but they all have family in the villages. Something must have happened.'

Silence fell.

They were driving across the grassland where the zebra were grazing; the animals, obviously used to the sight of Harry's Land Rover, paid little attention to it. Ann felt her mood begin to lighten as she leaned out through the window watching the big herds milling by. Soon there were more than mere zebra to look at. Great dark-skinned wildebeest collected in massive herds lazily grazing and, on the low hillocks overlooking them, a pride of lions.

The camera clicked and clicked. The men in the front glanced at each other without a word.

They reached the first village within half an hour. It was as deserted as the house had been. They stopped. They searched. The huts, made of wattle and daub with wooden doorframes exquisitely carved, all stood empty. Stripped. Not a rug on wall. Not a stool on hard earth floor. Not a copper pot by cold hearth. Not a cow or a goat in the stockade nearby.

The three of them stood side by side at the entrance to the thorn stockade which surrounded the huts and Harry looked north across the plain. 'That's where they went,' he said. 'Every mother, child and mother's son among them. I don't know why, but that's where they went.'

'What about your men in the lorry?' asked Ann.

Harry's eyes were chilly as they regarded her. 'They went east, to the next village,' he said. 'They were here after the villagers had gone so they found the same as us. They didn't stop, though. Their tracks just go straight over the tracks heading north.'

'Then they must have been expecting something like this,' Ann observed. Harry gave a minuscule nod of agreement.

'Let's get on,' said Robert. 'The day is wasting and we don't want to be out here in the dark.'

Half an hour later, at the second village, the same thing. This time Harry only stopped for long enough to ascertain that the truck's tracks went on eastwards with no sign of having stopped.

'They knew,' Harry said. 'Whatever message came, however it came, told them to go to the third village. But half of them had relatives in those first two. Why didn't they even stop?' He hit the steering wheel with his clenched fist as though it knew the answer but would not tell him.

'What's that up ahead?' asked Robert suddenly. 'Smoke?'

'You've got good eyes. No. It's birds. Vultures. Judging from the way they're flying, they look pretty full to me. Miss Journalist, I hope you got some spare film for that camera after you shot all those zebra and wildebeest and lion. I think we may get you some pictures here to make the papers in London and New York sit up.'

'What sort of pictures?' asked Ann, though she knew the answer well enough.

'The kind they like best,' spat the game warden bitterly. 'Dead niggers.'

'Robert?' said Ann uncertainly. She was unsure about this suddenly. Unsure about Harry Parkinson, about the situation he was hurling them into. The local representative of the UNHCR reached up and tugged the big rifle out of its retaining clips above the windshield.

'Remington,' he growled. 'I'd rather have an automatic.'

'I'd rather be driving a Chieftain tank. You use what you've got.'

'Shells?'

'In the glove compartment. Give me a box for the handguns.'

The third village crouched against a backdrop of forest, as though seeking some kind of shelter from the tall, dark trees. Rising and falling, first invisibly against the foliage and then etched clearly against the evening sky, a column of darkness wavered. Like Robert, she would at first have assumed that it was smoke, but Harry's words caused the scales to fall from her eyes and the seeming clouds resolved themselves into individual black shapes. She was obscurely offended. The place was near desert, at least to her eye; how could it carry the weight of so many scavengers? The size of the herds behind her was answer enough. Something here had been powerful enough to call all the vultures in the area under Parkinson's Law to assemble in this tiny village they were approaching with increasing caution.

'Can you see anything?' asked Robert when his busy fingers had finished checking and loading the Remington.

'Vermin. Scavengers. No people. It's very busy up there though.'

'You could hide an army in those trees.' Robert's voice was cool.

'Yes, you could, but then the jackals and hyenas wouldn't be running in and out so happily.'

Craning to see over the square shoulders in front of her, Ann suddenly realised that the ground all around the village seemed to be seething. Through the open window at Robert's side there suddenly came a sound like open warfare between a dog's home and a cattery, and a stench which turned her stomach.

'We're going to have to go in hard,' said Harry. 'Hang on.' He put his right foot on the floor and straightened his arms, wedging his shoulders against the back of his seat. Robert dropped the Remington onto his lap and grabbed the dashboard. Ann held on to the back of Robert's seat with all the strength at her command.

The Land Rover hurtled up the beaten earth track towards the main break in the thorn bush wall round the little village of huts. But suddenly Ann could see that there were many breaks in the stockade. Unlike the neat, picture-postcard defences round the two deserted villages, here the circle of high-piled thorns was ruptured in dozens of places and gaped widely. Through the breaks, animals were slinking and scuttling. Harry's words had warned her that there would be hyenas and jackals. She had not expected to see foxes, what looked like wolves; was that a lion? Surely not a leopard . . . They hit a pothole and for a moment it was difficult to see anything clearly at all.

Harry punched the horn and started yelling at the top of his lungs. The creatures leaped away from whatever they were doing, incredible numbers of them scattering back out like muddy blood escaping through gaping wounds. The light was just beginning to thicken now. The sun was behind them. Shadows hid much, but there were enough areas of ruddy light to show that not all the escaping animals were leaving empty-handed.

They exploded through the main gate and immediately Harry was swearing and swerving. The effect was painful and deeply unnerving, for he did not lower his voice at all and his wordless yelling suddenly became obscene invective screamed madly at the top of his lungs. Ann all but broke her ribs on the back of Robert's seat and was lucky not to knock herself out against the back of his head.

The Land Rover jumped and bucked and for a moment she thought it was going to roll, but Harry held it upright apparently by main force until it came to a stop. Had she supposed the drama of their entrance would have scared off all the animals, she was wrong. The ground around them still seethed. Vultures, some with wingspans in excess of two metres, hopped and flapped, too gorged to fly. Hyenas skulked towards shadows and jackals snarled. Three lean lions stood their ground until Harry leaned out of his window and opened fire. He seemed to be aiming high; the animals flinched and turned away at the sound his gun was making, but none seemed to have been hit. Then Robert kicked open his door and the Remington joined in. The deep boom of its report was like an echo of his basso profundo shouting. A flapping, hopping vulture exploded into a mist of blood, flesh and feathers. A hyena's head vanished and its body jumped high into the air, tumbling acrobatically. A jackal sprang open as though it had swallowed a live grenade.

All the animals that could move vanished then and a kind of quiet came. The three Remington shots echoed distantly. The vultures flapped and squawked. The barking, spitting, hissing of the frustrated scavengers whispered from the edge of the forest like a faraway tempest. In the village there was relative stillness.

Except for the scuttling, humming whisper of the insect world at work. The presence of the larger creatures had blinded Ann to the fact that everywhere there were flies. Big, black, bloated flies filled the rank air, as though giving body to the fetid stench. Ann pulled an end of her head-scarf over her mouth and nose.

'Watch it when you get out, Harry,' Robert grated. 'I've never seen so many nasty-looking ants. You have soldier ants here like we do in the Amazon?'

Harry didn't answer. As though in a daze he sat, filling magazines for his automatic pistols, looking away to his right, at the centre of the village. At the tall pile of black corpses there. Then he slammed a magazine in place and pushed his door open. He hesitated, then reached into the glove compartment and pulled out a pair of heavy-duty rubber gloves. 'Stay here,' he ordered. 'Both of you.'

He stepped down delicately and moved off. Robert stepped down too and pushed his door closed; then he took a couple of steps and leant across the bonnet of the Land Rover, covering Harry with the Remington.

Ann seemed to jump awake then, though she was in fact deep in shock. She shuffled across to the side of the vehicle which overlooked the village and the slowly moving game warden and she raised her camera. Framing what she could see through the camera viewfinder brought the overpowering enormity into focus somehow. It chopped the general horror up into a series of sharply focused images. The central pile of bodies could have been a hillock of slowly congealing tar, and the scattered individuals just shadows of various shapes and sizes. But the camera made a sort of sense of it. A visual sense of what was unutterably, obscenely senseless in every other regard.

She framed Harry on one knee in a nearby doorway, tenderly lifting in bright-gloved hands a child of two or three years, whose blood and brain was splattered brightly in the sunlight over the exquisite carving of the hard wood jamb. She pressed the button. The shutter clicked and the motor whined.

She framed Harry booting a bloated vulture off the body of a woman exactly like the woman she had first interviewed beneath the dead acacia on the outskirts of Mawanga; the vulture had been feasting on her baby. One bullet had been enough for both of them by the look of things. Ann pressed the button and the shutter clicked.

She framed Harry beside the central pile – or as much of it as she could fit into the trembling square. The wiry little Englishman stood five feet seven or eight. The pile of corpses was taller than he was even though the scavengers had pulled so many away. She found she could take the shattered limbs and the bright chests with their lungs like strange pink flowers; the lazy serpentine loops of intestine and the dark clots of internal organs so beloved of the flies. It was the faces which made her cry. And especially the wide eyes. She pressed the button.

Then, terrified that her weakness had made the camera tremble and spoil the shot, she wedged her elbows against the metal frame and took it twice again.

She framed him on his knees and throwing up, although she suspected there would be a lawsuit if she published. She framed Robert standing with the Remington, his elbows on the Land Rover hood in a puddle of his tears.

When she swung the camera back, Harry came into close-up so abruptly that she jumped. 'Robert. Come and witness this. I need an official witness. But put on gloves. There's AIDS everywhere.'

'Can't we do something?' Robert seemed dazed by it, made helpless and indecisive, too shocked even to register Harry's warning about AIDS. But he too pulled on heavy-duty rubber gloves as though preparing to wash dishes.

'We can look. Remember. Report. Report in detail.'

'Bury them or something?'

'There are too many and we haven't enough time. It'll be dark soon. There won't be much left by morning. Listen to them out there.'

As the shadows lengthened, the horrific chorus in the forest gathered new strength and volume.

'Burn them?'

'With what? The only fuel we have is in the Land Rover and we need it to get home. And we still haven't found my askaris, remember. They went that way.' The warden gestured over his shoulder past the pile of bodies towards the jungle.

'We're going in *there*?' Robert was clearly stunned by the thought of going where the terrible, inhuman cacophony was coming from. He caught up the Remington again as though it were a security-blanket.

'Certainly. Once we leave, they'll all be back out here, won't they? But do hurry up, old man. I want to at least try for a head count. Some kind of solid facts for the report.'

'Jesus *CHRIST*!' yelled Robert and he threw the gun down. Harry flinched as the weapon, loaded and primed, hit the vehicle. It did not go off and he straightened.

Ann framed the pair of them searching. Lifting a doll-like child, one arm each. Rearranging the edges of the pile. Checking that the pile was composed of bodies to its oozing core. Sorting. Counting. And at last the distance was too much. Hiding behind the safe glass of the Land Rover's windows was cowardice when the men were doing what they were doing. They were striving to compute and to remember. She had a function here: to feel and to record.

She opened the door. Flies and stench. The ground crackled as she stepped down onto it and not only because it was covered in dry grass. She crossed to the nearest doorway. She lifted her camera as though it was a shield and framed the bright spray of blood. In the shadows of the interior there were other children who had had their brains dashed out. She had not realised that. A pile of ten or so. She framed the huddled little bodies and then the bright spray of their blood. It caught the sun so vividly because it was alive with green-winged flies. She had not realised that.

She crossed to the woman and the baby. She was sitting up so straight because her back was supported by more corpses. Ann framed the mother with her almost headless baby but the camera was no kind of shield. Her hands were

shaking so much that the camera case split her lip. She
sucked at it automatically and her mouth filled up with
blood. It was only when she tore the scarf off her mouth
and started throwing up that the two men noticed her.
Robert stumbled over to her, took her by the shoulders
and pulled her erect. His broad face twisted with such rage
that she thought he was going to strike her and she flinched. The movement made him realise what he was doing
and he stood, gulping in fetid air and bloated flies until he
calmed. His fingers bruised her shoulders. The pressure of
his thumbs beneath her collarbone made it crack.

'What are you doing?' he asked at last, his deep voice
raw and ragged.

'My job! The same as you are doing yours. People need
to know about this. You report to the UN. I'll report to
every programme and paper in the world. Everyone who
will listen to me and print my pictures. You have to do it. I
have to do it. Otherwise what's the point?'

'She's right, Robert,' called Harry. 'She's right and you
know it.'

He let her go. His gloved palms made a tearing sound as
they peeled away from the cotton of her shirt and at once
the flies began to settle on the bloody hand prints there.
She tucked the end of the headscarf back across her
mouth. Her hands shaking with reaction, anger and shock,
she went rapidly, brutally, through the routine of emptying
and reloading her camera. 'Don't touch anything,' called
Harry. 'We've no more gloves.'

Robert returned to his grim work and she followed. She
brought the camera up and crushed it to her cheek. She
framed a naked body face down where he had laid it beside
half a dozen others. It bore a series of wounds which were
striking in their regularity. Low on the back, almost
between the buttocks; mid-back, shattering the spine; just
below each shoulder blade; the back of the head. She
framed and pushed the button.

Harry was crouching by another pile. She framed him as he worked. He had pulled his neckerchief up and looked like a bandit. The cloth and his cheeks beside it were smeared red. He looked up and she caught the white channels running downwards where his tears had washed the blood away. He was arranging the corpse of a girl whose upper chest and face had been blown away as though her heart had exploded like an anti-personnel mine. She framed and pushed the button. The shutter clicked and the motor whined.

'There are only women and children here,' she said.

'The old men and the boys are over there.' He nodded towards the section of the stockade nearest to the forest. 'Looks like they made a stand but they didn't have a chance. Whoever did this just walked right over them and moved in. Then they took their time with the women and girls.'

Whoever did this. The flat phrase echoed in Ann's head. What had happened here seemed so colossal that she had viewed it as some kind of natural catastrophe. In some part of her shock-numbed mind she had been treating this as though it was the result of some earthquake. Now Harry's words brought home to her with terrible force that this had been done deliberately. That there had been a pattern to it. A sequence. That the horror, terror and agony on these faces was not put there by the exercise of death but by someone who had done things to these people which had horrified and terrified and agonised them.

There were men out there in the forest who had done this thing. Men perhaps close nearby. To her feeling of horror was added a new one: terror.

She found herself beside the Land Rover and knew that she had run away. Holding herself still, holding every quivering muscle of her body still by the same exercise of mental power which had enabled Harry to hold the Land Rover upright when he had swerved to avoid the first body, she made herself stand there. Her stomach clenched agonisingly as though she had contracted the most virulent food poisoning. She needed the toilet urgently. She needed to vomit again. Instead, she stood absolutely still while she willed her heartbeat to slow down. After a time, she thought it might be safe to move. She tore open the door and reached inside for her carry-all. She ripped it open, pulled out a roll of film and reloaded her camera. Then she took a deep breath. Turning round was the bravest thing she had ever done. Walking back took so much courage it was worth a Congressional Medal of Honour.

Harry looked up as she returned. There was profound respect in his eyes: he had never seen terror more ruthlessly overcome. Ann noticed nothing of this. 'I want to get the sequence right while I still have the light,' she said. 'A series of pictures in the right sequence to show what order it happened in.'

'They came out of the forest and through the torn stockade,' he said. 'I don't think they used vehicles. Just large numbers and automatic weapons. There were only old men and boys here.'

She framed the distant forest with the sun glinting off tall trunks and eyes and teeth in the lower shadows. She framed the pathetic pile of tumbled thorn bushes. The untidy jumble of riddled bodies. A withered hand still holding a carved club. A young fist holding a shattered spear.

'Then they wiped out all the old women and the children.' Robert took up the story as she finished recording the single-bullet executions made so much more simple when the babies were clutched to withered breasts and a brain shot became a heart shot and carried on right through. 'Then they rounded up the young good-looking ones and took their time. Did some raping and played a couple of games.' He was worrying more nubile bodies out of the centre of the pile and placing them beside the ones

Ann had already photographed. Time after time the strange pattern of wounds was repeated.

'Tell me,' Ann demanded, alerted by the tone of his voice.

'Target practice.' He rolled one of the bodies over gently and the pattern of wounds on the front immediately made its own obscene, horrific sense. 'Stand them against a wall. Restrain them if necessary,' said Robert, his voice dead. 'Use six bullets. Got to be quick. Accurate. It's a sort of ritual. Only a certain kind can do it.' Robert pointed distantly, his whole body as far away from the dead N'Kuru girl as he could practically get and still be clear in his explanation. 'One shot through the pubic bone, one through the belly button, one for each nipple and one for each eye.'

Ann's knees buckled and she found herself kneeling by the ravaged corpse. Her camera dangled at the end of her numb arm, the last vestige of its fictitious protection gone. What she really wanted to do was scream and scream.

'And these poor girls stood there? And *allowed* them to do this?'

'They'll have let some off, maybe taken them with them,' said Robert. 'Held the rest in place with ropes tied round their wrists.'

'And those who refused got an alternative.' Harry gestured to the pile of corpses he had been dealing with. The strange wounds in their upper chests, shoulders and faces made all too much sense now. They were all exit wounds where bullets had torn out. There were no entry wounds. No obvious entry wounds at all. 'That's what happens,' said Harry quietly, incongruously, as though he was talking of gardening or cricket. 'That's what happens when you're raped with a rifle.'

Ann went out then, as though she had been clubbed over the head. It was simply too much for her to handle. Her brain shorted out like an electric machine on overload. She pitched forward into a bundle on the ground, seemingly as dead as the rest of the women in the compound. Harry reached over and pushed his hand under the scarf covering her neck. His fingers, thickly crusted with dried blood, felt the powerful surge of her pulse. 'She'll be OK. Put her in the Land Rover, would you?'

Robert picked her up with the same tenderness he had shown the corpses. She had left the back door of the Land Rover open and so he had no difficulty in lying her along the back seat, using her hold-all as a pillow. He twisted her legs enough to allow the door to close so that she would not get covered by flies before she came to. The last thing he did was to take her camera.

As the western sky, full of red dust from the dry farms, went the same colour as the blood leaking from the pathetic pile of corpses and the short sharp tropical evening closed down upon them, they finished sorting the corpses into some kind of order. Robert used the last of the light to complete the series of photographs that Ann had begun. Made ruthless by the depth of his outrage, he spared the potential viewer nothing, filling the viewfinder with close-ups of faces with their eyes blasted out of their sockets. Of heads riddled from beneath soft chins by point-blank automatic gunfire.

Then, as the whole landscape around them seemed to sink in a sea of blood, the two men stood back, knowing that the darkness had beaten them in the end.

'I counted two hundred,' said Robert.

'About that. Two hundred women, children and old men. I wonder where the warriors have gone.'

'The word in the camps is "taken by the Lions".'

'Taken as in recruited? Or kidnapped? Or killed?'

'Christ knows.'

'I think we're going to find out, though. Soon.'

'Yeah. No way round that.'

'Still . . .'

The first lion, made brave by the thickening shadows, leaped over the ruined thorn stockade, like the vanguard of a new army.

'Time to go,' said Robert as the sound from the forest swept towards them like the charge of a screaming horde.

They walked slowly back to the Land Rover, their eyes everywhere, knowing they were relatively safe because they were surrounded by so much easily taken food, but concerned that sudden movement might trigger some reaction from the blood-crazed animals around them.

In the Land Rover, they peeled off the crusted gloves, then sat, side by side, too stunned and emotionally drained for decision or action. Mercifully, the night came quickly and, although there were stars, there was no moon due until much later. It was a mercy that they could not see the sights which accompanied the cacophony of sickening sounds with which they were soon surrounded. Like corpses propped up on the Land Rover's seats, they stayed for an uncounted period of time, and it was not until a leopard charged up onto the bonnet, making an escape with its prize stolen from an angry group of hyenas, then leaped up onto the roof to feed, that the men were jolted out of their shock. The vehicle rocked forward as the big cat leaped up, then the heavy canvas roof sagged dangerously beneath it as it settled just above Robert's head. The eyeless head and burst torso of one of the girls who had been used for target practice slammed face down across the windscreen mere inches from the black man's eyes and he jumped awake with a scream. Harry exploded into wakefulness beside him. 'Go!' screamed Robert. Harry fired up the ignition and the Land Rover quivered into life. He stamped on the clutch and shoved the big old gearshift into reverse. Robert slammed the Remington's barrel up into the snarling softness above his head. 'Go!' he screamed again and pulled the trigger, so that when the Land Rover leaped backwards towards the opening in the stockade behind them, the cat and its meal were blasted up into the air to tumble back down upon the flat bonnet and away. As the vehicle shot backwards, both of Harry's hands upon the wheel, Robert leant forward and hit the lights. Twin beams of brightness wavered wildly over the unspeakable feast going on there but all that could be seen clearly was the group of thwarted hyenas moving in around the headless leopard. Over the sound of the shrieking engine, the mad cackle of their victorious laughter followed the horrified humans into the night.

Ann jumped awake. She was inside a long box being thrown around like a die in an energetic game. Her legs were twisted so that each movement of her body hurt her knees. There was absolute darkness nearby but a kind of a glow above her illuminated the head and shoulders of a man a metre or so away. She couldn't remember what she had been dreaming about but the terror of the nightmare filled her with an almost uncontrollable dread. Somewhere, perhaps in her fleeing dream, a group of creatures were laughing the sort of laughter she had always imagined Jack the Ripper must have laughed when he was at work upon the bodies of his victims. Whatever she was lying on came up and smacked her in the back of her head.

The head outlined against the darkness turned to profile and faced another, smaller, head outlined beside it. 'Where the fuck do you think you're going, Harry? This isn't the way back.'

'We've still got to find my askaris, Robert.'

'Are you out of your mind? Out here? In the dark?'

'There'll be no dangerous animals in the forest for miles around. We'll be safe if we're careful. And the moon'll be up soon.'

'The *moon*?'

'Full moon tonight. It'll be as bright as day.'

'You're out of your fucking . . .'

Abruptly the two figures in the front were wrestling together. The box Ann was trapped in really began to get thrown about. Her stomach rebelled and she felt her throat flood with burning liquid. She jerked upright, choking. 'I'm going to be sick,' she said urgently. 'Harry, I'm going to be sick *now*!'

The Land Rover juddered to a halt and she threw the door open just in time, hurling herself forward to hang over a pool of darkness into which she emptied what little was left in her stomach. When she was finished, she just hung there, feeling the stillness wash over her. Stillness and, apart from the rumble of the engine, silence.

A wind stirred and leaves whispered peacefully far above. 'We're in the forest,' she observed dreamily and pulled herself up to look around.

'Are you OK?' asked Robert, turning to look at her, his face invisible in the shadow except for a flash of teeth and a gleam of eye. 'You were out cold for more than an hour.'

'Fine, I guess,' she answered. 'But bits of me won't stop shaking, and other bits of me really want to know if there's a john around here.'

'Behind every bush,' said Harry. 'But take a torch and look out for scorpions, spiders and snakes. If you can hold it steady enough.'

'I think I'll cross my legs just for the time being, thanks.'

'Suit yourself.'

Harry engaged the gear and the Land Rover rolled forward again. Ann was sitting up now and she could see that they were following a wide beaten track through a forest of tall trees. On either side, framed by the shadows beyond the headlight beams, the low scrub gleamed palely. Every now and then there came a scurry of movement and a flash of reflected light. Up in the shadowy canopy above, dark shapes fluttered, and occasionally the power of their song broke through the monotonous grumble of the engine.

'This is quite a road,' said Ann, after a while.

'It's an elephant track,' explained Harry. 'Shortest way from the grassland down to the Blood River.'

'And you're sure they came this way?' Robert still wasn't happy to be following the lorry full of Harry's askaris.

'They didn't stop at the village for long,' answered Harry tersely. 'This is the way they were coming.'

'But what's down here?'

'The river. Dry now. Congo Libre beyond. No border guards or checkpoints for a couple of hundred kilometres in either direction. That's about it. The message must have told them that whoever did the killing would be down here too.'

'You wouldn't need to be Sherlock Holmes to be sure that it's the likeliest bet,' growled Robert.

The elephants came running out of the darkness dead ahead straight into the headlight beams just as Robert said 'bet'. The lead animal was a huge male, trunk high and ears spread. His tusks reached out in two yellow bows two metres long from jaw to rounded tip. To Ann's startled eyes he looked to be four metres at least to the shoulder and another one and a half to the top of his head. He was on top of them at once and Robert, yelling, leaned across to help Harry wrench the wheel over in a kind of power steering. The game warden's right foot went flat on the floor, perhaps in reaction to the shock, and the vehicle spun sideways out of the monster's path to crash into the undergrowth at the side of the track. Ann half fell, half jumped out of the door, to see the long legs and high flanks of the rest of the little herd flash by. 'Get back in here,' Harry was yelling. 'Get back in here, you stupid bitch!'

She stood, entranced, watching as they vanished through a sudden patch of moonlight into the impenetrable shadows behind them, silent as a dream.

A hand fell on her shoulder and she jumped. Turning, she saw Robert. There was moonlight further down the road but only darkness here. The Land Rover's headlights were pointing directly into a thick bush and one of them was broken. It was impossible to see the expression on his face. 'Get back into the Rover now, at once,' he said. His voice was calm, but even more compelling than Harry's fulminations. 'Elephants are incredibly dangerous. We were lucky those ones didn't trample us. If they smell you, it's a fair bet they'll come back and tear you to pieces.'

Numbly, she climbed into the back of the vehicle. Harry had got a grip on himself now, but it was clear that he had had more than enough today. The atmosphere was thunderous as Robert climbed in the front.

'Are you both all right?' he asked quietly.

'Yes,' snapped Harry as he reversed out of the bush.

'Yeah, I guess,' answered Ann. 'Why?'

'I think I cracked my ribs. My side hurts like a son of a bitch.'

Harry grunted. 'If you start to cough blood, tell me about it.'

'If I start to cough blood, I'll tell the world about it.'

Harry drove more carefully now.

It must take something fairly big to panic a herd of elephants, Ann was thinking. And whatever panicked them might still be down here.

'I'm just going to switch off the lights and roll forward in neutral,' said Harry suddenly. 'It's all downhill to the river from here and we don't know what's waiting down there.'

As the Land Rover rolled down the incline, the forest canopy fell back and the bend of a wide, shallow, dry river valley was slowly revealed. The moon had risen during their drive through the forest and it was as bright as Harry had said it would be – easily bright enough to illuminate the scene in front of them. The river bed curved away like the leg of a giant, slightly bent. They were approaching the curve of the knee where a little promontory jutted, like a kneecap above the dry ground. Here Harry braked and they came silently to a stop.

The solid mud was as grey, cracked and wrinkled as elephant hide in the silent moonlight, and it stretched away on either hand north to the arid source of the dry river and south to the solid sandbar which stopped the lake in the game reserve from draining back down here. On the far bank of the mud channel lay more shadowy forest, belonging to the People's Marxist Republic of Congo Libre. On this bank, at the foot of a cliff which must have been carved by a current in happier times, lay Harry's lorry, twisted, burned out, on its side. The marks just up ahead told their own grim but simple story. In the middle of the track, dead ahead, was a crater, such as a land mine might make. This side of the crater was marked with tyre tracks. The far side showed gashed impressions such as a vehicle tumbling end over end might make and circular scorch marks such as might result from a petrol tank igniting. The bankside vegetation was blackened; it had obviously ignited as the blazing truck slid past and then mercifully burned itself out without starting a forest fire.

Harry opened the door. Stepped down. Took one step. Took another. He moved jerkily, like a robot in an old science fiction film. Robert, however, was liquid grace and speed, out of his door and up behind the little man to catch him by the shoulder and pull him up short. 'Harry. You don't know what did that. There might be mines, for heaven's sake. You understand, Harry? *Mines!*'

Harry stook looking up at the intense, dark face. 'What is going on here, Robert?' he asked. He sounded old, plaintive, confused.

Robert looked back at Ann, his face in the moonlight desperate. She moved to help him at once, sliding out of the Land Rover and onto the solid mud. The night air was cool. A light breeze eddied from behind her, full of forest fragrances. Then the wind changed, and so did the smell. The stench brought back too vividly the sights and sounds and emotions she had felt immediately before she passed out in the village. She screamed at the top of her lungs and turned to run away.

'Ann!' The desperation in Robert's voice brought her up short. Whimpering like a terrified child, she turned to look at him, unaware that she was continuing to back away. 'Stay here!' he called urgently. 'If you go off alone you'll die. You'll die, Ann. I promise you!'

When she started to scream again he thought that his brutal words had driven her over the edge of hysteria.

They hadn't. The forest wall of the Dr Julius Karanga Game Reserve two hundred and fifty metres behind him was behaving in a very peculiar way. The trees were leaning of their own accord, preparing to topple out and down into the dry river bed. Something behind them was pushing them, shrugging them aside with thoughtless power as it strove to come out towards them.

All she could think of was that the elephants were coming back. Robert's words by the pathway in the forest had been correct. His prophecy was coming true. The great grey tusker with its wide-spread ears and mad black eyes was coming back to tear them limb from limb and trample what was left of them into the ground. In her mind's eye she could see the great grey bulk of it shrugging the trees aside as it came roaring into the open trumpeting its warcry, its trunk high and its tusks reaching out.

But that was not what happened at all. The monster that emerged from the forest shadows over the trunks of the fallen trees was grey but unwrinkled, not animal but machine, and what reached out in front of it was not the trunk of an enraged elephant but the barrel of a 125mm smoothbore gun extended by a bulky flash-guard. What was coming out of the jungle towards them was not an enraged and maddened tusker, it was worse.

It was a Soviet-made fully armoured T–80 main battle tank.

Stream

THE NORTH ATLANTIC
OCEAN

*And the gilded car of day
His glowing axle doth allay
In the steep Atlantic stream . . .*

John Milton, *Comus*

Chapter Thirteen

'In the south-western quadrant of the North Atlantic, here, between Bermuda and the Bahamas, there is a hill made of water. It does not stand very high, this hill; perhaps two metres above the level of the rest of the ocean at its peak. It is covered in sargasso weed and it is the Sargasso Sea. The hill of water is caused by currents flowing into a circle very fiercely, and, although the mass of water making up the hill is very still, there are currents also flowing out of it, and currents flowing around it. A strong current comes westward from the coast of Africa, driven by the trade winds. Just as this current reaches the southern slopes of the Sargasso, it is joined by the outflow of the Brazil current which pushes along the coast of South America from Natal to Caracas . . .'

'The Spanish Main,' supplied John Higgins.

'As you say,' agreed Professor Yves Maille with a Gallic shrug of his slim shoulders. He glanced round the table in Richard's day room to see whether the interruption had disturbed any of his audience at the first full captains' briefing. All eyes were fixed on him. His own eyes lingered on those of Captain Katya Borodin whose looks particularly appealed to him. A slim, slight, lined, dark-skinned Mediterranean man himself, he was drawn to the blonde Nordic farm girl type, of which she was a perfect example. Dragging his eyes away at last, he gestured at the Atlantic chart before him. 'But now, look. The currents meet.

Their speed is augmented by water flowing out of the southern flank of the Sargasso. They run westward and, because of the Coriolis force, they wish to run northwards, and here before them is a land mass which guides them further northward over a shallow continental shelf. So the currents turn and run up the coast of the United States at five knots and more, past Florida and up the coast to Cape Hatteras. And so the Gulf Stream is born. It is a ribbon of water moving very fast, powerful, like the outflowing of a fire hose.'

'When it is moving at speed, it even throws up a wall,' added John, the practical sailor as well as the nautical historian. 'Whether there is much to see at the surface depends on the conditions, but I have heard sailors talk of a west wall and a north wall on the outer edges of it. And they mean a wall of water. Something that can stand up above the level of the rest of the sea. Like the professor's Sargasso Hill.' The faces round the table were grim. They all knew they were due to start crossing the North Wall at about midnight tonight. At their current speed, if *Titan* went over on schedule, *Achilles* would be crossing at breakfast time. The iceberg would be passing through the wall of water for eight solid hours. There was much dark speculation as to what that would do to the massive piece of ice.

'Yes indeed. This so-called wall is a reflection of very strong changes in temperature, salinity, water speed and so forth at the interface. It can be very powerful indeed. It will be the first great test of Manhattan's true strength. But look, we have calculated on this, Captain Mariner and I. We will not be crossing the wall at right angles but coming in along this confluence with the Labrador Current here.

'Regard. The mass of the Gulf Stream turns away from the American coast here at Cape Hatteras, and no one is quite certain what happens to it then. It changes its name, to begin with, and becomes the North Atlantic Drift. Perhaps it changes its nature too, but I think not much. It wavers and spins and twists. It goes up and down in massive waves. For your purposes this does not matter too much because the current is there and running at some speed at one depth or another for most of the time and, even more importantly, at this latitude it runs under the constant weather coming across from the west and heading eastwards for Europe.'

'So,' Richard summed up the meeting so far, 'if we can get Manhattan over the North Wall out of the Labrador Current and into the Gulf Stream – North Atlantic Drift – we will have the help of water and weather moving eastwards at some speed.'

'*Oui!* The current will be moving at a mean five knots, the surface features – the waves – at a mean twenty knots if the wind averages force five on the Beaufort scale. Of course at that force the wind itself will be moving at nearer thirty knots and will be pushing at the exposed section of ice as though it were a sail. You wish Manhattan to average ten knots . . .'

'More if we can manage it. The water will be warm.'

'Perhaps. I have two thoughts on that. First, the main current may not be all that warm and in any case, as I said, it will come and go, wavering up and down and from side to side. And secondly, as the iceberg melts, it will automatically lower the temperature of the water around it. Even though you move it faster than the current, you may still find that the more it melts, the more slowly it will melt. It is a huge thing, you see? It will create its own climate. But in any case, all of these factors will help the berg move quickly. And more quickly still when the last two ships arrive and become attached.'

Richard nodded. 'That'll be within the next couple of days. We need them to drive Manhattan forward through the Stream – or the Drift – while we guide her down across it.'

'Again, the size of the berg and the enormity of the

forces you are dealing with will help you. As the Coriolis force makes the Stream turn north off the Gulf of Mexico, so it will make Manhattan pull southwards as you move it at speed. The Gulf Stream tends southwards itself, though it sends eddies to the north. The main bulk of the water movement is pulled southwards across the Western Approaches to La Manche – what you English call the Channel – and becomes part of the Canaries current which then goes into the current which flows west below the Sargasso. It is one huge circle. What my friends of the Oceanographic Institute in Woods Hole call the North Atlantic Gyre.'

'And once we get on it, we will ride it to the Canaries and catch an offshoot called the Guinea current down to Mawanga.' Katya Borodin's voice was cool. Her English correct. Her pronunciation had a combination of Russian roundness and American nasality which Yves Maille, for one, found irresistible. Her tone was one of not so mild amazement that any set of apparently sane captains could possibly be engaged upon such a hare-brained enterprise as this.

'But you are riding it already, you know. The Labrador Current which carries us south as we speak is but an off-shoot of the North Atlantic Drift returning from Baffin Bay.' Yves did his best to make his answer sound seductive.

'Right, thank you, Yves,' said Richard, bringing the meeting to order. 'Any questions?' His eyes also lingered on Captain Borodin, but only because he sensed her lack of faith and wished to allay it at once. But she did not accept his invitation, so he continued. 'No? Any observations, John?'

'No. The navigation is theoretically simple, in the big picture, certainly, but I suspect we'll find it challenging enough when we get down to the detail. We'll need to know exactly where we are at all times if the information Yves is promising about water and weather is going to be used properly.'

'Yes. I see that.' Richard nodded. 'And, of course, it will be of absolutely crucial importance with regard to sailing orders. Over to you, Bob. Propulsion?'

Bob Stark leaned back in his chair and stretched his long legs under the table. He brought his broad palm up his forehead to sweep the golden cow's lick out of his eyes. Katya Borodin observed him in much the same way Yves Maille observed her, and they made a striking couple as they sat side by side: Nordic farm girl meets Kansas cow hand. But the good-looking New Englander was unaware of her gaze; he was concentrating absolutely on the matter in hand. 'It's taken us two days and more to get Manhattan up to a mean speed of seven knots, and we've only been sailing in a straight line. We've got to try and turn left off Flemish Cap tonight. How will that work? As Yves has said, we're reckoning on a lot of help from the Labrador Current swinging east at that point to push us through the North Wall and into the main flow, but the whole plan relies upon picking up speed. What we haven't had to face yet is how on earth do we actually control this amount of momentum once we build it up? Have you done your sums on that one, John? How much force is actually involved in moving one and a half billion metric tonnes at ten knots? How long will it take us to stop it, if we can stop it at all?'

'God knows. But it has to be moving with enough momentum to do some serious damage to any poor sod who gets in the way,' observed John.

'Or any poor island. Or any poor cape. We don't want to arrive off Africa with Cape St Vincent and a couple of Azores wedged up against our bowsprit,' Richard commented wryly.

A chuckle went round the table, though they all knew Richard was only half joking. Then Colin Ross met the chairman's eye and, on Richard's tiny nod, stepped in. They were brushing against his areas of expertise now. 'In fact,' he growled, 'it would be a mistake to see Manhattan as being particularly solid. Not now; certainly not later on.

Under the circumstances Professor Maille has described, with warm seas and following weather, average winds of force five and waves of twenty knots, we can expect a good deal of water loss through melting and runoff – runoff depending on sunshine and air temperature too of course – but most of all from wave erosion. We'll have to choose the anchorage sites for *Kraken* and *Psyche* with extreme care because they'll be at the rear of the ice island above the surface and the following seas will smash that section to pieces.' They all nodded. Richard, Colin and Kate were due to be scouting for those very locations in the Sea King with Tom Snell the engineer this afternoon, in fact.

'You'll have to keep an eye on Manhattan's bow section as well,' the glaciologist continued. 'Remember, the bows are just hard ice, they aren't steel or rock. They'll wear away fantastically quickly. We're just hoping they'll wear away evenly, or all the Coriolis force in the universe won't swing her onto the right course.' He looked round the table. It wasn't quite a glare, but it was an expression of warning. 'You'll have to watch the ice all the time. Don't let the size of these boats fool you. One bad ice fall and even *Titan* would just vanish. Don't think of it as a hulk you're towing. Think of it as an enemy. Take your eye off it, turn your back for a second, and it will kill you.'

'So far in this project,' expanded Richard, 'it's killed one man, crippled another and landed a third in hospital. It did that for openers on the first day. Colin's right. Watch your course. Watch your instruments. But, above all, watch the ice.'

Titan's Sea King helicopter hung low in the restless air over the cliffs at the blunt northern end of Manhattan. Richard, Colin, Kate and Major Tom Snell looked down gloomily. Long grey rollers rode down the back of the Labrador Current, making the sea look like a huge dull file. For fifty kilometres further to the north, the submerged section of the iceberg acted on the water like a reef and its existence was revealed by a disturbance in the otherwise regular pattern of the waves. On the distant horizon, looming out of the freezing mist, the twin hulls of *Ajax* and *Achilles* rode astride the white islet of the far end of ice.

Immediately below the helicopter, at the foot of the square cliffs, was a seething maelstrom as the waves, propelled by the fresh breeze, foamed up against the white ice in a dazzling surf. It was clear to the watchers that all that stopped the cliffs from being undermined in short order was the pale reef of ice which swept from a brief, smooth beach away beneath the worst of the foam into the slate-grey depths beneath the serried ranks of freezing water. Finding anchorage points for the last two ships was going to be more difficult than they had expected. Working on that foam-weltered glass-smooth beach was clearly going to be impossible and, in any case, putting all too fragile hulls so close to submarine ridges of ice was unthinkable, especially to someone like Richard who had come within an ace of joining *Titanic* in her grave two miles down in the Western Ocean south of here.

Colin Ross beat Richard on the shoulder and bellowed over the deafening combination of engine, rotor, wind and water, 'And it'll get more complicated. As the berg melts it will rise – float higher in the water. That little beach will be a kilometre wide in a week and the reef which is two hundred metres down will be one fifty metres down. If you anchor your boats above submerged ice, they'll end up aground.'

'That's another thing you'll have to watch anyway, even with one as big as this,' added Kate anxiously. 'It will keep going straight up out of the water as it melts until its centre of gravity gets too low to support it. Then it will roll over. It's difficult to predict and there'll be no warning. It'll roll right over on top of you.'

Richard nodded. He knew about the instability of icebergs, but they had problems which needed to be dealt with before they had to worry about the whole berg turning turtle on them.

'What we need, then,' yelled Tom Snell, 'is a matching pair of steep-sided bays with no ice bottom. One on each side. They have to be big enough to berth the last two boats. The bays have to have a wide enough beach to tether a line fore and aft and maybe midships as well. The back ends of the bays really need to be open – sufficiently so, at any rate, for the ice not to interfere with the thrust of the ships' screws. This is particularly important because the two ships are oil-powered single-screw jobs, extremely powerful but not as flexible as the other four. They will be the main motive force for your dash along the North Atlantic Drift. So their placing is of paramount importance.'

Richard nodded again. There was nothing more to say, really; Tom had summed up the situation perfectly. He roared through to Doug Buchanan, the pilot, 'Take us down.'

The Sea King dropped over the western edge of the cliff and started working south along the fifty-kilometre flank of ice. The wall before them varied in height and sheerness – it was not all vertical by any means. Some of it reached out in dangerous overhangs, extravagantly fanged with massive icicles, the longest of which dropped off to stab the ocean as soon as the rotors disturbed the air around them. Sections of it were honeycombed with massive caves into which the waters washed, losing their dull greyness at once and taking on the hues of blue and green so spectacularly lacking in the mass of the dead-white ice. In some places the cliffs fell back into broad bays backed by gentle slopes and apparent dunes. The bays were floored by ice running like white sand beaches far, far out into the dull grey water. Only one tenth of the iceberg's enormous volume was visible in the ice island – the dry ice, they called it – above the surface of the sea. The rest was submerged and plunged out as well as down, in those huge submarine reefs. Because of the dictates of chance, augmented by the work of the engineers and explosives experts, the submerged ice reefs which swept out like wings for two-thirds of the iceberg's length vanished altogether for the one-third nearest to the bow section. For the thirty kilometres of the high, artificially created forecastle, the cliffs plunged vertically into the depths.

After ten kilometres flying south towards this forward section, the edge of the reefs became visible, swinging up and in to meet the side of the island, and after sixteen and a half kilometres, the reefs ended altogether – and so did the protection they afforded to the sheer sides of Manhattan's main island.

'Take us down closer,' ordered Richard.

This was the area which Colin, Kate and he had discussed at such length, for which they had great hopes. Here the dry ice lost its submarine protection from the battering rams of the surf, and the effect was all but inevitable. Under the solid overhang of cliffs, a great eye socket had been carved by the action of the following waves. They had chosen to start here because this was the side which had been best protected by the hook of ice blown off by Paul Chan and his men. And there it was. The very bay they had been looking for. The perfect place to start.

'Take us up and over,' Richard yelled. 'There should be a matching bay on the other side. If there is, then we can really get to work.'

There was.

The two bays were similar in structure as they had been caused by the same forces working in similar circumstances upon material in the same state. As the waves swept in over the last edge of the submerged ice reef, it thundered against vertical walls of ice. Such was the force of the collision that the cliffs inevitably yielded and so the bays were born. At first, no doubt, they had been more like caves, with beetling overhangs of ice cliff, but as time wore on and ice wore away, so the spray-weakened overhangs began to collapse and at last the caves opened out enough to be called bays. The process which Kate Ross had warned about took a slight hand here and the ice rose sufficiently to cause a relative fall in water level; the last shoulder of the reef rose up and broke the force of the waves for a while, and a beach – a simple, near level slope of ice which had been beneath the reach of the waves' action – was revealed.

So matters stood at the moment. All Tom Snell and his men had to do was to blow the overhanging slopes down into the sea and make the upper sections of the ice safe, and the very bays they needed would be opened up. The beaches and the last dry heaves of the ice reefs would make perfect anchorage points. The bays would easily accommodate the awaited ships, and could hardly be better placed. Richard felt a huge swell of hopeful excitement as he looked onto the giant white eye socket staring blindly down towards the writhing back of the serpentine Stream which they were so soon to join. It was quite possible that the positioning of the two great ships just at the point where the greatest force of the upper sea pushed hardest against the ice would make the counter-thrust of their great engines all the more effective. It seemed logical. He would have to check it with John and Bob; if it did work like that, it would be quite a bit of good luck.

'Back!' he yelled. The Sea King swept out and up. Richard turned to Tom Snell and gestured at the overhangs falling away beneath them. 'You've got until the day after tomorrow.' If we get through tonight, he thought.

The soldier was no mind-reader. He grinned a tight grin and gave him a thumbs-up.

The Sea King pirouetted and dropped its nose, heading across the ice to *Titan*, thirty kilometres distant, invisible behind a wall of fog so solid it resembled the ice cliffs below; so huge it dwarfed them. Richard's elation cooled further: the swirling vapour marked the first tentative meeting of the southward-flowing Labrador Current and the strongly eastward North Atlantic Drift.

Niobe hit the North Wall first, at midnight on the dot.

Richard was standing on *Titan*'s bridge, staring tensely out into the dark while Sally Bell and the other navigating officers tended the banks of instruments around him. There was nothing to see. The long deck before him carried running lights as required but they and it were cloaked in fog. The foghorn was hooting and out on the bridge wing it was possible to hear *Niobe*'s horn answering like the call of some mythical beast. He remembered reading of the fogs in these waters being 'so thick you could cut them and spread them on your bread, like butter'. They were there because of the mixing of cold water and warm somewhere in the depths. There was no sign of the Wall yet. But soon, soon.

'Signing on now,' said Sally, and he knew it was midnight.

His hand was actually resting on the cool black box of the walkie-talkie when it squawked. His fingers jumped away, then grabbed the instrument, almost fumbling with tension.

'Yes?'

'It's John here, Richard. Encountering very strong eastward current. Turning to counter it as agreed . . . Now.'

The collision alarm radar screamed. 'He's drifting down on us fast,' warned Sally.

'Steady as she goes, please, helmsman. You're coming down fast, John.'

'Yes, I can see. Christ, but this is fierce, Richard. You'd think we were white-water canoeing here!'

'It'll catch us at any minute. Any report from your line watch?'

All the ships had deployed a watch on the tow line; the

greatest strain of the whole voyage was likely to come now as the tankers were jerked eastwards by a force which the iceberg did not yet feel. Richard had ordered the lengthening of the tows so that the ships would stay well ahead of the ice at this point. The alternative was to risk *Niobe* being crushed against the ice cliffs down-Stream of her.

'Line's fine. Still drifting down on you. *Niobe* doesn't like this. She's very hard to control.'

Titan's deck quivered. Richard's heart leaped.

'If *Niobe* comes closer than three kilometres, then give me a countdown, Sally. I want lots of warning if we have to get out of her way.'

'Aye, sir.'

The deck quivered again.

'Helmsman, watch for—'

'Bugger me! Sorry sir, but—'

'Three kilometres now and closing. My God!'

Titan's head slammed round as though America had punched her on the jaw. 'Line watch, we're coming left hard!' snapped Richard into his walkie-talkie. Then he reached down for the engine room telephone and pressed it to his left ear. 'We've hit the Wall, Chief. Watch her!'

Titan groaned. It was as though she was alive. Her decking trembled, the whole of her long body shook. The stress on her sides and frame twisted towards her design capabilities. She was almost half a kilometre long. In spite of the care with which they had angled their approach to this point in the deep trench east of Flemish Cap, the sternmost two hundred metres of the ship wanted to go south and the forward two hundred wanted urgently to go east.

'Still coming down on us. Two and a half kilometres.'

'Thanks, Sally. Come left, helmsman, take us into it. Line watch, report.'

'Capstan's groaning a bit, Captain, but it's holding. I've never seen a cable so tight.'

'*Niobe*'s falling back a bit now. Two and three-quarter kilometres.'

'Good.'

'How is it with you, John?'

'All right, Richard. I see you're running east as agreed. We'll swing round as soon as we're right in. We can't fight it, really, in any case. You're the lucky one just giving in!'

'RICHARD!' A new voice on the walkie-talkie breaking into the tense conversation on the open channel. Richard felt his heart clench.

'Yes, Colin?'

'Can you hear thunder?'

'No. There's no weather—'

'Captain! Line watch here. I can hear . . . My God!'

'Sally! You have her. Steady as she goes. I'm just going out . . .'

Richard ran to the bridgewing door and wrenched it open. As he did so, he reached across, with the walkie-talkie hanging from his wrist, and snatched a pair of binoculars out of their pouch by the watchkeeper's chair.

He ran out into clear air where moments before there had been impenetrable fog but he was too concerned to notice the change in the conditions. He raced along to the overhanging end and turned. Looking back from the furthest point port, squinting along the side of his ship from a position well outside her hull, he could see the tow and the capstan. More importantly, he could hear. There *was* thunder, gathering on the calm air. A deep, unending rumble of it, intensifying.

He slung the binoculars unhandily round his neck. Pressed the walkie-talkie to his mouth.

'Colin? I can hear it! What is it?'

'It's the ice! It's shaking!'

'Sally!' he bellowed. 'Check the bottom.'

'Three thousand metres.'

'We haven't run aground then, Colin, we're still well clear of the Cap.'

'Then what is it? It's getting louder here. The ice is shaking! It's like an earthquake!'

The whole of *Titan* lurched left hard enough to make Richard stumble. He slammed his binoculars to his eyes. The tow line, a black, gleaming bar in the moonlight, jerked and swung, like the second hand on some giant watch. The great ship's wake was snatched away, the straight line coming after them out of the fog bank, broken like the fault line in a cliff, where it crossed the North Wall.

Comprehension dawned. 'It's the current! The Stream must be running further northward the deeper it goes. We're in it here now on the surface. The ice must be coming into it below the surface!'

As he spoke, Richard looked up and what he saw snatched away his breath and his words alike.

From out of the foundations of the solid fog wall astern, out into the clear blue moonlight here, came the prow of Manhattan as though she was a ship standing three hundred metres sheer to the forecastle head. The black cables leaped forward from their claw-like handholds to the groaning capstans on *Niobe* and *Titan*, and quivered visibly with the strain of holding firm. Below the handholds, the cutwater fell into the slick, bright surface of the sea. And as he watched, the glassy curve of the water's back exploded upwards against the white bow as Manhattan surged on out of the fog with a foaming bow wave at her bow foot made up of white water piling against her starboard quarter and tumbling down a metre or more into the hole in the water at her port. Even as he watched, stunned by the scale of this meeting of iceberg and Gulf Stream, the bow wave in Manhattan's teeth exploded anew. A school of sleek dolphins, gleaming, almost luminescent, flew into the air and tumbled with the blue-white surf. Time and again they jumped out of the wild swirl of water, flying, tumbling and sporting there, until the wave began to settle as the bow came well and truly into the new eastward flow. But still the sound of the thunder boomed as more and still more of the ice fought back against the pressure of the water, the huge sound of its victory over the crushing current booming across the clear rushing waters of the North Atlantic around them.

At last Richard turned his back on Flemish Cap and Newfoundland and looked due east three thousand kilometres towards Europe.

Right, he thought. Biscay, here we come!

Chapter Fourteen

Thirty-six hours later, they had just crossed forty degrees west, heading east with Manhattan still in one piece and all the lines in place, when *Kraken* and *Psyche* came steaming down from the north towards them.

As far as Richard was concerned, conditions could not have been worse. There was an Indian summer in the mid-Atlantic and the air was calm, the skies clear, the sea warm and dazzlingly blue. The North Atlantic Drift meandered lazily eastward, sometimes helping, sometimes not. It was becoming difficult to maintain speed and impossible to slow the deterioration of the ice. Even the runoff which Yves had promised would form a cool, protective pool in the thick salt water around the berg and slow the process of melting was only causing restless clouds of fog which came and went mysteriously, inexplicably and, above all, irritatingly.

The arrival of the two ships, therefore, could not have been better timed to lighten Richard's darkening spirits. It gave him something to do other than worry. It gave him a project, moreover, whose speedy and successful outcome would go a long way to alleviating the difficulty with which he found himself faced. He had been waiting for this moment since they turned the corner off Flemish Cap, but even talking to the captains of the vessels as they raced westward on the northern counter-current did not put his mind at rest in the way that the sight of them, hull up and side by side over the northern horizon and steaming south, gave him.

As soon as the two ships hove into view, he was back to his old self, feeling more in control of events again. He went through into the bridge, leaving the port bridgewing door slightly ajar behind him. 'I'll be going onto the ice to help with the securing of *Kraken* and *Psyche*,' he told Sally Bell. 'You can take the con and dog the watch if you want. I don't know how long I'll be.'

He left and the first officer looked after him with narrowed eyes, deciding whether or not to take his advice and rearrange the watches to break at two and six instead of four and eight, hand over the watchkeeping responsibilities to her juniors and take overall command herself. It might be a good idea, especially as the captain would be off the ship all afternoon. He would probably be back by six, though, she reckoned. No matter what jaunt he was up to, he always came back by Pour Out – not for a drink (she had never seen him drink anything alcoholic) but for a chat, a bit of socialising and psychological pulse-taking before working dinner and late meetings and reports.

In fact, Sally Bell was staggered by how hard her captain worked. She was a Belfast girl born and bred and no stranger to the Protestant work ethic, but she had never seen anyone pour so much time and energy into anything in all her life. Richard was up at six, woken, according to the chief steward, with a cup of tea the colour of teak. He was about the ship by six thirty, and put in a swift tour of inspection before breakfast at seven thirty. The tour formed the basis of his working breakfast with her, for during it he noted everything that needed doing or checking around the ship. When she reported to his table in the saloon at eight, usually a little drowsy after four hours' sleep, she would find, beside his coffee cup, a neat list of things he wished to refer to her notice, and as she ate – always a full cooked breakfast for Sally – he went through them with her. By eight thirty he was in the radio shack and he first contacted his other captains, checking what was happening aboard their ships and centralising their reports about the tow. Then he talked to Colin Ross and Major Snell up on the ice. Then he made a radio report to the United Nations building in New York and to Heritage House in London. Routinely, also, he called his wife who was usually getting their twin children Mary and William ready for lunch by the time he got through to her.

By eleven, he had assembled all the facts he needed in order to write his reports and he would routinely spend two hours typing ferociously in his day room. He shared a working lunch at one with the chief engineer who was expected to give the most detailed report on the state of the big RB211 turbine engines which powered the complex variable-pitch, twin-screw configuration deep beneath the counter.

From fourteen hundred hours he would be about the ship again, checking that the work listed this morning was under way, and then he would check with the other captains again, and tell off Doug Buchanan the helicopter pilot for duty – on almost every day so far, there had been a meeting of all the captains, Major Snell and the Rosses either on board or on the ice. But wherever he was during the afternoon, as she had observed, he was down in the officers' lounge by eighteen hundred, sipping sparkling Malvern water and taking the pulse of his command. For he *was* in command here, more so than any captain she had served under. Not fussily or dominatingly but supportively and absolutely; and if he habitually straightened every pencil on the chart table to regimented neatness whenever he passed, that was simply because he wanted to know where even the least thing aboard might be in case he needed it in an emergency.

During dinner he would complete any business left over from the afternoon's meeting and then share his coffee with her, checking up on ship's business. Then he would spend another hour at least in the radio shack making radio reports which, from twenty-one thirty or twenty-two hundred, he would put onto paper in his day room. At twenty-three hundred hours exactly, on the dot, he would put through his final call, to the lucky woman in Ashenden, that house of his high on the cliffs above the English Channel. Then he would retire. As often as not, however, Sally would find him prowling the bridge, sipping cocoa, checking the log and straightening the pencils when she came on duty at midnight, so he got little more sleep than she did – and she would usually catch up in the afternoon during a siesta which he allowed her but never himself. She was beginning to wonder how long he could keep it up, but in her bones she knew. He would keep it up until the job was done, no matter how tough it got, no matter how much it took.

She crossed to the telephone by the helm and buzzed the second officer's number. As she did so, the first fingers of mist crept in around the edge of the bridgewing door and the huge airy bridge itself was suddenly filled with the smell of slightly rancid cucumbers.

Captain Gendo Odate had come a long and varied way from his birth in the town of Tsu overlooking the bay of Ise-wan, on the south coast of Honshu, to the command of the supertanker *Kraken* currently nosing her way east-south-eastwards through thickening fog into a tiny bay on the north side of an iceberg proceeding towards Europe at slightly less than seven knots. He stood solidly in the middle of his bridge, looking steadfastly forwards into the dazzling impenetrability ahead, listening to the disciplined flow of information, all of it in English, which was coming via his officers from the electronic equipment all around him, and thanking various deities for the tall form of Richard Mariner who stood beside him.

Richard had come to *Kraken* first because she would take up her position first. *Psyche* had run ahead of the convoy when the two ships drew near and was now falling back into place as they worked *Kraken* into her allotted position here. About the only thing visible through the clearview in front of him was the bright yellow glow of the Sea King on the foredeck, sitting waiting to take him off again in due course. He was not simply halfway between a pilot and an idle observer. He held in his right hand a walkie-talkie tuned to a closed frequency on which he could liaise with Major Snell on the ice and direct his efforts as necessary. But at the moment, he was in pilot mode, talking to the Japanese captain.

'We have to position *Kraken* fifty metres offshore and hold her course parallel at just less than seven knots,' Richard was saying gently. 'Major Snell and his men will fire the lines across fore and aft. We can pull them aboard by winch and capstan and take it from there. John Higgins, Bob Stark and I have drawn up the disposition diagrams for optimum patterns of attachment, but I'm sure you will want to study them and discuss any points of concern.'

'One hundred metres and closing on the starboard side,' sang out the first officer who was crouching over the collision alarm radar. 'Ice across the stern at one hundred and twenty-five metres and closing.'

'Come to seven knots, please,' said Captain Odate. 'It seems you are maintaining a better speed than you thought, Captain Mariner.'

'Seven knots,' said the helmsman, his words coming under Captain Odate's observation and Richard's surprised grunt of agreement.

The pounding of the great oil-fired motor below moved up a beat.

'Perhaps a degree further south?' suggested Richard.

'Steer one degree further south,' said the captain.

'One degree further south,' said the helmsman.

'Ready with the thrusters, fore and aft.' Captain Odate was willing to listen to Captain Mariner, but he would be ready to take evasive action if his tall adviser got it wrong. How could even this legendary seaman pilot a supertanker into a floating dock alongside an iceberg?

'Ready with thrusters.'

'Seventy-five metres and closing on the starboard side.'

'Steady as she goes.'

'Fifty metres on the starboard. Steady at one hundred metres astern.'

'Very good. Bow thruster ready if we go nearer than twenty-five metres.' Odate was a little more relaxed now; perhaps Captain Mariner was as gifted as they said after all.

'Fire away the forward line now, Tom,' said Richard into his walkie-talkie, and even as the Japanese captain began to relax, he instantly tensed up again.

An arc of light suddenly cut through the mist as though a sky rocket had been fired a month early to land somewhere beyond the brightening glow of the Sea King. At once the walkie-talkie in the fourth officer's hand squawked, and the young Senegalese officer reported to his captain that the first line was aboard.

Captain Odate nodded once. 'Take it to the windlass and winch the main cable aboard,' he commanded. 'Steady as you go, helm, and watch in case the weight of the cable is sufficient to pull you further over.'

Richard thumbed the SEND button. 'Line well aboard now, Tom,' he said. 'It's going down to the windlass now. Stand by.'

He listened to Tom Snell's monosyllabic acknowledgement, then he stood and watched silently, knowing that the carbon fibre cable was nowhere near heavy enough to affect the stately progress of the great ship. His feeling of elation was at a new peak now, though combined with a certain amount of tension. For a start, he was surprised to find Manhattan was picking up speed. Perhaps they had lucked into a surge of the current; perhaps there was something else going on. He would have to check later, though. Tethering a supertanker to an iceberg was something no one had ever done, and God alone knew if they were doing it right. The plan was simply to get the bow attached, then allow the hull to swing in. Both *Kraken* and *Psyche* had come with enough buffers to stave off an avalanche and these were now disposed along the great ship's starboard side to protect her plates from the rough embraces of the ice. Tethered at the bow, with her side well armoured, she would settle in against the ice itself and be tethered again from the stern. As the same process was being completed with her sister nine kilometres south, the black lines would be finally adjusted and, on Richard's order, hopefully tonight, the six ships would slowly begin their run up to full speed, moving Manhattan right along with them.

The walkie-talkie spoke again and the young fourth officer – the UN could afford larger crews than Heritage Mariner, Richard observed – informed his captain that the main cable was coming aboard. Unable to stand as stolidly as the Japanese captain, Richard crossed restlessly to the starboard bridge wing and opened the door. The bridge filled with the smell of cucumbers. 'What is that odour?' demanded Captain Odate, surprised out of his studied imperturbability.

'It's Manhattan,' answered Richard. 'Apparently all icebergs smell like that.'

Silence returned – or partly so, at any rate. The opening of the door admitted more than Manhattan's smell. It let in some of the sounds she was making. The cascading of runoff, as though *Kraken*'s bow wave had suddenly leaped much closer. There came a grating rumble as though her well-buffered side had struck already. There came a sharp crack as though the line had parted. Richard caught Captain Odate's eye. 'It's safer than it sounds,' he said, and stepped outside.

As soon as he did so, he felt the kiss of the wind on his

right cheek. So that was why Manhattan was moving more quickly. Some sailors know there is wind about because they hear it, magically, in the far distance; others, like John Higgins, could find wind with their eyes, reading sky and sea with uncanny accuracy. Others used their noses. Richard used the skin of his cheeks, which was fortunate since all the other alternatives were out of the question under the current circumstances, with sight, hearing and smell overwhelmed by the nearness of Manhattan. Richard moved his face like a blind man, searching the damp, cucumber-smelling air for another kiss. It came, and he smiled. There was some weather swinging in behind them at last.

Suddenly the mist was snatched away and Richard found himself looking into one of the cavernous bays they had been exploring in the Sea King less than forty-eight hours ago. From the helicopter it had seemed little more than an impressive natural formation, like a cliff-backed cove on a rocky coast. Now, it took his breath away. It stretched out on either hand, curving like an archer's bow bent slightly out of true, not quite into a half-pear shape one kilometre long. Before him, the limpid blue water washed up against a beach a hundred metres wide, sloping gently up from an edge of ice falling sheer into black darkness in the ocean's depth. The beach ran up into the curve of a cave as shadowed as anything made of lucent white can be, then sloped up into an overhang which took into its gleaming opacity every shade of blue from the sea. And, above that outward curve, towering above his head in a carefully dynamited slope back to the crest and the skyline, was a hundred metres more of ice which reflected almost to the point of being unbearable every liquid hue of the cerulean sky. And liquid was an apt word to apply. The blast-slick slope was running with a river of runoff and a waterfall hung like a jewelled curtain a kilometre wide before the mouth of the broad, shallow cave.

From a point the selection of which was the result of almost Einsteinian calculation came the first line, reaching forward through the pouring brightness to the windlass on the forecastle head, overseen still by Tom Snell's men upon the ice. Just less than a full ship's length behind, the second of Snell's teams was ready with the equipment to send the second line aboard. Beyond them, perched apparently precariously on the square dry shoulder of the raised ice reef, sat the Bell Iroquois helicopter from *Achilles*, ready to lift them across to the other shore in due course.

Richard found himself swept in and in, until the waterfall was so close he could have put his hand into it had he reached out from the furthest end of the bridge wing. Instead he was content to stand, feeling the wind steady, looking down through the dancing drizzle to the shadowed ice below. Stretched out and hammered home, the iron points of eight claws dug into columns of carefully angled concrete plunging down into the white shelf. Even as he watched, *Kraken* gave the slightest shudder and he looked straight over the edge to see the fenders between the ship's side and the sheer ice bulge upwards and become slick with spray and runoff as they were nipped between the sides of two of the largest things ever to float across the Atlantic Ocean.

He thumbed the SEND button again. 'OK, Tom, let go the aft line now.'

A flat report warned him that the second line was on its way aboard, and he walked back onto the bridge just in time to see the fourth officer report the fact to the captain. Richard's job aboard here was finished for the time being. And quite successfully so, from the look of things.

'I'll go across to *Psyche* now, Captain Odate,' he said, 'and let you get settled in here. There will be a full meeting of all captains on *Titan* at sixteen hundred and it will last until Pour Out at eighteen hundred, when I hope I shall be able to buy you a drink.'

Captain Odate looked around the bridge but his eyes clearly took in everything beyond his command as well: the glacial bay, the overhang, the cliff and the runoff, and the eight-pointed anchorage of two unbreakable cables tethering himself and his command immovably to the side of the iceberg.

'Yes, thank you, Captain Mariner,' he said. 'You can most certainly buy me a drink. A whisky. A double whisky. Suntory, twelve-year-old, if you have it.'

Things started going wrong for Major Tom Snell, Royal Engineers, and his men as soon as they started trying to get *Psyche* secured in the second little bay. For a start the wind was freshening and although he was by no means a nautical man, Tom knew nasty-looking squall clouds when they started building themselves up all too close behind him in the west. Probably because of the wind, the Huey helicopter's pilot had the devil of a job getting them down on the southward facing reef. On their first pass, the helicopter – in no way a thistle-down aircraft – was whirled right to the forward end of the bay, and the dazzled eyes of the officer were treated to the sight of a honeycomb of little caves which marched up from the waterline, the biggest of which presented him with a bright white cave mouth a metre and a half high, backed with a cavern of cobalt shadows. He thought no more of it as the helicopter jerked up into the air to speed back along the length of the ship to the outthrust of dry reef astern of her.

Once they were down, they leaped out of the trembling craft and began to unload their equipment only to find that the freshening wind was bringing an icy, stinging spindrift over the low crest from the nasty-looking surf behind. In a moment, everything they wore and carried was drenched. A moment more and their hands were becoming clumsy with numbness.

The gloomy, threatening atmosphere in the little bay

could hardly have been more different from the bright blue seaside feeling which, after the mist had lifted, had filled the first bay on the north coast of Manhattan. But Tom and his men were soldiers. Atmosphere – weather conditions – meant nothing to them. Following orders and getting the job done, that was all that counted. And if conditions were deteriorating for them, so were they for the supertanker and the two captains in charge of her, Peter Walcott and Richard Mariner.

Tom was very keen not to let Richard Mariner down, for the tall, almost visionary captain had filled the hard-bitten, widely travelled soldier with a respect that bordered upon awe. And Tom had spent enough time in the desert hell-holes of Africa, watching in helpless fury as the United Nations just failed to stop situation after situation sliding into war, to come as near as he could to praying that Richard could pull off this wild, wonderful project. For Mau, for the UN, and for all those poor hopeless people who would die if they failed.

It was fortunate that they had done the really dangerous digging, filling and blasting in the bright warmth of yesterday. All they had to do now was repeat the smoothly efficient operation they had just achieved with *Kraken* all over again with *Psyche*. But that was far more easily said than done. The wind for which Richard had been praying arrived half an hour too early and its very presence made the replay of *Kraken*'s flawless docking a nightmare for *Psyche*. For a start, it blew the thickening waterfall of melt-water down into the faces of the soldiers on the sloping, slippery beach. Then, no sooner had the two captains got *Psyche* into some sort of position and Richard warned Tom over the walkie-talkie to get ready with the forward line than a blustering gust took the supertanker so hard on her high superstructure and tall, unladen side that she had to sheer off. The infinitesimal effect of the wind force on something of her size and weight was puny but nevertheless sufficient to disturb the exact calculations going on in her bridge. And when the long-suffering captains got her back in position again, riding steadily, able to make allowance for the increasing squally bluster from behind, the wind took the first rocket and blew it halfway to Biscay anyway, far beyond the forecastle head of the mighty vessel in spite of the fact that it was riding so unnervingly close to them.

'How did you manage to miss that, Sergeant Dundas?' snarled Tom in bitter frustration. 'I mean, it's only half a kilometre long!'

'Dunno, Major,' answered the Scot phlegmatically. 'Wind must'a took it like.'

'Pull the line back in and set up another one. Aim aft of the Sampson posts this time, just in case.'

'Yessir!' answered Dundas, busily pulling the icy, soaking line in hand over hand with his two private soldier colleagues. He hesitated, then, 'Ah, whit d'you mean aft o' the Sampson posts, exactly, sir?'

By the time they got it set up properly again, *Psyche* had drifted off station and they were back to square one.

'Coming in again, Tom,' said Richard distantly over the walkie-talkie. And just as he did so, it began to rain in earnest.

The walkie-talkie squawked again and Tom put it to his face, expecting more instructions from Richard, but it was the helicopter pilot. 'I've got to go, Major. This lot will blow me over into the sea otherwise.'

'Now just you wait a minute . . . Dundas! I'm going back to the chopper for a minute. You fire again on Captain Mariner's order. Behind those bloody great mast things halfway down *Psyche*'s deck. Understand?'

'Yessir! Halfway down *Psycho*'s deck. Yessir!'

Tom set off at a slipping, staggering run across the sloping ice, past the second little team crouching shivering at the second anchorage point. 'OK, men?' he bellowed in passing and received a shivering thumbs-up. Normally that lack of soldierly propriety would have earned a reprimand. Not now. He ran out onto the foam-washed reef and kept his footing in spite of the push and suck of the ankle-deep foam. He half fell into the side of the helicopter and took out his considerable, mounting ire upon the pilot. 'Now just what the hell are you talking about? You can't leave us here, you nasty little man!'

'Either you get aboard now or I do just that, Major. I'm sorry, but I'm not joking. I'll be off the ice inside five minutes, either flying or floating, and I know which I'd prefer!'

'We can't leave until they have the lines aboard *Psyche*. It'd put the whole show behind by a day at least.'

'Look, Major, I'm sorry, but I've got no choice. Get the survival equipment and the rubber dinghy out of the back just in case. I'll be back for you the minute I can land here again.'

Tom reached in and tore the two big bundles free, then he fell out into the surf, dragged himself to his feet by an exercise of pure rage, and staggered ashore. It was not until he was crouching there, gasping for breath, that he realised the mouthful of foam he had choked on while trying to get back up had been absolutely fresh water. While he crouched there, licking his lips in wonderment, he felt the numbing buffeting of the wind on his back intensify and he knew that the helicopter was gone.

He took the survival equipment up to the very back of the beach and wedged it against the curve of wall where, in about half a metre, the steepening curve of beach took wing to become the soaring overhang of the roof. Then he turned and began to fight his way through the buffeting maelstrom of rain, saltless sea spray, runoff and wind to crouch beside Sergeant Dundas again.

The sergeant and his team were paying out the last of

the line and preparing to stand back as *Psyche* winched the black cable aboard.

'Yon bastard's away wi' the chopper then, sir?' enquired the sergeant.

'Yes,' answered his commanding officer, who until today had never been heard to swear, 'the bastard is.'

The walkie-talkie buzzed angrily and Tom picked it up only to drop it again at once. Sometime during the last few moments, his fingers had gone completely numb. He beat his hand against his thigh and found that it was equally insensible. It was a moment or two before he could pick up the walkie-talkie and hold it to his face.

'Christ, Tom, what is going on over there? Are you all right?'

'It's pretty cold here, Richard. And we're stuck. Didn't you see the chopper lift off?'

'No I did *not*! Right. We've got the forward line aboard and we're drifting in fast. Can you take care of the stern one or shall I sort something out from this end?'

The cold was really starting to get inside Tom now. It was fogging up his brain and making that section of it still functioning fill with waves of agony from every single joint in his shaking body. He gritted his teeth. 'No, it's OK, Richard. We'll fire it aboard.'

'Right. Do that. Then just hang on. I'll have a team of men from *Psyche* ready to come down there and get you off the instant we're in position.'

'Right. Understood.'

He didn't bother switching off the machine, he just dropped it and watched it skitter down the steely curve of running ice. He staggered over to the second group, falling twice and arriving on his hands and knees, though they were only three hundred metres distant.

The great stern of the supertanker swung in towards them with nerve-stretching rapidity. Tom was torn between wanting them to hurry it up and extreme concern as to what would happen if they hit the ice too hard. As the rear of the ship, standing high because she was running only in ballast and augmented by five storeys of bridge-house, closed towards the sheer cliffs, it created a wind tunnel which none of the men involved had counted upon; the mounting gusts of the squall rushing down upon them from the west were forced relentlessly into the narrow channel, increasing their speeds pitilessly towards hurri-cane strength.

'FIRE!' yelled Tom at last, not when ordered to, or even when he thought *Psyche* was in the correct position, just when he could take the power of the terrible gale no longer. The rocket whirled away down the wind. 'Leave that!' he ordered in a hoarse scream. 'Get up to the back of the cave! Quickly!'

He led the way himself, making the last few metres up to the piled survival equipment on his hands and knees, his bright blue uniform beret long gone.

Richard realised how serious matters had become only when it was almost too late to do anything about it. It was the firing of the stern rocket line that alerted him, for neither he nor *Psyche*'s equipment, or her captain, the Guyanese Peter Walcott, had thought her in the correct position yet. Richard had been on the bridge, wrapped in deep concentration, completely unaware of what was happening other than that the helicopter had leaped off the foam-washed reef, certain only that the great ship was behaving very strangely and at a loss to explain exactly why.

The news of the fired line sent him out onto the bridge wing and into the unrelenting grip of the freak wind – a wind which only blew here and below, where *Psyche*'s instruments could not even tell of its existence. He ran back onto the bridge in a breathless burst of action. 'Cap-tain Walcott! Our movement is causing a severe intensification of the wind between our port side and the cliffs. It must be coming through force ten out there now. I would like to lower the port lifeboat at once and go after the men on the ice before they simply get blown away.'

'Of course, Captain. Number One, take a team and help the captain. You watch yourself though. I know what hurricanes can do!'

The two officers ran down through the companionways as the captain's voice broadcast orders around them. No sooner had they reached the correct deck than the lifeboat crew arrived beside them. Between urgent gasps for breath, Richard explained the situation and gave his orders. They all nodded various understanding and burst out into the tiny, vicious hurricane.

Richard was the only one really expecting it and he was the only one not literally staggered by the power of it. But the others soon fought their way into position and released the automatic davits of the lifeboat, allowing it to swing down and out. Richard and the first officer scrambled in unhandily through the top hatch as the solid vessel jerked viciously against its blocks and the winch hooks groaned to let it go. Two of the team followed them as quickly as they could while the last two held the tricing-in pendants and bowsing lines until Richard ordered them to let go. The winches whirred and clanked. The boat began to tumble out and down, the gravity brakes refusing to let the wind tear it free of the falls. One gust swung it in to batter against the buffers on the ship's side and everyone aboard tumbled around like stones in a huge maraca. Then their wild ride stopped abruptly. The hull jerked into motion three more times, falling less than a metre each time, and then it stopped for good, its keel just kissing the surface of the water and the strong curve of its lower port side thumping against the steep shore of the ice.

Tom Snell had no idea that anyone would – could – be

coming to his rescue. The moment he had got the second team crouching together enjoying some kind of protection from the bundle of survival equipment, he was off again, still on hands and knees, to check on Sergeant Dundas and his men. Well before he had suffered the full three hundred metres of wind-ravaged ice, he saw that Dundas had led the small contingent up to the only promise of shelter, the low back of the cave, and here they were huddled together, wedged between the curves of floor and roof, with their backs to the wild whirl of the wind.

It was only now that Tom remembered the glimpse he had had of the cobalt-throated caves less than a hundred metres further on along the ridge. He battered on Dundas's numb back until he had the soldier's full attention and then he began to lead the bedraggled little group down the slippery beach of ice. As they moved, the curve between floor and roof began to widen and the back wall along which they were moving rose from two metres to three in height, then four, five and six. The cliff was all but vertical above them by the time they reached the mouth of the nearest cave. They were on a tiny ledge now, a mere metre and a half of gently sloping ice, then a cliff lunging down into the sea at least as sheer as the one above their heads and five times its height in depth. The wind showed no sign of relenting and was doing its best to push them off, so they had no choice and, consequently, no hesitation.

Tom turned, thinking somewhere distantly, no doubt, that he should see his men in first, like a courteous host, but as soon as he faced the wind he knew with bone-deep certainty that to hesitate was to die. Leading from the front as always, therefore, he stepped through the portal first. He took one crouching step on safe, firm ice through a blessed calm of solid-walled windlessness, then a second round a sudden twist in the low, tunnel-like cave – just enough to take him beyond the immediate sight of the next man following. Then he took a third step into an abyss. He pitched forward and down so suddenly, he didn't even have time to call out. The second man, as disorientated as his commanding officer by the sudden windless silence, took the same steps and met the same fate. As did the third.

The fourth and last man was Sergeant Dundas and he was just that little bit more hesitant. He went through the doorway and hesitated. 'Major?' he called.

Silence. Still air here. The storm immediately behind. The roaring of wind and water. 'Major Snell? Harry? Jock?'

No reply.

With every sense on the alert, with every hair on his long, Lowland body erect, Sergeant Dougie Dundas lay on his belly and slid forward over the slick ice. He came to a twist in the low tubular passageway and eased himself round it. Light came through the walls, a green light, surprisingly gloomy. God in heaven it was even coming up through the floor! Light enough to show him the walls of the tunnel for a metre or two ahead as he eased himself round the corner. Suddenly, atavistically, he was very worried indeed. He hesitated, in two minds whether to stretch out his hands and run the risk of having them grabbed by whatever horror had gulped down his CO and his squaddies, or to go round the corner head first and come face to face with it. Never a man to do things by halves, he pushed his face round first and head-butted the roof with a glancing blow as the tunnel vanished downwards like a wormhole a metre wide into an apparently bottomless black pit.

'Jesus Christ!' screamed the sergeant, overwhelmed with as much horror as if he had met the Loch Ness monster face to face. The sinister throat of the tunnel bubbled and hissed at him and it took only a moment to realise that it was full of water. Black, seething, restless water which he knew well enough from the rivers of his childhood. Rivers in full, deadly spate, which would suck in the unwary like liquid quicksand and gulp them away to their doom in a second. Water was doing in here what the wild wind was doing outside. Enraptured, like a child touching the picture of a monster, caught between horror and fascination, he reached his right hand down to touch the quick black liquid. It was a long stretch down a one-metre slope to reach the braided surface with his fingertips. Halfway down, something gleamed and caught the sergeant's eye.

On a ridge of ice halfway down the slope there appeared to be a pile of large, rough crystals. As though in the grip of a vision or a drug-induced dream, the sergeant reached down and took the largest of the crystals. He brought it to his face. It looked like glass. Surely it was far too big to be a diamond. And it was dark, almost black. Was it full of tiny metallic flakes? He looked down at the rest of the little pile. Were they glowing? It seemed as likely as anything else going on around him. Without taking his eyes off the black water, he slid the first of the crystals into his sodden blouson jacket, then reached downwards again, inconsequentially thinking of chocolate.

His fingers had no more than brushed the topmost of the strangely gleaming pile when a broad hand burst up out of the rushing blackness and fastened round his wrist. He screamed and hauled back, fighting to get away. An arm came up out of the water and the pale threat of a face. Dundas, screaming at the top of his lungs, backed wildly out into the mouth of the cave, fighting with all his strength to break that deathly grip, certain that this was some kind of monster escaped from a nightmare buried deep in his subconscious. Only terror such as this could have given him the strength to move backwards.

Only the grasp of a drowning man on a straw of flesh and blood would have kept that iron grip unbroken as the terrified sergeant pulled him back.

They were still locked together when Richard and the

men from the lifeboat arrived moments later to rescue them.

It was only when they were back in the warmth of *Psyche*'s little treatment room that they were able to break Tom Snell's grip.

Chapter Fifteen

Yves Maille was the diving expert and only the foulest of luck would have taken him so far away when he was needed so badly. The French deep-sea explorer had no interest at all in the berthing of big ships and, quite correctly, had assumed that everyone else would be intimately involved in the operation. He had therefore taken the opportunity presented by the arrival of the two ships to do some of the work he had been brought aboard to do.

Before dawn, the Frenchman had headed off in the largest inflatable, together with the small team of seamen he was training to assist him in his work. With an absent-mindedness worthy of the most stereotyped of professors, he had taken no radio with him and so was impossible to contact now that an emergency had arisen. Nor had he bothered to inform the watch officer when he was leaving, so they didn't know exactly when he had gone. All they knew was that he was somewhere on the ocean ahead – *on* rather than *in*, because he had not taken any diving gear – aboard a vessel capable of twenty knots, taking readings of sky and sea.

Richard didn't want to wait any longer for him to return. He knew that inaction would only make a bad situation turn sour on them, and he wanted to press ahead. And, as far as he could see, they had no real reason to wait any longer. There were three others near at hand who could do the job perfectly well.

Richard had learned how to scuba dive in the Seychelles. Bob Stark had learned at his family's summer home in Hyannis Port. Katya Borodin had learned at a Komosol dacha on the Black Sea. All three routinely kept their qualifications up to date, though none of them had ever, in their wildest' dreams, supposed they would be called to dive down into the cavernous heart of an iceberg.

Tom Snell and Dougie Dundas were in the care of Asha Higgins MD who had helicoptered over from *Niobe*, which was under the command of her husband John; she was ensconced with the comatose men in *Psyche*'s sickbay. *Psyche* herself was snugly in place with the grey squall wind running outside round her southern-facing starboard flank and the grey surf thundering under her counter. John Higgins in *Niobe* was in technical command of the fleet as the six mighty ships beat the following seas with their massive propellers, fighting to bring Manhattan's huge, inertia-shackled bulk up to a speed in excess of ten knots.

Psyche's great black bow reared above and abaft the little group now as they stood on the dull ice in the blessed wind shadow, considering the blast-widened opening to the ice cave and wondering what they would find down below.

No survivors, that was for sure.

It was four hours since the accident – the quickest it had been possible to arrange things safely and sensibly. Neither Tom nor his sergeant had made much sense in the interim, but a quick inspection of the little cave had told its own story, especially to the wise eyes of Colin Ross. It was the big glaciologist who had overseen the engineers of Tom's command as they blasted open the cave mouth to reveal the braided, sibilant rush of the water. It was he who would now be in charge of the group on the ice while the divers went down after the bodies below. Bob and Katya would be diving first, with Richard as reserve and back-up. The divers would be tethered to long lines as there was no knowing what conditions would be like down there. All of the divers wore bulky one-size dry suits routinely kept aboard Heritage Mariner tankers for small jobs over the side. The water temperature would be exactly at zero degrees Celsius and even a wet suit would be little protection in that temperature. And the dives would be short. Kate Ross, second only to the statuesque, red-headed Asha Higgins in medical qualifications, was there to make sure of that, and in case of the unexpected. *Psyche*'s lifeboat, loaded with emergency equipment, dry clothes and hot liquids, rode immediately at hand.

At last there was nothing left to say or do other than to get wet. Katya and Bob crossed to the sinister black hole in the ice, pulling again at their safety harnesses and testing their regulators, their long, braided orange polyester safety lines trailing like tails in their wake. Together they sat on the edge of the ice, putting their feet into the obsidian rush of the rogue current with all too obvious reluctance. In concert, already working in unconscious mirror image, as though they had been diving as a team for years, they settled their full face masks, flashed their heavy duty, underwater torches, and checked the tightness of their light equipment belts. Then they gave each other a swift glance and offered Richard and Colin a thumbs-up to show that they were ready.

Colin depressed the SEND button on the walkie-talkie he held tuned to the wavelength of the tiny transmitter-receivers in the divers' headgear. 'Katya, can you hear me? Over.'

Her head bobbed. 'Yesss,' came her reply, distorted by the machine already.

'Bob, can you hear me?'

'Yesss.'

'And can you hear each other?'

'Yesss.'

'Loud and clear.'

'Lines tight,' ordered Richard quietly. 'Ready all.' He

glanced back to where the three teams of mixed soldiers and seamen stood beside the tripods they had hammered into the ice. At the top of each tripod hung a block and tackle through which the line was fed. Behind each tripod stood the three men who would let the line out grudgingly – and be prepared to gather it in swiftly – as occasion required.

Richard tapped Katya on the shoulder and she rolled forward into the water. Her team staggered as the current took her, and then began to pay out line.

'Wait!' snapped Colin to the men. 'Katya. What can you see?'

There was a short pause as she orientated herself and looked around, then her voice came strongly through the hissing of the open channel. 'Tunnel. Narrow upstream, widening downstream. There is light here. Is not too cold.' She paused, then added, 'The roof of the tunnel is uneven. There are holes in it, from air bubbles I guess. Big enough to be handholds. It would be possible to pull oneself along for a little way, even against the current, I think.'

Richard's eyes met Colin's. So that was how the quick-thinking Tom Snell had managed to save himself. They had been wondering.

'Right. We're going to pay out more line and put Bob in behind you. Good luck.'

Richard crossed to Bob, his eyes straying constantly to the quivering tension of Katya's orange line which was already eating into the rim of the ice hole as her team continued to pay it out.

At Colin's nod, Richard hit his old friend on the shoulder and the black water swallowed the American. Both the divers were important to the project, but the order of their going had been dictated by the difficulty of replacing them if anything went wrong.

When Bob had vanished, Richard stood looking down into the hole, lost in thought. The triangular edge of his headgear bit across his forehead and squashed his cheeks together. The face mask dangled on his upper chest, the top of it pressing up under his chin. The suit was bulky and uncomfortable around him, but he noticed none of this. Colin was listening to what Bob could make out of the tunnel and of Katya ahead. How warm he felt the water was. How quickly he wished to catch up with his Russian colleague. But Richard noticed little of that, too.

He crouched down, as though fascinated by the hissing surface of the water, staring into the heart of it like a seer of old looking for the future in a magic bowl. What would they find down there? he wondered. What was hiding down there waiting to be found?

Asha Higgins swept the luxuriant thickness of her long chestnut hair out of her dark eyes and frowned down at Sergeant Dundas. There was something just not right here but she simply could not put her finger on it. She had worked for years as a doctor – in hospitals, briefly in general practice, and since the mid-eighties on a whole range of ships, most of which belonged to Heritage Mariner. In the last few she had been there not only as ship's doctor but as wife to the captain, and she missed John now. She had got into the habit of talking things through with him, bouncing ideas off his relative ignorance but availing herself freely of his fund of simple wisdom and solid good sense. She said he played Watson to her Sherlock Holmes, which made him smile with wry amusement because for years he had been cast as Little John to Richard's Robin Hood. Always the sidekick, he would complain, never the romantic lead.

She bitterly felt his absence now, for there was something wrong with the sergeant she simply could not put her finger on. Could the slight discolouration of his upper right cheek and the bridge of his nose be wind burn? Could the cracks on his right hand be a kind of frostbite? And what in the name of Allah could have caused the rash of blisters across the pale expanse of his chest?

She had looked through his clothing for clues when she first noticed the strange symptoms, but had found nothing. Well, she would just go down to the ship's laundry and go through the clothing again. The sergeant's and the major's, just in case. She crossed the room purposefully and swept out through the door.

Dougie Dundas's eyes opened to the merest slit and, through a haze of nausea, he watched the doctor depart. A fine figure of a woman, he thought dreamily. When he was rich he would surround himself with lots of others just like her. But he hadn't liked the way she had searched through his clothing when she thought he was asleep from her drugs. She must suspect something about his diamond, he thought. And if she did, then who else did? He had been right to hide it. It was so big and so rough that he had almost choked to death getting it down his throat, but it would be safe enough inside him until he worked out where else he could put it when Nature returned it to him again in due course. And in the meantime, not even Dr Higgins would find it unless their relationship became a great deal more intimate!

Katya Borodin found it very difficult to swim at first. The current kept pushing her forwards down the slope of the widening tunnel, and in spite of incipient claustrophobia, she would have liked to lie forward and fin along easily in the middle of it. But every time she tried to do so, the rope pulled her up short and her legs would swing under her until she was almost hanging vertically again.

There was very little to see in the tunnel. It was roughly round, slick and featureless, though the walls, floor and roof were honeycombed with holes of various sizes where bubbles of air must have risen through the apparently solid medium. And the lack of absolute solidity was borne in upon her by more than her sense of sight. Behind the crackle of the open channel in her earpieces she could hear the sighing bubble of trapped air on the move, the sloshing rumble of water washing not just over the ice, but through the very heart of it. When she touched the walls or the roof above, even through the thickness of her diving glove she could feel them faintly vibrating as though, among all the other sounds she could hear, there was one too deep to be audible, which the mighty berg could feel.

The crystalline ice was lucent, but as she went down, the light faded fast. What brightness there was came in gathering shades of green. Behind her, Bob was outlined in viridescence which flared and dimmed with the passage of clouds or waves. On either hand, the walls darkened from jade to emerald shot through with the lighter tracks made by the captive air bubbles fighting upwards; ahead, the darkest bottle-glass darkened further. But never to absolute darkness, and never to formlessness. As she fought her way further down against the tugging of the safety line, she could see where the tunnel ended.

Ended not in a wall but in an opening.

'Can you see this, Bob?' she asked, her voice quivering.

'Looks like we're coming down to the mouth of this particular river,' said the American, his words distorted by the static on the little radio. But surely his voice, too, had been quivering just a little.

'We must go there and take a look.'

'Only if we've got enough line.'

'You have used less than half the available line,' came the even more distant voice of Colin Ross. 'How much more do you need?'

'It is difficult to judge distance. Not only is there the effect of the water to be considered, there is the lack of any recognisable scale. I do not have any idea how big anything which I can see actually is, therefore I cannot tell how distant it may be.'

'That isn't much help, Katya.'

'It's the best we can do, Colin. Katya's right. No way can we judge distance accurately down here. Give us as much line as you can, we'll keep updating you as we go.'

'No sign of the missing men?' asked Richard's voice reedily over the set in his suit.

'No,' answered Bob, his voice deep with sadness. 'Like it says in that old hymn, Richard, "Time, like an ever rolling stream . . ." '

' " . . . Bears all its sons away." '

'That's the one, old man. They're long gone, I'm afraid.'

'Then you should come back at once,' said Colin, his voice loud and his tone urgent.

'But no!' answered Katya Borodin at once. 'Dr Ross, how can you say this? We must look. How can we not? We must!'

The silence then told how deeply Colin was torn. Had he been down there in that unique position himself, he would not have hesitated for an instant. There would have been no force on earth great enough to pull him back from discovering what lay beyond the debouching of the underground, submarine river. And having Katya and Bob report to him in detail what lay beyond the tunnel, at the heart of the iceberg, might well add significantly to his understanding of the mechanics of its monstrous construction. He was a scientist, an explorer in the minutiae of ice crystals and the tiny forces that made snowflakes form as they did as well as in the enormities of frozen continents and what made glaciers the size of Amazons create icebergs the size of countries. He had spent his life discovering the facts he was now so expert in, no matter what the cost.

And yet the cost was potentially so high. Manhattan had already claimed too many lives, but their loss had not slowed the project and put at risk the hope of the dying millions in Mau. Bob and Katya were different. They were the best in their field. If they died, then the project might well die too and Manhattan would be left to waste itself in the warm water, and Mau would be left to tear itself apart. The responsibility weighed very heavily upon Colin, for the situation was of his making and the project the result of his work. Ultimately, they were all here because of him. Those who were no longer here had died because of him. And any more who were injured or killed would weigh like lead upon his conscience until he died.

He met Richard's eyes, not asking for advice, but summoning the moral courage to proceed. Richard advised in any case. 'Go for it,' he said.

But his voice was drowned by Katya's sudden exclamation, 'There's something moving down there! Bob! Do you see it? There's something moving just beyond the tunnel mouth!'

Katya was hanging upright in the water, kicking lazily against the current to keep her legs from sweeping on downstream. While waiting for Colin's decision, she had switched on her torch and shone it around, marvelling at the way its light changed the colours of the ice all around her. Lost in wonder at the new rainbow of blues that the torch beam seemed to trap just above her head, she had played the beam on down the tunnel roof until, with a shock, she saw the light vanish and realised she was shining it straight out through the tunnel mouth. And as her dazzled mind was just beginning to come to terms with that, something flashed across the broad brightness of the beam. Something bright, vivid with movement. Something alive.

She had called out to Bob in her excitement, but it was Colin who answered her. 'Right,' he snapped crisply. 'Give me depth reading and remaining oxygen time before you proceed, please, Katya.'

She looked at her depth meter and was surprised to see

that she had descended less than ten metres – the tunnel had given the impression of sloping more steeply down. But she still had lots of oxygen left, especially as she would clearly have no real problems of decompression at this rate.

The realisation that she was so near the surface did nothing to dull the wonderment she felt, but it subconsciously added to her confidence. When Colin said, 'Take care!' she took little notice. As soon as her line slackened, she was off, moving purposefully after the pointing finger of light towards the gape of the tunnel mouth. As the beam of light plunged into the shadows beyond, a whirl of movement was revealed and her eyes fastened upon it, dazzled and increasingly mesmerised.

When she reached the tunnel mouth, instead of recognising the fact, stopping and taking stock, she swam on out without a further thought and the body of Jock McGann, dead for six hours now but still spinning wildly in the swirl of the buried whirlpool, collected her in his icy arms as he swept by and jerked her bodily out and away. It felt strangely as if she had been pulled into a particularly energetic dance. The length of his body slammed against hers and the pair of them whirled out of the horizontal position in which she had been swimming into an upright position. There was an instant in which she thought he might miraculously be alive, but then the brightness from her waving torch revealed the gaping sockets of his eyes. His mouth was wide and screaming, as though he could feel the small fish there feasting on his lips and tongue. Overwhelmed with revulsion, she pushed away from him only to shove herself backwards against the side of the cave they were dancing round. She felt a stunning blow against the back of her head and surrendered to the dark.

The woven polyester line stretched taut along the tunnel, then it parted and Katya was gone.

The first Bob knew of it was the disorientating moment when the loose line suddenly became bar-taut, crushing him against the roof. 'Katya!' he called into his face-plate microphone, only to be answered by her wail of shock and surprise. Then the line was loose and he knew with a cold certainty what that meant.

'She's gone!' he called up to Colin. 'Give me enough slack to follow. I'll make an assessment from the tunnel entrance. Quickly!'

As soon as the line slackened, he fought his way forward, but unlike Katya, he was very careful indeed to note where the tunnel mouth was and he did not let his vision probe beyond it until he was firmly wedged within it.

'There's some kind of cave here,' he gasped. 'I can't really see how big it is. I can't make out the far side. I can see a little of the ice immediately outside and it looks as though the tunnel debouches near the top of a sheer ice wall, but I can't tell how deep it is. I guess it must be open to the sea, though, because there's a lot of stuff in here. There's a kind of slow whirlpool. Everything I can see is swirling around. I can't see Katya, though. I guess I need to go . . . My God!'

'What is it? Bob!' Colin's voice was sharp with much more than concern now. He glanced across at Richard who was rapidly preparing to go down into the tunnel.

The American's voice came back onto the airwaves. 'It's OK. I cut my hand, is all. There's some kind of metal wedged in the ice here. Bit of plate from some old wreck, I guess. Son of a bitch, that's a sharp edge. Maybe that's what parted Katya's line. It's well enough honed, God knows. Colin, there's all kind of stuff washing around in here. I still can't see Katya, though. Wait a minute. Let's have absolute silence.' On his command, there was silence on the air. They all held their breath. There was the faintest whisper of respiration. 'That's her. She's still breathing. Must be unconscious, though. I guess I'm going to have to go in. How much line do I have?'

'Less than five metres. Wait a minute. What, Richard?'

'If we secure the end of his line to my safety harness, it'll double the length available to him. I'll go straight to the end of the tunnel and we can take it from there.'

'Sounds good. Did you hear what Richard said, Bob?'

'Yup. Sounds good to me too, Colin.' There was a slight pause. Then, 'Katya, it's Bob here. Can you hear me? Katya. It's OK, we're coming to get you. Hang on. Stay calm and hang on.'

While he was broadcasting his message to Katya, one of Richard's seamen was securing the end of Bob's line to the front of Richard's safety harness. Richard gave Colin and Kate a wave and slid into the water.

Like the other two before him, he was struck by the smoothness of the air-shafted walls, by the quality of the light coming through them; by the strength of the flow and by the unexpected warmth of the water creating it. It wasn't exactly hot, but it wasn't icy cold either.

Where the others had taken their time, exploring with some care – to begin with at least – Richard knew what was down here and he hadn't the inclination to linger. And the men in charge of his safety line would not pull him up short before he reached the tunnel mouth. He was able to do what Katya had wished to do, therefore: he fell forward into the heart of the flow and finned purposefully down the tunnel as quickly as he was able. 'I'll be with you in a moment, Bob,' he said as he swam swiftly down the tunnel. 'Wait till I get there before you move.'

'I hear you, but hurry it up.'

As he swam, Richard collected the slack line in great loops so that when he did come up behind Bob, he was ready and able to control the speed at which the American went into the cavern beyond. 'Anchor me,' he ordered, and his safety line tightened at once. Following Bob's gesture, he saw the curved blade of metal protruding from the tunnel's mouth and he angled himself so that his body would ensure Bob's rope came nowhere near it. In order to do this efficiently, he had to come very near the mouth of the tunnel and so, as his American friend stepped out into the whirl of it, Richard found himself perfectly placed to observe the cavern and almost everything within it.

It was just possible to see the far wall, about seventy-five metres distant, – although as Katya had observed it was difficult to judge distance down here. His first glance out gave him an instant impression of being able to see the whole shape of the formation, however, and he carried that in his head as he concentrated on keeping an eye on Bob as he fought against the whirlpool current.

The shape of the cavern seemed to be like the top half of an hourglass. There was a roof, domed and shadowed, quite close at hand above, then walls which fell inwards as well as downwards to shadows which made their foundations impossible to fathom. Richard guessed he could see more than two hundred metres straight down, however, before the green light failed. And even then, there was the quicksilver gyre of the current reaching further downwards still. The mouth of the tunnel in which he was wedged was but one dark spot among many, though as far as he could see it was the topmost.

What was happening immediately around him and what he could see and understand of what was happening further out in the cavern made it quite easy for him to understand what was happening in this part of the iceberg as a whole. The cavern had begun to form because the honeycomb of tunnels crossed here and one at least opened out to the sea far below. In the flow of water – meltwater, sea water – a small gyrating current had been set up. Richard knew that until the hook had been blown off the cliffs fifty metres or so behind his back, the iceberg had moved around in circles, so perhaps the swirling current had been born of that movement. Or it might have begun to swirl because the iceberg had stopped doing so. Either way, he had no doubt that the force of the internal streams producing the whirlpool current would have been increased by the faster melting and the greater pressures caused by driving Manhattan at ten knots through the Gulf Stream.

The chamber had been shaped and filled by the whirlpool of water, fed by the streams endlessly spewing inwards from countless tunnels opening in its walls like the one he was standing in, and pouring out at its base, no doubt, the detritus which eventually fell down the quicksilver swirl of water at its heart. The outpouring below would intensify the suction above so that the tunnel rivers could never fill the place, no matter how fast they flowed, or satisfy the whirling suction of the gyre.

Bob was finning as hard as he could into the force of it and was just about holding his own. From Richard's point of view he was soaring away across the current in bird-like flight, falling back slightly as though riding down a strong wind, but remaining more or less level with the tunnel mouth. But the wind was not a clear wind. Like an autumn gale, it was full of bits and pieces, hard and soft, with and without life. Bob's torch showed the unexpected thickness of the detritus here. Much of it, blessedly, was weed. Unnerving sheets and streamers of brown; clumps of the stuff, torn loose to swim like huge brown octopi and giant men o' war. In amongst the slow, sinister reaching of the ten-metre arms of the weed were dazzling dartings of tiny shrimp and fish which caught the white torchlight and gleamed like falling stars. Shoals of them darted, riding the dark force of the current with agile ease. And where the small, bright-sided sparks of life darted, larger fish hunted singly and in shoals of their own. Mackerel with flanks like oil on water, thick-finned hake, steely-sided cod. As insidiously as the trembling rumble of forces ill contained, of air bursting out and water gushing in, the iceberg had been unexpectedly filled with life down here as well as outside in the brightness and the air.

Suddenly, abruptly enough to make him shout with fright, the ragged wreckage of a dead seal tumbled past, trailing a bright cloud of shrimp.

'Richard? RICHARD?' Colin, distantly, and Bob, calling his name together.

'It's all right. Dead seal gave me a bit of a fright. That's all.'

'See anything, Bob?' asked Colin.

'Nothing of any use. I was hoping I'd be able to make out the beam of her torch but I'll be damned if I can. How much time has she got left?'

'Depends on how deep she is.'

'Yeah. I guess it does at that. OK, Richard, cut me some slack. I'm going on down.'

Richard watched the angle of his friend's body change and he suddenly swooped down, the extra speed of the dive pulling him forward through the current for a while. Soon his body became difficult to distinguish against the dark, and only the bright blade of light remained clear. Even his voice began to break up so that Richard only caught snatches of commentary.

'Hell . . . all sorts of rubbish . . . here . . . wood too . . . packing cases I guess . . . flotsam . . . wreckage . . . not so many fish down . . . colder too . . . noisy. Can you hear? Hell of a . . . See the bottom now . . . more of a narrow . . . say again, narrow crack . . . wide funnel sides . . . narrow crack . . . ridges down the funnel . . . all sorts of shit . . . HEY! I SEE HER LIGHT! I SAY AGAIN I SEE HER LIGHT . . .'

Only the certainty that he could see Katya's light would have made Bob risk going down further. He had kept up a constant report to Richard and Colin as much to ease the tension he was feeling as to keep them informed and even then he wasn't certain they had heard him; certainly, he had heard no replies. The current was getting very strong here and he would have to be careful not to get sucked into it. As he had been explaining to Richard, it looked as though the chamber bottomed out here at the back, off axis. Immediately below was a wide funnel with shallow, ridged sides on which was piled all sorts of junk which must have drifted down over the years, but it looked to him as though the actual current exited the chamber through a long, narrow crack in what he reckoned must now be the west-facing quadrant of the lower wall. The wide-throated funnel in the floor was below the bottom of the gyre, there-fore, and caught anything drifting down out of its clutches into the bottom ten metres of relatively still water. And it was here that the light of Katya's torch tempted him to brave the fierce suction towards that long, tall, ice-fanged, deadly looking crack and head for the ten metres of still water below it.

In fact, as he found out immediately on arrival, the water wasn't as still as he had calculated. Even down here, there was an appreciable drift towards the roaring suction of the crack, but he was able to hold himself still enough to follow the beam on down. Because the beam was shining directly up at him, he was dazzled by it and could not see what lay behind it at all. He simply prayed that it would be Katya, lying stunned but otherwise uninjured on the icy hollow of the floor. And, as he came closer, it seemed that he might well be right; he could see a shape in the strange shadows made by the ever so faintly glimmering ice ledges. 'It's OK, Katya,' he crooned, 'I'm here to get you. It's OK . . .' He reached down and grabbed the light, moving it with ever such gentle hands.

'JESUS CHRIST!' he shouted.

Bob's bellow of shocked surprise jerked Richard out of a reverie induced by the hypnotic effect of the whirling, dancing life in front of him and by the drone of Bob's monologue, which had had the further effect of stopping

Colin Ross from breaking in for updates and reports. And it could not have broken the spell at a more opportune moment for as he leaped into shocked wakefulness, the entwined bodies of the unconscious Katya and her dead partner drifted past, having just completed their first circuit of the hellish ballroom this place had become.

At first Richard simply could not believe what he was seeing. Their entwined bodies, bound at the waist by the bright serpent of Katya's lifeline, slowly swirled towards him out of the shadows and into the beam of his torch with all the balletic grace of a spacecraft in orbit or a tiny planet spinning round a dark star.

He supposed Bob must have called him on purpose to warn him. But no, surely Bob was too far down to see what was going on up here. He would be looking up through more than a hundred metres of thick, whirling black water at what? At four feet dancing on air! Such was Richard's stunned confusion that he almost let the nightmare vision sweep by.

As the Soviet sleeping beauty floated past in the arms of her dead beast in United Nations fatigues, Richard launched himself forward, dangerously stretching his own lifeline to the limit and provoking a roar of protest from Colin. The loops of Bob's lifeline that Richard had been holding tumbled into the cavern as he closed his fists like steel grips round the cut end of Katya's lifeline.

The reciprocal tug of the contracting line was augmented by a sharp tug from his team. He performed a half-flip back into the tunnel entrance like a miraculous high diver returning to the board. The jerk of Katya's line brought him up short with a shock which nearly dislocated his shoulders but he was ready for that now, having shrugged off the last dangerous dreaminess under the old familiar imperative of urgent action. His fists did not relent, nor did his wrenched wrists, his torn elbows or shocked shoulders. He had no idea he had shouted in pain until Colin bellowed 'RICHARD! What is going on? First Bob, now you!'

He did not reply – and he noted that Bob was saying nothing more for the moment either. Instead he concentrated all his massive strength on holding onto the bright, braided rope as the forces unleashed by his wild dive transferred themselves to the gently floating, weightless, fairytale couple at the far end of it. Suddenly their dream waltz picked up speed, took on the features of a wild, whirling tango. On axis, like a planet, they spun in the void twice, three times, faster and faster, until Katya was brought up short by her harness, provoking a gasp from Richard that sounded as though he had been punched hard below the belt, and Jock broke free in a whirl of arms and legs to perform a gruesome Highland fling away into the merciful black shadows.

Richard tugged gently, hand over hand, until he held Katya cradled in his arms, as tenderly as though she had been his daughter.

'I've got her, Colin!' His voice throbbed with relief. 'Bob, it's all right. I've got Katya.'

Bob Stark knelt on the bottom, right down in the ice-green, dead cold throat of that wide funnel on the floor of the cavern's hour-glass shape. He held Katya's torch beside his own, both of them shining downwards. Richard's voice distantly began to penetrate the layers of shock which surrounded him like deadly cotton wool. His dark eyes came alive. His wide mouth choked in a breath. Bubbles rose again from the vent beside his head. His heart fluttered painfully and continued to beat, his blood moved in his arteries and he felt the hot surge of it as though it had been stopped for a while. He moved his face a little, shook himself, looked down anew at the body lying supine between his knees, at the white overall clinging in rags to the wreckage of bony limbs, at the grinning, eyeless death's mask face with its Nordic farm girl's wealth of long blonde hair stirring and floating in the current, home to a host of darting fish, and he said, 'Richard, if you've got Katya up there with you, then who in hell's name is this dead broad I've got down here with me?'

Chapter Sixteen

It took them a week to cross the North Atlantic. Seven days and nights of hard sailing and grinding effort as everyone began to put in the sort of hours Sally Bell had observed Richard Mariner working and he worked even harder. The better part of two hundred and fifty people were directly involved here, but it was the senior officers who worked the hardest. They battered out the routines which fitted with the requirements of ship handling, general sailing, weather and ice. The crews followed their orders, did their jobs and took their food and rest. They watched the monster they were towing with a kind of proprietorial awe, but it seemed that only the upper echelons felt the responsibility, the urgency.

Tom Snell recovered quickly and moved his men off the ice – it was getting too wet and dangerous up there for camping any more. As the surface of Manhattan began to weather, so the foundations of the huts began to weaken and there came a distinct worry that they would blow, or simply slide, over the edge one night. The ice was always covered in a skim of runoff, even on the rare days when the constant flow of frontal systems which swung in behind them after that first squall did not bring a good deal of rain to accompany their welcome westerly winds.

Colin and Kate Ross moved off their encampment, last of a series that had been on various locations on the berg for nearly a year, and took up residence in *Titan*, although

Colin was often called to *Psyche* or *Kraken*, especially during the early days when the two ships closest to the ice required constant advice and assurance about everything from dealing with cascades of runoff thundering onto their upper works with the sound of avalanches to the rate at which Manhattan could be expected to rise in the water as it melted – the rate, consequently, at which the unbreakable lines needed to be paid out to stop the ships being picked up out of the water. In the early days, such a horror seemed entirely possible.

After the discoveries in the underground cavern, anything seemed possible.

The cavern was the first of their difficulties. It was obvious that they could not just close the hole in the ice and forget about it. There were at least three bodies in there, though the presence of a second woman was the cause of much speculation, not least that Bob Stark had imagined her. It was equally obvious that none of the divers who had gone down in fact had the experience to deal with the situation. The conditions could be expected to worsen in any case. The iceberg was picking up speed. The currents feeding the whirlpool would only be getting stronger, making it that much more dangerous.

When Yves Maille hove back into view, he was astonished that his lack of simple precautions should have had such repercussions. Truthfully, he told Richard later, he had gone off incommunicado on purpose. He found all the close proximity a little overpowering and longed to be away from the rest, with only the smallest group of men required for safety this far out on the ocean. He shrugged resignedly. He would be more careful in the future. And, in the meantime, if Bob would help, he would guarantee to bring the dead men out of the cave tomorrow. The dead men and Bob's phantom woman.

It was a hard dive in difficult circumstances, but the Frenchman was as good as his word, a fact which went a long way towards rehabilitating him in the eyes of the crew and most especially in the eyes of the soldiers currently berthed aboard *Kraken*. By noon watch, just less than twenty-four hours after the arrival of the two ships, three sopping body bags were resting in *Psyche*'s cold store, awaiting offloading and official post-mortem examination in England as soon as possible.

Not all of Tom Snell's men were on board *Kraken*. Dougie Dundas was still aboard *Psyche*, too ill to move and in imminent danger of joining the three in cold storage below. Asha Higgins, assisted by Kate Ross, toiled unceasingly over the comatose soldier. He was isolated, of course, in case whatever was killing him was contagious, but none of the medical books available to the two women described anything like his symptoms. One particular manifestation of his illness might correspond to one type of disease or other, but the whole pattern fitted nothing they could find out about. The bleeding round his gums might be the old-time sailor's dreaded enemy scurvy; the sores around his mouth, on his tongue, throat and skin did seem like some sort of vitamin deficiency, but he showed no response at all to vitamin doses. And his increasing jaundice didn't fit in, nor did his uncontrollable incontinence or his dramatic weight loss.

Exhaustive tests on various samples proved little more helpful. His blood was increasingly anaemic, but there was no organism there to cause it. His liver and bone marrow seemed to be failing but there was no sign of leukaemia. His vital bodily functions seemed to be closing down inevitably as his major organs failed one after the other. And all for no discernible reason. Pan Medic calls got them no useful advice; and although there were other ships in the area, some with doctors aboard, it proved impossible to get Dougie Dundas off or further help on. So Asha Higgins scratched her head with increasing sad perplexity and slowly tried to come to terms with the fact that she was going to lose this patient.

Time and again, as they surged eastwards with the storm

winds battering along behind them, Tom Snell took the uncomfortable helicopter ride over from *Psyche*'s sister ship to be with his sergeant. Together, Tom and Asha went over and over the events in the ice cave, looking for clues, but there was none to be found. Tom went over it with Richard too as he wrote up the accident in *Titan*'s log, which doubled as Manhattan's log. And Tom wrote his own reports for his superiors in London and beyond. But there was no clue to the dying sergeant's ailment, for there was no way that any of them could even begin to imagine what he had done.

Asha had no X-ray machine, no scan of any kind, in fact, and short of an operation, nothing else was likely to reveal the fact that Dougie Dundas had a highly radioactive rough glass ball wedged in his digestive tract. Only a Geiger counter might have given a clue and, although Kate had brought one off Manhattan with the rest of her scientific equipment, neither of them thought to get it nor to use it on their dying patient.

'Any news of Sergeant Dundas?' asked Richard at the opening of his first full captains' meeting since turning the corner at Flemish Cap four days ago, the second day since the two new ships had joined. Tom shook his head. He looked tired, thought Richard grimly. So did they all – increasingly tired and depressed. They were making good progress. Both John and Yves had positive reports to contribute, he knew, but there was an air of gloom which seemed to be seeping rapidly out of *Psyche* in spite of anything they could do. It was too late to move the dead to another ship now. There was no question of moving poor Dundas at all. But Richard could think of no other answer to the situation. He would talk it over with Peter Walcott in private immediately after this meeting. The Guyanese captain was cheerful and open with a wide, welcoming smile which was always at the ready, but even this could not disguise the increasing wariness in his eyes and the deepening lines of strain around them. They all knew that *Psyche* had acquired a nickname. Everyone called her *Psycho* now, transforming her from a Greek maiden to a mad murderer. It was only half in jest. She was beginning to be viewed as a Brute, a Death Ship.

'Right, then.' Richard called the meeting to order. It was getting cramped in his day room these days, but there was just space for the eight of them round the desk which had been augmented with a table from the dining salon. But the new arrangement still could not accommodate the current chart, so, in preparation for his part of the meeting, John Higgins was securing the big square of blue, white and sand-coloured paper to the wall. As he waited for his friend to finish and join them, Richard looked into the eight other varyingly weary pairs of eyes. Colin Ross's clouded blue gaze was distant, his thoughts, no doubt, still up on the ice. Bob and Katya clearly hadn't got over their adventure deep beneath it yet. Obviously Tom hadn't either. He had only been allowed out of bed this morning. Peter Walcott was clearly worried, but Gendo Odate seemed more relaxed, as did Yves. The Frenchman had been quick to forgive himself for his absence when needed so badly and now even gave Richard the ghost of a wink, eliciting a weary grin in reply.

They were only one-third of the way, Richard thought. They had better get sorted out better than they were or the whole project would turn into a fiasco. A cold dry wind thundered up to gale force from the west. *Titan* shook in the grip of it, the whole of her massive length surged and jerked in an action most unlike anything a supertanker normally performed. The tea cups in front of the assembled men and women chimed, sliding in their saucers, struck by their silver spoons. John sat down at Richard's right. They were ready.

'First let me welcome Captains Walcott and Odate to

the team,' Richard began. 'I do regret that your arrival should have been attended by such tragedy, gentlemen, but I'm certain that now you are in place and running at speed, we can look forward to a very quick crossing indeed. And, on the subject of propulsion, I'll hand over to you, Bob.'

'Placing *Kraken* and *Psyche*, as you say, has made an enormous difference almost at once.' The tall American leant forward, frowning with the intensity of his thoughts. 'It is just under forty-eight hours since they were secured to the ice and already our mean speed has doubled. I know both Yves and John have more to say on the reasons and the situation, but according to my current log, we are proceeding at more than thirteen knots, with every chance of continuing to do so at least until we begin to turn south. Fuel shouldn't be a problem, we're exactly on projected consumption in all ships, even though the engines and motors are having to do more work than we estimated. But it will be conditions further south which will really be testing. This was supposed to be the easy bit.'

'Perhaps it will be,' said Richard quickly. 'We should get a steady run during the next three days which will give us a chance to shake down the routines we'll need to have in place when the going does get tougher. Still, that's a good report. Good news. Thanks, Bob. John. Navigation?'

John got up and crossed to his chart. 'We're here, and doing bloody well, in my submission,' he said bracingly. 'Even as we speak, we're just swinging past twenty degrees west longitude, sliding down off the back of the mid-Atlantic ridge here into the north-east Atlantic Basin at forty-four degrees north latitude. I couldn't do a noon shot in this murk, so these are the satnav's best figures, you understand, but it still looks pretty good. We've come the better part of two thousand and seventy-five kilometres in the last four and a half days, and to have pulled ourselves south of Bordeaux is particularly good. We'll be down level with Corunna later tonight. Bang on track.' He met Richard's eyes and gave a tight grin.

Richard returned an infinitesimal nod. How absolutely he could rely on his 'Little John'. For once, John had given a less than clinical navigation report, pulling in references to locations in France and Spain calculatedly, hoping to lighten the atmosphere by bringing Europe, and the next section of the voyage, closer.

'Yves?'

The Frenchman availed himself of John's chart. 'As you know, I fly ahead in the helicopters and take readings of sea and sky. I also take the inflatables if I need to examine the state of the sea more closely.' He paused, but not even Tom rose to the challenge. Yves took it as confirmation that the others had forgiven his absence as readily as he had forgiven himself, and he proceeded. 'My readings show that we are in the following situation, which I must say is extremely fortunate. As we come down off the mid-Atlantic ridge here, so we are crossing a whirl of cold Arctic water. As you may know, as the Gulf Stream ages, so the straight line of the water's flow breaks off into whirls, like enormous whirlpools. Warm water pools run westwards to the north of the main flow, up here towards Cape Farewell. Cold water pools run eastward and southward, here, towards Biscay. And the current which currently carries us east and south is a large one of these. We came into it, by my calculation, yesterday, and I may say that even as I was diving in the chamber beside *Psyche*, I registered a sudden drop in water temperature. I mentioned this to Bob who was with me, did I not?'

Bob nodded. 'It suddenly went very cold in there,' he confirmed.

'The mean temperature of the water of the Gulf Stream is twenty-five degrees Celsius,' continued the professor eagerly. 'The mean ocean surface temperature for this section of the ocean at this time of the year is sixteen degrees, but the temperature in the pool which we are crossing is three degrees. I believe we can expect that all serious melting below the waterline will now slow, perhaps even stop.'

'For how long?' asked Richard.

'When the weather clears, I will take the helicopter and fly on ahead. Such features can be many hundreds of metres in diameter. Thousands of metres, even. But there is no way of knowing how large this one is until I look ahead. I cannot be certain, but the way we are riding and the speed at which we are moving leads me to believe that we are going round the outer edge of it, at the south, along the strongest part of the flow. As we proceed, we will have to watch for a northward pressure of the current. But by then it may not be so strong, and the wind and the geostrophic force – the Coriolis force – will still be pushing us south. The wind is also colder than the mean air temperature for this time of year. We should be expecting mean temperatures of ten degrees. If you go outside, you will find that it is four degrees. But tomorrow, this depression will have passed, the sky will have cleared and the air will be warmer. More than this I cannot tell you at the moment.'

Colin Ross rose without Richard's bidding. 'A slowing in melt rate below the waterline fits in with what I have to report,' he said, his voice a low rumble carrying effortlessly over the raving of the wind outside. 'Since we turned east at Flemish Cap, the mean melt rate above and below the water has risen from negligible amounts to a much more serious one point five per cent per day. I had expected to warn this meeting that we were faced with a two per cent daily loss, rising further, but, as Professor Maille has observed, things have slowed down again. This is very good, because otherwise our friends aboard *Psyche* and *Kraken* would have to keep a very close eye on their lines indeed. The iceberg has lifted by little more than two and a half metres since we came east. When it gets hotter and the melt rate increases, I will be projecting lift rates of anything up to five metres a day, which will mean much careful slackening of lines, much less efficient towing regimes and a much increased danger that the whole thing will roll right over.

'But that is looking well into the future. As I said, the mean melt and lift rates have slowed dramatically over the last twenty-four hours. Which is very good news indeed.'

'Thank you, Colin. Any questions?'

There were none.

'Right. Let me sum up, then. We are in optimum position, travelling faster than anticipated, but using exactly the predicted amount of fuel. Projections of the continuation of this situation seem excellent and, in the short term at any rate, the situation will only get better.'

'I think that says it all,' said John. He looked at his watch. 'Time for Pour Out. Can I buy anyone a drink?'

Richard could not make an opportunity to talk to Peter Walcott over drinks or dinner, so he accompanied the quiet Guyanese back to his command that evening.

'As soon as we get within anything like helicopter range of England, I'll have them off.' Richard looked up at the captain's anxious face, and for the first time saw how worried he really was. 'That will be in two days,' he promised. 'Three at the most.'

Peter Walcott nodded, but he didn't look much happier. 'I'm worried she's getting a reputation,' he said. 'I've been worrying since I first came aboard. There's little things, you know? I'm not a superstitious man, but she's not a happy ship. Did you ever sail her when she worked for Heritage Mariner?'

'No. But I'm sure she never had a reputation then.'

'Well, I guess you'd be the man to know. But she's working hard at getting one now. Perhaps she didn't like being mothballed. Went sour off Piraeus.'

'I thought you said you weren't superstitious, Peter.'

'Yeah. Maybe I'm just tired, is all.'

'Well, is there anything else you think I can do for you? To ease the situation?'

Peter leant back against the outer wall of his day room. Behind his left shoulder, his window glimmered spectrally as the ice visible through it took and multiplied what little light there was. Wind thundered over the bridgehouse, its bluster hardly dimmed by the thick metal walls and heavy glass that cocooned them. A respectful tapping came at the door and a steward entered to close the curtains.

'I'm going to do my final round,' said *Psyche*'s captain without answering Richard's question.

'I'll come with you, if I may,' said Richard. 'I'd like a look over her again.'

'I thought you'd never sailed her.'

'I haven't. John Higgins has. I've visited him aboard.'

'You two go back a long way, huh?'

The two men crossed to the door and exited side by side. Richard chatted as they crossed to the lift and waited for the car.

'Yes. I first met him more than fifteen years ago on a ship called *Prometheus*. I was running a firm called Crewfinders at the time. We were employed to replace a crew decimated by an industrial accident. John was on my firm's books as a second mate. I hadn't met him but his references were good so I sent him out then I went out myself as master. We had an eventful voyage during which I met my wife Robin, quite apart from anything else. We stayed friends.'

The lift came. They got in.

'And he joined you when you took over the Heritage Mariner fleet?'

'That's right. I'd known Bill Heritage, my father-in-law, for many years. When I transferred into the Heritage organisation, John came with me. Now that it's Heritage Mariner, he's our senior captain. He's sailed everything from supertankers to tramp steamers. He met Asha when she nursed him after he'd been wounded by terrorists in the Gulf. They honeymooned on a cargo vessel refused permission to dock anywhere because the atomic waste aboard was so dangerous.'

'The leper ship *Napoli*. Yes, I read Ann Cable's account of that. You were on board too, I understand.'

'Briefly.'

The lift doors hissed open and the two of them stepped out onto the bridge. From here it was possible to see just how snugly berthed against Manhattan *Psyche* really was. Although there was no moisture in the wind at all, it blew a steady stream of runoff across the clearview and down the shadowed deck. It was almost as though the great super-tanker was moored beneath a waterfall. The noise was intrusive, if not overpowering. 'It's been improving all day,' said Peter, gesturing at the falling water. 'But I don't think it'll ever stop. At least it's fresh.'

He introduced Richard to his third officer, who was holding the watch, and checked the instruments, the charts and the logs. Then the two captains went out onto the starboard bridge wing where it was blustery and cold, but dry. 'I've started to do a full inspection at weather deck level,' confided Peter. 'Bridge and line watches before I retire. It seems to be the most sensible way of going about things.'

'It's what I do,' Richard told him. 'But I don't have to go all the way up to the forecastle head.'

'The forecastle head watch changes every hour at night. We found on the first night that it was a bit too much for the men out there during a full four-hour watch, and things have got worse since then, of course.'

'Do you go there first, or do you go to the poop-deck line watch first?'

'Capstans first, then windlass. I find I have to build up to the forecastle head, somehow.'

'Right then.' Richard gathered his cold-weather gear

more snugly about his massive frame. 'After you.'

They went down the external companionways sternwards to the first deck which stood at the base of the great funnel, side by side across it, deep in conversation, then down and aft again, five decks in all, finally coming down a central stair onto the poop behind the massive bridgehouse. All through their shadowy journey, they had seen no one; all the curtains were drawn except on the bridge, and they did not even see a light. But it was not dark. The clear skies promised by Yves had arrived, though the wind showed little sign of abating. The stars were out and the moon was glimmering promisingly on the distant, southern horizon.

The capstan line watch had rigged a shelter, half tent and half hut, open to one side to let the line ride out and up onto the white shoulder of the ice. The shelter was designed to keep the worst of the runoff away, but because the open side was, perforce, nearest to the iceberg, this was only partially successful and the three men of the watch sat huddled in unhappy silence while a fine spray drifted unceasingly in upon them. They said nothing to each other and only answered their captain's questions in sulky mono-syllables when he addressed them directly. Whether they were naturally taciturn or moodily mutinous, Richard had no way of knowing; the duty offered little in the way of opportunities for conversation in any case. The meltwater fell, the ice grumbled distantly; the wind blustered, some-times with enough force to make the rope hum and the capstan groan; the ship's massive motor rumbled like the onset of an earthquake, setting the deck to throbbing and the deck furniture to jingling and tinkling; the surf arrived at the reef astern with a piercing sibilance and an arhyth-mic lack of pattern, and thundered beneath *Psyche*'s coun-ter like a tidal wave, where the monotonous thudding of the propeller blades battered it to death.

'Where did you get your crew from?' asked Richard as

they began to walk down the length of the weather deck, side by side.

'From Piraeus. But of course they arrived in Greece from all over the world. Most of the stewards are Hong Kong Chinese who are particularly concerned that we are giving ship room to a white-haired ghost. The GP seamen mostly come from Pakistan and they would prefer, I think, that water claim the bodies of the deceased as is common practice in India. But amongst them there is a contingent from Haiti, of all places, so we have some *voudon* aboard as well. The officers are the usual mixed bunch. I haven't sailed with any of them before.'

'You must find it a bit lonely.' The wind battered around them, whirling past the port side of the bridgehouse. In the distance there was a howling sound which wavered and died away.

'Sometimes. A little. I have no family of my own. You haven't brought your wife along? I hear she's got her captain's papers too. Didn't she fancy a cruise?' The ice groaned as though weary of life. They glanced up involuntarily, looking across the tall, blind front of the bridgehouse.

'No. She's at home with the twins. She had enough of this berg when she pulled her ship up on the ice to fix its propeller earlier in the year. Especially as she lost a good few people doing it. At least one of them is still up there somewhere.'

Peter Walcott glanced up at the sheer cliffs. 'She must have had powerful winches.'

Richard gave a bark of laughter. 'No,' he said. 'There was a shallow bay. It came out in a kind of hook. Near perfect dry dock. She did brilliantly to make use of it as she did, though. I don't think I would have coped half as well. Anyway, we had to blow it all off to make Manhattan ship-shaped. We'd never have been able to control it as it was shaped originally. That was when we knew we were in

business, really, when we got it drifting in a straight line.'
The wind thundered up against the ice cliffs and the waterfall was snatched upwards suddenly and hurled like a great
handful of stars up into the blue velvet sky.

'Then it was just a case of controlling the course and
speed of the drift. I see that, yes.'

'A kind of intellectual game given form and urgency by
circumstances. A problem of practical seamanship put into
practice because Colin sold it to the United Nations as a
viable way of combating a drought and averting a civil war.
There was no other way a project like this was ever going to
get off the ground really. The cost is so enormous that it
could only seem worthwhile to an organisation confronted
with the prospect of sorting out another Somalia, another
Bosnia, another Congo. The political implications must be
enormous even outside Africa, too. Consider the amount
of ice-cold water we're putting into the North Atlantic
Drift even now. What effect will that have when it hits the
coast of Ireland? Only the UN could have got the Irish
government to take the risk of agreeing or we'd have farmers from all over the place suing.'

'Do you think it will have as destructive an effect as all
that?' Peter glanced across at Richard, and found his tall
companion's shape silhouetted against the first white ray of
the rising moon.

'Who knows? It's possible that there could be enough
meltwater there to affect conditions briefly, yes. Whether it
will do so, heaven alone knows. But, looking at the other
side of the coin, only the UN could have got so much
positive input from all over the world. Look at the range
of nationalities involved already. Even the Russians, and
they've got troubles enough of their own, God knows.'

'Well,' Peter said cynically, 'they've got a lot to play for in
Moscow, haven't they? They want the West's help still,
economically and socially, and that means politically. Of
course they're going to be falling over themselves to help

with something as high-profile as this. They've had their fingers in this particular African pie for a long time and it won't do them any harm to be seen either by the Americans or the Africans to be helping now. This way they get the kudos of supporting a great humanitarian endeavour without having to pay out too much. And if Mau is pulled out of the mire, you can bet the Russians will be in there bidding for business. Of course, if it isn't pulled out of the mire then you just know their armaments men have already been in there bidding for business. Not just in Mau; Angola, Zaire, Congo, Guinea, Congo Libre, all of the local areas. They may not be selling Marxism any more, but they've got a lot of military hardware and the expertise to back it up. Hardware they don't need now, foreign currency they do need. You know that, and even if Moscow wouldn't sanction it, what about the republics? They say there's even nuclear stuff up for grabs. A Ukrainian nuclear physicist gets paid about the same as a part-time janitor in the West; a full general earns less than the seamen down the deck, for God's sake. And they've just been hit by capitalism in all its glory. Market forces for all.' He swung round suddenly to face Richard, his expression creased with concern, his features etched by dead white moonlight reflecting off his glossy black skin. 'For less than it cost to fit out this ship we could probably have bought a regiment of tanks equipped with battlefield nuclear arms. Or a nuclear power station with all the staff to run it.'

'Chernobyl, perhaps,' Richard temporised. In the near distance there was the sort of scream, long and unending, that had echoed over the freezing ocean for hours after *Titanic* had sunk. Richard's scalp prickled. Peter continued to speak passionately, as though he had heard nothing of the dreadful sound.

'Well, maybe. Or Tomsk Seven. They're probably all that's stopping all sorts of people falling over themselves to buy it all in.'

They walked on in silence for a moment. The screaming died away. The wind shouted in the Sampson posts suddenly and Peter exploded again.

'And finally, if we pull this off, establish that there is a market, then think about it: in the northern hemisphere, the greatest number of naturally occurring icebergs is in the Davis Strait, but the greatest concentration of ice is in the Arctic Ocean and who has the longest Arctic shoreline? Who could just sail up there and start blowing chunks of the stuff off and shipping it out through the Norwegian Sea or the Bering Strait? No, apart from the United Nations, I'd say the Russians probably have the most to play for.'

As they talked, they had been walking up the four hundred metres of *Psyche*'s length and apparently into a different, more sinister, world. The ice was no closer to the ship here than it had been at the stern, but it seemed to be so. All the comforting presence of nearby humanity which had cast its protective mantle over the little poop was missing here. Even the throb and shudder of the motor was a distant indiscernible thing. There was no hiss or thunder of surf. There was the ice, and it cast a terrible, terrifying spell.

The four men on the watch had not bothered to build a shelter. They huddled away on the starboard rail of the forecastle head, close enough to see the winch, which they had illuminated with a stand of electric lanterns, but as far away as they could reasonably get from the ice. The wind thundered down the deck and swirled the constant waterfall away forward, but the friction this caused with the cliffs sucked the water inwards as well, as though Manhattan wished to reclaim what it had lost. The battering of the wind along the open deck, its hollow whimpering and hissing among the long sheaves of pipes and around the deck furniture came to its natural conclusion in the wavering, unremitting howl it made as it played against the straining black rope. Across the long, taut line it sobbed and screamed with the voice of a creature in unnamable torment. It was the voice, said the crew, of the woman with the long white hair, calling them from below.

But the ice made noises of its own. The open mouth of the cavern which had gulped down the soldiers gibbered and chuckled with the kind of lunatic intensity that the dangerously insane in horror films use. Behind and below the chilling sound, the ice rumbled, thundered and roared. It spat, hissed and cracked. There was never any pattern to the sound, nothing that the imagination could comprehend and deal with. The rumbling of air movement within the caverns of the ice seemed independent of the blowing of the wind. And indeed maybe it was, here, Richard thought. But who knew what winds were stirring fifty kilometres behind them, pushing their own dark forces through the ice, preparing to explode out of the cliffs in avalanches when least expected. Who knew what black currents from the icy depths where night-time was perpetual nine hundred metres below were being forced at incalculable speeds through the narrow honeycombs of tunnels into whirlpools, lakes or oceans entombed? Was it the manic gibber of the water which was to be most feared, or the sibilant, almost silent, surging hiss of great force fighting to break free into the thunderous glory of destruction? What was the sound they were to listen for particularly, the most dangerous sound of all? He had better check with Colin, who had warned him of the danger. He had better check with Colin soon, though he doubted that even the great knowledge locked in the glaciologist's astounding memory would supply exactly the sound that an iceberg could be expected to make in the instant before it reared out of the water and toppled over like a white whale breaching. A white whale weighing more than a billion tonnes.

As Peter Walcott talked to the quiet group, Richard

found himself lured across the broad green deck by the mesmeric power of the ice. He could never go so close on *Titan*, had never stood so solidly under the spell of it. He was a sensitive, imaginative man. He was fascinated, not only by the aura of naked danger which the iceberg seemed to emanate, but by his own atavistic, visceral reaction to it. Both Robin and their friend Ann Cable had been up on the ice. Ann had been lost up there, alone with a murderous terrorist and lucky to survive. It was this man, the deadly Henri LeFever who was still up there, somewhere, frozen into the ice. Ann and Robin had both described to Richard at length and in detail how the ice had affected them, and yet he had never imagined that it could actually be so powerful, so sinister, so overwhelming.

He was still standing there, lost in thought, when the relief watch arrived and Peter came over to touch him on the shoulder. 'The relief line watch brought a message,' he said. 'Dr Higgins would like to see us. I don't think it's good news.'

Dougie Dundas stared wide-eyed at the ceiling but he would never see it again. Between his cracked and darkened lips, the point of his tongue protruded far enough to show that it was swollen with cherry-dark sores. The skin on his yellow, black-jowled face was sickly yellow except that the bridge of his nose, cheekbone and forehead on the right side were more darkly discoloured. His chest was uncovered, and the light, antiseptic bandage did little to hide the open sores and blisters on his chest. His hands had been folded but the bandages had leaked a little so that fluid from the splits in the skin on his fingers formed a pool at the base of his still breastbone. He had lost weight in the days of his illness and, slim to begin with, now looked skeletal.

'Still no idea?' asked Richard.

'No idea at all,' admitted Asha wearily. 'But whatever it was, he never stood a chance.'

'He'd a wife and child in Glasgow,' said Tom Snell quietly. 'They're his next of kin. There's no record about parents.'

The four of them stood in silence, looking through the glass wall section into the clinical brightness of the isolation room. 'What are we going to do now?' asked Peter. 'We can't just leave him there, can we?'

'No,' said Asha. 'He'll have to be bagged up and go down into cold storage with the other three.'

'I'll look for some volunteers . . .' Peter's doubtful tone said it all. He could look. He wouldn't find any.

'No,' said Tom quietly. 'If you bag him, Asha, I'll move him.'

'I'll help,' said Richard. 'It'll take two to do it properly, even if we wheel him down on a stretcher. Asha, will the bag be germ proof?'

'Yes. Wait here. I won't be long.' She opened a door leading into the vestibule of the isolation room, climbed into her protective clothing, pulled on a new pair of gloves and a mask and went in.

'It's incredible,' said Richard quietly. 'I've never seen anything like it. What on earth could it be?'

The other two shook their heads in sad incomprehension, then they turned away until Asha had completed the task of washing the corpse in disinfectant and placing it expertly in a bag of yellow plastic which was so thick as to be almost opaque. She wheeled the corpse into the little vestibule and closed the door into the isolation room. She pulled off her protective clothing, binned it and opened the door.

'That's it,' she said. 'The best I can do. I really can't think of an organism which could break out of the regime we've had in place over the last few days. And, in any case, no one else has shown any symptoms. Unless exhaustion is a symptom,' she added. 'Plenty of people are exhibiting that one.'

'When Tom and I have put Sergeant Dundas safely

away,' said Richard gently, 'we'll give you a lift back to *Niobe* and John. You'll feel better after a good night's sleep.'

Aṣha gave him a grin of thanks, but shook her head. 'No, thanks, Richard love. I'd better kip down here. I have to run checks on the rest of *Psyche*'s crew for the next few days in case anyone shows symptoms like poor Dougie's there. If we do have any kind of infection spread, then I'll want to know at the earliest moment. And I'll have to keep monitoring you, Tom. It might conceivably have been something in the ice cave itself, some organism, infection . . . The ice is, what, twenty thousand years old. There could be anything in there. I know it sounds fanciful, but face it: four men went in there together and you're the only one left alive.'

Nobody spoke during the ride down with the late Dougie Dundas. Asha seemed to have come to the end of her tether; she looked at the floor as she followed the two quiet men wheeling the stretcher along the corridors from the medical rooms to the cold storage which was a clinically isolated section of the galley's main cold storage facility. They positioned the trolley carefully between the tables which now carried more yellow plastic body bags than even the most accident-prone voyage usually supplied.

Dougie slid off the trolley with a weary sigh, as though the plastic wrapping was speaking for him. With Richard at his head and Tom at his feet, the sergeant, his body as light as that of a child, settled onto the table top beside the body of the mysterious blonde woman who was only marginally more skeletal than himself. They placed him tenderly, reverently in place, but even so, as though still wanting the last word even now, Dougie settled further after they had laid him down. Romantic to the last, he shifted slightly towards the supine woman he shared the table with and seemed in this slightest of movements to nudge her. The yellow plastic which had been wrapped round her parted, showing rough edges where it had been half cut, half sawn open. Out of the wound, her white hair tumbled, matted, thick and stinking. It had weight enough to jerk her head round after it and, from her neck, something clattered onto the floor.

Richard, who was nearest, automatically bent and picked it up, holding it up to the light, wondering in shocked surprise how the corpse of a woman discovered on an iceberg at the top of the world could be wearing an ornament which seemed to be made of ebony wood and feathers.

But then Tom Snell was standing by his side speaking in a low, tense monotone. 'We'd better warn Captain Walcott to tighten up security in here. We don't want any more of that superstitious filth. And I don't want it coming anywhere near my men.'

He snatched it out of Richard's fingers and showed it to Asha, explaining in a voice shaking with rage, 'Just look at this, would you? It's a juju charm. Some kind of magic against the dead!' He swung round to face the stunned pair still standing, looking as though they didn't understand a word that he was saying. 'Juju!' he repeated fiercely, crushing the black trinket in his massive fist. 'Voodoo! Black magic! Christ! You'd think we were in the middle of the fucking jungle already!'

Chapter Seventeen

The sight of the tank, coming on top of all the other sights to which she had been subject that day, should have finished Ann Cable but it did not. She should have fainted dead away on the spot as she had already done earlier. She should have run away screaming, as she had been so close to doing at the very moment when she saw it, but she did not. The new crisis, in spite of introducing an air of unreality into the situation, sobered her up like a slap in the face is said to do with an hysteric. There was no doubt that the tank was real, though. No doubt of that at all. It sat there, squatting silently as the sound of the last falling tree echoed across the wide dry river bed of the Blood until it whispered away into the forest shadows of Congo Libre on the far bank. Its grey sides glittered all too solidly in the gleam of the jungle moon. A scent of hot metal seemed to come from it, of oil and cordite and burning, though these may have been the smells from the burned out wreckage of Harry Parkinson's askari truck. What came from it most clearly, unmistakably, was the sharp mechanical whine as the turrent swung round to bring the gun to bear on them.

The sound, carrying clear and sinister on the still African air, galvanised them all into action at once. Three people with but one mind, they ran for the Land Rover and leaped into its stuffy interior. Harry released the break, hit the motor and, because they were facing the dry river bed, drove straight down into it at breakneck speed. The bank fell away steeply, but the wreckage of the askaris' burned out truck had carved a slope for them; they got down because of that and also by the grace of God. They made so much noise and kicked up so much dust that it took Ann a moment to realise when she looked back that the tank had fired a round to land exactly where they had been standing when they first saw it. 'Quick!' she screamed. 'They've opened fire!'

Harry wrestled the bucking vehicle round in as tight an arc as it would manage and they thundered off up the dry river bed, bounding from parched rut to smooth river boulder in a storm of protesting tyres and complaining suspension. Something solid battered its way along the vehicle's underside and Robert yelled, 'Watch your axles!'

The second shell erupted in the dry mud exactly behind them. Harry swung the screaming vehicle into the first river bend and out of the tank's direct line of sight. 'They'll come after us,' yelled Ann. 'They have to!' She scrabbled in the rubbish on the back seat for her camera. She was a reporter. She would die reporting this.

'Either that or they have friends they can send!' yelled Robert. 'Harry, can you get this thing up out of here?'

'Half a mile,' yelled Harry. 'There's another old elephant track. Tight squeeze. Too narrow for tanks.'

The river bed immediately on their left exploded into a column of earth. The force made the Land Rover leap sideways. A burning wind ripped the canvas with the ease of a leopard's claws and threw Ann across the back seat. Robert's window cracked and struggled to come in – only the fact that it was half open saved him. The force whirled by him and the windscreen trembled.

'Lobbed it over on spec., canny buggers,' yelled Harry impenetrably. 'Look back behind us, would you, love? They hit my rearview with that if nothing else.

Ann pulled herself breathlessly round in her seat, held on tight with one hand only, tried to put the smell of burned hair out of her mind, squinted through the view-finder of the camera and concentrated on the deceptively peaceful scene behind.

The wide bed of the river lay clear and quiet under the full, low moon with the forest standing in Stygian clouds on either side, like smoke that had rolled into place on either bank and then, magically, stopped. There was a distant promise of flat veldt with steep-sided hillocks in the V behind the overlap of forested banks in the distance, and above the shimmering hillocks shone extravagant pearl-bright stars.

The tank swung into view, sitting like a steel toad in the middle of the river bed, grinding forwards along their tracks. She pressed the button, praying that there was light enough. It clicked and whirred twice before she spoke.

'Here it comes!' she yelled. Harry swung the wheel hard left.

'What I would like to do . . .' he bellowed at the top of his voice. The wheels hit a log about the same size as an adult crocodile and the Land Rover's bonnet slammed up into the air and down again. Harry wrestled with the steering until the shoulder seam of his bush jacket split open with the strain. 'What I would like to do is lead this bugger up to the bank that's holding the lake in place. Trick him into putting a shell through that!'

The log the size of a crocodile, still dancing from their passage, vanished in another column of black power. This one had a bright yellow and white heart, though. And, for the first time, a voice. A flat bellow which drowned out the click and whir of the camera photographing it.

'The lake'd come down here like a tidal wave and drown the buggers if I could do that!'

Harry had the wheel on hard right lock now and the Land Rover was screaming at full speed for the precipitous black bank.

'Could you do that?' yelled Ann hopefully.

'Not in a thousand years. Pure bloody fantasy, I'm afraid.'

The barrel of the tank's gun was pointing directly at them; then, as it was obvious they would have to sheer away from the high bank side, it swung one degree to the left. Ann framed it and pushed the button, holding it down as the shutter clicked and the motor whirred. A puff of smoke belched out of it, glowing with a greenish luminescence which was actually very pretty indeed. 'Incoming!' yelled Ann, and wondered inconsequentially where she had heard the word used like that. She pulled her eye away from the camera and looked back over her shoulder between the men in the front.

The black bank parted in front of them and the Land Rover's square bonnet lifted again – lifted and kept on lifting. Ann hadn't thought the engine could make any more noise but suddenly Harry was kicking at the pedals and shifting the gears. The huge motor screamed and howled. Ann was thrown backwards by the vehicle's wild movement up the sheer slope and then forwards by the explosion of the bank almost beneath their left rear wheel. She bashed herself in the face with the camera. Dust and chunks of earth roared past, collected the canvas roofing and tore it away like tissue. She found herself suddenly looking up at open sky where there had been dusty cloth an instant earlier. There was a strange tearing sensation at her breast. She registered it without any understanding of what it might mean. Then she was jolted back down onto the seat to discover that the metal backrest was twisted and hot. The air smelt of burning leather and the seat was covered in clods of dried mud which burned her through her jeans. She rocked forwards and the tearing sensation returned. Her whole chest moved strangely and for a terrifying instant she thought she must have been wounded after all. But then the Rover jolted again and her breasts bounced and she realised she had only burst the catches on her sport bra and broken her straps.

It was just dawning on her how lucky she had been when the tank's turret slammed into view again, gun pointing directly up the short, narrow track towards them. She framed it and hit the button, screaming a warning as she did so.

'HARRY!' It was all she could think of to say, but it was enough. He swung the wheel to the right and crashed into the thorn scrub. With tough-branched bushes and saplings screaming and clawing along the sides and bottom of the vehicle like an army of wildcats being crushed beneath its wheels, the battered old Rover forged its own track through the forest while the tank's last shell set fire to the dry trees behind them.

'That's sorted him,' Harry yelled as they burst out onto the old elephant track they had followed earlier. With the engine still racing wildly, Harry turned the Rover towards the ruined village with its slaughtered inhabitants. 'He'll never get back round now. We're OK for the moment.'

He rearranged the gears and the Land Rover settled into her accustomed steady rumble, chewing up the trackway at the fastest possible speed. Harry hit the lights. Tree trunks appeared dazzlingly, like the legs of tall elephants standing still among the scrub.

'Is that a good idea?' asked Robert. 'That T–80 may have friends.'

'Will certainly have friends. There were no tank tracks around the village. There's some kind of guerrilla squad out here somewhere and I reckon the tank is backing them up.'

'Where did it come from?' asked Ann, who was just beginning to shake with shock again.

'Congo Libre,' said both the men at once. Then Harry continued, 'Has to be. No tank tracks this side of the river that I've seen.'

'But why?' Ann asked, and for the first time her question

included the village as well as everything else. 'Why is all this horror going on?'

'It's a message,' said Harry. 'They want to drive the people off the land.'

'But *why*?'

Robert turned round. 'You know why,' he said. 'You're just not thinking clearly. They want the population on the move. The N'Kuru people starving and drought-stricken, moving down to the coast looking for help. But all they'll find there is Kyoga roadblocks run by Nimrod Chala's state police and Moses M'Diid's tank regiments. The N'Kuru will explode. It'll be civil war.'

'But what will they fight with?' cried Ann. 'They haven't any weapons!'

'With sticks and stones,' said Robert wearily, 'until the Lions arrive. Where do you think all the men from the villages were? They're in Congo Libre being trained to fight the Kyoga, being armed with Kalashnikovs and the odd T–64 tank, I'd guess. They'll come in and the real slaughter will begin. It'll be just another local African war unless the UN gets fully involved – and why should they? If they try now and it doesn't work, why shouldn't they just wash their hands and walk away? Then Mau will be just another bloody Senegal, another Angola, another Sudan, Rwanda or Somalia, except the war won't last nearly as long. After a while the Congo Libre troops will come in and clean up with their brand new T–80 main battle tanks and their battle-hardened troops who specialise in putting six bullets into women and children before they hit the ground.'

'But if you know all this why aren't you putting a stop to it?' she screamed.

'What do you think I'm doing here?'

'No! Not *you*! The United Nations!'

'Because it takes information. Organisation. Money. Commitment. Political will. *Publicity!* Because the guy from Gary, Indiana – or wherever they do all those US political surveys – and the man on the Clapham omnibus, they have to be made to see, to know, to *care*. They've got to tell the politicians that they care, and the president and the prime minister and all the other premiers and politicians have to get up and get organised. They have to do it before it's all too late! That's what it's all about. That's why you're here. Christ, look what happened when that little girl in Bosnia hit the news! Think what we could do with a ravaged village and a T–80 main battle tank!' He beat the dashboard in front of him with an uncontrollable overflow of passion.

'Harry,' he said, 'just get us to the airstrip as fast as ever you can and we'll have those photos on every newsdesk within the next two days, I promise!'

His words struck Ann with powerful force. She sat back then and began to search through the wreckage of her belongings, checking for those tiny, irreplaceable spools of film while Harry took them far faster than was safe back westwards along the trackways towards the little bush landing strip, trusting on the one remaining headlight to warn him of obstacles and potholes and to warn any animals up ahead to clear out of the way. She couldn't remember exactly how many pictures she had taken or how many times she had reloaded, but she found six films in all, four exposed, two still wrapped, and had to be satisfied with that. In the last of the moonlight, she stowed five of them safely in her camera bag and ripped open one of the still unused ones. She had no idea how many frames were left on the film still in the camera, but she rewound it and changed it for a new one anyway. She had come across some batteries for the motor, so she changed those as well.

By the time she had finished, the moon was setting behind the hills in the north, so when she looked between the men's shoulders dead ahead, she thought the glow in the sky must be dawn.

But no.

'This looks bad,' rumbled Robert.

'Very bad indeed,' Harry agreed quietly.

A spike of ice suddenly thrust down from the pit of Ann's throat into the very depths of her stomach.

They drove on in silence as the glow intensified and crept inexorably up the western sky.

'Do we need to look any closer?' Robert asked at last.

'Better to be sure. What have we got to lose?'

'Don't ask!' Ann intruded herself into the conversation on as light a note as she could manage. 'If they were laying a trap for us,' she continued, 'they wouldn't be advertising their presence, would they?'

'True,' said Harry. 'But there's still short odds we could meet them by chance.'

'Dancing round the bonfire,' she said.

'It's a bit early for Guy Fawkes,' Harry observed.

'Or trick or treat,' she agreed.

'It'd be a bit dangerous to dance round that much aviation fuel anyway,' said Robert wearily. 'And your place is probably next on the list. No fires over that way. Yet.'

'But they mightn't have torched everything,' persisted Harry. 'There might be some petrol left in the second hut. Enough to give Rover here a bit of a drink. I took the last of the petrol at my place this afternoon. There's nothing else there that I need now.'

'We have to risk a closer look at the landing strip, then. We have to check there,' said Robert.

'That we do, that we do,' said Harry. He switched off the lights and the engine and they coasted to a halt in an invisible cloud of coarse dust which would have been kept out by the canvas cover if they hadn't lost it to the tank. The fall of silent dust emphasised to Ann just how exposed she was now, and she looked around the star-bright bush to check for the presence of dangerous animals. The moon had set now, but there was still light enough to see the nearest rolls of grassland quite clearly. Their upper slopes were painted garishly, almost gruesomely, by a combination of bright fire and red dust. The hollows between were relatively shadowed, but even here the stars gave enough light for her to be sure there was nothing large nearby.

While she was looking round, the men had begun a quiet conversation. 'I'll go in first,' Harry was saying. 'I've got the bush craft to get close enough for a detailed recce before anyone sees me. And I know where to look.'

'Yeah. I see that.'

'So, you cover me from the ridge with the Remington. If the coast's clear, I'll signal and you can bring Rover down.'

'Makes good sense.'

Harry turned to her. 'Ann, the Remington doesn't have a decent telescopic sight. Does your camera have a big lens?'

'Well, yes. I guess it does . . .'

'Fine. I'd like you to put it on and use it to spot for Robert, please. The Remington will kill at a kilometre but only if the person firing it knows there's a target there. You use your longest lens like a telescope and you watch my back in the biggest close-up you can manage. OK?'

'OK,' she said.

'And if I do anything really heroic,' added the dapper little Englishman, 'then you will get an excellent photograph of it.'

They all laughed, and the men climbed down. Ann took an instant longer screwing the biggest of her camera's lenses in place, and then she followed. They left their doors open. So did she.

By the time they were approaching the crest of the low hill overlooking the airstrip, she had caught up with the men. They slowed down and fell into a crouch. Harry motioned her to keep down too and, feeling faintly ridiculous, like an adult caught up in a childish game, she crouched like them, lower and lower until she was lying flat out beside them on the very crest, only just peeping over the top.

'Right,' whispered Harry, his voice little more than a breath, 'you check it out, Ann, and I'll be off on your all-clear.'

'OK.' She began to move, but his hand fell on her arm.

'Just before I go, I want you to take this,' he said. He held up one of his automatic pistols. 'Seven shots. Automatic. Flick this switch at the back and you'll get a red dot up on whatever you're aiming at. Bullet goes where the red dot is. Understand?'

He sensed rather than saw her hesitation. 'Self-defence only,' he whispered. 'Remember what we're dealing with. I don't see you lying back and thinking of England, so you'll have to do some fighting. Get one back for the girls in the village.'

She agreed. Pacifism, she suddenly realised, could be taken too far. She took the gun. It seemed to be made of moulded plastic and it was heavy. It fitted in her palm as though it had always been there. 'Bullets go where the red dot is,' he reminded her, his voice as light as dust sliding over silk, only just audible over the sullen rumble of the fire. She shoved it into the back of her shorts until the barrel rested snugly in the cleft at the top of her buttocks. Then she edged up to the crest and looked over.

The slope fell away shallowly to the end of the runway where the two little huts had stood. Robert's plane leaned, blazing and broken, beside the hut which had been filled with aviation fuel, and both were brightly ablaze. The fire gave light enough to show the details of the ground for quite a way around, certainly bright enough for them all to see the threads of smoke rising from the roof of the second hut as it smouldered up towards its own flashpoint. Even here they could feel the heat on their foreheads, and when Ann put the camera to her eyes for the first time, the brightness in the telescopic lens came near to blinding her.

She was an imaginative person and, although of extremely peaceful nature, had seen enough war films, empathised with enough tough warriors to have a good idea what to do first. Prompted by what she had seen today and perhaps by the snug coolness of the gun into accepting a role she had mistrusted since early maturity with all her fierce intellectual strength, she mentally split up the ground below into a grid and used the close-up pictures in her viewfinder to sweep across the quadrants until she knew no area had been left unchecked and was certain there was no one down there.

'All clear,' she whispered to Harry.

She felt the slightest stir of movement and he was gone. At once Robert slid closer to her and side by side they peered over the hillcrest, searching the stark brightness below for any sign of their friend – or of any enemies. The heat and stench of the destruction eddied around them, the roaring of the flames overwhelmed them, keeping the rest of the vast night at bay. Robert looked over his shoulder from time to time – it would have been all too easy for someone to creep up behind them with his presence masked by what was going on at the bottom of the slope. Ann concentrated on the scene before her, however, scouring the brightness for movement and checking the shadows with her telescopic lens.

Harry appeared after ten minutes or so. His first movement in the corner of her eye nearly gave her a heart attack, but her lens soon showed the top of his bush hat and she breathed a little more easily. She nudged Robert to make sure that he had seen too. The hunter moved from shadow to shadow, like a lizard. He moved swiftly when he had to move and was absolutely still when at rest. Once or twice she looked away when he moved and had trouble focusing in on his absolutely still outline crouching in a new location. When at rest, his rough, dusty bush clothing blended perfectly with his surroundings. When he crouched flat on the ground, even his shadow gave little away.

He scouted all the way round the blazing wreckage. Then, satisfied that he had covered the area fully, he pulled himself to his feet and dashed towards the smaller, smouldering shed in a weaving, crouching run. When he arrived, he stood up straight-backed to his full height, looking around for one last time, then he tried the door handle. The door opened infinitesimally. He swung it open and jumped back all in one motion. The door slammed wide and bounced closed, all in silence, its noise buried beneath the roaring of the flames from the Cessna and her flaming fuel. At last, satisfied that there was no one nearby and that the little hut was also safe, Harry began to wave slowly, facing up the hill towards them.

'Right, let's go,' said Robert and pulled himself to his feet.

Harry dived out of sight into the shed.

As she prepared to pull herself to her feet, Ann realised she hadn't taken any pictures of the heroic little figure after all. She paused and focused on the distant door. 'You go on and start up the Land Rover,' she said. 'I'll be there.'

'Hurry,' yelled Robert.

'Don't wait for me!'

Harry emerged, hauling a pair of jerry cans which were obviously full of petrol. Ann focused in on him, waiting for a good photograph.

'Hurry!' yelled Robert, more distantly.

'Don't wait for me!'

Harry staggered free of the heat between the buildings with a can swinging from each hand. She had him solidly framed. The shutter clicked.

Later she would swear she saw the shot but it must have been her imagination that drew the thread-thin black line which was there and gone, streaking across the picture as Harry suddenly stopped.

THUD, went her heart.

A stream of petrol arced brightly out of each can, looking ridiculously like urine in the yellow light. Just as she was sure she had seen the bullet going through them, she was certain the curves of petrol from the cans hung lingeringly in the air, falling elegantly out and down from the level of his hips.

THUD, went her heart.

Sharp and clear as the breaking of a bone in her own body came the sound of a single shot. It was only then that she started screaming, 'NO! NO! NO!'

When the very first drop of the orange liquid touched the smouldering grass, it ignited and the cans exploded, with Harry still standing stricken between them. His slight frame was wreathed with fierce yellow flames in an instant. He toppled forward onto the ground and a sea of flame swept out across the grass towards the second hut.

Still screaming, unaware that her rigid finger was holding the button down, she swung the lens wildly around until the viewfinder picked up a group of men who had appeared out of nowhere. There seemed to be several of them standing on the grass at the edge of the shadow, with two in violent argument, gesturing as though they were yelling at each other.

THUD, went her heart.

The second hut exploded, ignited by Harry's funeral pyre, and the light flashed across the smouldering grass to the tiny group just in time for Ann to see one of the arguing men pull out a pistol. He put it to his opponent's chest, across which was held a smoking rifle, and pulled the trigger. The second man fell down, flat on his back, with his rifle still held tight across his chest.

Then the man with the pistol was screaming at the others, pointing at the burning hut, and gesturing towards the hilltop, apparently right at Ann herself. He was a tall man, cadaverously thin, and his hawk-like face was burned deep into her memory. Unlike the other soldiers, he was white.

Exactly ten seconds after Robert had turned away to go and get the Land Rover, Ann tore herself up off the ground. She had been screaming for five seconds but the first agonised cries of 'No!' had been lost beneath the noise – the suddenly louder noise. In the three seconds which had elapsed since he realised that there was something wrong, Robert had stopped, frowned and turned. He still had five metres to go before he reached the Land Rover. The sight of Ann running pell-mell towards him made him turn and break into a sprint too but, even so, they reached the vehicle side by side. 'Drive!' she screamed, and he was far too wise to hesitate, question or argue.

Fortunately, he was a frequent visitor here and was no stranger to Harry's Land Rover. He chucked the Remington into the back seat and slammed the rear door while she clambered into the front and paused to pull Harry's pistol out of her waistband. Robert had the elderly vehicle in first gear while Ann was still settling in the seat at his side and was rolling forwards almost as soon as Harry would have been.

'Which way?' he yelled.

She pointed out across the bush and he took her at her word, slamming up through the gears and keeping his right foot hard on the floor – very hard, for the seat was set in Harry's driving position and Robert's legs were half a metre longer.

Ann swung round, searching the shadowed slope with wild eyes. The flame-etched rim was still so close. What had Harry said about the Remington? It would kill at a kilometre! What sort of guns would these people have? She could see the shape of the rifle clutched across the dead soldier's chest, with its strange butt and long, curving magazine, but she didn't know enough about guns to identify it; certainly not enough to assess its killing range. She put the camera to her eye and everything swam out of focus at once. Horror gripped her. The camera was broken! She was going blind! She lowered the camera and wiped her face, rubbing her eyes fiercely with the back of a trembling hand. She was crying.

She looked back with her eyes clearer just in time to see the first figure top the rise behind them. It was impossible to judge the distance, but there was no way it could be a kilometre yet.

The figure came up to full height and brought a rifle up.

'NO!' she screamed again, howling more loudly for herself than she had done even for Harry. She never even thought of trying to shoot back with the pistol, or of trying for the Remington. 'NOOOQ!' she screamed.

Robert tried to swing the wheel, but he lacked Harry's wiry strength and bludgeoning technique. The Land Rover continued sedately along the straight line of its path.

The soldier on the crest put the rifle to his shoulder and took aim at them. Ann stopped screaming then, gulped, and watched, fascinated. Knowing that the gun was pointed straight at her, knowing it could not miss, knowing she should be cowering down and getting out of the line of fire, she watched as he drew his bead on her.

And hesitated. Looked around, down the slope. The barrel wavered and fell. The soldier stood there uncertainly until another man joined him then together they turned and looked after the fleeing Land Rover. A third figure joined them, began to gesture, wave his arms. The same scene began to play itself out on the top of the hill behind them as Ann had seen in the seconds after Harry's death. It continued as she and Robert made good their escape. But the man who hesitated and let them go did not meet the fate of the man who had murdered Harry and sprung the trap too soon.

Or at least he had not done so by the time they were out of sight.

'Where are we going to go?' asked Ann wearily when the

dawn at last showed them that there was nothing more threatening nearby than some zebra and a few distant giraffe, and allowed them to roll to a stop.

'I've been thinking about that,' he answered, his voice rusty with fatigue and thirst, and the roughness resulting from discussing over and over again what had happened to Harry and what Ann had subsequently seen. A conversation interrupted only when she hurled herself periodically over the door top to throw up down the Land Rover's side. 'We have to go north.'

'*North!* But we need to get to Mawanga city. On the coast. That's west!' Her voice was also weak. She had not had a drink in several hours – even the slightest sip started her vomiting again, and she couldn't work out whether it was exhaustion, shock or a gastric infection. It could even have been motion sickness, she supposed; the ride had been rough enough, for they had tried to keep clear of roads.

'I know we have to get to Mawanga, but we'll never make it if we go directly. First, we'll run out of petrol and although I've got local currency and cards, there's no guarantee that we'll be able to get any if we go west. They built great roads but no gas stations on them. Secondly, with or without Rover here, we're bound to get mixed up with the refugees heading that way, which will mean going through a police or army checkpoint. They'll have that camera off you in a second. You wouldn't stand a chance. They'd detain us at the least. Maybe disappear us, if you know what I mean. Especially if we still have the guns on us. And of course if we don't take the guns we'll get mugged by the refugees. No. It's too risky.'

'OK,' she said slowly. 'What's north?'

'Two things. First of all, Harry hid petrol and supplies in caches on his domain. Never knew when he or his askari would need them.'

He pulled out a battered map case from the pocket in

the Land Rover's door. 'Marked on a map in here. Some of them must still be there, though I doubt he's topped them up for months.'

'That's one. You said two.'

'The N'Kuru townships. We'll still stand out like sore thumbs but we'll have a better chance. There aren't so many refugees in that area and as far as I know there are no roadblocks yet.'

'So we can get in. So?'

As he had been speaking, he had been unfolding Harry's map. Now, holding it across the steering wheel and letting it flap up onto the windscreen, he pointed with a bright pink fingernail. Leading from the townships, across a bridge just below the Leopold Falls then on down to the coast, following an apparently insane course halfway up the tectonic cliff above the river was a long dark line scarred with short cross-marks. She knew it, though she had to reach right back into fourth grade geography to name it. 'It's a railway line,' she breathed.

They found petrol at the nearest cache marked on Harry's map, which was lucky but logical enough: they were working northwards from the game reserve now, coming into more populous regions. This was therefore the cache least likely to have been found and robbed by the desperate population. There was enough petrol to get them up to the nearest township, but nothing more. They filled up and pressed on. The game roaming the outskirts of Harry's jurisdiction was thinner but there were still wildebeest and zebra and once, in the distance, elephants. Ann's camera stayed packed away. She had more important things than animal photos on her mind now.

Seeming to interweave with timeless inevitability, the last few wild herds and the first few scarecrow figures shared the same barren scrub. As they left behind the last family of emaciated little gazelle they passed the first dispirited family of starving N'Kuru, sitting round a fire of thorn scrub cooking something in a copper pot. Probably a bit of gazelle.

The people of the bush gathered dejectedly round the outskirts of the town; more like beggars, never really achieving the status of refugees. There were not enough of them and there was too much food – not enough to keep them alive, just enough to stop them from dying at once. Their encampments thickened and began to form patterns as the tracks became roadways and as the strange grey hillocks in the distance suddenly gleamed dazzlingly as the sun caught their windows. Then the tracks were metalled, or at least tarmacked, and the hillocks were revealed to be clumps of high-rise buildings.

'But this is a city!' exclaimed Ann. She was feeling much better. She hadn't vomited again since they'd found Harry's cache. 'Couldn't we get things rolling from here?'

Robert looked down at her. 'I have no contacts here. I wouldn't know who to trust. Where do you suggest we start?'

'Embassy? Consulate?'

'Not here. This is upcountry. Certainly nobody of ours. Nobody from Europe either. Only the Angolans, the Russians and Congo Libre have limited diplomatic representation here. The rest are down at the coast.'

'Firms? Companies? Anyone with a darkroom and a fax!'

'Plenty of those. One or two oil companies with American staff. One of those new concerns with people checking out local cures and forest plants for new drugs. Very green, but an unknown quantity. Old-fashioned drugs firms. Copper works. Beer factory. Freedom Brand cigarettes – tobacco was a big cash crop here once upon a time. Sweat shops. Clothes of course – labour even cheaper than Taiwan. They make TVs and hold some local franchises for computers, videos, and of course cars and trucks. All a bit shabby since Julius Karanga died. You know how it goes. Western companies sensing a profit but they don't train the locals properly. Short-term moneyspinning; nothing solid at all. Big plans fallen flat. Lot of people pulled out, gone broke. It's been a while, but I can ask around. If you can do your own developing it will be much safer.'

'I can't. Well, I can but I'd hate to risk it. I'm not very skilful and one mistake would blow the lot.'

'Dangerous, then. If anyone even dreams we've got those photographs, the chances are we'll simply disappear.'

'Oh, come on . . .'

'You got any contacts in the government?'

'Well, no . . .'

'Anyone powerful? Influential?'

'No.'

'Then who's to stop it? Those photographs prove that this country is on the verge of civil war. That it can't govern itself properly. Have you any idea what getting them out into the Western news media is going to do to people in this country? How many people it's going to inconvenience, maybe destroy? Powerful people. Ruthless people.'

'Oh, come on . . .' She wasn't so sure now. What had been done in the village was all too real. What had been done to Harry. She would not have believed such things could ever happen in her ordered world. Until yesterday. Until last night. Robert was right. She had to widen her horizons here over what was or was not likely to happen.

'So if the wrong people find out about this we will probably never be seen again.'

'We'll disappear,' he repeated. 'And most likely not too slowly or comfortably.'

'You mean the police or the army would arrest us, torture us and kill us.'

'Probably. Or the Lions. Lots of them around here. Fifth

columnists from Congo Libre. Probably rape us too. You, certainly.' His voice was flat, matter-of-fact. Utterly believable.

They entered a suburb. Corrugated iron twisted itself into huts. Clapboard held garish paint, flaking. Beaten-mud footpaths. The first fat date palms, stripped. Two children and a dog ran into the road screaming. Robert braked and a battered Mercedes overtook him on the wrong side, narrowly missing the dog. In the quiet after the Merc's blaring horn, a transistor radio played loudly enough to drown out the Rover's engine and Robert's colourful language. He swerved to avoid a broken beer bottle in the road.

'It's make up your mind time,' he said. 'We're in civilisation now.'

The railway station was right in the centre of town. Its white marble portico stood between a tall building whose frontage was decorated with Arabic writing in gold and a Mercedes-Benz car dealership which presented the latest models, all white, on velvet behind thick dark glass, as though they were pearls. They parked and Robert had to go through the ridiculous process of finding enough change for the parking meter.

As they got down onto the pavement, they were given a pointedly wide berth by half a dozen young Arabic men in Italian suits hurrying towards the skyscraper. 'But there's so much money here!' whispered Ann, feeling suddenly badly out of place not because she was white but because she was so untidy.

'There always is, for the right people. That's part of the attraction.' He looked around, hawk-eyed. 'Take everything you can carry. Keep the gun hidden in your camera case. I'll take the Remington and we'll pretend we've been doing a spot of hunting if anyone asks.'

He jerked the gun out of the back as though it was a

suitcase. She did the same with her camera bag. Robert put the rifle casually over his shoulder and strode up the white marble steps with all the thoughtless swagger of Ernest Hemingway coming back from Kilimanjaro. She followed just behind him, trying to emulate his ease without seeming to do so. She was very scared indeed.

If they turned any heads or raised any eyebrows, the fact was not obvious.

The great cool marble hall of the station was packed with people and the noise they were making echoed overpoweringly in the white vaulted caverns above. In front, beyond the throngs, waited the maw of the departure gate. To the left, at the head of a shuffling, raucous snake of women, lay the ticket offices. On the right had once stood a parade of neat white shops. One or two still retained some kind of hoarding or counter but most of them had been ripped open and now contained market stalls laden with local produce which few here could afford, which no one in the shanties beyond the suburbs would ever see. Mangoes, pawpaws, bananas and oranges. Green plantains, dates and coconuts. A wealth of jewel brightness. And beside the fruit stalls were the travelling oven men with their half-barrels made of steel and filled with glowing charcoal. Roasted plantain, fresh cooked bread, various types of meat, their mingled fragrance filled the air. Two young women, scarcely more than children, attended a fat-uddered goat, selling fresh milk. Behind the goat, incongruously, stood a crate of Coca-Cola. Ann's mouth flooded with saliva, her stomach cramped fiercely enough to make her stagger.

Before she could pull herself together and look for Robert, she was surrounded. A mob of little boys varying in age from five to fifteen descended on her with ruthless single-mindedness. Their cries – offers, suggestions, imprecations, demands – were overpowering. They waved pieces of cloth at her, leatherwork, shoes, pots, jewellery, craftwork made of wood, skin and horn. In a range of broken languages and dialects, they begged, cajoled and offered – their fathers, their brothers, themselves.

And she had nothing at all to give them.

She looked around desperately as their demands became more insistent, threatening. She saw a sea of black faces all frowning with terrible single-minded desperation. Hands pulled at her clothing, demandingly, pleadingly, intimately. She felt the camera bag jerk once, twice. Then, like a fisherman feeling a fish on the line, she felt the hands begin to pull the bag away from her with irresistible purpose. She swung round and tore it free. In the distance she saw Robert, unconcerned, unaware, shouldering his way with lordly disdain towards the ticket office. Hating to be reduced to this, she made a break for his protection.

In fact it was the women waiting in the queues who saved her, for in order to get to Robert she had to go among them and when the mob of boys followed, with the determination of a pack of wolves chasing a wounded deer, it was the women they disturbed. The hubbub on the air intensified briefly. Shrill N'Kuru was augmented by the sound of slapping and screaming, and a good deal of laughter, and she was alone, struggling past the patient lines, half blinded with tears, tripping over bundles of possessions, clothing, chickens, babies.

'The next train to Mawanga will depart within the hour,' the clerk in the ticket office was explaining to Robert in perfect English. The slightness of his stature and the lignite gleam of his skin proclaimed him to be of Kyoga extraction. A perfect civil servant. 'No, there is no first class. Nor any other class, sir. Those days, alas, are gone. You may purchase either a seat or simple passage. Purchase of a seat permits you to ride inside the carriage. We do not guarantee you will actually be able to sit down, however.'

Robert looked at him for an instant. 'Have you ever worked for British Rail?' he asked.

'No sir!' The clerk seemed much offended. 'Now, what will you require? I should inform you that the queues are for passage only tickets.'

Robert looked back. There were perhaps a thousand women waiting – or so it seemed. 'Two seats,' he said at once.

'Two seats.' The clerk began to leaf through a box of tiny cardboard rectangles. 'Will that be single or return?'

'Single.'

The clerk stamped the tickets carefully and handed them over. Robert paid. The clerk counted the money twice and handed over the change. 'Persons in possession of seat tickets may board at their convenience,' he informed them. 'The train is at platform number one.' He smiled and rose, crossed to a table a metre or two behind him and poured himself a cup of tea. Ann began to understand why the queues were so long.

With the tickets in their possession, their next priority was to get aboard the train. They had to be strictly disciplined about this, for their bodies were making increasingly urgent demands upon them. For drink, food, relief and rest. But as all travellers who do not hold specific reservations know, mistaken priorities at this stage could all too easily lead to a complete journey standing wedged in a corridor. They passed through the barrier at once, had their tickets inspected and clipped punctiliously by a Kyoga in a heavy serge uniform, and crossed through a seemingly undiminished throng to platform one.

It was already almost impossible to see the sides or roofs of the carriages because so many people were hanging or sitting on the outside of each one. Up and down the platform itself surged a river of people calling up to the passengers, offering as wide a selection of items for sale as had been offered in the main station itself – by the shops and by the boys. Robert shouldered his way through all of this, followed by Ann who was perforce content to use his physical strength as a kind of shield. They crossed slowly to the nearest carriage and climbed up into it. It was packed, a long, noisy, glass-sided tunnel full of people – mostly women – children, chickens, goats, vegetables, fruit, anything which could be bred, reared, grown, made, found, collected, created, and sold. 'Market day special,' bellowed Robert wryly, and plunged into the throng.

Two carriages down, they got a seat courtesy of a huge woman who chucked two sulky boys off a broken-sprung bench by the door and gestured at them to sit, beaming cheerfully. They sank gratefully onto the lumpy, uncomfortable seat, but no sooner had they done so than Ann said, 'How long do we have?'

'Half an hour.'

'I've got to find the john, Robert. Guard the seat, will you?'

'OK. I think I saw a Ladies at the back of the platform. Cut straight across from here. And hurry, would you?'

She opened the door and fought her way down onto the platform again. After pummelling her way through the throng for about five metres, she turned and looked back so that she would recognise the door again. Robert, at the window, smiled and waved. She turned and plunged on. Without the camera case she found she could move much more quickly, and as soon as she saw the door with the female figurine upon it, she had surprisingly little trouble in crossing to it. Civilisation at last, she thought, and pushed the door. She stepped through it and stopped dead. She looked around. She looked back at the slowly closing door. She began to laugh, hysterically, tipped over the edge at last.

There was nothing there. No room, no cubicles, no basins, no marble floor or roof. No roof at all, in fact. There was a wall behind her and a door closing in it. Before her was a small field with a low mud wall across it; a wooden walkway made out of planks led across the sop-

ping, stinking, fly-crawling earth to the mud wall. Beyond
the wall she could see a row of heads where women were
squatting. From the smell pervading the stagnant air, it
was obvious that they were squatting over an open latrine.
Ann stopped laughing and took a deep breath to steady
herself, which was a bad mistake. She looked around desperately but there was no help for it. This was the Ladies.
She should use it or go on her way.

At least the plank led right round the wall and was firmly
bedded in the mud beyond. And it was quite clean, a fact
which was of great benefit to Ann's shorts as she gathered
them round her ankles. Burning with embarrassment, she
blinkered her mind during the next few minutes, refusing
to admit to herself the comings and goings of the other
women around her, even though she could sense them
pointing at her and giggling.

It was only when, at last, she felt fully relieved that the
unkindest blow of all occurred. In her confusion, disorien-
tation and simple ungovernable need, it hadn't occurred to
her that she would eventually require toilet paper of some
kind. In a panic she looked around, wondering what on
earth she was going to do. And the woman beside her
swam into view. She was a young N'Kuru woman, thin as
a wraith, who had settled herself wearily into place, half
supporting herself on a great hand of green plantains
which she was obviously taking somewhere to market. She
saw the look on Ann's face and understood it all too
clearly. Shyly, as though fearing that an offer of help would
insult this strange white skin beside her, she reached
towards the plantains and tore off a handful of green leaves
– and gave Ann the most welcome present she had ever
received in her life.

'My turn,' said Robert cheerfully as she pulled herself back
aboard. He heaved himself out of his seat. 'Will you be
all right?'

'Fine.' Ann meant it. She was feeling much refreshed. She paused beside her seat which was now piled with newspaper and food, looking down with wonder.

'I got some food while you were away,' he said. 'The oranges and bananas are particularly good. There's some bread and cold roast goat. Leave some for me. Oh, and the beer is mine; don't you dare touch it. I got the Coke for you.' Then he was gone.

She quickly arranged the food so that she could sit down and then she put the flat-topped camera case on her lap so that she could use it as a table. Her hands shaking with anticipation, she began to arrange the food in piles: meat and fruit; main course and pudding; his and hers. She glanced up at the woman opposite, gave and received a massive smile. She picked up the first piece of roast goat and brought it slowly, ecstatically to her lips. Her eyes closed and tears squeezed out of their corners at the ecstasy of that first bite. When she opened them, she found she was looking, not at the woman opposite, but at the crotch of a pair of trousers.

When she looked up, she found herself staring at a suave young man in his early twenties. His skin was dark but his face was long and handsome – a mixture of tribal blood. To go with his blue cotton slacks he was wearing a short-sleeved shirt in bright ochres, browns and greens. It was open and there were gold chains lying like oil on his dark skin to match the bright rings on his long fingers. His hair was cut Western style and parted on the right. He gave her a grin which did not reach his eyes and slowly reached for the waistband of his trousers. Languidly, with all the confidence of a practised gigolo, he pulled the trousers tight enough to show how well equipped he was, then, in a flash, he was sitting beside her, filling Robert's seat. 'That seat is taken!' Ann said, feeling at a terrible disadvantage, under far more threat, suddenly, than from the boys in the station with their wares.

He eased forward until his trousers were tight across his powerful thighs. Ann looked up at the woman opposite, desperate for help. The woman was looking out of the window.

The young man's hand brushed the bare skin of her forearm. She flinched. Turned towards him. 'Get away from me!' she spat. Spat, literally, for her mouth was still full of saliva summoned by the succulent roast goat.

He flinched and his face darkened with rage, losing all of its confident good looks in a moment. His nostrils flared and he swung round to face her. Shocked by what she had done, she stared at him and when he reached into his pocket she numbly assumed he must be reaching for a handkerchief. He pulled out something made of black wood and silver. She looked at it uncomprehendingly and it was only when he pushed the button and razor steel flashed out of it that she realised it was the largest flick knife she had ever seen.

The abject horror on her face triggered a new expression in his. He sat back a little, fitting his shoulders into the corner of the seat, and leered at her, stroking the white steel and the black wood slowly and suggestively.

Wildly, Ann looked around the carriage, but nobody seemed to notice that anything unusual was going on at all. The woman opposite stared steadfastly out of the window and her sulky children teased a piglet on the floor. Everyone else was fully occupied with loud, amusing conversation. The man waited, caressing his flick knife arrogantly, knowing that her eyes would inevitably be drawn back to him again. As indeed they were. First to the knife, held so suggestively in his tight, bulging crotch, then to the supercilious, sadistic gaze.

It was the sort of expression, she realised, with which the soldiers in the village would have looked at the naked N'Kuru girls before they started playing their games with them.

311

With that thought, Ann's hands were in action, almost independently of the rest of her shaking body. With short, ugly, brutal movements, she shoved the food down onto the seat between them, revealing the camera case. The black eyes flicked down then up again, speculative greed warring with stirring lust. She jerked the zips with convulsive movements like punches until the sides gaped open. His eyes fell languidly again, and lingered on the seductive shadows of the interior – the black leather, the expensive-looking plastic. He licked his lips. His fingers stopped sliding up and down his knife.

And Ann pulled out Harry Parkinson's pistol. With one flowing movement, as though in some previous existence she had been a master gunfighter, she pulled out the automatic and, two-handed, slammed its butt onto the top of his nearest thigh, pointing downwards at point blank range. Her whole face was aflame, her skin literally burning with rage as though with sunstroke. She looked at him through a faint blood mist and his eyes when they met her red gaze had lost all of their arrogance. His knife drooped in his numb fingers and his skin was suddenly dewed with great drops of sweat.

She flicked her right thumb upwards and he jumped and began to whisper. Perhaps he was praying. A bright red dot pointed unwaveringly to where his trousers strained at their tightest. The bulging cloth began to look looser very, very quickly.

She looked up again, feeling a little calmer. The knife was gone and so was the last vestige of that arrogant expression.

'Goodbye,' she said, her voice like a rusty hinge.

He understood but he did not move until she lifted the gun off his trembling thigh. Then he was gone, silently into the sudden, overwhelming silence.

In the middle of that silence, the train jerked into motion. Ann jumped as though shocked awake by the unexpected movement. The carriage gave another lurch. The seat patted her firmly in the back. The noise of wheels squealing and couplings straining stormed across the air. Ann's head whirled. She thought she was going to faint. The thought of being trapped alone in this train, so utterly, absolutely alone, brought a wild scream to her throat and tears flooding to her eyes.

In the last twenty-four hours, Africa had reduced the confident, worldly-wise reporter to the level of a confused, lost and lonely child.

When Robert tore the door open and hopped easily in, she swept him into a wild hug, oblivious of the fact that the camera bag tumbled to the floor between them or that she was still holding Harry's gun.

A few half whispered words served to acquaint him with what had happened in his absence and to explain the reason for her well-armed and unexpectedly enthusiastic greeting. His black visage set sternly and his dark eyes raked the carriage, though Ann was unsure whether his ill-contained rage was aimed at the vanished gigolo for importuning her in such a way, at her fellow passengers for failing to defend her, or at herself for reacting in the manner she had. The last one, she concluded gloomily. Her panic had attracted even more notice than her skin had and the gun, protection for ten seconds, was now a massive liability. They would have to be very careful indeed throughout the journey – especially if they met any of General of Police Nimrod Chala's checkpoints.

After they had finished their meal, Robert took the first watch and suggested that she sleep. She would dearly have loved to do so, but she was still too full of adrenaline. She settled herself back in her seat, half closed her eyes as though at least trying to rest, and watched through the window at her side. The township's outskirts fell back rapidly to reveal the red earth of the same sort of country that they had crossed in Harry's Land Rover. But instead of the scrub and brush of the grassland, here it was covered in orchards and grassland badly run to seed. There was some sign of farming, but it seemed ill-organised and increasingly desultory, a far cry from the great communal farms of Julius Karanga's time, though the fact that they were still producing marketable fruit and vegetables so long after his death testified to the way they must once have been. The train snaked through the farmland as it slowly surrendered to the bush proper. Soon there was no sign of any trees other than baobabs. The fields became rough grass filled with herds of ubiquitous goats guarded by sharp-eyed teenagers armed with rifles.

As the train escaped from the last vestiges of civilisation, the straight track began to twist from side to side. At one moment Ann could see the whole profile of the train, all the way up past the festooned carriages to the great puffing monster of the engine itself. The next, she could see nothing of the train itself but was instead granted a spectacular view of the great tectonic cliff towards which they were heading. Tall and damson-dark, even at this time of day, it towered across the northern horizon and rolled towards them with all the power and inevitability of a great slow wave.

Soon enough, as the train coiled round in front of her dazzled gaze, the jungle-green foaming crest of the great rock wave seemed to be about to break over the very top of it. Not long after that, the train rattled hollowly over the huge span of the Stanley Bridge which stepped across from the plain to the cliff over the valley of the River Mau. The river should have been in full flow, brimming dangerously close below them, greeny-brown and still carrying the quick lace memory of white foam from the Leopold Falls ten kilometres upstream. It should have been a sweep of water reaching out from the swift currents of its heart where only the great fishes lived to the slow, shallow bays at its sides where the hippos sported and the crocodiles waited patiently in the lush foliage along the slick, verdant banks.

Instead there was a stinking trickle in the midst of interminable mudflats where indistinguishable corpses had rotted into unrecognisable skeletons and even the scavengers that had scattered the bones were long gone.

The train swung wearily to the left, as though it bore all the responsibility for the failure of life below, and began to toil along the cliff face, following a wide ledge which occasionally allowed a glimpse over a scrub-strewn, black gravel edge down into the vertiginous, mud-bottomed depths of the dying river. And whenever the wind dropped – and there was precious little wind – clouds of flies would rise in search of a replacement for the food sources which had dried with the blood of the great river animals.

The last image Ann was aware of was that of the massed bodies of the hungry insects as they oozed across the window pane immediately in front of her like melting tar, or cooling blood.

Robert's firm hand shook her out of a nightmare in which she actually witnessed the destruction of the N'Kuru village. She awoke with the sound of her own cries of horror in her ears. She looked around in groggy confusion, never at her best on first waking. It took her some moments to register his look of deep concern and the fact that the train was first silent and secondly absolutely still.

'Are we there?'

'No.'

'Well, what—'

'Ssssh!'

Distantly on the still, faintly buzzing air came a shot and a long, falling scream. The sounds accorded so horribly with her dream that her flesh crawled and she shivered convulsively.

'What's going on?' she asked, her voice a feathery whisper.

Robert shrugged his ignorance and then looked across at the woman opposite and raised his eyebrows.

She met his look of mute enquiry and at first it seemed that she was going to maintain the same distance that had protected her when the gigolo accosted Ann. But this was even more dangerous. She relented. 'Sometimes,' she said in a rich contralto voice which half-sang a liquid mixture of French and N'Kuru which Ann could only just follow, 'the police stop the trains looking for Lions.'

'And do they ever find Lions?' asked Robert, frowning, his eyes sliding busily around the carriage already, looking for an avenue of escape.

'Always. Or N'Kuru men and women who they say are Lions.'

'And do they arrest these people?'

'No. They make them fly away home.'

The distant, falling cry was repeated. Ann had spent a lot of time on or near the sea during the last few years. The noises made her think of gulls who had forgotten the art of flight.

This cry was much nearer than the last one had been. A wind of concern blew through the carriage. Robert was in action at once. He reached up and grasped the Remington with one hand while pushing her roughly with the other.

'Out.'

Without thinking, she obeyed, opening the door and rolling through it with her camera bag clutched to her belly.

She stepped down out of the high train onto the very edge of a sheer cliff. On her right the black rock reached out into a stubby pulpit as though a high diving board had been started but never finished. On her left, a ridge of rock spread in a thin pie-crust over the abyss. Immediately in front of her was next to nothing. A metre of gravelled black rock ledge, surely no more, then a sheer drop of hundreds of metres straight down to the cracked mud of the river bed. Spewing stones over the black rock lip as she moved, she hurled herself backwards under Robert's feet as he climbed down. He came very close to tumbling over her and pitching right over the edge himself. Instead he collapsed straight down between her and the side of the train, rolling backwards under the carriage as he landed. This was only halfway towards being an accident. As soon as his square body was on the cinder road bed, he scrabbled further back beneath the carriage. 'This way!' he hissed. She was glad enough to follow, but it soon became obvious that there was nowhere, in fact, to follow to. The inner edge of the train was almost as near the foot of the cliff as the outer edge had been to the drop. The inner side might have felt safer, but it was every bit as exposed. The best cover offered was a thin mess of scrub lying defeated in the angle between the horizontal and the vertical rock.

Robert swore once, foully, and began to push her back beneath the train. She took the lead now, rolling across the hot, stinking cinder road bed and out onto the narrow ledge between the pulpit and pie-crust overhang. This time, her face came close to the sheer drop and her hair actually swung out into space. She made to jerk her head back as though her hair would suck her down after it. But then she stopped. The drop was not sheer. The vertiginous smoothness of the cliff was an illusion. The same forces which had pushed out the thin overhang of rock had also fashioned a second ledge beneath it. Invisible to all but someone lying here with their head hanging over the edge, the rock folded inwards sharply to a depth of a couple of metres.

Made desperate by the lack of any alternative other than surrender and death, she swung outwards and dropped over the edge. She landed with a thump which covered Robert's gasp of horror, and shuffled backwards as quickly as she could, pushing detritus off the rock shelf with the soles of her desert boots as she moved. A moment later, his head thrust out over the edge and an instant after that he was swinging down to join her.

Like gulls nesting in the cliff, they wedged themselves into the narrow mouth of black rock. From this position it was obvious that the cliff was nowhere near as smooth and glassy as it seemed. The black rock was riven with cracks and crevices from side to side and up and down to depths which varied widely. All that lay below and in front of them, however, was the thick hot air. It stretched out to the quivering tawny and blue distances ahead; it reached temptingly, seductively, down and down and down to the hard red river bed.

And the air here was as crowded with ravening hordes of flies as that around the train had been. They settled on Ann's body as soon as it was still; landed and crawled and bit with agonising power, each pair of jaws apparently armed with a red-hot needle to be thrust deep into her tender flesh.

As much to keep her eyes from tempting the rest of her over the edge and down that long fall to safe oblivion, Ann wriggled round so that she could see past Robert's hulking shape and understand something of the rock surfaces surrounding her. At once it became obvious that, although there was no direct line of sight up to the ledge above their heads, it would have been possible to see this place if they had ventured out to the end of the pulpit and looked carefully, for the end of the short rock platform was clearly in their view.

Any further speculation was brought abruptly to an end by a spray of cinder and black gravel which spat over the edge of the cliff as impatient military boots strode along the outer edge of the carriages above their heads. Raucous voices shouted orders in Kyoga-accented French and N'Kuru. A resigned grumble of protest answered and it became clear that a number of people were being ordered out of the carriage.

Orders, questions – incomprehensible to Ann who could guess their meaning only from their tone – were bellowed. Grudging answers were given in a range of voices which fell silent one by one until only a liquid, French-accented contralto persisted. The Kyoga voices yelled and snarled more and more forcefully, but the soft N'Kuru voice maintained a steady flow in a tone of innocent ignorance. And indeed, thought Ann grimly, if the police were asking about Robert and herself then the fat woman who had sat opposite them, the owner of the beautiful voice, was indeed ignorant. No one on the train could possibly have any idea where she and Robert had vanished to.

But the woman's protestations were clearly not enough to satisfy her inquisitors. There was the sound of slaps and blows, and the rich contralto rose in a shriek of outrage and pain.

The gravel spat over the edge of the precipice once again as a large body was obviously moved under close restraint. The contralto tones faded into the middle distance still protesting innocence, ignorance and outrage.

New voices entered the conversation, cold, commanding voices. At once the woman's tone moderated. The outrage left it to be replaced by naked terror. The N'Kuru word for chief, one of the few that Ann understood, began to feature prominently. And, once or twice, incongruously, 'milor' in French. Now who in heaven's name, Ann wondered, could the powerful N'Kuru matron be calling 'my lord'?

The cold tones soon ran out of what little patience they had ever possessed. The voices became abrupt, dismissive. The woman's voice rose to a wail of protest. The cold tones rapped out orders like a rifle on automatic.

And incredibly, shockingly, the bustle of motion became not only audible, but visible. A group of bodies worked their way out along the pulpit. Two solid Kyoga men in immaculately pressed blue uniforms dragged the writhing bulk of the unfortunate passenger out to the end of the rock pulpit. They released her and retreated at once. She whirled and would have run back towards safety, but the two soldiers were replaced by three other men. Both Ann and Robert hissed at the sight of these three, but they did so for varying reasons.

Ann's first hiss of surprise came from the sickened recognition of her would-be assailant in the carriage. The same Western haircut, gold chains, bright shirt and pale blue slacks. The young man was shouting and gesturing to the woman and to the other two men. The other two men were obviously the possessors of the cold, commanding voices. Both wore the immaculate, razor-creased uniforms of senior officers, though one uniform was blue and the other green. The officer in blue was a squat, square man whose black skin and full face showed him to be of Kyoga descent. The man in green was white. Everything about him was albino white, cadaverous, consumptive; distastefully sick-looking.

Ann's hiss of surprise became a gasp as though she had been kicked in the belly hard. All at once she was scrabbling for her camera and pressing it to her eye. Even without the telescopic lens, she could see the white man clearly enough in the trembling viewfinder to recognise him as the man who had killed the soldier for firing too soon at Harry Parkinson last night. But there was more. In the brightness of daylight, that thin, hawk-like profile was familiar from another context. She had seen him before. She knew who this man was, if only she could remember.

The N'Kuru woman stood transfixed on the end of the pulpit with these three standing quietly opposite her. The young man asked another question. The woman's answer was negative. Desperately, she looked around, her mahogany skin gleaming with the sweat of terror. The two senior officers, white and black, pulled pistols from their belts. The young man asked his last question and this time the woman stood in silence. She had said all there was to say.

The certainty of what was about to happen hit Ann like a blow in the face. She jerked in her breath to call out, to tell the terrifying men with their pistols that she was down here. That she would give herself up at once, betray Robert even, to save this woman's life.

But she was too late. The pistols spat once, together. The woman, struck in the upper chest, staggered back with the impact, and those few faltering steps were enough to take her over the edge. The three men almost ran forward, avidly following the fall of the silent body with bright, excited eyes. Ann pushed the button, catching them in clear profile, then she pulled the camera down to show what they were looking at so fixedly. By the time she found it so far below, the body had already landed and the dull thud of its arrival was echoing upwards loudly enough to drown the repeated sound of her shutter clicking. She took enough pictures to show the slow spread of darkness around the shattered, ruptured frame.

By the time she pulled the viewfinder up again, the three men were walking back along the pulpit, the young gigolo still protesting in animated monologue that the woman must have known more than she would tell. Abruptly, the white man seemed to run out of patience with the native. He turned his death's head profile towards the man and yelled at him with a broken, wheezing snarl. The young man stopped, his face a dark echo of the expression he had worn before pulling the flick knife. He opened his mouth to protest, but the white man's fist moved with terrifying speed and the lethal accuracy of a snake striking. He punched the gigolo in the chest. That was all. One blow immediately in the middle of the sternum.

The gigolo stepped back, more surprised than hurt, only to find that there was no rock to step on behind him.

Waving his arms as though he might fly, he turned ballet-ically on one toe and toppled off the side of the pulpit.

Where the woman had fallen backwards and silently, the gigolo dived off head first with that wild, seagull scream. He plummeted through one lazy somersault before hitting the ground. It was all so sudden and so unexpected that Ann never even considered trying to take pictures.

Where the woman had been tightly wrapped in swathe after swathe of tribal costume, the gigolo was wearing only his open-necked shirt. Where she had landed flat on her back, he landed head first and face down. His head exploded on impact and his chest burst open immediately behind it. Great gouts of blood and soft matter splattered out in a vivid circle all round him, showering not only the deceptively restful corpse of the woman but also the widely strewn collection of bones nearby. And Ann realised that what she had fondly believed to be the remains of animals, strewn by long departed scavengers, were the bones of N'Kuru who had been made to fly away home by the Kyoga soldiers of Nimrod Chala's paramilitary police force.

The sound of the train departing covered the noises she made as she sent her lunch to join the remains of the unfortunates below. Only Robert's iron grip stopped her from going over herself.

'Well,' he gasped, as soon as he saw some kind of intelligence glint back into her desperate eyes, 'what do you think of your first introduction to our revered conservator of the law of the land?'

'What?'

'Didn't you recognise him? The officer in the blue uniform? You must have seen his picture on posters. That was *him*. General of Police Nimrod Chala himself.'

Ann was shaking her head, desperate to impart her own news. Truth to tell, she had hardly bothered to look at the black officer, so fascinated had she been by the white man in green. 'The other one,' she gasped. 'I recognised the other one. The white. He was in charge of the ambush that killed Harry Parkinson!'

'What? Son of a—'

'But that's not all. I know him, Robert. I know who he is!'

'What? How . . .'

'Years ago. When I was working for Greenpeace full time. They got tapes of the Chernobyl trials. Everyone involved in the Chernobyl fiasco was either tried or gave evidence afterwards. He was there. He gave evidence. He was in charge of the circle of tanks they had in place around the complex on the night of the fifth and sixth of May! That was General Valerii Gogol of the Soviet Army General Staff, one of the greatest tank commanders of his generation. The Patton of the Soviet empire. The Rommel of the Ukraine. The Russian Horrocks.' She paused in her wild rush of information and her eyes, fully alive now, filled with almost limitless speculation as she asked the question which was burning at the forefront of both their minds.

'What in hell's name is General Valerii Gogol doing here?'

Heat

HORSE LATITUDES AND DOLDRUMS

'An uneasy throne is ice on summer seas.'

Alfred, Lord Tennyson, *The Idylls of the King*

Chapter Eighteen

The air above the globe circulates not only in great whirls round the points of the compass, wandering across the northern and southern hemispheres, but also in massive waves upwards and downwards between the ground and the troposphere which step north and south in unvarying series. Over the equator, hot air rises fiercely and continually, until it reaches the solid impenetrability of the upper reaches where its upward pressure is channelled northwards and southwards and, as it moves, is cooled and gains enough weight to fall again until it reaches surface level between 20 and 30 degrees north and south. Here, independently of the actual conditions on the ground, the air pressure is always high, for the cooled equatorial air is pressing downwards in untold, invisible masses. This is a system which not even the turning of the earth and the consequent power of the Coriolis force can seriously disturb, though circumstance and local conditions can undermine or intensify it from time to time.

Where the air presses down upon land masses between these latitudes, the result tends to be aridity, for the circulation of atmosphere required for regular rainfall is hampered by the weight of the pressure, and the frontal systems of the middle latitudes cannot break through the walls of air and the steady breezes which tend to blow at surface level north and south from their lower edges. In their hearts, under the massive weight of the air, there is a great stillness. Where this falls over the land, it is the cause of what the geographers have called the great hot deserts; where it falls over water it is the cause of what sailors have called the Doldrums.

During the autumn of this year, the sun, declining rapidly towards the Tropic of Capricorn, nevertheless shone with unremitting heat upon the equatorial jungles south of troubled Mau. Great masses of air rose into the sky and raced invisibly northward until their energy was dissipated and all that was left to them was exhausted weight. Downwards they plunged onto the Sahara which stood naked, dry and cold. Already the night-time temperatures in the white sand and red rock of the desert were plunging well below zero. It so happened that a combination of fallout from Chernobyl, Tomsk Seven and several severe volcanic eruptions was still trapped high in the jet stream, forming a layer of dust thick enough to give spectacular sunsets to the northern hemisphere, and solid enough to turn the daytime rays of the lowering sun off the desert, reflecting away both light and heat with millions of minute mirror surfaces. Even at midday, the Bedou shivered as they walked beside their camels across the great sand sea; and in the battered lorries rumbling southwards out of Ghardaia down the trans-Sahara highway across the Erg, the slight, dark-faced Tuareg drivers narrowed their eyes and checked the settings of the air conditioning in the cabs.

The weather man at the airport at Tamanrasset high on the Hoggar tapped his barometer and frowned, for the ambient pressure of the unusually cool air was worryingly high. He reached for his phone and, still frowning, began to ring round his colleagues at the airports of Oran, Tangier, Casablanca, Santa Maria, Funchal and Las Palmas.

But it was an old female camel, taking her ancient ease on the dry slopes below Tindouf, who first noted what was beginning to happen. At noon, when the heat should have been fiercest and her rest at its most uncomfortable, some atavistic memory jerked her long head round until her dull eyes and wise nostrils were pointed south. Slowly, she turned her head from side to side, disregarding the stench and noise of traffic from the ridge above which bore the roadway north to Bechar, and read the southern quadrant with the fine hairs and acute surfaces of her nostrils. Moving in on the air from the south-east, she found just the hope of distant water from some oasis, no more than a promise, far away. From the south-west, the planes within her nostrils detected the oven odour of hot rock surfaces and, beyond it, the familiar sand grains of the Yetti and the Erg Iguidi. But from the south, due south, she recognised the grains of sand from distant deserts, from the Erg Chech, from El Khenachich, borne upon a wind which had blown for more than a thousand kilometres to bring them here. The camel turned her head and sneezed, then she pulled herself erect and limped away. No beast wise enough to read the wind would remain on a south-facing slope while the harmattan was blowing north.

Psyche's helipad was a bustle of activity, and Captain Peter Walcott looked down upon it with a mixture of wonder and relief. He was standing on the starboard bridge wing, away from the ice cliff, watching as Richard Mariner managed to make order out of the apparent anarchy attendant upon the refuelling of the incredibly thirsty long-range helicopter from the naval air base at Culdrose in Cornwall two thousand kilometres north-east of them and the loading into its extremely limited capacity of the four plastic body bags which were the reason for its long flight south. The helicopter itself was standing well over to the starboard side, where the constant drizzle from the overhang of ice cliff was its weakest, but in fact, they were all getting used to it now and either disregarded it or varied their activity in order to avoid it.

During the ten days it had taken to reach this point, all the routines had shaken into place, and none of the Guyanese captain's dark fears had come to obvious fruition. A close watch had been kept on his superstitious crew, but no more juju dolls had turned up. Tom Snell had replaced the one he had found – on Richard's orders. Although the major had been offended by what he saw as superstitious disrespect for the dead, Richard had astutely calculated that Tom would be spending most of his time on *Kraken* or on the ice; the men who had placed the doll, for whatever reason, would be spending most of their time on *Psyche* with the corpses. And if the doll gave them a measure of relief from their worries, then it was performing a useful function.

It had been a wise decision. And Peter found that he was becoming more and more impressed by the simple wisdom of the leader of their enterprise. The big Guyanese had been prepared to dislike Richard Mariner in spite of – or perhaps because of – his reputation, but the Englishman had proved impossible to hate for any length of time.

Peter had worked for the United Nations for a long time, however. The association had made him a little cynical. He liked Richard Mariner, there was no way round that; liked him and respected him. But he was all too well aware that on the great stage of world politics, it was only too easy for even the most able to be broken by forces far beyond their control; Peter had seen it happen too often. And the tall English captain had all the open, boyish, almost naive confidence of a man riding hard for a very bad fall indeed.

Though, to be fair, the confidence had been wearing thin over the last few days. Ever since they had lost the current, in fact.

The whirl of cold water from the North Atlantic Drift had swept them east and south for more than a week until they had swung almost imperceptibly onto a due southerly course reaching down on an arc inside the Azores, and there, three days ago, it had dissipated. The movement of the water had ceased with surprising abruptness. According to Yves Maille it had simply tripped over the submarine heave of the Cape St Vincent ridge which reached up from the seabed like a range of mountains below them. That sounded plausible enough to the Guyanese captain who knew well enough how the undulations of the seabed could affect the currents flowing over them. Whatever the reason, they had awoken two mornings ago to find themselves pulling the increasingly inert bulk of Manhattan across water which was every bit as dead as the mysterious, skeletal woman in the cold store below.

'They've loaded the bodies safely aboard and they're just off.' Richard strode onto the bridge wing so abruptly that Peter jumped.

'That was an incredibly quick turnaround,' he observed.

'Well, in spite of everything, we're still heading away from their base at more than ten knots,' Richard said. 'We're at the limit of their range as it is. They'll be lucky to make their scheduled refuelling stop in Corunna if we leave it any longer. The pilot didn't even want to think of the paperwork involved in taking all those dead people for an unscheduled ride into Portugal looking for fuel. Can't say I blame him.'

His last words were all but drowned by the surge of power as the helicopter lifted off. The two captains stood side by side in silence and watched it heave its bulk up into the blue sky with apparent effort and grinding slowness. It came level with the upper galleries of the ice cliff, laboured into the upper air, turning its blunt nose away towards *Ajax* and *Achilles*, sixty kilometres to the north, pulled itself wearily upward a few hundred metres more, and was abruptly snatched away, like a leaf in an autumn gale.

After the time and effort it had taken for the helicopter to achieve level flight, the speed of its departure was striking, and the brows of both captains folded into frowns of surprise tinged with concern. 'There's something going on up there,' said Richard.

'Big wind, by the look of things,' agreed Peter, speaking with all the experience of a man who has faced hurricanes since childhood. His eyes narrowed and he found himself wondering whether the removal of the cursed corpses was in fact going to bring about a change in their luck after all.

Richard nodded once, decisively, and was in action immediately. 'Strong southerly at about a thousand metres up. I'd better get back to *Titan* and get ready to sort it out if it comes down here. It's time we made a determined effort to find the Canaries current in any case. I want us out of this dead water as soon as possible. Especially if we've got to deal with contrary winds.'

The frown remained on Richard's face as he strode out of the bridge and crossed to the lift which would take him down to the weather deck, the helipad and his own helicopter. He was by no means as confident as he appeared. Things were not going to plan – if a vague desire to pick up the Canaries current as soon as the impulse of the North Atlantic Drift began to fail them over the Cape St Vincent ridge could be called a plan. He was very much aware that they would soon begin to fall behind schedule and that the ice was beginning to melt too quickly, a fact emphasised by the increasing tension on the long black lines as the anchorage points inevitably began to rise. He was also too well aware that the exhaustion which held them all in its grip meant that they were on the verge of drifting mentally as well as physically, losing impetus, like their massive charge, in the dead water between the two great currents they were supposed to be riding southwards. Now the threat of a contrary wind, a southerly which would be bound to be hot, seemed to crystallise all his misgivings.

Richard stepped into the lift car and punched the button marked 'A'. As soon as the lift was in motion, he lifted his walkie-talkie to his lips and thumbed *Titan's* wavelength. The black machine was not powerful enough to communicate with the distant ship from within the bowels of *Psyche*'s bridgehouse, however, and he had to wait until he stepped out into the still, heavy air on the main deck before he could raise Sally Bell on his own navigation bridge.

'Any further word from Yves?' he asked as soon as she answered his call.

'Nothing new. He's with me here, though. Want to speak to him?'

'Yes. Put him on, please. Yves, I'm coming across in the chopper. Any thoughts about the current? Is it possible that I could see it if I get high enough? I mean, would it be obvious to the naked eye?'

'Yes. That is an extremely good thought, Captain. I can see nothing from down here and there has been no variation in sea temperature for some kilometres ahead, so I have found nothing working at sea level. But you may be lucky enough to see a change in surface colour or wave formation if you can get high enough. And if you see nothing on your way over here, then perhaps I can borrow the helicopter and go south myself.'

'Perhaps.'

Certainly, now that *Psyche* was free of her unwelcome cargo, the necessity of hopping from ship to ship should be reduced, freeing the helicopter for other duties. And the loss of the current suddenly gave added priority to Yves' work. Perhaps this was the time to let him have the chopper. He had been asking for it for long enough. Ever since his untimely absence during Tom Snell's crisis, in fact.

Richard crossed the deck from the port bulkhead door to the helicopter which crouched just beyond the range of the incessant drizzle from the melting ice. After he had signed off, just before he climbed aboard, he paused, looking up at the tall white slope. There was a haze high in the sky, but it hardly cut the power of the sunshine and cer-

tainly did not detract from its brightness. The brightness of
the ice cliff was painful to look at, but Richard forced
himself to look up steadfastly for the few seconds it took to
establish that the upper galleries still looked absolutely
solid – as far as could be seen. The thought of an avalanche
thundering down onto the deck of *Psyche* or *Kraken* on the
far side was another nightmare he wished to keep firmly in
his dreams and out of their actual experience – together
with his fear that the whole berg might turn upside down
and pull them all to sudden destruction. This last was a
worry which was growing little by little in all their minds as
they began to pay out the two lines metre by metre as the
iceberg rose out of the sea.

'We'll have a look at the ice cliff from close up,' he
ordered as he climbed aboard.

'Yes, sir,' answered Doug Buchanan. He reported in to
the bridge and alerted Peter Walcott that Richard was
aboard and they were just about to take off.

Richard strapped himself in and settled back into his
seat, his mind checking through the list of immediate
priorities. He would give the upper slopes a close visual
check on this side and the far side. Merely looking at the
ice would tell him little enough, but the fact that everyone
would see him checking on their safety would do no harm
to the morale on the two ships. Since they had withdrawn
Colin and Kate Ross's team from Manhattan, the massive
berg seemed to have attained almost a threatening air in
the estimation of the crews most closely associated with it.
Richard knew this as well as Peter Walcott did and was
concerned to boost morale on every possible occasion.
The most effective way of brightening everyone up would
be to find the Canaries current and renew that sense of
urgency which had dissipated with the North Atlantic
Drift nearly seventy-two hours ago. Once they had
checked the ice, he would order Doug to fly them over to
Titan and then he would get the pilot to take them straight

up into the sky until he could see the sea for a hundred miles ahead. They had to find the Canaries current before nightfall. Before that mysterious wind which had whirled the RAF chopper away so rapidly at a thousand metres up came down to sea level and began to push them backwards along the course they had just sailed so laboriously.

The upper slopes of the ice cliffs revealed nothing of immediate importance, even after the closest possible inspection. They fell back at thirty degrees from the horizontal, flawlessly carved into the safest possible angle by Tom Snell and – so long ago now, it seemed – Paul Chan and their explosives. There were no obvious cracks or loose ice boulders, though the smooth white surfaces were beginning to surrender to the relentless power of the runoff and the featureless skim of water was being channelled into increasingly obvious river valleys. This gave Richard some pause and he lapsed into deep thought as the helicopter flew south towards his command. If the runoff began to carve deep valleys into the ice slopes, then there would soon come a time when the ridged sections between the slopes might begin to break free and fall off in dangerously solid chunks. He would have to set up a routine for checking the slopes on a regular basis.

His eyes remained busy as they ran low above the white shoulder of Manhattan for kilometre after kilometre. No matter how deep in thought he was, his gaze could hardly fail to register the fact that the whole berg was beginning to change shape, and not just because the increasing height above the water was revealing slopes of beach reaching out at the waterline to echo the slopes up here. He would have to get Colin to give a detailed estimate on the current and projected rate of water loss. Or, to be fair, an updated estimate. Colin had been feeding rough figures into the regular meetings every day. They had been accurate enough to form the basis of the paying out of the line on a twice-daily routine, but it looked as though they would need more detailed and accurate figures as soon as possible. They still had ten days' hard sailing – a fortnight's if they failed to find the current. How much water would they lose in that time? Without detailed figures, it would be impossible to make any kind of realistic estimate.

And of course they had to come up with more than a mere estimate. The Mau Club at the United Nations would begin to demand accurate figures soon; they needed to know exactly what size the berg would be when it reached the harbour at Mawanga, for it was going to be no mean feat to arrange for Manhattan's reception. He had hardly begun to think about that yet – not that he needed to: they would arrange things at that end, he had no doubt. All he would have to do would be to get Manhattan there and then fit in with the plans they had made for it.

The ice below chopped into a point and he realised with something of a shock that they had skimmed above Colin's old camp site without him having noticed. So much for the closeness of his inspection. The ice vanished as the white forecastle head disappeared behind them. The two tankers reached out hugely, their long hulls parallel, cutting through the dazzling blue water like long green swords. Richard reached down and picked up the binoculars which fitted beside the walkie-talkie at his side. 'Take us up,' he ordered. 'And look out for that wind at a thousand metres.'

The helicopter swooped upwards, its motion translating itself into a sinking feeling in the pit of Richard's stomach and a battering clatter of increased engine noise in his ears. He pressed the binoculars beneath the frowning ridge of his brows and began to sweep them from side to side, focusing on the horizon as it jumped near in the magnification, and then began to fall away again as they climbed steadily through the still air. At first there was nothing to see other than the bright blue of the water marked by the silvery ridges of the swell. The set of the sea was westerly, apparently coming in from America. The shoulders of the waves were bright and their faces dark, as though picking up shade from the Dark Continent towards which they were heading in regular series. He concentrated on looking due south, sweeping the binoculars a little eastwards and westwards. If he looked a little north of west, he knew, he would see the distant specks of the Azores beyond Doug's profile. He felt that he could see so far that he should have been able to see Gibraltar or Morocco a little south of east on the opposite side. In fact all he could see was the featureless surface of the ocean to the south.

Except that . . . There, on the furthest edge of his vision, away down in the south-east . . . 'Doug. Take her up a bit more, would you?'

'Yes, sir.'

The thunder of the motor intensified. 'But watch out for the wind . . .' Richard said the words automatically, his mind actually far distant as he concentrated with all his might on what he could see in the distance.

'We're nowhere near a thousand metres yet,' Doug said calmly, but Richard was hardly listening.

Hope welled almost painfully within him. The regular series of waves was interrupted far to the south-east. The whole character of the water changed down there. The pattern of the waves was subsumed into a broad ribbon of brightness like a calm river flowing through the serried pattern of the swell. A river apparently kilometres wide, flowing southwards.

Richard reached down again and this time he lifted the walkie-talkie to his lips. He thumbed *Niobe*'s channel.

'John?'

'Here, Richard. What can I do for you?'

'I think I can see the current. We're only five hundred metres up, but I can see it quite clearly. It must be the better part of fifty kilometres south-east. If you come round a point or two we should pick it up by dark.'

'We've just been too far west all along?'

'Heaven knows. It probably wavers from side to side like the North Atlantic Drift did.'

'But we can pick it up by dark?'

'I'd guess so, but it's impossible to be certain of the—'

The helicopter seemed to fly into a wall. Its nose lifted and it was swept backwards so rapidly that Richard lost the current, almost lost the horizon. He dropped the glasses and the walkie-talkie and grabbed the sides of his seat. The sky reared over him like a wave breaking and he bashed the back of his head on the seat.

'Doug . . .' He said the word in a tone of surprise, hardly more, as though what was happening was of mild interest.

But this was not the case. As Doug wrestled with the controls with all four limbs and extremities, swearing at first under his breath and then more loudly, the Bell tried to loop the loop backwards, and then settled for standing on its tail while moving northwards and seawards with incredible rapidity. Inside the cabin, the two men were hurled back in their seats as everything around them sprang bodily up and back though ninety degrees. Everything that had been vertical was now horizontal and everything that had been floor was now wall. It was as though they were trapped in an elevator which had fallen on its back and was dropping at an incredible rate.

Before Richard could even begin to assimilate what was happening, the helicopter toppled onto its right side like a felled tree, and Doug miraculously managed to swing it round so that the cabin returned towards level before putting the nose hard down and dropping the game little craft, barely under control, hard down towards *Titan*'s broad green deck. At once, they were in still air again, and it was as though the terrible power of the wind had been a kind of nightmare shared between the two men and the machine. As though, in fact, it had never actually happened.

Richard reached for the binoculars and the walkie-talkie,

but could find neither of them, for the wild dance of the helicopter had been enough to send them irretrievably under his seat. The movement was enough to establish, however, that the muscles of his shoulders and neck had been torn as though by whiplash, and that the tight seat belt had bruised him painfully across the stomach. Automatically, not a little shocked, he loosened it.

'Son of a bitch,' said Doug. 'I did not like that one little bit!'

Richard shook his head and winced. 'That was one hell of a wind,' he grated. He glanced across at Doug and was surprised to see a vivid line of blood running down from the corner of the pilot's mouth.

'Too fucking true,' said the pilot. 'That's the closest I ever want to come to flying into a tidal wave. Christ knows what it's done to the old girl . . .'

As though he was a gifted prophet – or at least in psychic contact with his machine – the engine died on his word. There was not an absolute silence, for the rotor continued to thud through the still air, but the sudden cessation of the pounding engine was utterly shocking. The continued whir of the rotor, though little louder than the thump of Richard's heart, was enough to keep the helicopter steady and Doug continued to pilot the craft unerringly towards *Titan*, whose deck represented the nearest safe landing place.

Inconsequentially, Richard thought of surf, and was surprised to note that the sea was calm below them and the steady progress of the ships so measured that there were actually no waves breaking down there at all.

The helicopter was angled downwards and there was no doubt that even though it had stalled, and even though there was no sign of the engine restarting, Doug had it under control.

'I'm going to put her down on the forecastle head,' he said, psychic again, as though reading Richard's mind.

Richard nodded, his mind still distant, wondering whether he was still in shock. He had hardly heard Doug's words, reassuring and poignantly welcome though they were, because of the persistent roaring. Of course, he thought, there was no surf, it was simply the shock of the near-disaster making the blood pound in his ears.

No sooner did he realise this than the thought vanished as the blunt point of *Titan*'s forecastle head swung into view close below them. Richard's eyes narrowed as he automatically began to estimate which would be the safest point to touch down. The supertanker's forecastle head was a rough, slightly bow-sided triangle sixty metres wide at its base and forty metres deep from the point. The forecastle head was an idea more than a fact for there was no raised section, merely a narrowing of the flat deck. But in any event there was no way of putting the helicopter down on the forecastle head itself for the big green triangle was too full of equipment. There were two huge anchor winches, not to mention a range of vents and tank tops. Furthermore, a solid little mast stood right in the middle of it.

Doug could see the danger as clearly as his passenger, and he lifted the Bell's nose a little to skip back beyond the complex of deck furniture and set down on a square of uncluttered deck beside the long sheaf of pipes which reached down the centre of the ship. The rotors continued to turn, moved by the momentum which had brought them safely this far, but the undercarriage settled solidly as the weight of the machine met the green steel deck. Richard unloosened the seat belt and turned to Doug. 'Well . . .' he began.

The roaring broke over them then. It was not the thunder of the shock in Richard's ears at all. It was the sound of the wind which had followed them down the last five hundred metres to sea level. The wind swept across the forecastle head and plucked the helicopter off the deck once more.

'Jump!' yelled Doug as he began to wrestle with the controls.

Richard swung the door wide and leaned to one side. The seat belt was loose and it fell back to allow him the movement he needed. He half stepped, half fell out onto the deck. The steel was moving past at considerable speed and Richard hit hard. He rolled sideways, trying to minimise the damage which the unforgiving steel was all at once trying to do to him, only to be brought up short when the back of his head came into violent contact with the raised edge of a hatch cover.

He never saw the Bell, with Doug Buchanan still wrestling fruitlessly with the controls, collide with the top of the mid-deck Sampson post, explode into flames and whirl away downwind into the suddenly stormy sea.

The last wreckage from the blazing helicopter had fallen, hissing wildly, into the choppy sea, before the first crew-member was on his knees by Richard's side. This was Cadet Wally Gough, currently on deck duty. He arrived in a flurry of sand which would have graced a seaside beach and crashed onto his knees beside the inert figure of the commanding officer which lay, as though crucified, face-up to the thick brown sand-filled sky.

Wally was studying for his First Aid certificate in his spare time, however, and he knew just what to do. He checked around for near and present danger but there was none. The helicopter had taken its debris far away out to sea. Apart from the Captain's lifeless body there was nothing of it left.

First, Wally gripped the big man by his shoulders and shook him gently. 'Captain! Captain, can you hear me?' he shouted at the top of his lungs. His voice was snatched away by the power of the wind and hurled after the blazing wreckage of the helicopter. Richard Mariner made no response at all.

Working by the book, Wally eased the great grey-templed head back until the square jaw fell and he could check that the Captain's tongue was not blocking his airway. Shocked, increasingly terrified, the boy leaned forward until his chilled cheek was a couple of centimetres above Richard's lips and his wide-eyed gaze reached down the great barrel of his chest. There was no sign of breath and no stir of breathing – although the wind interfered with both sensation and vision. The clothing billowed massively but Wally had no doubt that the Captain's chest remained still.

It was with a rapidly sinking heart, therefore, that he placed his chilled fingers against the cool flesh of the Captain's neck and began checking for a pulse. He could find no sign of life at all and he shouted out loud as the full shock hit him. With trembling fingers he reached for the dead man's collar. Only rigid self-control kept Wally from tearing the buttons wide, for he knew how dangerous such a movement could be if the Captain was still alive but his neck or spine was injured. But even in the hollow of his throat the terrified cadet could feel no pulse. No pulse at all.

When he looked up, he was horrified to find himself utterly alone. It had never occurred to the young cadet, only on his second voyage, that the deck of a supertanker could be so lonely – that the bridge house could be so far away.

He took a deep breath and choked upon a mouthful of airborne sand. Then, fighting to control his breathing, his heart-rate and his panic, he lifted Captain Mariner's left arm and laid it on the deck above his head, angled away from his face. He took the massive right arm, folded it across the barrel chest until the back of the hand was by the left cheek and the palm was facing out. He raised the right leg until it was bent with the knee pointing upwards and he carefully rolled the body onto its side so that it lay – uselessly, pointlessly, but by the book – in the Recovery Position.

Then he pounded off towards the distant bridge looking for help. Or, more precisely, looking for Sally Bell, First Officer and ship's medical officer.

She was on the bridge, seemingly unaware of the full horror of the accident, going through a series of checks over the phone with the Chief Engineer designed to ensure that the impact of the helicopter against the Sampson post had not damaged the fabric of the ship.

Wally looked wildly around the shocked faces on the bridge around him. 'Number One, the Captain's on the deck,' he babbled. 'I saw him fall out of the 'copter as it went over the side but I think the impact has killed him. I can't see any respiration and I can't find any pulse!'

Sally Bell lowered the phone. 'What?' she snapped. '*Where* is the Captain?'

'He's on the main deck by the Sampson post but I can't find any signs of life.'

'Tell the Radio Officer to contact Dr Higgins at once,' Sally ordered, though it was not clear exactly who she was talking to. 'Tell her to get over here as fast as ever she can. Tell her it looks like Captain Mariner is dead.'

Then she was gone out into the sudden sandstorm on the deck to see the truth for herself.

Chapter Nineteen

The RAF helicopter skimmed in on fuel vapour and a prayer on the back of the evening wind. Porthleven heaved up lazily out of Mount's Bay below and the B3304 unwound like a grey ribbon across the mile or two of Cornwall leading up to Helston town. They followed it, passing low over the sleepy, gloaming-shaded countryside, before falling away to the right towards their final destination. The pilot had picked up air traffic control at the naval air base at Culdrose away over the Scillies and they guided him down onto the pad as the last of the light died away.

The chopper was met on the pad by an ambulance. The four yellow body bags were lifted reverently out, loaded and transported at once to the camp's medical facility. Here they were placed in cold drawers where they remained through the night because the helicopter had arrived well after sunset, the duty medical officer was out at a formal dinner in Falmouth, and there was apparently no real need for haste in spite of the mystery surrounding the death of one and the very existence of another.

The camp's senior medical officer was the first one to see them in the morning, for he arrived, full of a traditional English breakfast as dispensed by the mess, at the same time as his orderlies so that he was there right from the undoing of the first zip. Bodies taken from the sea were commonplace enough here, for the big Sea Kings squatting on the concrete apron outside were all too often called for air-sea rescue work in the Channel and the Western Approaches. Bodies discovered on icebergs had a certain amount of novelty, but not enough to arouse much interest in the blue-uniformed breast of Captain Edward Penmarrick MD. The body of Sergeant Dundas, however, was more intriguing, he thought as he glanced up from the medical notes which had arrived with the bodies. Two of the bags were open now, and the still, marble-pale faces of the drowned soldiers lay open for the first time since they had been bagged up on *Psyche*. Penmarrick glanced down again, wondering if either man was this Dundas, but there was no immediate evidence of the discolouration noted by the doctor. What was the name? Higgins. Asha Higgins.

Now, what on earth was a woman with a Middle Eastern name doing as doctor on a tanker towing an iceberg? Sidetracked by the speculation for an instant, he didn't notice the sound of the last zippers coming undone. When he glanced up at last, his gaze flicked over the featureless skull-face of the skeletal woman to the profile of the last corpse.

He went cold. His breath departed in a gasp as though he had been hit in the stomach. He gulped in enough air to fuel a word or two.

'Get out,' he ordered. 'Clear the room at once!'

The two medical orderlies looked up at their normally easygoing chief and hesitated. '*OUT!*' he rasped. 'Get next door and wait.'

They went and he lingered for a moment himself, looking across the three cold corpses to the one that was obviously not so cold. There was a telephone hanging on the wall behind him. He lifted the handset.

'Security,' he requested.

He was through before he had blinked twice, though shock was slowing time around him now as the details of

Dundas's radiation-ravaged countenance were beginning to burn themselves into his stunned mind. He was far away from speculating how and why as yet.

'Security here.'

'I need two armed guards over at the medical facility now, please.'

'Yes, sir.'

'And tell them to bring a Geiger counter.'

An infinitesimal pause, then, 'Yes, sir.'

'Transfer me back to the operator.'

'Sir.' The word was cut short as the order was obeyed, and the operator's voice returned, echoing the mono-syllable.

The doctor hesitated for another instant, his mind racing. But, other than speculation, there was little to think about. The procedures had been laid down in the sixties as to the correct reaction to this sort of thing both in wartime and in peacetime. The standing orders were clear. It might be some kind of exercise, he thought. But even if it was, he still had a clear duty to perform.

'Get me the Ministry of Defence,' he ordered.

The man from the MoD arrived twelve hours later. He was a rumpled, dyspeptic little man called Jones, with thin hair and thick glasses. Penmarrick had heard of him; he was a professor of forensic medicine with an international repu-tation. On the one hand, the captain was confused that the MoD's reaction had been so slow; on the other, he was impressed by the stature of the man they had sent, if not by his personality. Professor Jones did not drive. He had had to take the intercity express train from London to Exeter. At Exeter he had been forced onto the local service through Teignmouth, Newton Abbot, Totnes, Plymouth, Liskeard, St Austell and Truro. Four dilatory hours, he complained bitterly, on a second-class ticket in old-fashioned, uncomfortable carriages without the luxury of either a refreshment car or a toilet. This bloody corpse had better be worth all the inconvenience and discomfort.

Penmarrick picked him up at Penryn British Rail station, carried his little leather case to the car and drove him down to Culdrose himself. In the interim, the whole naval air station had been put on alert – heavily irradiated corpses were by no means as run-of-the-mill as drowned ones – and Penmarrick was eager to make a detailed report of what he had done in the length of time it had taken for the expert to arrive. He was, perhaps, a little over-anxious, because his reaction to Sergeant Dundas's body had been exactly by the book – which had not stopped it spoiling the camp commander's day and putting the doctor's general popularity seriously at risk.

But the professor wanted no reports or self-justification. He would see what had been done for himself and would make up his own mind as to the procedures they would follow then. He was in any case here to perform an autopsy, not to comment on naval security procedures. The only thing about the navy which did attract his attention, however, was the quality of the camp mess and his chance of a decent dinner after this thing was all over.

Penmarrick had formed no high opinion of his grumbling visitor by the time he pulled up at the security barrier on the main gate. Whether the professor was interested in naval security or not, he was quick enough to produce his security pass and gave the soldier's crisp salute a curt nod.

He treated the camp commander with a grudging courtesy, but made it plain that he wished to get on with his business rather than exchange social chit-chat. The doctor felt his popularity plunging lower with each rude professorial monosyllable.

Professor Jones's pale blue eyes were busy about the arrangements which Penmarrick had made inside the medical facility as well, though the beleaguered doctor hardly knew what to make of the raised eyebrow which

348

greeted the sight of armed security guards in white anti-radiation suits. 'If they need those, then we'll need them too,' he prompted, as the two of them stood outside the door. 'It'll make things difficult, but we'll manage. You'll assist me.'

So, thought Penmarrick, some of the details of his rudely-dismissed report had sunk in after all – the Geiger counter readings, for instance. At least the professor hadn't actually questioned anything he had done so far.

It took them ten minutes to kit up and for the professor to place a cassette in the little tape recorder he proposed to carry with him, along with the battered leather case. Then they went in. Professor Jones placed his case on the floor and approached each body with the Geiger counter first, tutting to himself as the readings rose. Naturally enough, he spent the longest time checking out Sergeant Dundas. But he kept returning to the nameless, skeletal woman too. The doctor watched him, grudgingly impressed by the transformation which action seemed to bring to the professor. The little man's movements were suddenly precise and economical. His concentration impressively absolute. To and fro he went between the corpses which lay on the tables like strange aliens half emerged from yellow plastic cocoons. At last he switched the machine off and turned to Penmarrick.

'You were right,' he conceded. 'This is very strange. Your sergeant here is certainly the primary source. The other two men have been irradiated secondarily, and only slightly. There's something else about the woman, though. Something I don't understand. Still, time for a closer look . . .'

He placed his case on a worktop on the far side of the room and stood the tape recorder against it, out of range of interference from the radioactivity being emitted from the corpses, and switched it on. In a loud voice, he intoned the date and time, their names and the names, as far as they knew them, of the people they were examining.

Side by side, they lifted the bodies and pulled the bags out from beneath them. Then, slowly, carefully, working as a team, they pulled off the corpses' clothes. The outer clothing came quite easily, but they needed to cut the underwear away. Professor Jones opened his case to reveal that he had brought his own equipment with him: enough knives and scissors to dissect a deceased army. He used a pair of scissors with blades like a hummingbird's beak rendered in steel. It was a filthy, deeply unpleasant job and Penmarrick was grateful for the body suit – though it was designed to protect him against radiation, not liquid putrefaction. The uncut clothes went into one bag. The ruined underclothes into another. The rags from the woman's skeleton into a third.

Jones began with a careful visual inspection of all four, talking in a loud voice so that his description of what he was looking at reached his tape recorder. Then he moved from observation to exploration. He began with Sergeant Dundas. A careful series of probes and pressings resulted in a sudden, surprised grunt. 'What do you make of this?'

Penmarrick crossed and pushed his fingers into the cavity beneath Dundas's skeletal sternum. The protective gloves deadened the feel of his fingertips, of course, but even so he easily felt a hard protuberance at the junction of oesophagus and stomach.

'Any thoughts?' asked Jones.

'Could be anything . . .'

'Not likely to be a sandwich, though, is it? Bit of pork pie?'

'Well . . .' Penmarrick was swept back to his days as a junior houseman under the tutelage of a particularly cantankerous surgeon.

'Quite right, though; quite right. It is likely to be something carcinogenic.'

'Yes, but—'

'But there's only one way to be sure, isn't there?'

Jones bustled across to the far side of the room and began to rummage around in his case while Penmarrick looked down at the concavity between Dundas's chest and navel as though the lump would be as apparent to his eyes as it was to his fingertips. Jones began to whistle tunelessly and it was only after a few moments that the bemused doctor realised that the professor was sorting out the contents of his case to the tune of 'Mack the Knife'.

'Done much post-mortem work?' he asked cheerfully five minutes later and Penmarrick said 'No' very faintly indeed. His eyes followed the line made by the big scalpel as it moved from the hollow of Dundas's throat in one sure sweep down almost as far as the navel. Then two shorter slices created an inverted Y shape and Jones slid his thickly gloved fingers into the sergeant's body cavity.

'What did you say? Speak up.'

'No, sir.'

'You won't like this bit then.'

Penmarrick didn't.

But then his fierce distaste was swept to one side. The grey-pink sack of the stomach was revealed, and Jones's nimble fingers were lifting the tube of the oesophagus into prominence. And the lump was much more obvious, though still concealed in the internal organs like a walnut in a sausage.

A delicate movement of a very much smaller blade opened the stomach wall and the lump slid into view. It was at once obscene and wondrous, like the laying of some rare egg. Automatically, Penmarrick reached for the gleaming, obsidian jewel as it slid out of the pale flesh and into the dark-walled cavity below.

'*Don't!*' snapped the professor.

Penmarrick looked up, surprised by the urgency in the older man's voice. He stepped back, his eyes still fixed on the strange contents of the dead man's stomach. There were silvery specks deep within it. They gleamed like a galaxy of distant stars in the blackest of winter skies. He did not look away until the end of the Geiger counter was thrust rudely into his line of vision. Jones's thumb moved and the machine screamed.

Only when he switched the machine off could the tutting sound he was making be heard. He crossed to the case again and returned. He was holding, of all things, a card. A white, pasteboard business card with plain black letters and numbers etched upon it. 'I want you to phone this number, please,' said Jones formally. 'You've done very well indeed, but we will be taking over now.'

It was only when he was reciting the number to the camp's telephone operator that Penmarrick's eye strayed up to the words above it:

THE DIRECTOR,
ATOMIC WEAPONS RESEARCH ESTABLISHMENT,
ALDERMASTON.

Halfway between Reading and Newbury, in the northern-most section of the county of Hampshire, just south of the River Kennet on the edge of a Roman road which has run north-west from Silchester for more than two thousand years, stands the British Atomic Weapons Research Establishment.

At dawn the next morning, the ambulance carrying Professor James Jones sound asleep in the passenger seat and the four corpses in lead-lined coffins behind, turned south off the A4 onto the A340, crossed the river and slowed as it pulled up the gentle slope and approached the security gates of the establishment.

Like the Royal Aeronautical Establishment at Farnborough little more than thirty kilometres south-east along the long-buried Roman road, Aldermaston sits on sandy-soiled heathland with low pinetrees surrounding it, giving it a faintly Nordic atmosphere – as though both establishments had been designed to make the German scientists imported at the end of the Second World War feel at home in case, like Werner von Braun and his Peenemünde rocket team, they were tempted into going far further west.

During the 1960s the high wire fence with which the establishment was surrounded had featured widely and regularly in a whole range of media as the British anti-nuclear lobby, under their peace signs so reminiscent of the incisions disfiguring the belly of the dead Sergeant Dundas, marched regularly down the A4 and demonstrated outside the main gate in the same way as, during the next decade, they demonstrated outside the United States Air Force base at Greenham Common. But the air base and the wire fence were redundant now, of course, because *glasnost* held sway. Even so, the guard at the gate examined the contents of the ambulance and the passes of the two men in the front of it as closely as he would have in the darkest days of the Cold War. The coffins, however, remained closed.

Two hours later, the Director reached across his wide mahogany desk, offering a cup of coffee to Jones, and said, 'You've no real idea what it is?'

'No. It's a crystal of some kind and it seems to have flecks of metal suspended within it. It is fearsomely radio-active. The sergeant's face was burned so severely probably because he looked at it closely. His fingers and hand have even more severe burns. And the internal sections of his digestive system which came into closest contact with it have sustained quite considerable tissue damage.'

'Quite so. And how did it come to be wedged inside the body?'

'Well, he must have swallowed it.'

'Yes, I see that. But where did he get it in order to ingest it in the manner you describe?'

'Apparently somewhere on the iceberg which the United Nations is having towed to the west African state of Mau.'

'How on earth could it come to be on – or in – an iceberg the mass of which is more than two million years old? Is there anything on record to indicate it might have fallen from outer space?'

'Nothing at all, as far as I know,' Jones answered, 'though you must understand that I have yet to offer it for close analysis by men in that particular field of expertise. What I am reporting to you is the effect of a crystal of unknown substance and of unknown origin upon the body of a man noted for his fitness up to a week or so ago.'

'Right. Have we reported to the people involved in the Mau project that what they are dealing with may be dangerous?'

'No. That's a decision which needs to be taken well above our heads, I'm afraid. I've recommended that we warn them that something is going on, especially because of the United Nations involvement, but as I say, it's not my decision.'

'I see. So you'll be working in detail now, I imagine.'

'Yes. I would like to start at once. I assume the rest of the teams are in place and ready to go?'

'They are. We called them in last night and they've been waiting for you to get here.'

Jones nodded once. 'Roadworks,' he said. 'On the A390, the A30 and the M5. What can I tell you? You don't even want to know about the M25.'

'Right.' The Director glanced at his watch. 'Everything should be ready for you. Good luck.'

By the end of the afternoon, there were specimens of tissue, fluid, bone, hair and nails from each of the corpses – several different specimens of each from Dundas – as well as samples of everything available from the mysterious skeletal woman. Slivers of the crystal itself were being analysed in various places throughout the establishment. Jones, having taken all the obvious samples and sent them for analysis, turned from the corpse of Dundas to the skeleton of the woman. The sergeant's body was, apart from its unusual contents, absolutely unremarkable.

Not so the woman's body. Her teeth, for instance, were most unusual.

At about tea time, Jones came out of the laboratory where he had been working, washed up and tapped the Director's number into the internal phone system.

'Yes?' answered the Director at once, the speed of his reply giving a good idea of the importance attached to the work being done here.

'I suppose it's a silly question,' Jones began, 'but do we have a dental expert available who might be able to give us some help with what looks like Russian bridge work?'

In earlier days, the answer to such a question would have been no, but in these post-*glasnost* times, things were less simple. As it happened, there were men and women available on secondment from institutes in various parts of the old Russian Empire. Men and women to whom the vast majority of the establishment's rooms were still off limits but who were regularly accepted into low security areas.

'Yes indeed,' answered the Director. 'I'll probably be able to get someone down to you by dinner time.'

At seven thirty that evening, Pjotr Serbsky made his way down to the laboratory. The Russian was registered as a dental expert but in fact had far wider experience than that, experience which he was happy to offer to the security services of his country's erstwhile enemies, especially as they were now his temporary hosts while he studied at their world-renowned teaching hospitals. Serbsky was in his early forties, with thick black hair and a square cut beard. He spoke English fluently and roguishly, with a twinkle in his pale eyes and a curl to his sensual lips. He was on the Director's list of names because of the work he had done in the aftermath of the Chernobyl disaster – he was a recognised expert in the field of radioactivity as well as in Russian dentistry.

His security clearance was high and the current security status of a soldier who had managed to poison himself on an iceberg under the aegis of the United Nations – of which Russia was a fully paid-up member – was low, so there was no problem about allowing him into the laboratory where Jones was working. He knew his subject too, and was able to give the professor a fairly detailed breakdown of the style and date of the dental work on the teeth of the blonde-haired cadaver.

Shortly before midnight, Jones, much impressed by what the Russian knew about dentistry and aware of his work on post-radiation sickness, swept back the cover over Dundas's stomach cavity which still contained the black glass fragment and said, 'I don't suppose you have any idea what this is, do you?'

Under the merciless light of the laboratory, the black glass nugget gleamed wickedly and Pjotr Serbsky regarded it with all the fascination of a bird eyeing a snake. His sensuous lips parted and his bright eyes shone.

After a few moments he shook his head. 'No,' he said. 'I have never seen anything like it before. I have no idea what it could be.'

The good doctor was lying. He had seen something exactly like it before and he knew precisely what it was.

Chapter Twenty

Paul Chan wrestled himself out of the lift onto the 38th floor of the United Nations building with a difficulty compounded by one broken thigh, lightly bandaged, two crutches and an extremely large bunch of flowers already bedraggled through the ministrations of the security guards downstairs. But Paul was a man in love, and it would have taken more than discomfort, discourtesy and the destruction of his posy to slow him down. He was upset about the chocolates, though; the guards had insisted on X-raying them to check for arms and explosives, and Paul really didn't fancy giving his delicious Inga irradiated chocolates. He had left them at the security desk.

In the eyes of Western men, even those in her native Dresden, Bonn or Frankfurt, Dr Inga Kroll was a dumpy hausfrau, unremarkable and unappetising. Paul, however, was an Eastern man of militantly Oriental aesthetic and his eyes saw her differently. To him her hair was a golden wonder. Braided – he had yet to see it down – it seemed like gleaming, intricately woven wires of the most beautiful of metals. Her high cheekbones and narrow, slightly sloping eyes held all the allure of an odalisque. When her bright blue irises caught the light and flared like sapphire behind thick, dark lashes, he found it difficult to breathe. Her short nose, full mouth and square chin simply completed the plump, almost Chinese beauty of her features.

Her short neck and square shoulders served as the most natural introduction to the deep perfection of her bosom. No matter what she wore, be her collars never so severe and her jackets never so tightly buttoned, he always descried – or believed that he did so – the most tempting hint of a cleavage there. And even when her clothes achieved pinnacles of modest conservatism, she was one of those women whose breasts had the facility of moving independently of the rest of her body, swaying and bobbing with hypnotising grace.

Her strong, thick arms ended in unexpectedly long and artistic hands which she seemed to know were her best feature and which she kept manicured and bejewelled to perfection. She had the most delicious habit, Paul had noticed, of putting her hands on her hips in an unconsciously Teutonic gesture which emphasised the breadth of her pelvis and the surprisingly narrow confines of her waist. Paul adored her hips. They were so square, so full. They supported a bottom which to his eyes could only be described as majestic and were in turn supported by thighs which – even though he had to imagine them – echoed this perfection, he was sure. Her calves, ankles and feet completed neatly the mental picture the love-smitten doctor carried with him down the corridor towards her office.

She had been the first thing he had seen upon returning to consciousness after the operation to pin the shattered bone of his thigh together. She had popped into the hospital with a get well card from the Mau team because it was on her way home. She had stayed to talk to the increasingly alert Paul, however, because there had been no real reason for her to rush away. And that talk, at first general, had rapidly become personal. Both of them had revealed a great deal about themselves – perhaps because they were such utter strangers in such an unusually intimate situation; perhaps because each of them, for one reason or another, had had their defences down. She found New York lonely and alien, as did he on his rare visits here. She had no real social life, no friends and certainly no partner. She earned good money and did not need a flat mate. The closest she came to socialising was when she went out with people from work, and they all had firm relationships and families. She had considered joining the music societies, the dinner clubs; she had even thought of cruising the singles bars but in the end she had been put off by fear of the sort of man she might meet there. So she went out rarely in the evening – she had stopped going to the cinema and neither Broadway nor the Met could tempt her as they once had done. She went home late and stayed there until she left early for work. She ordered in – usually junk food – watched the news channels to keep up with international finance, when it was reported, read the foreign sections of the newspapers she had delivered and the volumes of economic theory she purchased through her TV ordering service, and slept alone. She lived for her work, because that was all she had.

Evening visits to Paul's bedside became regular events. Even had there been no spark of attraction between them, it would have been a pleasant change for her. But there was no way she could have failed to observe the effect she had on him right from the start and by the end of the week, when he had been released, it was taken for granted that their relationship would continue.

But Paul had been housebound until now, and the tenor of her visits had changed. On his territory – even though 'his territory' was currently an impersonal, rarely-used UN flat downtown – she had been shy and defensive. He was uncertain whether this was because she did not return his obvious regard or because she did and could not trust herself to reveal the fact.

He had come out into the world today with the express intention of finding out. He had come out earlier than his doctor advised, motivated by his need to know and supported by luck as well as crutches. He had managed to book a table at the only local restaurant she had spoken of with approbation – Kampung, blessedly serving Malay cuisine – and was making what, in his long-gone teenage years, would have been his *big move*.

Inga glanced up from her work as he staggered through her office door and her long eyes widened with surprise. The door slammed back against the wall on his left. His right crutch pushed a padded chair back from the jamb so that it threatened to topple a small table nearby. Her square face blushed a vivid red, seemingly deepened by her fair hair and her usual pallor. She did not blush prettily. A red tide rose up her neck from her high collar and flooded out to the tips of her ears before vanishing under the golden helmet of her braids. He gave her his most insouciant grin and hopped forward, thrusting the bedraggled flowers towards her.

'How did you get up here?' she demanded breathlessly, half rising, her eyes checking her desk top for sensitive material. Her accent, miraculously soft Germanic, reminded him of a Brahms lullaby, but her tone was cold.

He refused to be put off this early in his campaign. 'I work for the UN too,' he reminded her.

'Why—'

'I'm inviting you to dinner.' He took another hop forward, still holding the flowers out to her. 'I've booked a table for eight o'clock. Please say yes.'

At the mention of the hour she automatically glanced at her watch. 'But it's only five now!'

'I thought you might want to change. I didn't know.'

She paused, obviously calculating. The door banged shut behind him and the little table decided not to fall after all. Such romance as he had wished into the moment was rapidly seeping away. He looked around the neat, Spartan room for somewhere to put the flowers she seemed reluctant to take. There was a tall ornamental vase on a windowsill further to the right and he turned to cross towards it. At once, the crutch currently bearing his weight slipped out of control. He hopped once and his automatic systems cut in, trying desperately to protect his injured leg. The flowers sailed lazily through the air and the second crutch hit the carpet. It had held him erect for just long enough to complete one full turn so that when he lost his balance at last he fell back into the soft safety of the chair by the door. The table went west, scattering magazines all over the floor. The chair legs creaked dangerously but held firm and he sat safely, a still point in a whirl of cascading magazines, fluttering papers and flying flowers.

The posy hit the desk top immediately in front of Inga and exploded. As though the blooms had been a grenade, Inga herself fell back into her very much more substantial chair and raised her hands to protect her face from a wave of long-stemmed roses.

Silence and stillness returned to the room, but they took while to do so. A connecting door opened and Indira Dyal's head peered round it. 'Inga,' she began, 'what on earth . . .' But something in the German woman's expression put Indira's mind at rest. Her almond eyes swept round the room once, then she withdrew and closed the door behind her.

Paul sat still, his heart thudding and his thigh throbbing. He was suddenly gripped by the enormity of the loneliness that was facing him now that he had failed with Inga Kroll. He looked across at her, as nervous as a boy, a wave of frustrated despair sweeping over him very much as the wave of roses had burst over her. Roses hung in her slightly dishevelled hair and clustered on her shoulders. Their sharp thorns clutched the fine cloth of her jacket. Three lay lengthwise in the valley of her breasts as revealed by the surrender of several blouse buttons, their leaves spread across the white silk of the blouse. She presented a slightly ridiculous and utterly irresistible figure to the smitten man.

He noticed first that the roses were trembling. The three in the cleavage trembled most and were in any case holding his attention absolutely. Such was his concentration on these as they shook and began to heave, that he hardly heard the sounds she was making. He thought it most probable that she was sobbing in any case.

But she was laughing. Her laughter gathered, grew, and it soon became obvious that she was not hysterical but genuinely amused. Suddenly the future looked brighter to Paul. He summoned up a chuckle, and at the sound she gasped, 'Are you all right?'

'Yes. You?'

'Nothing wounded but my dignity. But your leg . . .'

'It's fine. Honest.'

'Good. Then get over here and remove your roses please, Doctor,' she commanded softly, swinging her chair slightly to the right so that she was more easily available to him.

It was easier said than done, but he was more than willing to make the effort. Lifting green stems from her shoulders was no problem, but disentangling the sharp hooked thorns from the cloth of her jacket required him to lean close to her. Far closer than he had ever come before. She exuded an unexpectedly powerful warmth and a faint, dizzying scent which added mysteriously to the odour of the roses. Next he freed the roses entangled in her soft, golden hair. By this time his hands were trembling, and his breath was short.

The last of the roses nestled in the warmest, most intimate place of all and he looked up into her eyes before he dared reach down for them. Her expression was faintly challenging. There was a slight smile on her full lips which extended the shallow crow's feet at the corners of her eyes.

She had stopped laughing now, which was, perhaps, fortunate, for his hands were trembling so much he could
hardly grasp the stems where they lay between the soft
slopes. The tiny thorns along the spines of the leaves lifted
the silk of the blouse and his gaze fell inevitably upon the
skin revealed by the action.

He lifted the roses one at a time and the removal of each
revealed more and more to his dazzled eyes. Curves of
white flesh contained in delicate white lace. The warmth
of her burned his sensitive fingertips. The perfume of her
went into his nostrils like smoke from the finest opium.

When the last rose was gone, he stood there, transfixed,
until her long, elegant fingers moved languorously to
fasten the buttons which had popped wide and close the
cloth like curtains where the tiny mother-of-pearl discs had
torn off altogether.

'Well, I suppose that settles the time difference anyway,'
she observed softly, huskily. 'We will have to do a little
tidying up here and then I shall have to return home to
change my clothings.' This was the first incorrect use of
English he had heard from her; the first hint that she was
not, in fact, as cool and calm as she seemed. She got up
and slid past him in one liquid motion. 'Where are you
taking me?' she asked as she righted the little table.

'Kampung.'

The restaurant was small and intimate. Their table could
not have been better chosen or the service more solicitous.
The lighting was low but still bright enough to show every
fleeting expression on the faces of the couple as they kept
up an animated flow of conversation as though they had
been friends for many years parted for quite some time. As
they sipped their beers and attacked their food, the last few
flimsy barriers between them fell away and the seduction
of each by the other became complete.

Paul favoured Tiger beer from Singapore but Inga was a

Budweiser girl. In fact it was the strong European fore-father of that American institution that she favoured, and it was part of the magic of the evening that Kampung had some of both in stock. They sipped their drinks, as cold as any Martini, and contentedly ravished the menu. Inga had some experience of what the restaurant could offer, but Paul had intimate knowledge of Malay cuisine. So they guided each other through great classics and chef's specialities unerringly and the starters alone lasted them until after ten o'clock.

Elegant satays on bamboo skewers were ordered, slivers of pork, beef, chicken, duck; curls of fat prawn and crab all marinated and deep-fried and brought to the table in aromatic bundles to be dipped in fiery peanut sauce and savoured as much as consumed. The jewels on her long white fingers caught the light as they moved. The polished perfection of her long almond nails glimmered liquidly. *Kuay pie tee* came next, tiny crisp baskets of savoury pastry filled with bamboo shoots, grated vegetables and minced prawns. Her lips caressed them as her perfect teeth bit into them. She took away his breath, his self-control; everything but his appetite.

Kuay pie tee were followed by chicken wings, their bones pulled out and the flesh deep-fried to the lightest whisper of crispness. Then came tiny, exquisitely savoury spring rolls. Prawns returned, not skewered in satays but wrapped in pastry and deep-fried to golden crispness, followed by stuffed *won tons* and light-as-air prawn crackers. The sea-food theme was interrupted by spare ribs marinated in soy sauce and deep-fried; but it returned again in crisp, aromatic seaweed, in a *mau tan har* of prawns served with a chilli sauce even hotter than the peanut sauce which began this banquet of appetisers. By now they were leaning for-ward across the little table, their faces separated by little more than candle light. Beneath the crisp linen and the strong wood, their knees touched then leaped apart as though from an electric charge, only to come into contact once again. As they dipped their delicacies, their fingers, too, became used to contact. The tactile freedom thus achieved allowed for further intimacies. For every glance he sent directly across into her eyes, another fell lower, especially when she leaned forward.

She had exiled him to the sitting room in her flat and he had taken his ease lengthwise upon her sofa and waited while she showered and changed. The frustration of remaining immobile while sounds and movements beyond the closed door set his imagination afire was rewarded when at last she returned. Her dress had an air of fifties elegance about it as though she was Grace Kelly stepping out of a classic Hitchcock film. It was the brightest of emerald velvet, hugging her hips and thighs down to the tiniest swirl below her knees. Above the tight waist it was equally tailored, rising to square shoulders and a high collar which stood behind her neck before falling into two tiny lapels. And the lapels fell further, in a long V down towards her waist, revealing at last in all its glory the cleavage he had so vividly dreamed of seeing.

A dream which lay opposite him through all that meal, emphasised by a thin necklace of garnets, its slopes contained in emerald green, its warm depths clad only in candle shadows.

The main courses were preceded by bowls containing the accompaniments with which they would be eaten. For her a *nasi goreng* of fragrantly spiced rice flavoured with *ketjap manis* and *sambal oelek*, and for him a *bahmi goreng* of noodles full of clouds of deep-fried bean curd. To go with these they chose *rendang daging lambu* of beef in coconut gravy, *ikan masak asam* of fish in hot and sour sauce, lemon chicken, and sizzling king prawns which came to the table in a shallow iron dish which was so hot that the air above it wavered, the wood on which it sat smoked aromatically and the food within it bubbled and spat in clouds of mouth-watering steam. Thus, wielding chopsticks with equal adroitness, talking nineteen to the dozen and sipping their beer as though it was finest wine, they passed the better part of the two hours left to midnight.

For pudding – and they both turned out to be sufficient trenchermen to require pudding – there were *pisang goreng* battered banana fritters, *kueh dah* pancakes stuffed with creamed coconut, and *rambutan*, as scented as lychees, stuffed with fresh pineapple.

The cab dropped them off at her flat just before one and Inga said, 'Send him away and come on up for coffee.'

Her flat was quite spacious and very well appointed. He had been restricted to the sitting room earlier; this could not be the case now, the beer alone had seen to that. And she was content to let him wander into the kitchenette too, continuing their lazy, intimate chat as she made fresh coffee in a French cafetière.

They carried the coffee through into the sitting room and placed it on the low table there. 'Would you wish a drink?' she asked. 'I have here kirsch and vodka.'

He chose kirsch and she poured herself a vodka, then they sat companionably side by side on the sofa. They had hardly taken a sip of either liquid before he reached for her. Their first touches were as hesitant as their first social contact had been, but the shyness which both felt was soon overcome and fingers which had stroked tight braids on the first soft pressure of lip upon lip were soon sliding under green velvet lapels as tongue tip touched tongue tip.

The clumsy, increasingly irritating thigh could not dampen Paul's ardour, but it did threaten to cramp his style. It was bandaged – lightly but tightly to support the surgeon's work and still fit inside the trouser leg of his best suit. He could bend his leg, but only a little and not for long as the muscles were stiff and tender. Increasingly, too, there was an irritating itching on the outer side, where the long incision was. There was no way in which he could take things on the sofa to any kind of conclusion, or even escalate them appreciably beyond a kind of heavy petting. This point was made frustratingly obvious at last when his leg hit the coffee table and nearly upset the cups and glasses standing on it. At this point, Inga pulled away decisively and rose. She paused, looking down at him, her hands automatically straightening her much disarranged clothing, and he could not read her expression. She stooped, caught up the tray, straightened and left the room.

Silence and stillness without. Within, Paul Chan fought for some kind of control. He tried to regulate his breathing, calm the beating of his heart, rearrange the agonising tightness of his clothing – every bit as disarranged as hers had been. He concentrated so much on these things that he was only vaguely aware of the passage of time but as soon as he had restored himself to some kind of order, he found himself looking at his watch and frowning, struck suddenly by how long she had been gone. He had no sooner registered the length of her absence, than she returned.

On Paul's right, away beyond the end of the sofa, stood a tall double door, much grander than the single door leading out towards the bathroom and the kitchen. These doors opened now and Inga stood there, outstripping in every detail each point of his most erotic dreams. He looked up and looked again, breathless, feeling every hair on his body come erect.

She wore a basque of white lace which contained her torso by something close to a miracle and seemed to narrow impossibly from the dazzling generosity of its cups to the severe restriction of its waist. She wore white stockings which disdained any support other than that their tops clutched the marble swell of her upper thighs. She wore shoes with high heels, their toes made of the same dark velvet as the dress which she had just removed. And she wore her jewels, the square-cut garnets set in gold at her throat and round her wrists.

Behind her, framing her, glimmered a room designed to match her and the fantasies she walked out of. There were little sidelights covered in exotic cloths and tall candles with flames glittering like diamonds. There were dark curtains, long pier glasses and a brass four-poster bed liberally piled with silk and satin pillows. Paul took all this in with one dazed glance before his eyes returned to her, pulled by a force of nature beyond his control.

It was not so much the nakedness of the rest of her that gripped him – though the nudity was quite glorious – as its sculpted perfection. There was precious little fat beneath the white skin before him. This was not the body of a soft office worker but of a trained athlete, and when she moved now, it was with the unconscious grace of a gymnast or a ballerina.

Where she had discovered such a fund of self-confidence he would never know, but every trace of shyness had departed with her clothes. She took charge of him now, pulling him easily to his feet and supporting him through the double doors into her bedroom as though he weighed nothing at all. And every plane of her cool skin seemed to burn paradoxically through his clothing as they moved together so that it was as though there was nothing between the two of them at all. She sat him on the edge of the bed with his damaged leg supported on the firm mattress, then crossed to the door again with seemingly very little purpose other than to pull the wings of wood together and lean back against them while he feasted his eyes anew.

'I wanted,' he began, breathlessly, his voice little more than a whisper. 'I wanted to do that. To take . . . To remove . . .'

'No,' she purred, looking across the table at him, 'there was no need. It's all right.'

She was in motion again, coming closer, reaching for him, her fingers busy as she removed his jacket and shirt; flowing down to her right knee and placing each of his feet upon her left thigh as she unlaced each shoe. Peeled off each sock. So it was the sensitive pads of his toes that first came into intimate contact with the cool solidity and burning softness of her.

Trousers and shorts came off together, a lengthy and painful process complicated by his excitement. At last she pressed him back into the hillock of pillows at the head of the bed and swung herself up between his legs. Fractionally she hesitated, looking down at him slightly, her eyes just above his. Then she turned lightly and sat back, her pale buttocks between his thighs, her back fitting thrillingly into the curve of his belly and chest. Her position placed the golden helmet of her hair just beneath his chin. 'There,' she whispered throatily, comfortably. 'You wanted to take my clothing off. You may let my hair down instead.'

The release of her Rapunzel locks seemed to release something more inside her. Something at once dominant and subservient, demanding yet tender, wild yet thoughtful. He had brought protection. So had she. They threatened to run out, even so. After the first wild rush, they slowed and varied their positions so that his thigh would be protected from the strenuous heights of their passion. As they began to explore the gentler foothills, with just a bottle of Krug champagne to sustain them, his thigh began to gain in importance, for the itching he had felt on the side of his leg intensified. No doubt their exertions had covered this part of him, as well as the rest of him, in a liberal sprinkling of perspiration. The candles had burned low now, but they gave off heat as well as light. The radiators as well as the sidelights remained on and the temperature in the room was very nearly tropical. At last he broke away from her, hissing in ill-controlled agony.

'What is it?' she asked, all concern at once.

'The leg. I can't stand it any longer!'

'What is wrong with it?'

'I don't know. It just burns! God! How it itches!'

'Shall I take a look at it?'

'Don't tell me you're a nurse too!'

'No, but I will be able to tell if you need to go to the casualty, yes? If the wound is infected or tearing. This will be obvious, I think.'

'Yes. All right. Please. But be careful, *please*.'

'Of course.'

She pulled herself away and vanished. Moments later she was back with several pairs of scissors, disinfectant, dressings and clean elastic bandaging such as might be found in any well-stocked medicine cupboard. She turned on the main light so that she could see what she was doing and some of the wild romance left with the velvet shadows. She sat beside him, all efficiency and practical concern. Using the largest pair of kitchen scissors first, then smaller and smaller pairs in turn, she removed the bandage until the wound was revealed.

Just uncovering the flesh brought Paul some measure of relief and, exhausted, he felt himself sinking into the soft pillows as though they were quicksand, and consciousness began to fade away.

For Inga Kroll, the opposite was true. The last layer of gauze revealed a thigh almost as muscular as her own, covered in lightly furred ivory skin. Down the outside, from the hip nearly to the knee, ran a thin wound held closed by a combination of stitches and thin lateral bandages. The wound itself showed no sign of infection or any suggestion that their lovemaking had strained it in any way. But the flesh all round it, in a long rectangle, straightedged and square, was red and irritated, almost as if it had been burned. And, strangest of all, down the middle of the red-burned rectangle of skin ran a series of white blisters. Some had burst, some had been cut open by the surgery so that the sinuous line they might have made was no longer continuous but was pitted with raw wounds which were obviously the source of Paul's discomfort. But there was a pattern which was still quite clear. Shockingly so.

The strange white blisters spelt out several letters in mirror-writing. In Cyrillic, Russian, writing. She could read it with very little difficulty: 'Leoni'.

What did it mean? How could it have come to be there?

Inga had heard a certain amount about the bizarre side effects of the atomic explosions at Hiroshima and Nagasaki; it was part of her Soviet-inspired education in the East German city of Dresden. She was aware that some victims on the outskirts of the cities and on the slopes overlooking them had been found with the letters from the newspapers they had been reading at the moment of explosion burned into their faces. So she knew something about the ability of black on a white background to soak up far more radiation during a nuclear explosion, but she knew nothing at all about any nuclear explosion that Paul could have been involved in, or any nuclear explosion that might have involved something with the word 'Leoni' written on it.

But it was so striking, she thought she had better report it the next time she passed a message back to her masters in the one section of the STASI which was still operational, and they in turn would report it to their masters in Dzerzhinsky Street.

Chapter Twenty-One

Dr Asha Higgins had led a varied and exciting life. She had been born the elder of twin girls by less than five minutes, the daughter of a Kuwaiti prince. She had been brought up as a princess in an exclusive English boarding school. She had studied to be a doctor while her sister Fatima studied journalism. She had married and divorced one of Fatima's friends, the journalist Giles Quartermaine. She had worked for many years as ship's doctor with the Heritage Mariner organisation and met her second husband, John, when they had been kidnapped with his whole command, pirated by terrorists in the Gulf.

But of all the things she had done and been expected to do during the last five years, this was by far the worst. She clipped on her safety line and heaved herself up out of the pitching little dinghy onto the Jacob's ladder which swung and flapped up *Titan*'s massive side. Crossing a viciously choppy sea still foaming from the death of a blazing helicopter and its brave pilot and heaving herself up the better part of twenty metres of sheer black metal counted as nothing. Being called to certify the death of her husband's closest friend, her own good friend and husband of her own closest friend was a bitter thing indeed. Wally Gough, the ship's cadet, was there at the top of the ladder to haul Asha aboard and hand her the medical bag which had been pulled aboard separately. 'Where is he?' she yelled. And she did have to yell. Up here the wind was very nearly

373

storm force and it was armed with lethal whips of sand. Even though Manhattan was far behind, she could hear the power of the harmattan in the superstructure, the wailing hiss of the sharp Saharan sand, and the massive booming bluster of the gale against the distant icy cliffs.

'Down here!' yelled Wally and, although they had told her it was too late, she ran down the deck to Richard's inert body and the tall Irish first officer – captain now, if they were right about Richard – kneeling by his side. There was quite a crowd of crew men down here as well, all gathered anxiously, protectively, round Richard's body.

Asha shouldered through them roughly. Watching herself, studying her actions from that distance which shock can engender, she was surprised by the violence of her actions and at the same time recognised it as a reaction to the depth of her personal pain.

Richard was lying on his back, facing up as though fascinated by the low hazy scud of sand clouds. At least his eyes were closed. That was fortunate because the sand was falling out of the wind at an incredible rate and already the long still body was being shrouded in miniature dunes. It was a trick of the wind, however – one which they would soon come to recognise as being typical of its vicious character – that the only part of the deck near the body innocent of sand was in the wind shadow of Richard's head, where a thick pool of blood lay.

'Has anyone moved him at all?' bellowed Asha, thudding painfully onto her knees at his side.

'Only as far as we needed, in order to check his pulse and perform the standard resuscitation,' answered Sally. She was pumping powerfully on Richard's chest. 'Fifteen,' she said, apparently apropos of nothing. Then she leaned over and breathed into Richard's mouth.

Asha began to check for herself while Sally continued to pump Richard's chest, and her sensitive fingertips warned her that Sally might well be right. To be fair, she would have expected nothing else from a Heritage Mariner first officer – they were all fully trained to be acting medics. A doctor aboard was a luxury normally only granted to *Prometheus*, John's usual command, the flagship of the fleet. Deep concentration and sensitive exploration of low-fluttering life forces was almost impossible here in the teeth of this foul, vicious wind, but Asha thought that, deep in the muscle-twined column of the neck, something was stirring in Richard after all. 'We're going to have to move him,' she decided at last. 'I need a stretcher here. Now!'

A stretcher arrived surprisingly quickly and was slammed down onto the deck beside her as roughly as she had shouldered her way through the circle of onlookers. Sally and she were clearly not the only people aboard who held Richard Mariner in deep affection. But none of the roughness was apparent in the way they gathered Richard's inert form, folding his arms carefully across the barrel of his chest and cradling his still-bleeding head, and lifted it aboard the sandy stretcher. Equally gently, they strapped him in place and packed pillows round his head and neck.

Six men caught up the stretcher and ran it back up the deck with Asha, Wally and Sally in close pursuit. Skidding over the gathering sand dunes, they swung in through the bulkhead door into the A deck corridor. Still running at a trot, like a squad of marines, they went along the corridor until they reached the door to the ship's sickbay. Here at last they stopped to let their commander and the doctor through first. Then they, too, entered and laid Richard's body on the nearest of the beds. They stayed, anxiously, where they were until Asha ordered them out. Sally Bell's eyebrow, raised when they hesitated, added irresistible weight to the command. Wally went with them, obviously regretfully.

The two women began to unpack Richard's head and neck with great care. The frame of the stretcher came easily apart and the metal tubes were pulled out of the fabric so that the injured – dead – man was left simply lying on the bed. Then Sally was called up onto the bridge once more, and Asha, desolate, continued on her own.

Richard and she were old friends and she thought she knew every detail about him except those which were absolutely private between him and his wife Robin. She knew what had caused his aquiline nose to be broken slightly out of true. She knew why one of his fingers was shorter than the rest. She thought she knew the bulk of his medical history, but the moment she undid the buttons of his boiler suit and began to expose his upper thorax to the light, she stopped and reached for his medical notes once more. She had several pages to scan quickly, with frowning concentration, before she took the cold disc of her stethoscope and pressed it to the left side of his still chest. It was no wonder, she thought grimly, that his heartbeat was so hard to find. His right lower thorax was ridged with scar tissue. She moved the stethoscope up almost to his armpit, thrusting it mercilessly beneath the solid slab of his pectoral muscle.

She did not clearly hear a heartbeat, but she did hear just the faintest whisper of respiration.

Her long, golden, almond-shaped eyes flooded with tears of relief. She moved across the ravaged wasteland of that great barrel chest and yes, there at last, was a heartbeat. Slow and regular and blessedly strong. Automatically she crossed to her medical bag and began to get out the thermometer, the reflexometer, the blood-pressure gauge and all the other equipment she would need for the battery of tests she wanted to complete now that she knew there was a point in completing them. Then she stopped, turned and crossed to the telephone which hung on the wall by the door. She lifted the handset and dialled.

'Bridge here,' came Sally's unmistakable tones at once.

'He's . . . he's alive,' said Asha.

The news of Richard's near death and current condition went round the little fleet like wildfire after that, and there were few aboard any of the ships who were not cheered to hear that their admiral had survived such a close brush with oblivion.

Four of those who cared least, however, were the forecastle head line watch on *Psyche*. With the wind blowing so strong and so foul, they had perhaps the least enviable job of all and certainly felt themselves to be the most severely hard done by. The same wind that had whirled *Titan*'s helicopter to destruction had taken their new makeshift shelter and hurled it in rags and sticks back down the deck, leaving them as exposed as the little pigs in the fairy tale. The drizzling waterfall from the ice cliffs above them intensified at once, gathering the sand in the wind into a foul sludge which covered them and clung. Only at the outer edge of the forecastle head itself could the eternal drizzle be avoided and the men soon retired here to crouch and watch gloomily, their thoughts little short of mutiny, their ears assaulted by the banshee screaming of the wind in the haunted cave throats of the ice.

The unvarying battering force of the cold dry wind, surging northwards in a river a thousand metres deep, battered across the vertical surfaces of the iceberg, making them tremble like great drumskins and sound a note too deep for hearing but one which could be felt like the onset of an earthquake. Every hole and imperfection in the ice from pocks the size of pin heads to caverns larger than cathedrals set up their own hollow booming resonances. Air which had been stirred to the occasional whisper by the movement of the water through the internal chambers of the ice mountains went snarling and thundering now. And water which had been held solid by that chill stillness began to melt and murmur deep within the glacial heart of Manhattan.

The forecastle head watch pulled themselves grimly further and further out from the unutterably sinister sounds of the monster they were trying to control. Only one man, once in a while, according to the schedule agreed between the captains and Colin Ross, ran underneath the foul, sludgy waterfall and eased the howling black line which tightened again inexorably as the berg continued to rise up out of the water.

The wind had come suddenly, unexpectedly. The worried weather man at Tamanrasset had contacted his colleagues with questions; no one had contacted ships with warnings. Even Yves Maille had failed to see what was happening ahead. The great desert wind had brought with it a whole range of problems and disasters. There was no real chance even for a sailor as widely experienced as John to take full account of what it was capable of doing. John, in any case, was suddenly submerged beneath a pile of procedural demands which arose out of his hopefully temporary assumption of Richard's overall command while at the same time he tried to find the current Richard had been describing moments before the disaster. Sally Bell, likewise, had her work cut out for her. Captains Walcott and Odate had more than enough on their plates trying to ensure the safe passage of their ships under these new and dangerous conditions this near to their lethal charge. Bob Stark and Anna Borodin had to recalculate all their propulsion figures to meet the new situation. They were still in dead water, after all, and would not pick up the current until after dark even if John could find it under these conditions, and now they suddenly had an enormously powerful headwind pushing them unremittingly straight back along the way they had just come. Small wonder, then, that no one had any time to spare for the complaints of *Psyche*'s forecastle head line watch.

The line watch was led by a Greek called Nikos Lykiard-ropolous who shipped aboard at Piraeus but who originated from Lamia. Lamia he was called, therefore. Lamia was a square man with thick, twisted arms and short, bowed legs. These, with his stooped back, overhanging brow and underhung jaw gave him a darkly simian appearance. With his solid ball of a belly protruding from beneath his scrawny, tubercular chest, he looked like a black-haired orang-utan, a one-man argument in support of Darwin's theories as to the origins of the species. He had massive, scarred hands, a temper soured by a decade of severe dyspepsia relieved by nothing but Keo brandy, and a reputation among his peers as a vicious, unforgiving fighter to whom the concept of Queensberry rules was as foreign as cheerful laughter.

The others scurried under the filthy waterfall to ease the line as directed by the chart Lamia held, but he never did. Of all of them, he, the least careful of his personal appearance, was the only one who remained clean and dry. He slouched beside the starboard rail, turning his head into and out of the solid blast of the wind as dictated by his desire to roll, light and smoke a series of cigarettes unobserved by any officer. He more than most, therefore, stood erect, facing like a cut-rate figurehead into the full brunt of the wind, often when the others were huddled glumly round his legs, whenever he felt that the officers on watch might be observing him from the bridge. He was on the first officer's discipline roster already and any further infringements of standing orders would result in the loss of several days' pay. The time he spent like this was acutely and increasingly uncomfortable, and only the combination of extreme nicotine addiction and the threatened loss of earnings would have prompted him to do it at all.

But do it he did, made intrepid by his weaknesses. And as he stood there, filling his lungs with the bitter smoke they craved, he was uniquely placed to observe, if not to appreciate, the gathering of the darkness. The sun was falling westwards through a sandstorm many thousands of metres high. As the great orb settled towards the western horizon, it slowly lost both power and heat; it seemed to shrink, collapse, and its blinding gold became a lurid carbuncular red. The scene was one of gathering threat. The starboard quadrant of the sky seemed to be running with slowly coagulating gore. Shadows gathered and fled as the sand clouds thickened and thinned above, and the crimson stain leaked down out of the air and spread across the sea like some dreadful curse from Biblical times.

But if the starboard was filled with sanguine gloom, the port was even worse. The high flank of Manhattan, suddenly filthy and running with thin, sandy mud, took and darkened the thickest of the light beams until, horribly, the whole cliff acquired the dully gleaming aspect of a mountainous pile of offal awash with thickening, almost black clots of blood. Thick streams of the dark red foulness came pulsing downwards in titanic arterial rhythms as though Manhattan had been stabbed a hundred times and was slowly bleeding to death upon them, and the whole ship seemed to be sinking inevitably in an ocean of blood. The almost human howling of the wind across the hollows, caverns and caves took on an eerie, agonised, otherworldly nature, which even the unimaginative Lamia found almost impossible to endure.

By sunset, Lamia had had enough and, quite ready for a confrontation with the first officer – or even with the captain if need be – he led the bedraggled, filthy watch into the red-caked bridgehouse. But there was no trouble. The watch officer nodded dully when they reported in and sent them down to shower. The line watch had seen and heard the most, but the weird, haunting atmosphere emanating from the strange, screaming, blood-red mountain beside them infected everybody aboard.

John Higgins stood up on the bridge of *Niobe* and looked

forward into the thickening haze. He was a well-educated man of literary bent and his mind was full of images from Shakespeare's *Macbeth* which threatened to distract him from the many demanding tasks with which he was being overcome. The first one was to calm Peter Walcott. 'Yes,' he was saying into the phone with an assurance he was far from feeling, 'it is only to be expected. The weight of sand on the ice is bound to have slowed the rate at which the ice is rising. We will try and work out new tables as soon as possible. In the meantime, I suggest you try and ensure that the weight of sand on your decks does not begin to pull you down too fast either . . . Yes. Of course, I will send you the information as soon as Colin has completed the calculations. And yes, I shall report Richard's condition as soon as Asha gives me an update.' He broke off, frowning, as his command shuddered suddenly. Dear God, what now? he wondered. 'Yes, I guarantee it. As soon as I can,' he snapped and broke contact. At once the handset was buzzing again. He pushed the button. 'Wait!' he snapped, and let the importunate machine drop to arm's length. 'Helm, what's going on?' he barked irately.

'Swinging south-west, Captain,' came his helmsman's quiet voice. The answer was followed by the degrees through which they were now swinging, but John paid no more attention. Hope flooded his system, and a bubble of elation grew in him. He recognised the Ulster tones coming from the distant set and lifted it to his ear. 'We've picked up the Canaries current!' he and Sally Bell told each other at once, as excited as a couple of kids at the news.

As darkness fell, they pulled the great dull ruby mountain into the grip of the south-flowing current and began to make some serious headway against the northward pressure of the wind. John felt too tense to eat, so he stayed on the bridge through Pour Out and dinner, and was on hand to answer all the messages streaming in from the other ships and beyond. It was very late indeed when Bob Stark called in to say that it felt as though *Ajax* and *Achilles* were beginning to feel the benefit of the current and to advise a reciprocal diminution in revolutions which would, with the current's help, maintain their mean speed at ten knots in spite of the contrary wind. John phoned the orders round to the watch officers. And the watch officers woke the captains. And the captains woke their chief engineers. And the reduction in revolutions was co-ordinated.

It was after midnight before Asha got through from *Titan*'s sickroom. 'No change, darling,' she reported. 'Richard's still out cold. All the vital signs I can check on here seem fine.' She hesitated. 'Is there any way I can get him ashore if things don't improve?' Her voice was weary, guarded, full of worry.

'Not with this wind, I'm afraid. No way we can get a chopper up until it moderates.'

'That's what I thought.'

'We could put him in a boat, I suppose, if anyone could get one out to us.'

'No. I'm better placed to help him than anyone except a hospital with brain-scanning equipment. But it's not good to be out for so long.'

'We'll see how he is in the morning. Anything else?'

'Nothing. I love you, Captain.'

'I love you too, Doctor.'

This was the last of the calls on the walkie-talkie from the various ships, but it was not the last call of the night. Hardly had John switched the little machine off and returned it to its accustomed resting place on the console than the automatic incoming light lit up to warn him there was someone trying to raise the ship on the big radio. He walked through into the radio shack and switched the equipment to manual.

'*Titan* here, Captain speaking. Over.'

'It's Sally Bell here, John.'

'Sally! What on earth . . .'

'. . . sorry, John, I didn't catch all of that. I'm relaying an incoming call to you. It's supposed to be for Richard, but . . .'

'Hello, Sally? Yes? Sally?' He flicked from TRANSMIT to RECEIVE and back again, then settled on RECEIVE.

The set crackled fiercely, and John wished bitterly that he had woken up his radio operator. But then the big speaker sprang into life again and a new voice came across the air waves.

'Hello? Is that Captain John Higgins aboard *Niobe*? Are you receiving me? Over?'

'Yes. This is Captain Higgins. I am receiving you loud and clear, over.'

'Thank goodness. Now I want you to listen very care-' fully, Captain. My name is James Jones and I'm speaking to you from the Atomic Weapons Research Establishment at Aldermaston . . .'

Chapter Twenty-Two

Lamia Lykiardropolous shivered uncontrollably as he crawled across the ice. He was a hot-blooded man from a warm Mediterranean country and of all the things he hated most, cold ranked the highest. Of all the deaths which were most terrible, freezing to death was the worst. And yet he knew that he was dying here. The knowledge seemed to exist outside him, as though his mind was trapped in some other body. The body of a man marooned on eternal ice freezing slowly and horribly to death.

He looked up and narrowed his eyes against the awful glare. All he could see was an infinity of whiteness stretching in an unvarying plain to the horizon, formless, featureless, freezing. The agony in his hands made him look down with a cry. Where in God's name were his gloves? Not on his hands, that was for sure. The white fingers were distinguishable from the white ice only because their flesh was blue and the nails were black with frostbite. And because they were edged in a bright red outline of frozen blood. He must have been resting here on all fours on the ice for a little while, gathering his strength. But he could not remember stopping. He could barely remember leaving the ship, for that matter. It was as though time had just begun. Here. Now.

He tried to move and the tearing sensation as another layer of skin ripped away from his palm to remain frozen in place shuddered up his arm until his heart fluttered as though it would fail at once. He looked back. Sure enough, there were ghostly handprints in the ice behind him where his skin had torn off layer by layer to remain frozen in place on the glacial surface of the ice. And there was more: a long red trail as though he was dragging a brightly-slimed slug along behind him. He knew what that meant, and it was important. But he just could not remember. Sobbing quietly, he looked up.

The wind came in from the white knife edge of the horizon. It was full of tiny, razor-sharp spicules of pure ice. They acted in concert, seeming to form one huge knife which was slowly flensing the flesh off his cheekbones. In his mind's eye he could see the white flakes of flesh whirling back in the grip of the wind to go whispering like snow across the unforgiving ice behind him. Whimpering, he crawled on into the terrifying blast. Tears flooded out of his tortured eyes to freeze at once, setting his eyelids open to the blast, solidifying like super-glue.

How long he had been out here, crawling across the ice, he no longer knew. All that registered with him were the twin facts that his hands were being consumed by frostbite and his face was being flayed by the gale. What drove him on he had no idea. Where it was driving him to and why it was keeping him moving likewise had long since failed to register. All he knew was that he was freezing to death here and now because the cold from the terrible ice was burning through the skinless, frozen flesh of his hands and the fleshless, skeletal horror of his face.

But then in the far distance, his tortured gaze made out a black shape. Something with colour and form, something utterly out of place in this inhuman, alien environment. It was what he had been looking for, he suddenly knew. This was hope. This was life – or the chance of it. He altered the angle of his snail-slow progress and began to crawl towards the black beacon standing steady in the face of the blast. Determinedly, doggedly, he crawled, tearing himself forward. The hope within him engendered by this sign of life in the frozen wilderness was almost as agonising as the pain of the frostbite. He looked up: it was still there. Tears of relief flooded – and froze as swiftly as the tears of hopeless self-pity had done. His eyes stretched agonisingly wide and he felt the eyeballs beginning to freeze as well. The cold stabbed up his optical nerves and it seemed that his brain began to set solid too.

He began to crawl even more quickly, reduced to near insanity by the power of hope.

He could see it now, a low construction of wood and hide. The weight of the ice was beginning to make his eyelids tear away from the horror of his face. The hand-prints on the naked ice were no longer made of pale skin but of bright flesh. The bones were beginning to show through on his palms and fingers. The agony was inde-scribable.

He rammed into the flimsy wooden door with the top of his head and continued to crawl for a moment, unaware that he was no longer moving forward. But then the new situation slowly registered in the icebound cells of his brain and he stopped trying to crawl and began trying to pull himself up. Of course he could not move his hands for almost all of their musculature lay behind him, frozen into the ice. The wood of the door was as slick and cold as the ice and the last shreds of flesh tore off the bone of his fingertips as he scrabbled hopelessly to pull himself up.

The door was in the wind shadow of the rest of the simple construction, so Lamia could at least look upwards – for as long as he could bear the agony of his tearing eyelids, frozen wide as they were. What he could see was a cliff of wood halfway up. It was a simple door latch. Hardly more than a metre above his head, it stuck out tantalis-ingly, begging to be caught, lifted and pulled.

This is very stupid!

The thought entered his head as though someone else

had thought it – or whispered it – close by.

Stand up!

He began to obey. It was impossible that he should have the strength and yet he actually began to pull himself onto his feet, reaching up unerringly for the latch.

But as soon as he put weight on his left leg, he felt the shattered bones grating across each other and a thunderbolt of agony crashed up the left side of his torso, hurling him bodily down onto the ice with such power that he was knocked insensible.

And he sprang immediately awake.

It was an unutterably vivid transition, as though the act of falling had smashed him from one state of existence into another. As though it had not been a dream at all, but another level of genuine experience. Lamia remembered every detail of the excruciating nightmare, every lancing needle of agony in every nerve of his hands and face. He remembered it so completely that he still seemed to feel it now, even in the safe, warm, dark fug of his berth deep in *Psyche*'s crews' quarters.

'*Lamia!*' a voice whispered urgently, and the burly Greek jumped, for it was very much like the voice from his dream. 'Lamia! Are you all right?'

Only on the repetition did Lamia recognise the voice of his crony and berth mate August Lebrun, a weasel-like ex-smuggler from Marseilles.

'Of course! Why do you ask?'

'I heard you cry out. I thought perhaps you were having a nightmare.'

'Such things are for children. What is the time?'

'I am not sure. Sometime in the graveyard watch.'

The two men chatted in their less than perfect English, the lingua franca of the sea, already falling into severe disuse as Britannia no longer ruled so many of the waves. Time passed, and Lamia's heartrate began to ease. He stared upward in the darkness, his eyes seeing nothingness but his mind still full of the image of a door latch for ever far beyond his reach. It was soon clear to him that the terror of the nightmare had filled his body with so much adrenaline that further sleep would be out of the question, even had he dared return to it.

It was at about 6 a.m. that Lamia ordered Lebrun to switch on the light so that he could replace the haunting vision of that mocking door latch with the gaudy pictures of very much more easily attainable women which he kept pasted on the walls round his bunk. Lebrun did as he was told and Lamia was dazzled by the cabin light as he had been blinded by the brightness of his dream. He slitted his eyes against the light, then as his eyes adjusted he lay for a little longer, waiting for the memory of the agony in his fingers and face to fade.

After a while, the pain in his cheeks eased to a simple itching and, with his eyes fixed upon the gleaming orbs of a model's naked buttocks, he moved his right hand for the first time since he had woken, and scratched his cheek.

His mind was blank, save for that part of it which was lazily exploring the carnal possibilities offered by the naked model, so it took him a moment to realise that something was wrong. It was a question of feeling, to begin with. It felt as though he was wearing gloves and a face mask. The scratching failed to ease the itch in his cheek. He folded his fingers into a fist and scrubbed at his cheek with a little more energy. The effect hardly varied. He felt an unsettling sensation as though there were loose surfaces between the skin of his fingers and that of his jowl. Loose, silky surfaces which slid about independently of the movements of his hand and head.

He lifted his hand until the fat fingers swam into the space between his eyes and the bright pink curves of the model's buttocks. He refocused his eyes almost lazily. And for a moment wondered whether he *was* wearing gloves. Had he come to bed with a pair of white gloves on his hands after all? He thought back, trying to cut through the fog of forgetfulness engendered by the alcohol which he usually consumed between coming off watch and coming to bed. No. There was no possibility that he had put on gloves before retiring.

He brought the oddly coloured appendage closer to his face and looked at it more closely. His stomach twisted and vomit burned at the back of his throat. He shuddered with shock and the nightmare threatened to wash through into the solid reality of the cabin. His palm was covered in patterns of tiny blisters which spread into bubbles over his fingertips. He slowly turned the hand through one hundred and eighty degrees until he could see the back of it. Here the skin was completely detached and hung in wrinkles weighted by lymph, like a series of yellow balloons full of water.

Lamia jerked his left hand up. The back of it brushed against the blanket in such a way that it arrived in a warm rain of liquid as the blisters on it burst. Lamia screamed and this time there was nothing of dreams in the nightmare vividness of his horror. He sat up with such violent motion that he tore the muscles of his beach-ball belly. 'Lebrun!' he yelled and the Frenchman rolled over into full wakefulness and, horrifically, also shouted out with fear.

'*Mon Dieu!*'

'What is it?'

'*Merde*, Lamia.'

'*What . . .*' The Greek seaman's voice cracked as this long drawn out word spiralled towards a panicked scream.

Lebrun rolled out of his berth and crossed to the small chest of drawers built in against the far wall. Three strides took him to it. A wild wrench tore the mirror off the top of it. Three strides brought him back, holding the reflecting square in front of his chest.

Lamia's narrow eyes fastened with sick horror on the wavering image. He jerked back, his whole body reacting with revulsion against what he had glimpsed. He was, in common with many Mediterranean men, more vain about his appearance than the appearance itself seemed to warrant. He considered his round, heavy-jowled face with its oily, dark-hued skin and glistening, tight-curled hair irresistible even to such visions of beauty as adorned the walls round his berth. But his vanity was destroyed by what he saw in the mirror.

It was not that the flesh itself was swollen – this might almost have been preferable. It was that the skin seemed to have been pulled off the underlying structures and inflated into puffy yellow balloons all over its surface. The forehead was grotesquely swollen and the eyes beneath it puffy and narrow. The squat nose was all but lost in a soggy ivory bubble and the pale grey jowls sagged as though they belonged to some kind of hound. His mouth, too, was puffed out and his chins were doubled, trebled into pendant, trembling fullness. Only where he had scratched his cheek was the skin flat, hanging in shreds off his face and glistening where the lymph had burst from the broken blisters.

John lay, wakeful even at 6 a.m., with his arms folded on his pillow behind his head, sensing the stirring of his command all around himself as she plunged unhappily through the unvarying headwind, thinking of the responsibility he now bore for the other five ships and their mysterious icy charge, wondering how Asha was caring for Richard, and wishing there was someone to care for him now. The longstanding joke in Heritage Mariner that John Higgins was 'Little John' to Richard Mariner's Robin Hood was not a jibe against his stocky size or a wry comment about his undoubted intellectual stature; it was a comment about the relationship he had always had with Richard. But John did not feel like the definitive right-hand man now. The burden of his extra responsibilities weighed heavily upon him. It had been massive enough even before Professor Jones had phoned through from Aldermaston to warn him that the iceberg which it was costing so much in effort, ingenuity and lost life to move across the ocean might well be contaminated with a mysterious form of radioactivity.

'Watch out for any signs,' the professor had suggested.

'Like what?'

'Signs of radiation sickness. Nausea, diarrhoea, bleeding gums. Sores around the nose and mouth. Hair loss. Lassitude. Blisters.'

John had closed his eyes. As a first officer he had been trained to treat most shipboard illnesses, any number of which could show some or all of these symptoms, from toothache via scurvy and food poisoning to terminal malingering. Not to mention the self-inflicted varieties which arose out of sniffing, smoking or injecting illegal substances or over-indulging in any of the more legal ones. 'Professor,' he had said, hearing his voice taking on the overtones of one addressing a clinical idiot, 'have you any idea of the number of things which might generate those symptoms?'

The professor's tone had remained surprisingly understanding. 'Yes. But I'm afraid I can't give you any further guidance. If I were you I would send some men onto the iceberg with Geiger counters and see whether you can locate the source of the radiation. But I have no idea what the thing Sergeant Dundas swallowed was, or where it could have come from. I don't know whether you would be looking for lots of little bits of black glass or one enormous piece. God, I hope it's not in one big piece. But no, it can't be; you'd all be as badly off as the sergeant if there was one big bit of it.'

'That would depend on the size of the bit, I suppose,' John had snapped.

'Yes. And where it was located. I understand the actual

iceberg is more than a hundred kilometres long.'

'It was when we set sail. It may be smaller now. But yes, it is still extremely large. More than a billion cubic metres volume, as far as we can calculate. Only ten per cent of it above water.'

'Well, you'd better search as much of it as you can as soon as possible.'

'Any ideas what I should tell my men? "We're just going to check this iceberg we're all tethered to with unbreakable ropes because we think it may be radioactive?" ' He paused and then asked, 'Are you familiar with the term *mutiny*, Professor?'

Jones had given a dry laugh. 'I recognise that you have a problem of communication, Captain. I'm just trying to establish clearly that that is not the only problem you have. I can offer a little advice, however. One of the bodies you sent to us, that of the woman with blonde hair, was Russian. At least, she had Russian dental work, of a type routinely performed in Moscow during the early 1980s, I understand, though I don't know how one can tell. You might like to use that as an excuse for a more detailed examination of your . . . ah . . . cargo.'

'I'll take it under advisement. Thank you, Professor. Would you please give me a number where I can contact you if we have any more news from this end . . . Thank you. Good night.'

In fact he had not taken it under advisement at all. He had told no one of the professor's news, preferring to brood darkly all night, sleepless, increasingly perplexed and worried, missing Asha bitterly and wishing to God he could at least talk to Richard Mariner.

This last wish had been more than compounded by the fact that his last act before retiring had been to contact Robin, Richard's wife, and tell her of his condition. It was a chore he had been dreading and one which, frankly, he had been hoping to delegate to Asha, who was one of

Robin's closest friends. But in the end he had seen all too clearly that it was just one more of his duties as acting commander. He would have done the same for the merest stranger; how could he do less for his closest friend? But it had been hard. He had got her out of bed and in the background he could hear that he had also disturbed the twins who howled dismally. He could see Robin quite clearly in his mind's eye and could interpret every dull tone of devastated shock into a facial expression. When she took the walkabout phone downstairs to get away from the noise her children were making, he could imagine all too clearly the rooms through which she was moving, alone in the dark. He had visited Ashenden often enough to see in his mind's eye the route she would be following through the great, chilly, cavernous, empty old house. He knew from the whispers of background sound just before they broke connection that she had ended up standing by the French windows looking out over the lawns to the tall white cliffs overlooking the busy Channel; the wife of a seafaring man going through every sea wife's worst nightmare.

In the dark of his own cabin afterwards it had taken more time than he would have wished to clear that poignant image from his mind and return it to consideration of Professor Jones's far more pressing information. What was he to look for among the crew? Lassitude. Incontinence. Bleeding gums. Radiation sickness.

He was still deep in these thoughts when the phone beside his bed shrilled and the measured tones of Peter Walcott, each precise syllable telling of the exercise of the most iron self-control, informed him that one of *Psyche*'s crew seemed to have contracted a strange, disfiguring skin disease.

'What does it look like?'

'Like nothing I've ever seen, John. His skin seems to be coming off in great blisters.'

Blisters, thought John. Oh God. Professor Jones had warned him about blisters.

'All over his body?'

'No. Just on his hands and face.'

'Isolate him. Check the rest of the crew for similar symptoms.'

'Done and being done. It's the ice, isn't it? There's something wrong with Manhattan.'

'Are you alone?'

'Yes.'

'Thank God. You can't voice speculation like that in front of your crew, man!' He took a deep breath, aware that his shock had made him step over the mark with the UN captain. He moderated his tone. 'No, we don't know if it's anything to do with Manhattan. But I'll send Dr Higgins over at once.'

'Isn't she looking after Captain Mariner?'

'Yes. But this sounds more important.'

'Yes, I agree – for the time being at any rate.'

'What is the atmosphere on *Psyche* like?'

'She's called *Psycho* quite openly by her crew now. That should tell you.'

'But you and your officers are well in control?'

'Yes,' snapped Peter.

'Good. I'll get the doctor across to your man as soon as possible, then. After she reports back to me with probable cause and recommended treatment, we'll get everyone to work on sorting this mess out.'

'Right. I'll keep in touch.'

'OK. But I'll be moving out of *Niobe* across to *Titan* for the morning at least. Leaving at once, in fact.'

'Weather permitting,' observed Peter, but John had hung up before the phrase was completed. The weather was the least of his problems, he thought.

He thought again when he arrived on the bridge. Steve Bollom, his square, reliable first officer, was there. He should have been in bed hours ago but John knew better than to mention it. Mentioning anything was going to be quite a trick, in fact, for the noise of the wind was a con-

stant overpowering, reverberating roar, as though the
bridgehouse was trapped beneath a waterfall. There was,
too, just the faintest, most sinister, hint of a sandblast
whisper, which only seemed so quiet because the wind was
so loud.

'I was just going to call down to you,' shouted Steve,
pulling a hand the size of a spade back over his steel-grey
hair. 'It looks as though this mess is getting worse.'

John's eyes narrowed as he strode over to the clearview.
'It's difficult to tell,' he observed in a throat-tearing
bellow.

'Right!' agreed Steve. 'But it's past dawn now and we
should be able to see more than this.'

'You mean we should be able to see *something*.'

'Yes. Something like a deck, Sampson posts, forecastle
head. Sea, sky . . .'

'I agree. What's the mean wind speed?'

'Last recorded two hours ago at about sixty knots due
south. Steady. Not a gust or a fluke. It hasn't veered a point
in two full watches, just got steadily stronger. It's as though
it's coming out of a fire hose. Then when we tried for a five
o'clock reading we found the anemometer had seized. It's
solid. Full of sand. Nothing we can do.'

John looked into the whirling murk immediately in front
of his nose as though the glass itself was full of wildly
dancing dots and the darkness beyond was solid. He
checked with his watch and then doublechecked with the
ship's chronometer immediately above his head. It was
well past dawn. Where was the bloody daylight?

'I'll tell you what we can do,' he said grimly. 'We can
make that idle Frenchman earn his keep.' He strode across
to the pilot's chair and picked up the walkie-talkie beside
it. 'Hello, *Titan*?' he barked.

'*Titan* here, Sally Bell speaking. Is that you, Captain
Higgins?'

'Yes. Buzz down to Yves Maille, would you, and tell him

I need a detailed weather prophecy as soon as humanly possible.'

'I called him up at six, John. He'll give us a detailed report within the hour.'

'Good. I want to come over to you at the earliest opportunity and I want to send Asha back to *Psyche*.'

'OK. I'll pass that on to Yves. Any problem there?'

'We'll talk about it when I see you. In the meantime, how's your captain?'

'No obvious change. Asha checked in ten minutes ago. She hasn't done more than a visual check yet so he may be sleeping rather than out cold. We'll know more soon and I'll update you at once.'

Sally Bell broke off contact and John called through to *Psyche* again.

'Captain Walcott here.'

'This is John Higgins again. Any more news on that man of yours?'

'No. We're still checking through the rest of the crew but no one else has shown any symptoms yet.'

'Good. I understand what you meant when you said "weather permitting" just now. I'll get the doctor over to you as soon as possible, but obviously we'll have to wait for things to moderate.'

'OK, but you'd better pray for things to moderate soon. When I said my officers and I had things screwed down tight here I may have been being a little over-optimistic.'

Peter broke contact and it was all John could do to keep his shoulders square. Never had the weight of responsibility seemed so heavy. Never had the forces of nature seemed so set on keeping that weight so unremittingly and crushingly in place.

Suddenly he found that from the bottom of his soul he was praying that Richard Mariner would wake up now, right this instant and resume the burden of command.

Asha leant back against the wall nearest to Richard's bed head and looked down at her friend. He was heavily bandaged, more heavily bandaged than was absolutely necessary, perhaps, but she had been deeply worried yesterday and had reacted with more than usual concern.

He was wearing a hospital gown – not a very dignified garment but the only practical one under the circumstances. He lay on his back atop the pale green counterpane – she had kept the temperature in the little medical room high enough to make any covering of bedclothes redundant. He lay absolutely still and, but for the slow rise and fall of his massive chest and the placing of his arms at his sides, he might have been laid out for burial. The first bandage was wrapped round his left ankle, though the sharp-boned joint was little more than grazed. The same was probably true of his knees and elbows, all of which were bound up in thick white gauze as though they were actually broken. In the absence of an X-ray machine, only Richard could tell her whether there was any real damage there. And he could only do that when he woke up and could tell her in detail what he could feel. The last bandage was the most important in that regard; it was wrapped round his head as neatly as a Sikh's turban.

Where to start? she wondered. The damage – slight enough, perhaps – to his knee joints was complicated by the fact that they were actually held together by steel pins courtesy of a terrorist bomb. She smiled fondly, remembering the stories he had told of how the pins had more than once tripped off the security sensors at law courts and airports. That was Richard, she thought; a story for every occasion. Only he could have contrived to turn a terrorist outrage which had so nearly destroyed him into an amusing after-dinner story.

But there had been no such stories about the state of his

chest. The massive, star-shaped entry and exit wounds which marred the pale barrel curve of his right lower thorax, just beneath the swell of his pectoral muscle, had come as a stunning surprise to her. Even the medical notes in his personal file had been sketchy. He joked about his involvement in the Gulf War, occasionally held up the middle finger of his right hand to display the missing top joint, giving the impression that this was all the damage he had sustained; but there was never a mention of the wounds in his chest which, it seemed, had been severe enough to interfere with his circulation and make his pulses so difficult to find.

Well, that was the logical place to start. Find the pulse and check that. Then the blood pressure. Then the joints themselves. Check for freedom of movement and look for any reaction to the pain. If there was any discomfort, with luck it would wake him up.

She was aware of John's concerns, and the weight of the responsibility he now carried. She did not share her husband's worries about his adequacy to meet those responsibilities, however. She had seen him in a bemusing range of situations during the years of their courtship and marriage, and she had never seen him in a situation he could not cope with. Even wounded – with a bullet wound similar to though thankfully much smaller than the wound on Richard's chest – John had still been able to command and sail a supertanker almost single-handed. He was simply the steadiest, most reliable man she had ever known and she could see him now in her mind's eye, meeting each new problem with an increasingly squared jaw, holding his face as though he was still chewing on the stem of his beloved pipe. But the pipe had remained unlit for years and she had talked him into putting it away now. He had amiably acquiesced to her wish, though he missed it, she knew. Under pressure he would still reach for it and his expression would remind her irresistibly of pictures she had seen depicting the typically English faces of pilots in the Battle of Britain. He was a Manxman and the son of Manx-Irish parents; he was a seafarer and the son of a seafarer, so why he should remind her of young fighter pilots, she had no idea. But there was something about those narrowed eyes and that squared jaw that always reminded her of those intrepid young heroes ready and heartbreakingly eager to do battle against the Hun on high. Her eyes flooded with tears and she burned to throw her arms round him; to try and stiffen his resolve – or to lighten his load.

'Penny for them.'

The rusty, gruff voice was so unfamiliar, so unexpected, that she glanced across at the door, expecting to see one of *Titan*'s crewmen. Nobody was there and she looked down at the bed again.

Richard's eyes made her catch her breath, as they always did. She had forgotten how blue they were, how dazzlingly bright, like magnesium flares ignited behind thin panes of sapphire, their colour all the more striking for the contrast with the thick black lashes.

'Richard! Oh, thank God . . .' She ran to his bedside, as impulsive as a teenager, her whole body flooding with relief. 'How are you?'

He looked at her, his face immobile. Then the faintest of frowns gathered between the perfectly sculpted black wings of brows. Something moved in the depths of those hypnotic eyes. What was it? Confusion? Fear? That deep, rumbling voice came again, though he hardly seemed to move his lips at all. 'The question, my dear, is not so much *how* I am,' he grated, 'but *who* I am.'

John Higgins stood, thunderstruck, with the walkie-talkie crushed to his ear. 'Amnesia?' He simply couldn't believe what Asha was telling him.

' 'Fraid so, love. Total. Classic case.'

'But when will he get his memory back? I mean—'

'No way to tell, darling, I'm sorry.'

'But I thought most amnesia was psychological!'

'This is physiological, John; no doubt of that as far as I can see. Bash on the back of the head. Big bump. Complete memory loss. One, two, three; QED.'

'Anything else? I mean, how is he otherwise?'

'No. Nothing else at all. He's one hundred per cent otherwise. I've done a complete series of tests. Everything else is AOK. Couple of Band Aids and some tincture of arnica for the bruises. He's up and about already, looking for something to do. I'm having the devil of a job keeping him here in the sickbay.'

'So it shouldn't be long before—'

'No idea, darling, I really haven't. Sorry I can't be more help, but you're still in charge of the whole shooting match. I'll keep you up to date.'

'Well, I'm afraid it's not as simple as that, my love. If Richard's OK, then I've another job for you, an urgent one.'

'What is it?' Her voice picked up the tension in his own.

'No idea, but it's really having quite a negative impact over on *Psyche*. One of their crew men seems to have picked up some kind of . . . infection.'

'Infection?' She knew how devastating an uncontrolled infection could be in the enclosed environment of a ship at sea.

John glanced around the bridge, looking for somewhere to continue the conversation in private. At last he walked into the captain's day room behind the chart room and hoped that his navigating officers would assume he was just passing some private endearments to his wife.

'What sort of infection?' she was asking. 'Can you describe the symptoms?'

He did so, his voice unconsciously dropping to little more than a whisper as he did so.

. Then, checking that the dayroom door was tightly closed behind him, he unburdened the leaden weight of the news that Professor Jones had passed to him little more than eight hours earlier.

'*Radiation poisoning*?' Her distant voice rose several decibels. Thank God she was in the sickbay, he thought, alone except for the man who could no longer remember that he was Richard Mariner. 'I'll get right over and check. But how on earth I can do it without using a Geiger counter or letting this Lamia person or his friends catch on to what I'm doing, I just do not know!'

'Your first problem is going to be getting over there,' he said, walking back out into the howling, hissing bedlam of the bridge. As he broke contact, he noted that the light at least was beginning to break through the sandstorm. It was more than an hour late, but at least the day was beginning.

Asha's journey to *Psyche* was less of a problem than John had imagined it would be. The situation was resolved by Yves Maille, not through any miracle of meteorology but simply because he could not take satisfactory readings on *Titan*'s bridge. So, having been given direct orders from First Officer Sally Bell to provide readings, he went down onto the main deck.

Inside the bulkhead door at the starboard end of the lateral A deck corridor, he adjusted the bulky clothing he had donned to protect himself against the sand. Several men were detailed to help him should he demand it, but the one in attendance was now simply required to close the door behind him and then to await his return. The intrepid Frenchman was going to brave the vicious sandstorm in order to check the readings of the instruments he kept on the ship's distant forecastle head. These instruments were important not just because they were even more sensitive than *Titan*'s own, but because they were the only ones at deck level. All the others were located atop the bridgehouse more than twenty metres above.

Yves adjusted his goggles and pulled the filter tighter across his nose and mouth. He nodded once to his assistant and threw open the door. He stepped out with his eyes tight closed in expectation of inundation by whirling sand. He heard the door slam shut behind him. He had taken half a dozen stumbling steps before he realised he was walking in calm, still air. He opened his eyes and blinked. It was clear air too. From the sandswept deck, up through less than ten metres to a claustrophobically close, thick, sand-drizzling sky, there was a band of utterly still air. He ran to the side of the deck and skidded through miniature dunes to catch the safety rail and look down at the strange, sullen sea. It, too, seemed quite calm. Then he turned, thunderstruck, and looked around himself, consciously noting every detail he could discern for the exhaustive report he was going to write to the Geographical Societies in Paris, London and the United States.

The meteorological explanation for what was happening was simple enough, but it had never occurred to any of them, not even to Yves himself, that the forces they were dealing with were so enormous that the microclimates they were capable of creating could be hundreds of square kilometres in area. The harmattan, blowing north from the Sahara, was a cold desert wind, generated by the pressure of the air. It was relatively warm in comparison with the air around the iceberg, however; and that air was further chilled by contact with the ice and with the surface of the water all around Manhattan which had been itself chilled by runoff from the great berg. This had the unforeseen but almost inevitable result of forming a cushion of cold clear air some thirty metres high over which the sand-laden harmattan rode as though over a low hill. To the officers and men on the navigation bridges of the ships, the southerly wind, made impenetrable by the weight of sand it was carrying, seemed to be reaching from the wave tops upward for a thousand metres sheer, but down here on the weather deck, Yves alone could see that things were very different indeed and an utterly unexpected calm held sway.

The effect of being out in that calm was very disturbing. As he looked down the length of the deck, along the wide but terrifyingly shallow band of clear air, he could almost feel the weight of the sand above his head and he found himself crouching as though it was solid rock about to crush him like a mountainous press. But to compare it to rock was misleading, for the stratum a mere seven metres above his head was in frantic, liquid motion. To watch it was to feel reality being torn into inversion until one became almost like a watcher entranced above a silt-laden river in full spate. But in the place of cold spray rising, cold sand drizzled down, lightly, to land like a tawny cloak on everything around until the deck and the billows below it were barely distinguishable.

Asha, too, felt that they were moving through a long low cave as she and four crewmen from *Titan* powered the little inflatable west across Manhattan's mighty bow and then due north towards *Psyche*. They were moving northward at twenty knots towards a goal which was moving south to meet them at ten knots. They were travelling through still air, but even allowing for the southerly current, they still had the ship in sight in little more than an hour.

'There's *Psycho* now,' said one of the seamen quietly. None of them had wanted to come. Asha hardly heard and certainly missed the fact that he had mispronounced the name. The low brown roof of the wildly rushing sky seemed to join the rough wall of the sand-streaming flank of the iceberg and spread out into the dark, flat stillness of the water as though they were coming to the back of the dreary cave now, and the atmosphere of this strange meeting drizzled down on them with all the insidious penetration of the sand itself. Just as the fine grains crept with chilly silence down into every strand of hair and every fold of flesh and clothing, no matter how intimate, so the atmosphere crept into every corner of their minds and crouched there coldly, like shadow. And everywhere, just above them, the wind raved and the whirling sand hissed and the upper galleries of the ice boomed and grumbled and thundered.

If anything, the atmosphere darkened as they climbed up the accommodation ladder onto *Psyche*'s weather deck, and Asha was whirled back in her mind across the years to her honeymoon and a desperate, doomed freighter called *Napoli* with a mutinous crew and a deadly cargo destined for the coldest deeps of the Western Ocean. She shivered, for she knew how dangerous things could get on a ship which felt like this one did. The men she had brought with her suddenly grouped themselves round her like a bodyguard. Abruptly she realised that several trained medical assistants had been overlooked in favour of these four whose greatest qualification seemed to be their size. They fell in around her, two in front and two behind, as they hurried up to the A deck bulkhead door and then along the corridor to the lift.

Captain Walcott was tall, distinguished and very worried looking. 'We've got two more,' he said at once. 'Not as bad yet, but even so . . . We've isolated them all, of course, from each other and from the rest of us.' His voice was deep, lilting, and every bit as concerned as the expression on his lined, dark face. He took a deep breath, as though inflating himself, rounding his chest and squaring his shoulders. 'We don't know whether or not it's contagious. We're counting on you to tell us, Doctor.' His dark eyes swept round the wide, shadowy bridge, and the atmosphere, like the light, thickened sinisterly for a moment.

John had described Lamia's symptoms in as much detail as he had at his command and Asha thought she had built up a fairly accurate mental picture of how the man would look. Even so, what she saw as she lifted the bandages off him made her catch her breath with shock. The Greek seaman lay quiet, his eyes open but distant, heavily sedated. 'I'll just bring my bag over,' she said soothingly. 'I've got some ointment which will ease this at once.'

She opened her bag and pretended to be rummaging for medicine but in fact she switched on Kate Ross's Geiger counter which she had hidden in there. Then, holding her breath, she brought the whole thing over and actually placed it on the bed beside the drugged man.

Nothing. The little machine gave no reaction at all. A weight lifted off her shoulders and she began to breathe again. One less thing for John to worry about, apparently, but a new puzzle for her to solve. It was one which occupied her mind as she treated and re-bandaged Lamia's wounds, but she found no solution to it. There was nothing in the blisters themselves which offered any explanation, and the patient himself was too far gone to answer any of the questions she was burning to ask him. At last she was finished with him, and it was time to go and see the others, each of whom was in a separate room. 'Hello!' she called, and one of her minders from *Titan* came in at once.

'Where are the others?' she asked. 'I need to see them, and to talk to them in some detail.'

But before she could either see them or speak to them, the sickbay phone buzzed and she lifted it at once. It was Peter Walcott. 'I don't know whether this is good news or bad,' he said crisply, his tone making her suspect that he was in fact quite relieved, 'but Captain Odate has just reported men on *Kraken* with similar symptoms. So it's not just *Psyche*'s problem. It's something bigger.'

She found herself nodding, thinking, if it's not this ship then the next logical culprit must be Manhattan; the two ships that had reported trouble were the closest to it, after all.

But Peter Walcott was still speaking.

'I beg your pardon?' she said.

'I said that the wind has moderated suddenly. Lifted, actually, gone back up several hundred metres. Captain Higgins has called for *Kraken*'s helicopter with Tom Snell and his engineers. He said to tell you that he's taking a team of men up onto the ice. Something about looking for more Russian corpses like that blonde woman.'

Asha went cold with simple terror. She wanted to scream a warning, to order John to avoid the berg until she knew more about what was affecting the sick men's skin in this horrific way. Even if it was not radioactivity, it was still something that Manhattan was doing. Something horrible; something dangerous. But she would only be screaming at Peter Walcott, and he would never pass the message on to John. Even if he did, John would never listen. She took a deep breath. 'I see,' she said.

'Oh,' added Peter, as though this was an afterthought, as from his point of view it probably was, 'he said to tell you he's taking Kate and Colin Ross and Captain Mariner as well.'

Kraken's Westland dropped Tom Snell and his men off on the highest northernmost shoulder of the ice and then skipped low over the tawny sea to pick up the contingents from *Titan* and *Niobe*. John had called for Richard to be included in *Titan*'s specially selected team in the hope of jogging his memory. He suspected that Asha would have ordered that the sick man should remain in bed, knowing that this was the surest way to restore his mind. On the other hand, she had said Richard was physically one hundred per cent, and dying to get out and about, so, in her absence, there seemed no harm in bringing him along. If his mental processes were as acute as she had said they were, he would be an asset to them whether he knew who he was or not.

As John climbed into the helicopter's big square body,

his eyes eagerly sought out the tall frame of his friend, half convinced that the sight of the ships would have restored everything. Failing that, perhaps the shock of being back aboard a helicopter so soon after the accident would jog something back into place. Like Asha, he caught his breath at the almost luminous quality of Richard's gaze. The bright blue eyes seemed to be alight but there was no flicker of recognition, no wide smile of welcome when their eyes met, and John sat, a little deflated, in the seat opposite.

'I'm not sure that this is such a good idea,' said Kate Ross severely.

'Is he likely to do himself any harm?' John sounded defensive in his own ears.

'No,' her own tone moderated in the face of his. 'At least, not if we keep an eye on him. We don't know whether he understands about the dangers of the situation we're going into.'

'Yes I do,' said Richard, making them all jump.

'OK, old chap,' answered John at once. 'But we only have your word for that and we don't know how much you actually remember.'

'I remember about falling off bloody great lumps of ice.'

'Yes. I suppose that sort of knowledge runs pretty deep. Do you remember what one of these is?'

Richard's cocky self-assurance slipped a little. 'Telephone?'

'You remember about portable telephones?' John was stunned. Even Kate was looking surprised, and Colin's eyebrows were just distinguishable from his hairline.

But Richard was shaking his head. 'Asha answered one hanging on the wall by my bed. I asked what it was and she told me.' He looked at John. 'Do you know Asha?'

This was deeply unsettling. Perhaps it had been a bad idea after all. 'I'm married to her. Asha is my wife.'

'So you're John!'

'That's right. Captain John Higgins. Ring any bells?'

Richard pushed his cheeks out slightly and shook his head. He looked mildly regretful but not particularly worried.

'And you don't know what this is?'

'Not if it isn't a telephone.'

'Right. It's what we call a Geiger counter. Do you remember anything about radioactivity?'

Again, Richard blew his cheeks out and shook his head. John took a deep breath and began to explain. They were going up to the furthest extreme of the exposed section of Manhattan and walking south to the bow section; he had a nice long chopper ride to explain to his old friend just what was going on here.

Tom Snell had his men with him on a high point looking northward towards the barely visible shapes of *Ajax* and *Achilles*. They had not been idle while waiting for the helicopter and its passengers; they had already surveyed the immediate area. There were six engineers, a closed unit, who could be relied upon to discuss nothing with the crews of the ships they were on. A unit, moreover, which very much wanted to discover what had happened to their sergeant.

With Richard and the Rosses from *Titan* had come Yves Maille. John had brought Steve Bollom with him, trusting Sally to be senior officer in command of the two lead ships while his own extremely competent second officer guided *Niobe* on a steady course through a calm sea. Other than an unforeseen accident on the ice, only the unexpected return of the harmattan would make things difficult and the French weather expert was confident that he would see it coming early enough for them to get the helicopter back out. And even if that went wrong, they had scaling ropes and two tight-packed inflatables which would be more than enough to get them back to the ships. In this position, *Kraken* and *Psyche* would be the closest; when they got up to the bow section, then the lead ships would be their safest haven.

It felt unnatural to John to be taking command while Richard was with him, but only for the first few moments, then he simply got on with the job. His old friend was quite obviously not fit to command a rowing boat at the moment. But Richard had caught on quickly enough to the way Geiger counters functioned and to the fact that they must maintain the fiction that they were here looking for more mysterious Russian corpses.

'We'll split up into two groups,' ordered John. 'I'll take the seamen with me, and perhaps subdivide again if conditions warrant it. My second group would be led by you, Colin. Tom, you take your unit and do the same if need be. We'll go down the starboard side, you take the port. Colin here has two rough maps of the section above water, but we don't know how accurate they are after the last couple of days' weather. Over to you, Colin.'

As Colin Ross began to talk about elementary ice safety, the group of men and one woman looked glumly down the length of dirty, slushy berg. The island in front of them was still much the same size as the island of Manhattan. It was pear-shaped, with the long point facing south. On either hand of them, the ice reached towards fifteen kilometres in width. Here it seemed largely flat, but it was much more hilly in the middle, especially in the widest sections just aft of *Psyche* and *Kraken* in their anchorage positions three hundred metres below the mean surface level.

They were looking at a long, hard, dirty day's work. Only the fact that they were due to spread out and check the ice's surface with the Geiger counters for unexpected extremes of radiation made the proposed action at all realistic. If they had actually been looking for bodies, the task would have been hopeless. 'Above all, keep an eye on each other,' Colin concluded, the rumble of his voice easily carrying over the quiet tinkling of water which surrounded them like spring-time in the Alps. 'The ice is beginning to perish. God alone knows what fissures, caves and crevasses will open up now. If we were at either Pole in these conditions, I'd be inclined to stay put and radio for help. It will be very dangerous, so take care.'

There was nothing more to be said and they moved off.

Within the hour, John was forced to face the fact that the task they were all engaged in was well-nigh impossible. The ice island was almost as big as his native Isle of Man, and true Manx people never travelled from one end of the island to the other unless they could stay for the night. And no one in their right mind would dream of walking from Douglas to Ramsey unless it was for charity along the Millennium Way, perhaps. Searching the mountainous interior with a dozen companions armed only with Geiger counters and walkie-talkies would be considered the action of someone desperate or insane. It would be an utterly pointless waste of time here and now except that the Geiger counters might discover a source of radioactivity powerful enough to damage the crew of the ships at some range. And, of course, the main object of the exercise was actually to put the minds of the crews at rest by proving that there was nothing unnatural – or supernatural – on the ice at all.

John found these depressing thoughts sweeping over him as he and Richard entered the first real hill valley between rounded swells of ice. Colin and Kate were away on the coastal side of the central icy outcrop and Steve Bollom and his team were just entering the foothills on the inward side of them, between the Rosses and himself. Each team was exploring a notional swathe of territory about two kilometres wide.

411

The surface of the ice was dirty and dull, covered in a thick overlay of wet sand which the runoff was beginning to carve into channels and fans with glistening, crystalline floors. It was a strange, restless environment and it put John forcefully in mind of the strange geodes which he had seen in jewellers' shops all over the world. He had often thought of buying Asha one of those rocky coconuts which contained not white flesh but breathtaking crystals, but he had never had quite enough money in the right place at the right time. Now when he looked around him he felt as though he was walking on the dirty, rocky shell of one which was being slowly worn away to reveal the glittering jewelled interior. All around was the sound of running water and the slither of sliding sand as the fans of streams overlapped and whole slopes of dirt unexpectedly slipped down to reveal dazzling white scars. It was like watching a thaw in negative, with the brightnesses of frosty winter being uncovered as the surface melted.

John found it disturbing. It made it difficult for him to concentrate, and he needed to keep a close eye not only on the read-out of his Geiger counter but also on the massive form of his companion. Richard's every movement seemed to be informed with care and concentration, but John could not forget that his old friend still did not really know who either of them was. It was like walking along a dangerous roadside with a young child: he could never quite be positive that Richard would behave in a sensible, adult manner. Each time he glanced down or looked away, John feared that Richard might have done something stupid in the instant he was out of observation. Quite simply, he was beginning to regret bringing his friend with him at all; he should have followed the advice he knew Asha would have given him and left Richard safely in bed on *Titan*.

As the sides of the gully they were following got steeper, so the depth of the sand-clotted runoff through which they were wading deepened and John's glum thoughts were lightened by a glimmer of relief that he had insisted that they all wear full foul-weather gear and high boots. Richard, slightly ahead, sloshed on like a fluorescent yellow giant, in a world of his own. A turbaned giant – perhaps a genie – with his head bound in a simple bandage. Both men had hoods folded back on their shoulders. It was cold here, but not so cold that they needed their hoods up. John waved his Geiger counter from side to side, glancing down to see the needle staying solidly in the safe green. The constant visual checks were necessary because of the noise; the machine would have had to register a nuclear holocaust before the auditory signal managed to cut through the ceaseless, thunderous, hissing sloshing babble washing around them.

Such was the power of the sound that John did not at first hear the buzzing of his walkie-talkie. Richard did, however. The way in which the two-way radios functioned had been explained to him on the flight over here. 'Someone wants to talk to you,' he bellowed, gesturing.

John jerked the machine up to his ear. 'Higgins,' he yelled.

'Tom Snell here. We've got a reading.'

The chill against which John was so carefully protected suddenly seemed to be inside him. In a column between his heart and his bladder, he froze solid. 'They've got a reading,' he yelled at Richard and was unaccountably relieved when his friend nodded wisely as though he understood the implications of that simple statement. 'Tell me about it,' he ordered Tom Snell.

'Easier said than done, I'm afraid,' came the distant voice of the engineer. 'We're on a broad reach of open country. Pancake flat as far as the eye can see. And we have a reading with nothing to show for it.'

'You can't see anything at all?'

'Ice covered with sand. It's not even rolling. I can see both my other teams on either hand and then the hills you're in on the far eastern horizon. But it's like Blackpool beach here for God knows how many square kilometres. Except that there's no pier and no tower; nothing at all, in fact.'

Richard had come back to stand beside John, crouching slightly so that he could hear what was being said.

'It's under them,' he suddenly announced. 'If there's nothing to see nearby on the surface then it's buried in the ice under their feet.'

John found himself nodding in silent agreement. 'Did you hear that, Tom?'

'Yes. It's what we figured too. The only logical explanation. Was that Captain Mariner?'

'Yes, it was. How strong is the reading?'

'Nice to hear him firing on all cylinders again. The reading isn't all that strong here. Well under danger level . . .'

'But they don't know how deep it's buried,' murmured Richard.

'. . . but we don't know how deep the thing's buried. You think we should dig?'

'Negative. Certainly not. Mark it on your map. Make some kind of notation as to shape and size of the signal; it might be important.'

'Yes, we hadn't thought of that. We'd rather assumed it was going to be one point of emission, but you're right. We'll set to what?'

'Nought point five millisieverts,' said John.

'OK. We'll set to nought point five and trace the shape of the signal at that.'

'If it is one point of emission, they'll just get a circle,' murmured Richard.

John nodded again. 'That's it, Tom,' he said. 'I'll warn Colin Ross. You keep in touch with me.'

'Will do. Over and out.'

John lowered the walkie-talkie from his ear and looked speculatively up at Richard. 'You seem to have a good grasp of this.' There was almost accusation in his tone. 'Are things coming back to you?'

'Nothing you didn't explain in the helicopter,' answered Richard. 'Nothing at all before I woke up in the sickbay.' For the first time, he sounded worried about his loss of memory. 'It will all come back, won't it?'

'Sure to. Soon.'

Their eyes met and John tried to force all the sincerity at his disposal into his. In spite of Richard's brightness and his impressive grasp of the rudiments of radioactivity, John still felt that he had probably overstepped the mark by bringing him along. Whether or not Richard read this in his eyes, the tall man puffed out his cheeks and turned away. Then he was sloshing on up the dirty valley floor and John was following just behind him, looking down and dialling in Colin Ross's wavelength.

And so the day wore on. Morning became noon and afternoon. John realised that in spite of all the meticulously organised preparations, he had omitted to bring any food. He also regretted the decision not to bring skis or ski poles – both of which were available – because they were no use on sand. They would have been very useful on the slopes of soft ice which were so rapidly washing themselves clean, however, and as the afternoon wore on, John's legs began to regret that particular decision, poignantly. The apparent weakness of the walkie-talkies bothered him too; as the slopes above the valley sides gathered around them, so the range of his radio seemed to diminish. The outer teams faltered into incomprehensibility and soon only Colin and Steve Bollom were clearly audible; the military contingent was out of contact altogether, which, under the circumstances, was increasingly worrying.

The head of the valley they had been in when Tom Snell first reported his discovery sloped up to a watershed and then gave on to a high saddle which in turn fell away into another valley. It plunged southward between two parallel ranges of low hills, one running to the east of them and another to the west. High on the saddle, at the very point of the watershed, they paused. Here they had something of a vista to north and to south. Looking back along the track they had followed, they could see how much of the valley was now uncovered. A slow river of sludge, up which they had just waded, seemed to be running sluggishly away onto the outthrust of the plain upon which the helicopter had originally dropped them. Ahead of them, a precipitous valley seemed equally deep in filth, equally beautifully framed. The brightness reflecting off the clean ice slopes seemed to multiply itself from gallery to gallery, emphasising the dull depths of the slowly-moving sand sludge.

The brightness of the slopes was by no means a pure white, however; it was variously champagne, straw and gold. The light of the afternoon sun was still filtered through streams of sand which were being whipped northwards by the high wind. High in terms of speed if not of altitude; the steady thrust of the harmattan was still in excess of sixty knots but the lower edge of the sand was little more than two hundred metres above their heads, and it still gave the impression of being a feverishly active gallery of rock, as though they were moving through some strange kind of lucent cave whose walls glowed with phantom light mysteriously forbidden to the roof and floor.

'Good place to check on the rest of the team,' opined Richard, clearly thinking fast still. John nodded and brought his walkie-talkie to his chilled lips. His eyes narrowly inspected the strange airborne stratum so crushingly close above them as he began to call the teams in, hampered by the bright, thick gloves he wore.

He began with Tom Snell's because he was still waiting to hear details of the shape of their discovery. He soon got through, but heard more than he had bargained for.

'Hello, Tom, this is John, over.'

'Hello, John. Glad to hear from you; we've been trying

to raise you for an hour or more.'

'Any news?'

'Quite a bit. Our readings seem to be in the shape of an arrowhead pointing into the centre of the berg.'

'An *arrowhead*?'

'Correct. An arrowhead about twenty metres at the base and about the same from base to apex. Pointing to the centre of the berg, about five kilometres to the north of *Psyche*'s current anchorage. But there's more. My other teams have registered a whole series of readings. None high. All small. But lots of them. They seem to be in a series of circles all round the arrowhead. As near as we can judge.'

'Do the circles reach out to the cliff overlooking *Psyche*?'

'No. We've been all along that section of the coast but it's clear.'

Thank God, thought John as he clumsily thumbed Colin's wavelength and began to check on the conditions overlooking *Kraken* on the opposite side of the berg. They too were blessedly clear. Steve Bollom's report made John's usually open countenance fold into a frown again, however. The square, reliable first officer and his team were in a valley parallel to John's valley, shorewards and a little ahead. They were concerned about the quality of the ice. They had come across two crevasses already, their narrow mouths betrayed by slow whirlpools of sinking sand. And they had come upon a series of caves which reached back into the increasingly precipitous cliff faces on either hand. Beware, Steve warned. The ice which had borne the brunt of the harmattan was honeycombed, perishing and dangerous.

'Right,' said John decisively as he switched his walkie-talkie to GENERAL RECEIVE and hung it back on his belt. 'It's time to get moving again.'

'Right-oh,' said Richard cheerfully and stepped over the edge of the slope. He made no attempt whatsoever to go down carefully or in a controlled manner; he simply stepped out over the void as though he half expected the air to support him. He came down hard upon his right heel, for the slope fell away steeply into the throat of the high-sided little valley. This high, near the watershed, the sand had all washed away, so his heel came down onto hard ice and it skidded down the hill.

Richard pitched forward as his left leg collapsed at the knee. His weight went over his centre of gravity and the whole of his long body followed that injudiciously placed heel down the slope into the valley below. He was fortunate to topple onto his side so that at least he had the chance of pulling his legs together and in the end he went down riding on his backside, like a child too poor to afford a toboggan.

Had John not been adjusting his walkie-talkie he might have been able to catch his friend, but as things were, the wild leap to grab the rapidly vanishing left arm did nothing more than take John over the edge to join Richard in his wild, incredibly dangerous ride. But where Richard was lucky enough to gain some kind of control over his breathtaking downward slide, John simply went head over heels to land spread-eagled on his belly; and then he slid even more quickly downwards.

At first the wild career was an overwhelming mass of mostly painful sensation shot through with a piercing bitterness in the instant that John realised all his fears about Richard had been fulfilled and the pair of them would be lucky not to be crippled or killed here. He found that he was screaming at the top of his voice and was unsure whether the sound was the result of the bitter realisation or the shocking agony in his elbows and knees. His chin came in violent contact with granite-hard ice. His mouth snapped closed and instantly flooded with blood from a bitten tongue. He saw flashes of light all round the edge of his vision, then a wave of porridgy slush slapped him in the face and he saw nothing clearly for some time. His world shrunk to an internal mindscape of half imagined sensation as he slithered precipitously downwards through flashing lights like stars exploding above the curve of a barren planet; through a freezing, Plutonian sea of blood which sloshed chokingly down his gullet to be joined by bitter tasting sand whenever he tried to part his lips to breathe. The sounds of his overwhelming experience were, perhaps, the only things which truly came from outside, washing in through his ears like the blood washing down his throat – equally progenitive. It was as though he was being born anew, pushed back into an environment all liquid and sanguine, where everything was tearing, bitter and painful and he had yet to achieve that first, regenerating, lung-filling primal scream.

But before he could come back to earth or to life, the wild ride was halted. Had he tried to imagine, high on that icy saddle, what it was like to slide down the length of the valley below, he might have supposed the precipitous journey would have culminated in a slow, spinning slide out over the plain at the bottom into which the valley opened. No such luck. The only luck involved, in fact, was that it was his stocky legs and back which hit first, not his all too breakable arms and head. He was on his side when the valley's most perpendicular wall gathered him to itself and the sensation which was added to all the others was that of being dragged viciously across corrugated iron. First his heels, then his calves; the back of his thighs, his backside; then, punishingly, his kidneys and ribs.

He rolled onto his stomach and came to a stop. He raised his head slowly and spat. He had no idea what he might be spitting at because his eyes were still closed. He emptied his mouth of blood and sand, then continued to hawk and spit, trying unsuccessfully to clear his throat. His mouth hurt even more fiercely than his body and he found himself moving his tongue gingerly, trying to judge how much of it he had bitten off. Once he had established that, his slowly awakening reason suggested, he might try to move his arms and legs, just to see whether he still could.

'*PHEW!*' came an explosive exclamation so close behind him that he established that his whole body could still move by jumping nearly out of his skin. 'That was quite a ride!' the exuberant voice continued, oozing childlike excitement.

John rolled over onto his side and opened his eyes. He found that he was looking up the hill along a long brown tongue of mud which was creeping disorientatingly down towards him, like lava, still bearing the signs of his wild ride. Stiffly, he pushed himself to a sitting position and leaned back against the sheer, corrugated wall that had stopped him. From this position he could see across the mouth of the valley to the overhanging crest of ice opposite, where the foot of the slope ended, not in a gentle hillock reaching down to flat ice, but in a concave, over-hanging cliff face fanged with icicles like a big surf just about to break.

Maybe fifteen metres away, out towards the middle of the valley and further down the slope, sat Richard Mariner, unutterably filthy and obviously ecstatic. As John looked at him, the big man cast a speculative glance back over his shoulder, clearly calculating his chances of getting back up to the watershed for another ride. John folded his left leg in until his boot heel touched his bottom and tried to pull himself to his feet, but his boots simply skidded out from under him, so he rolled over onto all fours, ready to push himself up.

This simple act brought him face to face with the ice cliff he had been leaning back against. Like the far jaw of the valley mouth, it was a breaking wave with a steep overhang supported by stalactites of ice, huge columns too massive to be called mere icicles, which had been large enough to stand against the hot breath of the harmattan. Behind them rose a wall apparently of glass into which, as Steve

Bollom had warned, there reached a honeycomb of caves. And, like a real honeycomb, some of the cave mouths were sealed. Those nearest John, for example, were sealed with thick greenish panes of ice.

Against the inside of the nearest glass-clear pane, staring out from the mouth of a sealed cave with scarcely sane intensity straight into John's eyes was the face of a man. The ice was thick enough to bear the man's weight as he knelt there, leaning forward, clawing against the inner surface as though trying wildly to break out. It was thick enough to bear his weight but clear enough to hide nothing of what was pressed against it. The face was absolutely white where it was covered with skin but some of it, like the claw hands pressing palm out beside it, had been flensed down to red muscle and white bone.

John shouted aloud with shock. He lurched back onto his knees, knocked upright as though by an upper cut. The lips in the face, spread wide in a grinning grimace, were nearly black. The teeth were pearl white and square, seemingly huge between shrunken gums. The nose was fine, slightly hooked and skinless down one side. The cheekbones were sharp, the chin square. The eyes were wide and staring, like marbles; dead as doll's eyes. John shouted again and scrabbled backwards wildly until he was stopped by what felt like two tree trunks close together. He tore his gaze away from the hypnotically shocking vision frozen into the ice cliff and looked up at the figure of Richard Mariner towering above him. Richard reached down, gripped him by the shoulder and, as though he was weightless, raised him to his feet. Without taking his eyes off the figure which had so shocked John, he said quietly, 'So that's what happened to him. I wondered. We all did.'

Still deeply gripped by shock, John gasped and gobbled for a moment until the effect the corpse had had on Richard registered. '*What?*' he said. 'Who wondered what, for heaven's sake?'

'Robin, Colin, Ann Cable; everyone else who knew him.

421

Wondered what happened to him after they got away.'

'You know who this is? You *remember* who this is?' John simply could not believe what was happening. How could the shock of finding another corpse on this God-cursed iceberg possibly have jolted Richard's memory back into place?

But it had. 'Oh yes,' he said quietly, his voice even colder than the unforgiving ice around him. 'I remember everything about this particular son of a bitch. I never actually met him, but I've seen his picture often enough and I know all there is to know about him, now.'

Chapter Twenty-Three

The messages both found their way desultorily and at different times into the communications room in the bowels of 2 Dzerzhinsky Street, Moscow. One came direct from England and the other, more circuitously, from Washington via East Germany in the normal liaison between the STASI and the KGB. Thence they were passed to the records section as neither report was tagged urgent nor important. In the old days, they would have been filed – everything was always filed – and forgotten for years until some grey *apparatchik* made a connection on the third or fourth routine check. But not now. Now they were fed straight into the computer to join the millions of other random pieces of information in its almost infinite memory. Because the mainframe was only updated with non-urgent information once a month, it happened that the news of both Dougie Dundas's strange death and the form of Paul Chan's unusual scar were fed in together.

Seven years or so previously, in the aftermath of Chernobyl and before Tomsk Seven had demonstrated how little anyone really cared about nuclear accidents in Russia, a perpetual file had been opened especially to contain facts related to the disaster. The file had been tagged, in those far-off days when the disaster was still of major political importance, for the attention of the Deputy Director. So that, although the reports individually were of no apparent importance, coming together as they did they caused the computer automatically to reactivate the Chernobyl file. The original program was clear and the directive inescapable: into this file the computer had to place any reports of radioactive black glass and any reports of the words Leonid and Brezhnev when associated with ships, the sea or radioactivity.

And the fact that the file was being reactivated and thus updated rang an alarm bell in the Deputy Director's office.

Moscow was in turmoil. President Yeltsin was preparing for direct confrontation with the People's Assembly who were preparing to barricade themselves in the White House. There was a threat of revolution in the air and senior officers of both the armed and security services were habitually rushing hither and yon at a moment's notice, summoned for secret negotiations by one side or the other as the political situation slid rapidly out of control.

Even so, it was unusual for a senior officer in GRU Army Intelligence to be riding towards Dzerzhinksy Street last thing on a Friday evening – unless he was going to the Detsky Mir toy store to buy a doll for his daughter who was waiting with his wife at their weekend dacha out in the woods. This, indeed, was an idea which appealed to Lieutenant General Boris Bovary, for he did not relish being summoned to the offices of a rival organisation on such short notice. But he was an acute man, and he had not risen to eminence merely by being the most successful intelligence commander in Afghanistan. No, he thought as his Zil pulled up and his driver saluted him smartly out of the back, the KGB might be a toothless tiger, but it still had long claws. And an infinite memory.

He paused on the steps and looked across the wide road towards the bright bustle of the store where only the most privileged, the richest, and the foreign could afford to shop. Like most of the other big shops, in fact, during this painful period of post-Party reconstruction.

Bovary had been careful not to speculate about why he

had been summoned here. No one in his own office had been able to think of anything. His commanding officer had also been stumped but gruffly certain of the importance of whatever it was. The old man was tired and out of touch nowadays but Boris respected his contacts. Indeed, he respected his own contacts, too. So, if there was no glimmer of news, then this was either very secret or extremely obscure. Speculation would only serve to channel his mind into presuppositions which would blinker him and be counter-productive, perhaps dangerous.

With his mind absolutely blank, therefore, he presented his credentials and followed the shapely figure of a young secretary sent to escort him up to his destination. She had a fine-boned, intelligent face, a full chest which caused the buttons of her fine blouse to strain, a slim waist and wide, welcoming hips. In the lift, alone with her, he sniffed secretly but appreciatively. She smelt of soap, even in this heat. Most attractive.

But no. This kind of speculation could blinker a man just as effectively as any other kind. He wanted to be acute, not lustful. He blanked his mind again, automatically rearranging the already perfect lines of his sage-brown dress uniform – and failed to notice the speculative glance she shot him from the corner of her wide, violet eyes.

The office of the Deputy Director looked down towards the square where the statue of Felix Dzerzhinsky himself had stood until so recently. With his mind still carefully blank, Boris Bovary glanced across the room from the doorway, noted the view and then concentrated on the man who was standing idly looking down upon it. At least the KGB was not yet run by women, the soldier mused, unlike the British Secret Services.

'General Bovary, Deputy Director,' said the woman by way of introduction, then she shut the door behind her as she left.

The Deputy Director looked up, and the two men began

to take the measure of each other. Each one might have been looking in a mirror. They were both square, solid Georgians whose thick hair and long eyes spoke eloquently of Cossack blood. There was only a year or two between them and it would have been hard to say which was the older.

'What do you know about icebergs, General?' asked the Deputy Director.

Bovary stayed where he was, so close to the door that his shoulders might have touched it had he not been at parade ground attention. 'Nothing germane, Deputy Director.'

'Germane,' mused the KGB man. 'A good word. Well-chosen. Please sit down while I consider its implications.'

Boris marched to the chair indicated. He bent his knees ninety degrees and his elbows one hundred and twenty degrees, allowing his hands to cross in his lap, but remained at attention as he sat. He refused to let his mind speculate, though this was now something of a strain.

'By *germane* I suppose you mean in a relevant intelligence context. I see your point. How can icebergs be of any interest to the intelligence services? Well, I will tell you. Icebergs become relevant when they become politically important. You understand this?'

'So, we are discussing the iceberg called Manhattan which is currently en route to Africa under the eyes of the world's most powerful leaders and the United Nations, with the widely welcomed support of Premier Yeltsin and the merchant marine personnel he has graciously supplied.'

The Deputy Director's eyebrows rose appreciatively. They were square, shaggy eyebrows, like those of the late Comrade Party Secretary Leonid Brezhnev.

'Have you read the Red File on Chernobyl?'

'It was one of the files passed to us during the internal *perestroika* phase. We passed many Red Files back to you.

426

And, in any case, many of the facts in the Chernobyl file were originally supplied by us.'

'I will accept that as a simple yes, shall I?' There was an instant of silence. 'I'm beginning to appreciate your use of language, General. *Germane . . .*' The Deputy Director flicked open a humidor and the fragrance of Virginia tobacco filled the room. He gestured. Bovary accepted – American cigarettes were his only weakness. Well, perhaps not his *only* weakness . . .

The two men lit up, watching each other through the smoke.

'You are speculating about the links between an iceberg called Manhattan and the disaster at Chernobyl,' probed the Deputy Director.

As a matter of fact, Bovary was not. But the strain of keeping his mind blank was beginning to make him sweat.

'They can be encapsulated in two words,' persisted the Deputy Director as seductively as Mephistopheles whispering to Faust. '*Leonid Brezhnev.*'

Bovary jumped, struck against his will by the coincidence: he had been thinking of Brezhnev only an instant before – of his eyebrows.

The Deputy Director supposed that he must have struck a chord in his military audience. 'I am surprised you realise the significance of the name,' he said, piqued. 'I had not realised that the loss of the *Brezhnev* had reached your ears. She was so carefully . . . *non*-military. Unusually so; that was her only flaw. Or so we thought.'

Bovary's mind was no longer blank. It was making quantum leaps from one cryptic comment to the next, tying them together. How accurately he was making these links he had no idea as yet. He sat in silence, therefore, knowing how seductive that, too, could be.

'There was pandemonium here when she vanished, of course. But then the received knowledge, the best guess, came to be that she was somewhere at the bottom of the

Arctic Ocean near Novaya Zemlya. Which was where the black glass was supposed to be in any case. So. No harm done then, and everyone relaxed.'

But now things have started turning up. Bovary began to gain enough confidence in his understanding to predict the Deputy Director's words.

'But now one or two unusual reports have appeared in the Chernobyl file.'

Close. Black glass? On the iceberg Manhattan?

'Firstly, we have a report of a death on the iceberg Manhattan, caused by the ingestion of radioactive black glass.'

'Ingestion?'

'A soldier swallowed it. He must have thought it was worth a lot.'

Bovary nodded once. Smuggling was not unknown among his own soldiers either.

'It killed him of course. In the same report we have dental records from another corpse discovered on Manhattan, a very much older corpse whose dental records conform with those of the first officer of the missing ship.'

'Pretty conclusive . . .'

'And finally, we have a report from Washington that one of the scientists working on the ice seems to have an unusual radiation burn. It apparently looks like this.' The Deputy Director pushed a piece of paper across to Bovary who instantly recognised the rough Cyrillic letters even though they were reversed.

He sucked his cigarette and allowed his mind full rein.

'It was the computer,' said the Deputy Director, his defences destroyed by wonder. 'A couple of reports from opposite sides of the world. Nothing to do with each other. Nothing to do with anything. In they go to the computer and my alarm bells start ringing and the Director says, "Cancel your weekend, Dimitri!" Vodka?'

'The implications of the situation seem obvious.' Bovary's words were distantly academic, but he nodded yes as he spoke them. The Deputy Director reached into his desk drawer as he listened. 'The potential political damage is incalculable. If the situation is discovered and blame is apportioned here, then we will be drummed out of the United Nations.'

'Out of the international community,' supplied the Deputy Director over the sound of clinking glass and gurgling liquid. 'Goodbye World Bank. Goodbye international aid. Goodbye economy.'

'Hello revolution.' Bovary tossed back the vodka and slammed his glass down on the desk. 'Hello anarchy.' The fiery liquid seemed to have taken his breath away.

'Hello civil war,' said the Deputy Director, sipping his drink more slowly.

Silence fell, broken only by the sound of vodka pouring and the scream of a siren from Dzerzhinsky Street.

'The iceberg must be stopped, lost or destroyed before anyone finds out.' Bovary drank his second vodka.

'It represents a billion cubic metres of water. Remember, the one-tenth above the water alone is the size of Manhattan Island.'

'It is not a situation calling for subtlety, then.'

'Which is why we have turned to the GRU, General.'

'The Russian personnel already involved . . .' The vodka was tempting Bovary into thinking aloud, something he rarely did.

'A good thought, and one which is already being looked into.'

'But also there is something else. Something military.'

'Something relevant. Something elegant. You have a man out there. The right man. The relevant man. The man who started it all, so to speak.'

'*Gogol!* Mother of God, you want me to send in Gogol!'

'He is, as they say, in the right place at the right time.'

'But he's retired . . . Sick . . . Dying. He's a salesman, not—'

'He's within five hundred kilometres of the point of reception with a division of main battle tanks and a squadron of heavily-armed helicopters.'

Bovary sat, stunned, staring fixedly at the clear greenish glass of his empty vodka tumbler. The Deputy Director refilled it for him.

'Perhaps the first step would be to ask General Gogol to assess the situation.'

Bovary tossed the clear liquid back. 'Well, he could certainly take a look, I suppose.'

'And no one any the wiser, if he's careful.'

Bovary shook his head in wonder. 'Yes. He would have little trouble in arranging that, but I warn you . . .'

'Yes?'

'He's not . . .' Bovary paused, searching for a word that might impart his worry without divulging his knowledge. 'Not *answerable*.'

'You mean he's out of control?'

'No.' *Yes*, thought Bovary, and the Deputy Director read it in his eyes.

'A loose cannon, perhaps.' The Deputy Director moderated the phrase carefully so that the military man could accept it.

'Partly. Perhaps.'

'But you can communicate with him? Ask him to take a look?'

'I can order him to make a reconnaissance and a detailed tactical report, yes, of course.'

'But how quickly? How *soon*?'

'That depends on the clearance.'

The Deputy Director slid across the desk a document on the bottom of which were a series of signatures. Bovary recognised them at first glance, though he checked their authenticity closely. The last, least important of them, belonged to his commanding general.

He picked up the phone.

'Who are you calling?'
'First my commanding officer, then General Gogol.'
'You're calling Gogol? On the phone? From here? Now?'
'If he's in his tank or his helicopter I'll get straight through. If he's anywhere else they'll page him. He's on the Dark Continent, Dimitri, not in the Dark Ages.'

Chapter Twenty-Four

General Valerii Gogol stood on the rocky outcrop above the drought-withered River Mau and looked around with the slow, intense concentration which Ann Cable remembered from his behaviour in the witness box after Chernobyl. The intensity of that gaze, even at this distance, made it seem that the general could all too easily see through lies, persiflage, disguises and rocky hiding places. Ann slithered back into the crack which was concealing both herself and Robert Gardiner. But then, typically, the action, an almost unconscious movement towards self-preservation, immediately begot its opposite. 'Brace up, Cable,' she muttered to herself and began to move outwards again, scrabbling for her camera.

'What are you doing?' whispered Robert anxiously, still in the self-preservation mode.

'Going for a picture.'

'You're mad! Look what they've just done to those others! Do you want flying lessons?'

'Sod you, Gardiner. That's a five-star Russian general up there. This is big news!'

'But he'll kill us, Ann. God knows what he'll do! I mean, what if he's mixed up with the slaughter we've just witnessed upcountry? What if—'

'What if nothing! Of course he's mixed up in it. Who else is in charge of those tanks? And how could that village have been destroyed without the involvement of the tank? And

433

who else but the people who destroyed the village would also destroy the landing field? I mean I saw that bastard there when poor old Harry Parkinson was killed. The only question is whether General Gogol has gone out of control or whether this is official Kremlin policy! Can you imagine the trouble Yeltsin will be in if he's sanctioned this?'

Ann's manic wriggle to get into a good position for a photograph and the hissing conversation were brought to a halt as a spray of pebbles fell past their hiding place and they realised that someone was just above their heads, looking down.

They froze and for the next few moments it was as though the added weight of the man on the rock above them was enough to close the whole thing down on their heads with crushing power. As they lay, hardly daring to breathe, even had the weight of the rock allowed them to, Ann kept her eyes firmly on the general. And it became obvious to her that he was not the same man she had seen interviewed at the Chernobyl enquiry. The same person, yes, there was no doubting that, but the man himself, the physical man, had changed. Gogol seven years ago had been thin but strikingly fit-looking. Almost threateningly athletic, he had moved with a sinister grace and the slightest of bounces, exactly the type of movement she associated with a hunting cheetah. Then he had worn the battle dress of a full general as though it was a suit from the most exclusive of English tailors. Now he wore the ubiquitous battle fatigues which everyone with military pretensions – or dreams – could find anywhere in the world. But he did not fill them; they hung off him as though they had been bought for someone much larger, much fitter. Only the red scarf knotted round the turkey-skinned throat and the jauntily angled green beret gave a hint of the old style. Now there was something emaciated about him; a withered gauntness which was eerily apparent even from this distance, an aura of sickness almost as powerful as the febrile intensity of his gaze. The effect of such intelligence attached to such corporeal corruption was deeply disturbing. Nimrod Chala might be a sadistic power-crazed psychopath, but Gogol was a dead body looking for somewhere to lie down, a man with no life left and nothing left to lose. And he was one of the foremost tactical intelligences of his day. It seemed all too probable that the pair of them wanted to speak to her. Urgently. It was more than enough to restart her unconscious wriggling towards self-preservation.

The ledge was narrow and the cleft reaching back into the black rock tapered so sharply that it pinched their legs and especially their feet painfully as they tried to crush themselves more deeply into it. And their movement finally disturbed the creatures whose home the humans had temporarily usurped. The first sign of life that Ann felt was a rushing scuttle up her right thigh. It required all of her most gritty fortitude to remain silent and immobile as that first scratchy movement over her sensitised flesh abruptly warned her that there were insects running all over her legs. Quite big insects, by the feel of things. Robert lurched beside her and she looked into his face from a disturbingly intimate closeness, as though they were sharing a bed. His face seemed to be swelling as if his head was a balloon being inflated. Sweat beaded his glistening skin. He began to twitch as though gripped by the onset of an epileptic seizure.

Ann came near to panic then, not just because the invasive scuttle was forbidden complete intimacy with her body only by the tightness of her underwear, but also because she knew in her bones that Robert was about to scream. Wildly, guided by nothing even faintly like logic, she reached across, took his head between her hands and crushed her lips to his with all the power at her command. It was not really a kiss; it was a kind of oral gagging. It worked. She felt the trembling in him ease, and was in fact so shocked by her own action that she too began to put the visceral reaction to those intimately scurrying legs into some kind of perspective.

Whatever was running all over her with such frenetic activity was at least not biting or stinging. Visions of scorpions and soldier ants began to recede. Robert's lips began to move against her own and she correctly assumed that she had rechannelled some of his thoughts too. She broke away and turned back to her observation of the rocky pulpit. The grim, gaunt spectre of General Gogol was gone. Indeed, as her heartbeat slowed and her terror diminished, so the pattern of sounds going on above began to make some kind of sense to her. She lay down on her back, exhausted, and concentrated on what she could hear.

Footsteps were receding, grating over a cinder road bed. Then came the coughing of an engine being fired up and the thud, thud, thud of helicopter rotors. As they lay side by side staring upwards past the sheer edge towards the hard blue sky, concentrating fiercely and trying to envision what they could hear, the rotors achieved power and the helicopter lifted invisibly, clattering away down the distant, rock-hidden sky.

Silence surged slowly back into the afternoon, and the movement of whatever was crawling over them suddenly resumed its importance as the danger presented by General Gogol and General of Police Nimrod Chala receded. Robert began to move, preparing to climb back up over the cliff edge and out of this nest of busy creatures at once. Ann beat against his back until he paused. 'Be careful!' she hissed. 'They may have left a guard!'

He nodded, and began to move again, but this time with careful slowness, like a cat, pulling himself clear of the crack a centimetre at a time, and rising with absolute concentration to peer up over the edge of the rock. As his leg came level with Ann's face, she was given a very unwelcome close-up of the cloth of his khaki bush trousers stretched tight across his thigh. Hanging on the cotton fabric was a fat black spider the size of her spread hand. Her whole body bucked as a picture of what owned the scurrying feet filled her mind and she had to crush the back of her hand against her already bruised lips to stop herself calling out.

'There's a guard post!' hissed Robert. 'Three guards and a hut beside the track.'

Ann could taste blood and she suddenly realised this was because her teeth were fastened in the skin on the back of her hand. The spider fell off Robert's leg and was heavy enough to make a sound as it hit the rock surface by her ear. It scrambled onto its feet and scuttled away. 'They're keeping a careful watch, I think they've been ordered to search for us!'

He paused, probably waiting for an answer, but she didn't dare take her hand away from her mouth. She hated spiders even when they were small. The one on her belly, crawling from hip to hip at the moment, seemed even larger than the one that had fallen off Robert. It was moving across the upper swell of her stomach above the line of her panties, pausing for a moment to push one leg exploratorily into her navel. She could feel each of its eight feet and every single hair on its heavy black coconut of an abdomen. This was a section from one of her worst nightmares. If only she had been wearing long trousers like Robert. The shorts, cut loose for coolness, gave her no protection at all. The only thing stopping it crawling upward to explore her chest was the precious camera bag resting on her ribs.

'No, wait!'

A distant call echoed out over the railway track.

'They're going into the hut. All of them.' He paused. There was nothing to hear but the moaning of the wind, the calls of distant birds, the scratching of spider claws on the rock nearby and the rhythmic hiss of Ann's breath through constricted nostrils. 'Right! Coast clear!' He was in motion, scrabbling upwards, kicking spiders loose as he went. She lay rigid until his face was thrust out over the cliff face above her. 'Quickly!' he hissed. The word coincided with the final movement of the spider, scuttling across to tumble off her hip into the loose leg of her shorts. She was in motion at once, tearing her hand away from her mouth and rolling over onto her stomach. Then she was crawling along the ledge with the bag tucked clumsily under her left armpit and reaching up to grab his offered clasp.

On the cliff edge side of the ledge there was no cover at all so they were forced to scuttle across the tracks into the thin jungly scrub at the foot of the vertical cliff which reached up towards the high country above their heads. Here they both fell to their knees, irrespective of the danger, and tore at their clothing until they were certain that there were no spiders left anywhere near their super-sensitive skin.

After a few minutes of frenetic activity, they stopped, crouched with their backs against the trunk of the one tree nearby broad enough to support them both, and began to think their position through. Every now and again, one or the other of them would shudder and scratch, as though the spiders were still in place.

'We'll have to go back the way we came on the train,' hissed Robert. 'We'll never get past that guard hut.'

'Do you think they'll be looking for us?' She asked the question like someone probing at a cavity in a suspect tooth.

'They were looking for us on the train,' he said.

She thought back to her earlier musings while she had been looking at Gogol and had to agree. It could not possibly be a coincidence that the two people they had seen killed were the two people who had talked to them on the train. No doubt Chala and Gogol had stopped the train for their own reasons, but whatever their original motive they had also been searching for the two of them.

Whoever set fire to the landing strip would almost certainly have checked in the little Cessna, so they would know that Robert Gardiner from the UN was involved in the situation and witness to the massacre in the N'Kuru village. Nimrod Chala or one of his underlings could all too easily have checked the flight plan and found that the best-selling writer and investigative journalist Ann Cable was registered as a passenger and in all probability trying to get the story of village massacres and Russian battle tanks out to the news-hungry world. Gogol himself had seen that they were involved with Harry Parkinson and it wouldn't take Sherlock Holmes to link them to the dead man's Land Rover. Someone must have found Harry's Land Rover outside the station in the township and the Kyoga officials behind the ticket counter and the barrier would both have remembered them quite clearly. That Land Rover would have been the key of course: whoever had been driving the T–80 main battle tank in the dry bed of the Blood River must have been able to see it clearly in the bright moonlight, and so would the gunner through his gunsights, number plate and all.

'We've no chance at all if we stay up here,' Ann said, urgently. 'We've got to get down somehow.'

'Depends on where we're going . . .' temporised Robert.

'We're going to Mawanga city! Where else?' She was up and in motion at once, pushing on back along the path they had followed in the train. He followed, listening as she continued to whisper with vivid passion. 'It's the only place we've got a chance, though even there it's a slim one. We've got to get down onto the plain first, then find some way of getting back.'

'Try for a bush taxi?'

'Possibly. Hire a boat if we have to and go down the river

itself. But we can't wait around up here. And I don't think it would be wise to wait for the next train!'

He nodded. 'The only reason for the train to slow down here is for a police inspection. If it doesn't slow, we can't get on. If it does slow, we'd be lucky not to get caught as the soldiers go through it again. And this is just the first of the inspection posts. There must be another half a dozen of them between here and the coast.'

'What about the roads?'

'Same number.'

'What about the river?'

'There was a patrol boat but I don't think they use it any more. The river is dry to all intents and purposes. It's a mere shadow of its former self all the way down towards the coast, and it doesn't even make it to the sea any longer. It empties into a lake about ten kilometres upstream from the city limits and that's it.'

'It's still the best way back, though, isn't it?'

'In terms of avoiding police patrols and checkpoints, yes, it is.'

'Well, that's what we want to do.' She stopped and looked at him, her face drawn with desperation. Real, disabling panic welled up in her and threatened to incapacitate her. 'We can't let them catch us! There's no telling what they'd do to us!'

This time he had no dry riposte to offer. He gave a numb, defeated nod. She was right. They had very little chance of escaping the situation alive. If they were caught, death would be certain – and unimaginably protracted and horrible. He met the hopeless desperation in her gaze and frowned with fear in reply.

'How do people keep going in situations like this?' she whispered.

'One step at a time, I suppose,' he answered. His voice was rusty, as though he had been screaming until it broke.

'Right. Our first step is to get down to the plain. Any ideas?'

Under the influence of her impassioned fear, he refrained from making any grim suggestions about flying and seriously began to think about the question. Soon after they had left the N'Kuru township, they had crossed the bridge over the Leopold Falls. The river was running low and the falls themselves had been revealed as a series of rocky steps down to the plain. How far back were the falls? Pretty far.

'Wasn't there some kind of cable car affair a little way back?' asked Ann suddenly. 'I remember coming under some machinery. I think it was broken down.'

'Yes! I remember it. It was a bauxite lift or some such thing, designed to get minerals from the plateau down to the river for transportation to the city – in the days when the river was a reliable way of transporting anything. It's ruined and deserted now. There may be a way down there, though. Good thinking!'

The lift had been constructed on a widening of the ledge where it was possible for goods trains to stop and be loaded if there were no barges available. The whole thing consisted of three compounds, one at the head of the cliff high on the jungly escarpment, one here on the main ledge behind the railway track on a semi-circular spur line, and one at the foot of the cliff on the river bank far below. The middle compound, behind the track, was the smallest by the look of things, a couple of hundred metres square surrounded by rotting, jungle-covered fencing. Inside the compound was a big storage shed, a loading facility beside the rusty spur line and the winding machinery which controlled the big box lifts that raised and lowered the consignments of ore from the cliff top. Outside the compound, in a little area of its own on the far side of the main tracks, stood another winding house which controlled the lines down to the riverside. It was all deserted and, in the gathering evening when Ann and Robert arrived, chillingly eerie.

They had been following a rough path through the jungle, trying with marked success to stay out of the general view. They had cowered behind mercifully massive bushes on the two occasions when trains had thundered past and had been fortunate to be under such a solidly impenetrable canopy, for time and again helicopters had swooped unnervingly over the cliff edge just above them and blattered away across the river and out over the grasslands. The vegetation in the groin between the horizontal ledge and the vertical cliff face was surprisingly lush, fed no doubt by the constant rain of detritus from the abundant vegetation overhanging the edge three hundred metres above their heads. It was very light in animal occupation, however, and although there were vivid, occasionally shocking hoots and monkey calls from the jungle far above, here there were only the calls of birds and the chitterings, rustlings and flutterings of the insect world. The earth upon which they trod so silently was a strange, soft stinking mixture of rotting vegetation and bird droppings liberally intermingled with the shattered corpses of monkeys who had fallen over the cliff above and failed their flying lessons as spectacularly as the people from the train. There was nothing of real soil about the place at all, no earth, no sand, stones or rock fragments, simply this thick, incredibly fertile layer of rotting ex-life on the flat black basalt. Only the roots of the abundant vegetation held the whole microcosm together, and these were beginning to give way as the bushes and trees slowly surrendered to drought.

Dead or not, dying or not, the jungle had invaded the ancient compound and held it in its thrall. The rusted, rotten diamonds of the compound wire surrendered to the first tentative push as though there was no trace of true metal left within them at all. The concrete which had once graced the main compound area was crumbling and floury. The rails of the little spur were the colour of dry blood in the setting sun as the two lost humans followed them ever more slowly across to the storage facility. The necessity of keeping out of sight forced first Robert then Ann into the bush-bulging web-clouded tombs of the buildings. Broken windows and doors gave easy access to desolate offices, which still contained, apparently undisturbed in nearly thirty years, a few pathetic sticks of furniture, books and calendars. Like children in a haunted house, they wandered through the gathering shadows, glancing here and there at the rubbish left behind by men who had apparently been spirited away like the crew of the *Marie Celeste*. The whole place had a disturbing air, as though sometime during its long, lonely wait, the buildings had gone native in the worst possible way.

It was an impression intensified by the big warehouse behind the offices. Here, everything that had been constructed by humans had been taken over by other, older life forms, which had then died in their turn. The branches of the adventurous vegetation which had explored the buildings lay about like white bones, twisted and alien. In the square metal box girders high above, the huge untidy nests of nameless, long dead birds extended the shadows and were, seemingly, home to nothing but insects now. On the ground, low bushes, dead and skeletal, rose and fell over piles of invisible produce so worthless that no one had even bothered to stack it properly. There was a silence about the place, emphasised by the chittering of the insects high above; a silence so intense it seemed to whisper. Robert and Ann stood side by side on the threshold of the place, looking across the wilderness of dead things. Ann thought inescapably of the spiders that had run across her body earlier that day.

'I'm not going in there,' she said aloud.

The sound of her voice echoed briefly. The vibration of the words seemed to set dust to slithering down walls and settling through the strange dead sunbeams reaching across the dead air.

In the tiny silence that followed, something stirred. Something strange and close by.

'We don't need to be in here anyway,' said Robert more quietly, his eyes everywhere. 'We just need to see whether there is anything that will get us down.'

'If the winding gear is in this state, nothing mechanical will,' opined Ann, also quietly. The pair of them were backing out of the big room now, still side by side, their eyes searching for whatever was making that strange, snuffling movement.

'You know I still have the pistol in my camera bag,' breathed Ann as they fell back through the frame of the main access door into the corridor between the derelict offices.

'Forget it,' suggested Robert. 'Let's just leave whatever is in there well alone!' and the pair of them turned and fled.

Outside, they followed the sagging cables across the compound, over the spur line, out past a crazy gate, across the main line and out to the edge of the plateau. As they moved, glancing nervously over their shoulders, they discussed what the thing in the main shed might have been, but they had nothing to go on and could do little more than guess. In spite of the gathering darkness, the blustering of the increasingly boisterous evening wind and the way in which the red-edged shadows intensified the disturbing atmosphere, they tried to keep their speculation within reasonable bounds. It could be anything from a goat thrown off one of the trains to a big dog that had scavenged its way along the ledge from the township. It might even have been one of the monkeys that had fallen from the cliff edge above and flown a little more successfully than the rest. Whatever it was, it was left well behind them once they had crossed the main track, and their quiet conversation began to speculate whether or not there was a direct way down from here.

The door into the second winding house yielded easily.

There was an impressive bolt padlocked shut on the outside but the screws holding the bolt had rusted and the wood into which they were screwed was dust. At Robert's first push, the whole thing simply tore loose and the door swung inwards on screaming hinges. There was just enough light to see the machinery inside, and to register the fact that it was every bit as rusty as the bolt and hinges were. Caught between desperation and the grudging realisation that it had been a long shot that anything here could have been of much use to them, they went on into the big room.

It was the view ahead which claimed them first, for beyond the rust-red shape of the machinery, the wall was open to allow the cables access. Through the opening, it was possible to see in the glimmering blue distance the far horizon where the vivid sky crushed down upon the quivering, brick-red earth. After the claustrophobic closeness of the jungle they had been fighting through, the distances were breathtaking.

Ann blinked tears out of her eyes and looked away. On either side of them were two rooms, glass-panelled, containing the controls of the machines which squatted in front of them. Ann looked into the nearest of the control rooms, noting with wry amusement the posters on the wall above the main control board. One depicted a range of half-familiar black faces – the freedom fighters of a generation or two ago. Beside it hung a poster showing a huge black woman, stark naked, full frontal, with legs astride and hands on hips, all arrogant lip curl, overflowing curves and rich, dark promise trembling on the edge of threat.

The bull chimpanzee came through the door behind them at a full charge slowed only by the fact that it was crippled. The speed and noise of its entrance had all the impact of an attack by a mountain gorilla. The creature was massive of its kind, a metre and a half high, though hunched and twisted by injuries to spine and legs. Its bones were huge and made all too obvious by the state of the flesh and hide upon them – the one reduced to string and the other to mange by a combination of starvation and disease. Its face was emaciated too, making the size of its red eyes and the length of its yellow fangs all the more obvious. A foam of drool overflowed its thick black lips and spattered onto the black-haired breadth of its chest. Its cavernous belly heaved as it bellowed at them and, below, its gender and its rage were alike shockingly obvious.

The two humans ran at once, rushing to take refuge behind the hulking metal of the winches themselves. As each of them went a different way, the chimp was given pause and it fell forward onto the knuckles of its massive hands. The thunder of the impact seemed to make the wooden floor shake and it was suddenly borne upon Ann's mind that the solid foundation of the building ended just beyond the weighty machine. The wooden section which she and Robert were currently cowering upon was in fact built out over the sheer drop down which the cables reached. As if to emphasise the point, the hot red wind battered in through the open section immediately behind them and the cables groaned as though they were in eternal agony. The chimpanzee at once took up the cry, battering the floor with its knuckles, obviously building itself up to another charge. 'Give me the gun!' yelled Robert.

As though the creature understood the words, it ran bellowing round Robert's side of the machine at once, hurling itself at him bodily, long before Ann could free the weapon from the camera bag. It missed on its first charge and brushed past Ann as it rushed wildly across the open area of the overhang, the fetid stench of its rancid body, rotting flesh, and putrid breath making her gasp. It was slow to turn, giving her an instant more to rip the zipper wide. The gun came clumsily into her shaking fists as the rest of her precious equipment cascaded unnoticed onto the floor. 'Give it to me!' snarled Robert at her shoulder and she would gladly have done so, but there was no time left.

The beast hurled itself forward again just as her wildly twitching thumb found the switch which ignited the red dot. By sheer chance, the dot was on its left nipple. She didn't even register this consciously before she was pressing the trigger. Her wild attempts to switch on the red dot had set the gun to automatic and it spat a skein of bullets at the chimpanzee, which stitched up the left side of its chest, shattering its ribs and detonating its collar bone, hurling it up in the air, still screaming, and chucked it out through the open wall. Ann watched it go over the edge, utterly unconscious of the fact that the bullets were spitting through the corrugated tin of the roof, following the red dot across the ceiling above her head. The thunderous pounding of the impact was deafening and the dust billowing down the air was joined by a thickening rain of insects.

'STOP!' screamed Robert and jerked Ann back part of the way towards reality. She dropped the gun altogether. Then, still held by the dark magic of the moment, she stepped over the smoking gun and walked across to the opening. She stood against a low rail, looking down to see where the creature had gone.

It had not gone far. On the left-hand side of the wood-floored balcony which overhung the two-hundred-metre drop down to the river was a tall structure of wood and metal which had clearly once contained a lift car. On one strut of this, perhaps twenty metres down, the animal hung like a length of tatty black carpet. Even as Ann watched it, overwhelmed by a disorientating surge of guilt, the creature twitched, probably in its final death throes, and fell free of the strut to disappear down the hollow shaft. After a while, there came a dull thud, flat and final, carried up on the red wind.

Robert's arm came round her shoulder then and he folded her in against his broad chest. She began to sob uncontrollably. It was not simply the death of the creature which affected her, nor even the fact that she had actually killed it with her own hands; it was this coming on top of all the death and destruction with which she had been surrounded since she came out into the bush with him. He knew that. He probably also knew that the kiss she had pressed against his lips in the hiding place on the cliff had been nothing more than a ploy to keep him silent. In any event, his embrace was avuncular and bracing, designed to strengthen, not seduce. His gaze in any case was reaching out over the dark curve of her head and down the lift shaft which had just swallowed the body of the chimp. If the rest of this place was anything to go by, its fastenings were probably about as solid as that rusty bolt's. And the wood struts were probably so wormy they would crumble at a touch. But there was no getting round it: that was the best way down they were likely to come across.

He shook her gently until her sobs choked off. 'Come on,' he said quietly. 'Let's get out of here before Tarzan arrives looking for Cheeta there.'

Wisely, she would not venture onto the wooden structure without a safety harness, so after picking up the contents of her bag they spent the last half-hour of daylight searching for rope. They found it in a supply room off the late chimpanzee's indoor kingdom just at that trembling blood-red moment when the last of the light died at the end of the short tropical evening. There was an awful lot of it – more than a hundred metres. They searched desultorily in the dark for something to cut it with, without success.

'We'll have to wait now,' she said, not too sadly, as they walked back across the compound towards the main rail track, for she was bone-tired and envisaged a night's exhausted sleep.

'That's right,' he agreed. 'We'll go back to the winding shed then you can get forty winks. I'll wake you at moonrise.'

'We're going down in the dark?'

'It won't be that dark; it's coming up to full moon, remember. And anyway, we want to be out of here as soon as possible. Even if no one heard the shots, I still don't fancy being caught halfway down that shaft if a chopper comes by in the morning.'

She nodded wearily; she had to agree. Death had become a part of her life. There was no sense worrying, she just had to accept it as a new fact of her strange existence. Even if Nimrod Chala and the terrifying General Gogol failed to catch up with them, they were dead in any case should even the slightest thing go wrong.

She had expected to lie wakeful and worrying but instead she plunged into a deep sleep in which she dreamed of Nico Niccolo, first officer in the Heritage Mariner organisation and her sometime lover aboard the leper ship *Napoli* in the wonderful safe old days when all she had had to worry about were cargoes of nuclear waste going critical all around her.

At first when Robert woke her, she thought he must have waited until morning after all. The winding shed was so bright that she felt she could easily have read a newspaper or a book. Only slowly did her groggy mind register the colourless quality of the light. Everything yellow and red had been bleached out of it and only whites and blues remained. And yet it was dazzlingly bright, as though the whole room was trapped eternally in the light from an exploding flash bulb. She blinked owlishly and he shook her once again. 'Are you awake?' His voice was loud, its normal, conversational tone sounding like a bellow to her super-sensitive ears. She had become, she realised, one of the hunted; as much a quarry as a fox pursued by hounds.

'I'm awake.' Her answer was couched in a whisper.

'Good. It's time.'

They pulled themselves to their feet and she realised

449

that, although she had fallen asleep curled independently on the wooden floor, he had come close to her in the darkness and cradled her sleeping head in his lap.

She automatically began to tie the rope round her waist, preparing to wind metre after metre of it round her ribs, but his hand fell on hers. 'Not so fast,' he said. 'I think you'd better find the Ladies before we go. There won't be any rest stops halfway down the cliff.'

'Great. But where?'

'Anywhere. The neighbours won't complain, believe me.'

'The only practical places are the two offices, unless you want to go blundering around out there in the dark.'

'That's about what I thought. You take the one on the right, I'll take the one on the left.'

And so she squatted and relieved herself like a native in the bush, except that this was in a rusty old wastepaper bin from beside a desk in the corner, under the ironic gaze of the massive black woman naked on the wall. For some reason best known to Ann, it was the freedom fighters who got used as toilet paper.

Ann went first, exploring and guiding, and he followed on the safe struts that she had tested in the knowledge that if she fell, the rope round their waists would keep her from falling. As long as Robert could hold on. And, oddly enough, she had not a moment's worry on that score, even when the furnace breath of the evening wind tugged at her most powerfully. She did have some vivid worries, however, not about the strength of the wood or the security of the metal, but about the blood of the chimp she had murdered and the type of nocturnal creatures that might come out in the darkness to scuttle along the struts beneath her hands. Worries about scorpions, centipedes and spiders made her go slowly, and as soon as she gained confidence and started to speed up again, splinters slowed her down.

She was a fit woman, muscular and lithe. Her desert

boots were thick-soled and took firm hold of whatever she stepped on. What she put her weight onto held up bravely, and remained firm under Robert's greater weight when he followed her. Only her soft palms let her down and, in the absence of the nightmare creatures she feared, they did not begin to hurt until she was more than halfway down the crazy ladder they were steadily descending.

There was more than the pain in her hands to worry her by this stage, for as they descended they seemed to pass out of the hot boisterous air of the uplands into the hot, fetid, poisonous air of the dying lowlands. And, while the air was still, it was by no means as clear as the upper air had been. Nor as empty. Clouds of mosquitoes surged upwards, hungry for blood, and soon proved as intimately pervasive as the spiders had been. In fact, given the discomfort of their persistent bites and the literally maddening whine of them around her head, Ann would very gladly have carried a whole range of spiders on her burning skin if they had guaranteed to feast upon the crawling, biting insects moving there now. This was a thought which she held in her heart and treasured even before the word *malaria* occurred to her.

Ten metres up, the light of the lowering moon fell in behind the tops of the tallest trees which stood above what was left of the river. On the far bank the greenery stood half a kilometre distant, but on this side it crowded closer, overrunning the thin, intense bank which had been widened artificially into a landing stage. Higher up, looking down on a moonlit panorama, it had been possible to see that only the outermost reaches of the landing stage reached into the water now. But the wet, fetid air of the river still filled the valley sides even though the water hissed along quietly far out from either shore. The nature of the wood beneath her hands changed during the last few tens of metres. It became softer and spongier. The acutely unwelcome visions of centipedes returned, to be joined by

451

fears of ticks and leeches. 'This is truly foul,' came the gasping rasp of Robert's voice immediately above. 'You believe what they say about malaria?'

'What do they say?' Her own voice was strained and breathless from the exertion. Perhaps the gallons of sweat she was oozing would wash the damned mosquitoes off and give her some relief. Except, of course, that the salt in the perspiration only made the bites itch more fiercely.

'That if the bites don't itch, then you've probably got it.'

Ann considered the burning acres of her skin and feelingly said, 'I'll buy that. I didn't think it was possible to itch so much.'

'Me neither. Little bastards've bit my dick.'

'That'll be hard to scratch,' she said sympathetically.

'And we're fresh out of Waspeeze, too,' he moaned.

At the very moment he said this, her feet stepped down onto solid ground.

The rest of her body refused to believe what the feet were telling it, so she continued to move down, collapsing into a heap in the deepening puddle of shadow. At first she thought the sparsely grassed, suspiciously soft ground had managed to retain the warmth of the day to an amazing extent. Then she realised she was sitting on the dead chimp. She jumped to her feet and collided painfully with Robert just as he stepped down beside her. 'What is it?' he demanded.

'It's the . . .' She took a deep breath and choked on a mouthful of mosquitoes. By the time she had stopped coughing they were out from under their makeshift ladder and seated together on the dock itself while he tenderly untied the rope from round her chafed and itching waist. They were on a cool concrete area, blinded by shadows and all too aware that the setting moon had robbed them of any real chance of going further. Ahead of them, the concrete stretched out towards the river whose insistent voice now filled the air around them as persistently as the ravening mosquitoes. On either hand, the jungle gathered impenetrably as soon as the palely glimmering concrete ended. And the jungle was full of restless stirrings, slitherings, whirrings and whisperings. From the far bank, but close enough to make them jump, came the cough of a big cat immediately followed by a snarl, a howl and a scream. Large bodies battered about among light shrubbery and the screams choked off into a heart-rending whimper.

All in all, it seemed safer to stay where they were until it grew light. Sleep was out of the question. The ground was covered in a thin, sandy grit but it was still rock-hard. The air stayed hot and filled with a whole range of insects, all of which seemed intent on sucking as many liquids from their bodies as possible. Grimly, they sat face to face on numb buttocks with cramping legs, swatting unavailingly with swollen fingers and raw palms, and planning their next step as the interminable hours wore on. Immediately above, in the arch of smotheringly soft black sky which reached from the cliff edge across to the black skeletons of the trees on the far shore, extravagant stars slowly wheeled through their motions as Ann and Robert talked. But, for all the energy and hope they poured into their plans, both of them knew that their destinies might just as well have lain in the astrological dictates of the stars. No matter what they planned and how they acted, survival would just be a matter of luck.

Because of their position at the foot of a westering cliff looking south, the dawn came up over Ann's shoulder and suddenly flooded into Robert's eyes like a summer spate on the river beside them. From the very moment of its birth, it had a bludgeoning power as though the heat had some unnaturally powerful force.

As soon as it struck them, they pulled themselves to their feet. Ann tucked her camera bag under her arm and Robert tightened the length of rope into a kind of cummerbund round his waist. Then, staggering like drunkards, they walked side by side towards the river. The concrete of the loading facility was rough and cracked. The grey dust with which it was covered, and which now also covered the pair of them, was ample evidence of the extent to which it had perished. The far end of it was still in place, however, and although they were cautious and increasingly wary of simply falling through it, they made it out to the very end and sat down again, looking around themselves. Here the scene that greeted them had the remains of a wild splendour about it. But the splendour was raddled, diseased and dying. At their feet, and for more than half a kilometre, the river ran, dark, greenish and sluggish, clearly a dwarf where a giant had once rolled. Beyond it sloped bare mud littered with rubbish, bones, dead tree branches.

'It reminds me of Rudyard Kipling,' she whispered.

'What?'

'This. All this. It's from *The Elephant's Child*: "The grey-green, greasy Limpopo River all set about with fever trees." This is just what I always imagined it would be like.' She shuddered so much that he looked down at her in concern, wondering if the mosquito bites had tricked off a fever after all. But after a glance, his weary gaze was seduced away again to the terrible sight before them, and he found himself echoing what she had said: 'The grey-green, greasy river all set about with fever trees.' This was it, all right.

On their left hand, flowing down out of the dawn light, oozing past them and curving away into the grey jaws of the dying forest far back on the dry mud banks on their right, the stream slid, far too small to keep the jungle here alive, far too big for the two of them to cross. Above the curve on their right, the beetling black cliff made it all too obvious that the shore on which they sat had as little life left to it as the vegetation growing on it. There was no doubt in either of their minds that the northern bank of the River Mau would be washing against sheer black basalt in a kilometre or two. It was equally obvious that on their left, it had flowed against sheer rock face from the foot of the Leopold Falls all the way down here as well. They were, in effect, marooned here, trapped on a thin, manmade tongue of land with the cliff behind them and the cliff on either hand washed by half a kilometre of sluggish, uncrossable water. If they didn't find a ford or a boat, they might just as well climb back onto the ledge above and give themselves up to the soldiers.

'What do you think?' asked Ann, though she knew the answer perfectly well.

'We'd better go downstream first,' answered Robert. 'We have to find a ford or a boat.'

They sat and thought for a little longer as the sun began to weigh down upon them as though it was the gold it seemed to be. The river slouched past, thick, green and impenetrable, more like bile than water. The sluggish breeze brought the putrid stench up to wash over them but the movement of the air did little more than stir the flies and mosquitoes to a renewed frenzy. It seemed too much trouble to get up and get on with things; they were both far more exhausted, shocked and drained than they realised.

Their thoughts rapidly became so depressing and the weight of the day so enormous that at last they were glad enough to pull themselves up once more and seek some shelter in the trees, no matter what dangers might lurk beneath the shadows lingering in the dying undergrowth. Had it not been so near death, they would never have been able to get through the undergrowth. Clearly no human foot had been set here since the thirties, and they would both have needed heavy machetes had the vegetation been strong. As things were, the branches and fronds yielded to the pressure of their bodies with brittle weakness, and all they needed to be careful of was the shard-sharp edges which swung back into their faces like broken bottles in a pub brawl.

Keeping the sibilance of the river on their left, they wrestled their way westwards through the undergrowth, always alert for a chance to break out onto the bank of the river, eyes sharp for a crossing or a craft. To no avail. The river was much reduced and the bank on the outside of the curve was effectively a mud cliff ten metres high, but the nearer the edge, the thicker and greener the verdure. Tall trees stood strong and the bushes between them, with deep roots, had strong branches, long thorns and sharp-edged leaves. So there was no way to the edge, no way down the bank and no way across the river. Westward they plunged, through the dead grey forest, hoping against hope that there would be something to help them across before they ran out of shoreline.

But there was nothing. Forbidden all but an occasional look out over the river itself from an impenetrable wall of undergrowth, they fought their way westward through the first hour of the morning. The shadows protected their eyes but did little to cool them, especially as they were exerting themselves so fiercely. The movement of the branches, catching, scratching and cutting them, at least seemed to sweep the worst of the mosquitoes away. The canopy overhead remained thick enough to protect them from any prying eyes in the first low helicopter of the day, which swept in on the end of a long, sinister drone from the south-east, flying at no altitude from the direction of the Blood River and the border with Congo Libre.

At last, towards mid-morning, the forest around them thinned. The ground beneath them sloped down increasingly steeply. The bush began to die back and bare earth under their feet was briefly covered with a crisp pelt of dead grass, and they were out onto a long spit of dry mud which stretched westwards away to nothing along the foot of the black cliff, edged on the left with the sluggish surge of dull green water. The river turned in to the cliff foot here, but it was still a good three hundred metres wide and was just beginning to urge itself into something like a serious flow. Out towards the middle of the stream, the dull sage of the water was roused into sinister, lacy white by a series of irregularities which, had the water been shallower or quicker, would have been rapids.

On the far bank there was a wealth of debris, everything from lone trees through clumps of bushes, dead with their roots in the air, to a car tyre, an ancient wicker chair and an old divan bedstead. Had almost any of it been on this side, they might have made a makeshift raft. But there was nothing here. Nothing but a long, pointed tongue of stinking, sunbaked mud, as hard and red as brick. The pair of them staggered onwards, looking around themselves in dazed disbelief, going into slow motion like characters escaped from a *Tom and Jerry* cartoon. Down at the thin end, with five hundred metres of rock face reaching up sheer on their right while the shallow green water chuckled and sucked away busily within a couple of centimetres of their shoes on their left, they stood, looking down, defeated.

Then, round the corner, upstream, as though it had been following them down the river on purpose, came a felled tree, its roots in a wild, mad tangle, as if it had taken Medusa as a figurehead. With silent, powerful majesty it moved, sweeping along like a queen. Robert looked at Ann and the pair of them looked around themselves once again. They were alone. Exposed. There was no other help, no promise of help, in sight. 'I'm going for it,' announced Robert.

'Give me the end of your rope, just in case,' she ordered. 'If anything goes wrong I can pull you back.'

'Good thinking.' He was already pulling loops of it from round his waist, glancing alternately down at his stiff, clumsy hands and up at the stately progress of their one true hope. She caught up the end at once and began to tie it round her own waist. He paused, looking doubtful, but it was as clear to him as it was to her that she could never have held it with any firmness. And there was nothing down here to belay it round. She caught his look and shrugged. 'Needs must,' she said.

He nodded, his attention dwelling on her only for a moment, then his eyes were pulled back to the steady sweep of the tree trunk. It was nearly level with them now, out in the middle, less than a hundred metres away but swinging in towards them, moved by the current round the proto-rapids.

'Thank God I'm not at home,' he said, and began to wade into the water.

'What?'

He paused and gestured down at the water which was so thick and dark that his legs were invisible already. 'Piranha,' he said. 'Anacondas. They don't have either of them here.'

'That's right,' she said brightly. 'So you don't have anything to worry about. Except the crocodiles.'

He may or may not have heard her. He took another step and fell forward, preferring to swim than to wade. She regretted having said it, however. He was doing a brave thing and trying to make light of it. She had been joking, not supporting, and it seemed a little petty, somehow.

As he swam, the rope uncoiled and it soon became clear to her that she would have to get her feet wet too if he was going to stand any chance of reaching the tree. The current was swinging it round and in towards him as he swam, but there was only a hundred metres or so of the rope and it looked as though the bulk of the tree would pass nearly two hundred metres out. With the closest approach to quick thinking that her exhausted mind could manage, she began to run down the spit of land and out into the thick, warm water.

As soon as it flooded into her boots she stopped again, doing her best to calculate rapidly while making sure the blessedly watertight camera bag was done up properly. A mass of sensation swept over her in the breathless instants which followed, as though her fatigue-stunned mind nevertheless recognised the onset of violent action and was preparing her for it with an excess of information.

Above the waterline, the ground was rock hard. Below it, the mud still oozed, and it sloped away surprisingly steeply. No sooner was she standing in the busy shallows than she found herself slipping and sliding forward and down, no longer quite able to stand still and think. The tug of the water on her ankles was insistent, and it was easy to see how the tree, and Robert himself, were suddenly moving so fast out in the main thrust of the current. The rope was all in the water now, streaming out in a loop downstream, adding its strong tug at her waist to the sinister suck of the river at her calves and knees. It was becoming increasingly difficult to keep her feet and she found herself waving her arms like a tightrope walker in a high wind as she fought to stay upright.

But it seemed to be working. Robert was a little downstream of her now but the tree was still level and the two of them were coming rapidly together. The branches reached out in a welcoming tangle for a good ten metres on either side of the squat, thick trunk. Not only did they reach out, but as the whole tree spun slowly in the grip of the water, so they swung across to catch the swimming man. One moment Robert was chopping his way through the water in an ugly but effective crawl, the next he was floundering onto a trampoline of small branches and actually pulling himself out of the water. Ann drew in her breath to cheer.

And something massive hit her in the back. That is what she felt, and visions came into her mind of the chimpanzee horribly resurrected or some soldier from Nimrod Chala's army of police creeping up behind her. Thrust forward by the impact, she flew off her feet and out into the water. It was no animal or paramilitary policeman however, it was only the rope, behaving with the inevitability of anything caught up in the laws of physics; doing exactly what they should have known it would do, had they been thinking more clearly. There was no give in the line or in the knots she had tied. The rope was fastened at its far end to a big man solidly anchored in the branches of a tree moving westwards at five kilometres an hour, and as soon as the slack was used up, Ann sprang from rest to movement in an instant. For a moment or two her rate of acceleration exceeded that of a Bugatti and she was lucky not to crack a couple of ribs.

She hit the water hard and was pulled under at once. Shock allowed her to keep the lungful of air she had jerked in, in spite of the fact that she felt as though she had been thumped on the back. She kept that precious air in her lungs as she surged and floundered out into the stream. Once she was in the water, however, her movement became relatively slow; the water was moving slightly faster than the tree and the line which had been tight soon slackened, allowing her to fight her way to the surface. She exploded out of the water, waving her arms and fighting to keep her head clear of the thick green warmth of it. She breathed out and in, her mouth gaping, then heaved helplessly as she felt slimy drops cascade back onto her tongue. A wild phantasmagoria of fears whirled in her imagination – all the toxic chemicals used in farms locally, all the diseases the thick hot water would hold. The vision of the skeletons along the low waterline on the far bank returned and she wished acutely that she had not made that crack to Robert about crocodiles.

The perspective she had on the tree was very different now. It looked very large but suddenly distant – a great mass of twisted black limbs like a cloud on her waving horizon. And the horizon was waving too, for the tree was just coming out of the grip of the rapids now but she was being pulled across and into the busy water. She saw no alternative but to try and swim, so she floundered into action at once and understood immediately why Robert's style had been so brutally ugly.

Robert rose into her vision then, outlined against the hard blue sky, a black figure among the wild black branches. The rope round her waist tightened once again and panic returned for a disorientating moment before she realised he was pulling her in like a fish on a line. Gratefully she began to flounder towards him and within a very few minutes her plunging hands encountered the first branches of their safe haven.

What sort of tree it was or where it had come from was impossible to tell. It had a squat, thick trunk in the middle and a riot of thick branches at one end and equally thick roots at the other. The girth of the solid part was perhaps fifteen metres in circumference and the length of clear wood about the same. It sat solidly in the water and, although it was spinning when they first got aboard it, the current soon reclaimed it and it settled into a straight line of motion with the wild roots as the prow.

As soon as she had dragged herself out of the maze of small branches into the arms of the more solid boughs, and thence into Robert's arms, Ann led the way down, as though they were climbing out of a tree house, until they reached the junction of the lowest, thickest branches with the trunk. These made makeshift backrests and it was possible for them to sit side by side with their legs reaching down the trunk itself and their backs against the easy slope of the branches. It was by no means a comfortable situation, but they both felt relatively safe, especially after they used the slack line to anchor themselves in place.

Had Ann ever in her wildest dreams imagined that she would find herself drifting down an African river on a makeshift raft, she would have imagined herself standing intrepidly looking around, noting the finest detail of everything in sight for inclusion in her next book. As it was, she had no intention of doing anything but clinging on for dear life and waiting for the next thing to happen to her. What that thing might be she had no idea and did not speculate. Nor, apparently, did Robert. They simply sat side by side in stunned silence and allowed the day to wash over them.

The river swirled the tree trunk slowly and gracefully in against the foot of the cliff almost at once, showing them all too clearly that they would never have managed to come any further along the northern bank – unless they could have found a way of scaling several hundred metres of seamless, glassy black cliff. The movement of the water towards what was clearly the deepest part of the river bed also served to pull them well clear of the far bank, however. And any temptation they might have felt to use the tree as a launching pad for a second swim was nipped in the bud by the sight of a crocodile sunning itself on the muddy slopes which would have been their destination. It was difficult to be sure at this distance, but it looked to be about ten metres long. For a moment, the photographer in Ann stirred as she stared across at the great beast, but then she thought of the danger she would be putting her precious pictures in if she opened the camera bag here. She thought of the danger she herself would be in if she did anything but cower here and pray for deliverance.

And so the day passed. Apart from the occasional crocodile, they saw nothing alive on the desolate shores. On their right, the cliff continued interminably. Only occasionally, as the river made a desultory attempt to meander, was there any shoreline on that side, but it was never more than a bulge of red silt like the flank of some buried giant or the shard of some huge terracotta jar baked hard. And the only sounds which came from that side over the insistent rustling chuckle of the river was the thunder of trains rushing ahead of them to the coast.

On the left, however, lay a dying desolation whose atmosphere hung like a miasma across the water. From the green edge of the shrunken river, red mud rose seemingly interminably up a long, weary slope to a low cliff of ancient bank. The mud alone rose ten metres above the water level in three-quarters of a kilometre, and the long-dry cliff rose another ten above that. Above the red, overhanging cliff, the better part of eight hundred metres from the thick water, stood the tall jungle. It was grey and sere even against the hard blue sky, and the sun in the southern quadrant struck through the upper canopy as though it was a mist. Ann was American. She was more used to autumn in Vermont that to this hopeless surrender of lush leaves to grey death. She found the sight of the jungle distasteful; ultimately disturbing. Great trees stood as though wrapped in restless shrouds of dirty paper. Their massive limbs writhed in a mute agony of drought, as though begging the water for succour. But only the hot wind answered, and when it gusted it brought with it red dust from the naked grassland far beyond. So that beneath the ghostly grey giants, the dead scrub, as ghastly as the hopeless mess of limbs in the bauxite store which had been home to the crippled chimpanzee, was tinged with wind-channelled runnels of red.

And the jungle was silent. Dead. It seemed like one great creature to her, one massive entity which should have been composed of verdant leaf and burgeoning branch, pullulating with teeming insects and whirring flies; dappled and dazzling with the gleam of quicksilver wing and exquisite singing of birds, and heaving with the pulsating explosion of roaring, howling, trumpeting and calling animals.

But there was nothing. The whole thing was dead. They were sailing through the still heart of a corpse.

As the afternoon gathered around them and the sun came blazingly over their heads to glare down upon them, its terrible light and heat multiplied beyond bearing by the reflective quality of the black cliff just beside them, so the river, too, began to die.

The first sign of the onset of death seemed to be positive.

The depressing spectacle of the dead jungle fell back silently, unobserved, and the far bank slowly withdrew to more than a kilometre distant. Dozing, stunned by the lethal afternoon sun, hardly more than braising bundles of mud and clothing, Ann and Robert did not notice that the black cliff, too, was effectively withdrawing as the river itself spread out into a shallow lake and the flow which held the tree trunk began to meander and their steady progress began to slow. The branches under water began to scrape along the river bed, and the tree drifted to a dead stop.

It was the helicopter which woke them, swooping low like an inquisitive fly, monstrous not only in its size but by its vivid movement in this place of sluggish death. The clattering roar of its approaching rotor jerked Ann awake first and she peered out from under the sun shield of shirt and camera bag which was perched precariously upon her head. It was shockingly close, skimming in over the distant jungle, kicking up leaves in its wake like an autumn gale. 'Robert!' she screamed, feeling unutterably exposed at once. She had no idea whether the tree trunk they were on was a unique feature or one among many, effectively invisible. And she had no idea whether the two of them were visible upon it. She felt an overpowering need to run at once. She froze, fighting the panic, watching the hawk-swoop of the helicopter as it sped unerringly towards them. She could feel the weight of the pilot's eyes like sunburn on her skin. With a whimper she rolled off the log and into the water. The rope held her and she rose back above the surface, clutching a handful of roots and hiding as best she could behind the swell of the wood. A slithering splash and the gentle stirring of the wood informed her that Robert had followed suit. Terrified, she hung there as the helicopter clattered by, seemingly only a couple of metres above her head. The down-draught stirred against her scalp like a cold shower and she realised that, warm though it was, the water, too, felt cool against her parched skin. As the silence returned to the heat-weighted air around them, she felt her body beginning to relax, as though she was in a warm bath.

Then something brushed sluggishly beneath her dangling toe.

She actually screamed with terror. Gripped by a fear which was far more powerful even than her exceptional self-control, she went scrambling up out of the water, whimpering as she went, until she was crouching on the trunk again, looking around herself at the still, impenetrable water, sobbing with incipient hysteria. Only when she was safely out of the reach of whatever had touched her did she think of Robert. 'Robert,' she called, and only when she had said the word and it was echoing back from jungle and cliff alike did she realise that she had screamed it. There was no reply. 'Robert!' This time she knew she screamed. The thought that he might be gone was more than she could bear. She hurled herself wildly across the wood and hung over his side, barely restrained by her section of the rope. The thick dark water was still. His rope trailed into it, apparently attached to nothing. Making a kind of keening noise, far beyond sensible control, she reached a trembling hand down towards it.

Robert exploded out of the water immediately beside her, his face thrusting immediately up beside hers. 'I touched bottom!' he yelled, making her jump out of her skin. 'This tree's not going anywhere now. It's wedged in place. If we want to get on, we'll have to get off. We'll have to swim a bit and wade the rest, but we can get to the shore, I think.'

'Is it safe?' She asked the fearful question before she realised that the thing that had brushed her foot must have been the bottom of this shallow lake.

But it was a serious question. They would have to swim for quite a way and then wade for the better part of five hundred metres to gain the first slope of mud. The slope itself stretched for nearly a kilometre up to a cliff dead ahead and away to the west into a seemingly limitless field of dead reeds. And until they were actually out of the water altogether, they would be in very real danger of attack by crocodiles and whatever other monsters lurked here.

'No choice. We can't just sit on the log and wait for the next rains to wash us free. We could be here for years. Come on, untie us and let's get it done. And remember, that helicopter might well have spotted us.'

That, carefully calculated, spurred her into action. Within minutes she was floundering down beside him and the pair of them were moving as quietly as possible through the sluggish westward tug of the water. In her mind, Ann was reciting the names of all the demons which most terrified her, working on the superstitious assumption that if she named something it would be less likely to attack her. It was always, as Nico Niccolo never tired of telling her, the *unexpected* which got you in the end. And her Neapolitan lover's magic seemed to work, for no crocodile caught her, no snake bit her, no raft of floating insects, soldier ants, spiders or scorpions drifted down to explode against her unprotected head. No ravening fish – the African equivalent of piranhas, if such things existed – latched hungrily onto her legs. No electric eels came writhing to shock her to death. No swimming python came to emulate his cousin the anaconda.

This time she did not scream when her feet touched the bottom and as she waded out of the water onto the clear expanse of hard-baked, blood-red riverine beach, everything seemed to have passed off perfectly. They staggered across the rock-hard mud towards the distant earthen cliff. A wind, the evening breeze, rustled sinisterly through the hollow skeletons of the reeds away to their right. It brought dead leaves and a fetid stench from the jungle ahead of them and, had they not been so desperate, they would have stopped then or gone back. But if they stopped now, the next helicopter would definitely spot them; and there was nowhere to go back to.

Their shadows were long across the red ribbed mud by the time they reached the concave cliff of crumbling earth which had once been the shore. It had looked like the merest mud dune from the water's edge, but now it revealed itself to be a wall the better part of four metres high, concave and overhanging. Wearily, they turned until the westering sun was in their eyes and began to plod along it, hoping for a tributary opening before the vast, threatening forest of the dead reed bed overwhelmed them.

What they found was not a stream bed but an animal track which had broken down the high bank and churned up the red earth down to the distant water. It was still going to be quite a scramble up to the top of the bank but it would be possible to do it if they organised themselves. They would have to do this at once, for it was coming disturbingly close to sunset – and whatever had made the track would soon be using it again. In spite of the drained weariness they both felt, they prepared to scale the two-metre mountain in front of them. A very few half-coherent words sufficed for a plan: Robert would go first, with Ann pushing him upwards from behind; then he would pull her up. Simple.

For the first time since they had come out of the water he went ahead of her. He reached upwards towards the crumbling crest and she closed in to push him upwards. His shirt tail had pulled out of his trouser waist and as she bent to shove her shoulder under the swell of his buttocks, she saw the broad expanse of gleaming skin over his kidneys. And, beneath her dazzled eyes, the skin writhed and rippled with an obscene life of its own. Great blisters and welts raised upon it, black and glistening, *alive*. She froze and he turned, sensing at once that something was wrong. He found her pulling her own shirt out of her shorts with manic concentration and saw at once that the same obscene black welts, the size of his thumb to the wrist and bigger, were gathered vividly against the pallor of her skin.

'They're leeches,' he bellowed, his voice trembling with disgust. 'God! Oh God!'

She was shaking as though several thousand volts were coursing through her body and he, too, very nearly went out of control. Had they not been in such desperate straits, he would almost certainly have done so. But he knew with inescapable certainty that if he let slip then they were dead. He caught her by the shoulders and shook her with far too much savagery. 'We don't have time for this!' he snarled. 'We have to get up before the evening wallow or we'll be killed. Trampled to death. Do you understand?'

'Yes.' The word released a trickle of blood from the corner of her mouth, but when he let go of her the shaking had stopped.

'We'll get up and get clear,' he said, his eyes fastened on her as though he could mesmerise more strength into her. 'We'll get clear and we'll build a fire then we'll get rid of these things. We'll be all right. All right?'

'Sure.' Her eyes slid away from his. She did not believe they would be all right at all. But then, even if they did build a fire, she couldn't see how they were going to light it anyway.

In the end they lit it with the gun.

They scrambled as planned up the incline onto the animal track then struck west into the last of the setting sun at once, driven by the certain knowledge that something big enough to step up and down two metres of bank was coming to have its evening drink with several of its family and friends. In the last of the sunlight, from the eastern edge of the reed bed they looked back across a kilometre of empty bank to see a small herd of elephants move like the silent spirits of the dead jungle out of the grey trees onto the red mud. As the huge animals stepped down, the tallest one stopped and spread its ears, raised its trunk and looked at them. Red light glinted off long, curving tusks. A challenging scream came echoing on the evening air. Suddenly a kilometre seemed hardly enough.

By the time they found a place to stop, the sunlight was gone and the darkness was closing down like a door swinging shut. The warmth was draining out of the day as rapidly as the blood was draining out of their systems, and they had reached the time for decisive action. They were on a tongue of dry mud exposed to the sky between the outer scrub of the dead forest and the whispering field of dead reeds. The forest seemed marginally more welcoming, so they struck south until they reached the edge of it. Here they pulled together a pile of sere leaves and broke dry branches on the top. Robert had used the walk from the elephant track to rack his brains about lighting the thing, but had come up with no ideas at all. It was Ann, her memory of the muzzle flash as the bullets destroyed the chimpanzee twenty-four hours earlier still fresh in her mind, who suggested using the pistol.

Only their desperation to be rid of the clammy, unutterably disgusting creatures on their skin and the overpowering need for some comfort and reassurance could have made them risk doing it. But their world had closed down to such an urgent intimacy that worries about Nimrod Chala's scouts or the ease with which a passing helicopter would spot a fire in this shadowy desolation shrank to insignificance. Crouching, trembling, beneath the over-arching branches of the first broad tree on the edge of the forest, they thrust the gun into the pile of dry kindling they had assembled and pulled the trigger. The bullet exploded out of the other side, scattering twigs. A tantalizing smell of burning lingered on the air. Robert crouched and blew with increasing desperation. Nothing else happened.

After the third shot, he said, 'It's not going to work.

They won't catch. We need something which will burn at once.'

The thought of spending a cold night defenceless on the dark edge of this terrible place with no alternative but to pull the leeches off by hand was enough to inspire Ann even further. 'Film stock,' she said, reaching into the open camera bag.

'What?'

She pulled out the last of her unexposed films. 'This stuff. Film acetate. Burns like fire lighters,' she said, and jerked the ribbon of glistening brown out of the little tube. It was only a matter of moments before it was crushed into a loose ball and the pile of kindling was reassembled on top of it. This time, the explosion of the shot was followed almost at once by a crisp crackling and the smell of powder was subsumed below the acridity of blazing acetate and smouldering leaves.

Even now they had to keep themselves under rigid control, for the fire had to be nurtured, raised to a blaze, given at least the promise of some permanence and then corralled, restrained, stopped from running out of control. Only then could they turn to the almost overpowering urgency of the other matter in hand. And once they began, it did become overpowering. More important than hunger, thirst, dignity, modesty; more important than anything except, perhaps, death was the need to rid themselves of the creatures clinging to their skin. They stripped each other, all too aware that the loathsome things would be clustering in places where they could not be seen by their reluctant hosts. Then, with their clothing in steaming piles by the fire, first Ann then Robert stood with eyes closed and all their concentration focused on remaining still, while the other, with the glowing end of a smouldering stick, worried at the glistening, slug-like bodies until they reluctantly dropped free. Each time one fell, it was caught up and thrown immediately into the flames where it hissed and crackled like a toasting sausage.

'You've lost a lot of weight,' Robert said as he worked on her cool, pale body.

She said nothing, preferring to remove her mind as far from the humiliating present as possible.

'Those mosquitoes have surely made a mess of you,' he continued, more to himself than to her. The firelight showed every intimate detail of her and none of it was unscathed. But her face had suffered worst of all; her eyes and lips were puffy with bites and the first of tonight's mosquitoes were just beginning to arrive as he finished work on her. Compared to the leeches, the little insects hardly seemed worth a second thought.

At last, like Aborigines, they crouched side by side, naked and sluggishly bleeding from the myriad bites on their bodies, disregarding the thickening cloud of river mosquitoes hovering hungrily over their heads, holding their underwear as close to the flames as they dared until they at least were dry. As soon as some sort of dignity was restored to them, they began to arrange things around a circular blaze to give them some comfort. Ann set up makeshift racks upon which to hang the rest of their clothing until it was dry. Robert collected more wood to burn. Then they both pulled a log to sit on close enough to the flames to toast their toes, fingers and faces. They sat in silence, swatting desultorily until shirts, shorts and trousers began to darken in colour and to smell a little like toast.

Once they were vermin-free, warm and dry, they began to realize how hungry and thirsty they had become. The station in the township seemed a long, long way ago now; indeed, it was more than thirty-six hours since either of them had had anything to eat. But there was nothing to be done about it now. It was too dark to go hunting and although the jungle seemed dead, there was no guarantee that it was as empty of predators as it seemed. Stumbling about blindly with the gun would be a suicidal waste of time, even if either of them had been any kind of a hunter at all. Neither of them was. They banked up the fire, did their best to ensure that the circle of logs round it would stop it spreading across the jungle floor, made themselves beds of dry leaves with pillows of outer clothing and went to sleep hungry in their underwear. And, wisely, in their boots.

The last thing Robert did before sleep claimed him was to take the gun and some bullets from the camera bag which was supplementing Ann's shorts as her pillow. The cold metal added nothing to the comfort of his own bunched-up shirt, but it added a great deal to his peace of mind, even though he took the considerable risk of setting it to automatic after he had loaded up. He was so exhausted that even the gnawing in his belly could not keep him awake for long – nor could the sight of Ann curled seductively so close at hand. He was idly pondering the paradox of the way in which her brief plain cotton underwear enhanced the attractiveness of a body he had just seen utterly exposed with no conscious reaction at all when he fell into a deep, dark slumber.

The smell of the fire was enough to keep the herd of elephants well away from them and the tall pachyderms finished their wallow and returned through the dead strip of jungle to the red plains beyond to spend a restless night searching for something to assuage the hunger which had replaced the urgency of thirst in their massive bodies. They were not the only animals moving among the dead trees, but even the most desperate of the predators was wary of the fire and so the two defenceless humans slept on in relative safety for the first few hours at least.

The leopard was old. Wounded in a cull and crippled with disease, it had been reduced to chasing injured or sickly birds in the days when Julius Karanga was president.

In the years since, it had scavenged around the outskirts of N'Kuru villages, taking the odd goat, the occasional unwary dog, every now and then a child. It had been lucky to survive this long but now its luck was running out. The smell of the fire held no fears for its wise old nostrils, for this was not the stench of fire uncontrolled. Rather, it was a smell it knew well, which told of village camp fires, of offal to be scavenged, of soft, weak, unwary prey. Had it been capable of surprise, it might have wondered that there was no odour of roasting meat or boiling maize; but it was not. It was too hungry and intent upon feeding its hunger.

It came through the forest silently in the blackest moment of the night just before moonrise, and paused to look across the makeshift campsite from the edge of the forest. It noted the two still forms beyond the brightness of the fire and heard the restless rustle of their breathing. Saliva washed down the long channel of its mouth and all its claws slid out. Drooling with excitement, it filled the night with the hunting roar it had hardly used in the last decade and charged.

Robert jerked awake to see a bright yellow streak rushing towards him at unbelievable speed. He was sitting up almost before his eyes had opened and he was at such a point of tension that he fired the gun before he was properly awake. There was no thought of taking aim, no supple flick of switch, no red dot. He pointed at the middle of the thing and pulled the trigger.

'ANN!' he screamed as he fired, tearing his throat with the power of the sound he was making.

The leopard, recognising the muzzle flashes, turned, but too late. The bullets spat into its wounded shoulder and flipped it over into the fire. With its oily fur beginning to smoulder, the wounded animal writhed in the heart of the pile of glowing branches, scattering them hither and yon. From side to side it rolled, wildly trying to regain its feet.

Its mangy, shaggy coat was on fire before it pulled itself to its feet and, blinded by the flames as its beard and whiskers ignited, its nostrils blocked by the stench of its own pelt burning, its ears all but deafened by its own wild screams, it charged again.

Had Ann not been sleeping with the strap of her camera bag wrapped round her arm, she would have lost it. Like Robert she sprang from deep sleep into total wakefulness and, like him, she found herself facing a charge by a leopard. But this leopard was fiercely ablaze. The sight of it and the sounds it was making were utterly, overwhelmingly terrifying. She was on her feet at once and running wildly along the riverbank far beyond rational thought or the faintest hope of self-control. Because she was screaming at the top of her lungs, the leopard was able to follow her movements, and because it was mad with agony and rage, it continued its vain attempts to destroy her.

Robert abruptly found himself alone in the wreckage of their makeshift camp. Because of the noise, he too was able to follow Ann and the leopard. He was up without further thought and off after them at a dead run. Sometime during the first five steps he switched on the red dot, and he followed this along the top of the river bank, sweeping it from right to left. After five minutes of feverish activity he paused to draw breath and compose his thoughts. There was now neither sight nor sound of them. How could they have vanished so quickly and so utterly? he asked himself in an agony of worry. The low, bright stars gave him light enough to see a possible answer. He found himself looking forward and to his right down the slight slope into the massive featureless field of dry reeds which lay between the high bank and the mud slope down into the dry lake bed. The wind stirred the tops of the dead reeds as he watched and he suddenly realised that if Ann had vanished into this then he would never be able to find her again. 'Ann,' he bellowed as loudly as he could. 'Ann, can you hear me?'

He made a conscious effort to control his breathing, and even to slow his tumultuous heartbeat so that the could listen for her reply, but there was nothing. Nothing save the wind and the weird whispering of the reeds.

He pointed the gun up into the air above his head and pulled the trigger. A brief burst of bullets ripped up into the air. It was a short signal but a clear one, he thought. Surely she would hear. He listened, straining his ears.

The faintest mumble of sound above the seductive sibilance of the reed sea.

He raised the gun again and pulled the trigger. Nothing. He swore and yelled at the top of his voice again but there was no reply. Except that when he stood absolutely still, and listened with every nerve of his body, he could hear a quiet babble and the odd crackling of footsteps.

Just behind him!

Spooked, he swung round, expecting to see the smouldering leopard creeping up with Ann's arm drooping palely from its smoking jaws. But what he saw was much worse. He saw yellow brightness gleaming through the tall columns of the dead, dry trees, and he realised that the whispering and crackling were the sound a bushfire makes when it is spreading swiftly through undergrowth.

He stood for just a moment, calling to mind all the foulest swear words he had ever known. What the hell was he going to do now? 'Ann!' He swung round again, to look over the reeds. The wind gusted warmly from behind him, carrying smoke already; smoke and sparks. 'ANN! For Christ's sake! AAANNN!' All too close, the first tree exploded into flame and he was running. As though observing a complete stranger, he noted that he was running wildly along the bank above the dead sea of reeds. If there was any kind of a plan in his head it was this: to cut round behind the reeds away from the blazing forest and down across the wide expanse of mud to seek refuge in the sluggish water. Even the leeches seemed a fair exchange if he could escape the all-consuming fire which was exploding terribly into life behind him as he ran. And if he remained on the high mud crest he could keep an eye out for Ann, for he was still convinced that she was somewhere down there.

As he ran he kept swinging his head to right and left, for the starlight was not strong enough to reveal the details of the bankside path ahead and he was forced to rely on his more acute peripheral vision. Furthermore, he was half fearful that the path the leopard took between the dry stems of the reeds would burst into flames at any moment, ignited by the burning creature's fur; and in any case he wanted to keep an eye on the wildfire spreading through the woods behind him. When it got firm hold it would, he knew, be able to move at more than sixty kilometres an hour. Downwind. His way. Of all the things he feared most, fire ranked highest on the list and he had no intention of being outrun by this one if he could possibly avoid it.

When the next tree exploded into flame and sent a wave of red light rolling down the bank after him, he thrust Ann into the back of his mind, tucked his chin down and started to run in earnest. He was going at full sprint, the better part of ten kilometres per hour, when the ground gave way under him and swallowed him with one silent gulp.

He slammed down the throat of a shallow pit with stunning suddenness and dropped into a mud-walled little cave. A long hard balk of wood broke his fall and he found himself precipitated head first into a claustrophobically narrow corner where the hard earth of the roof pressed terrifyingly against the back of his head. The cave was clearly some kind of fault in the high bank, and was apparently prone to flooding for it stank overpoweringly of the river. He choked in the fetid air and scrabbled backwards until he could at least sit up straight and look around him. But there was nothing to see on either hand except the suffocating blackness. He looked up and high above his head he saw the grass-edged jaws of the hole through which he had fallen. The blackness surrounding it made it impossible for him to judge how high it was above his head, and without thinking he began to scramble to his feet, already reaching up to see if he could get some kind of purchase on the sides of the rim.

But as he moved, so did the balk of wood he was standing on and he lost his balance and sat down suddenly. Chillingly, close by, something stirred. In his mind's eye he tried to conjure the situation he now found himself in. The cave, low in the bank, open to the river though the water was long gone now. Open at such an angle that tree trunks and branches and balks of timber had been swept in here by floods over the years, like the tree which had brought them this far today. Great lengths of wood piled atop one another and stirring now uneasily under his weight. Great trunks beginning to rot and give off that fearsome fetor which almost smelt like rotting meat.

He was already whimpering with visceral, atavistic realisation when he switched on the red dot and saw it reflected off a cold, golden eye. He shouted with fear as his own eyes cleared just enough to reveal the length of the snout beyond that cold, cold eye and the length of the teeth around it. With trembling concentration he pressed the barrel to the patient eye, until the steel circle was mere millimetres from the bright red dot. Babbling a childhood prayer he believed he had long forgotten, he pulled the trigger. Nothing happened. Still praying, refusing to the last to believe that there was no way out of this, he pulled the trigger again only to hear the quiet click of the hammer falling on the empty chamber.

The eye closed, squeezing a fat tear from its corner. The mouth opened.

And he was screaming wildly all through the next few dreadful moments as his finger pressed and pressed the pistol's trigger – and continued to press it long after the hand controlling it was ripped from the end of his arm and lay nestling for ever in the belly of the largest of the twelve ravenous crocodiles into whose bankside nest he had fallen.

And the nest remained safe even from the apocalyptic inferno which whirled by above and without during the rest of that terrible night.

Ann had in fact fled into the field of reeds, some half formed thought inhabiting her panicked mind that cats feared water and if she could elude the leopard until she had gained the river, she would be safe. In fact the unfortunate creature succumbed to a massive heart attack brought on by the shock of its terrible injuries soon after it had entered the reeds behind her, but she did not know this as she plunged wildly through the tall grasses. Nor had she any idea that the noise of her own terror, of her gasping for breath, of her wild passage was drowning out the gathering rumble of the fire behind her. As she shoved her way by main strength through the sharp reeds, they chopped at the skin of her forearm and scored along the flesh of her triceps into her armpits. Within two hundred metres, the shirt which was all she wore apart from her underpants and boots was hanging in tatters from her and only the camera bag hanging round her neck saved her breasts from more serious damage. But she neither knew nor cared: she was running for her life, not just from the leopard but from everything that had happened to her during the last three days. She was running away, far beyond control, and she had no real intention of ever stopping again.

She burst out into a kind of trackway and paused, disorientated, just as a single scream, crystal clear and utterly terrifying, sang out through the night. So piercing was the scarcely human sound that it would have echoed hauntingly off the cliffs even though they were nearly five kilometres away, but the dull crump of an explosion – exactly like the shell from a T–80 main battle tank – killed the sound utterly. She looked around, half convinced that there must indeed be a tank following her. As she did so, the sound was repeated and suspicion became certainty. Fear of the leopard was replaced in her mind by the conviction that Gogol and Nimrod Chala had found her, that within a matter of mere moments she would be utterly at their mercy, with nothing to look forward to but six carefully-placed bullets.

A ghastly yellow light showed her a wall of reeds ahead and a tunnel of shadow leading away on either hand. She turned right and hurled forward with almost Olympic speed, so far out of control that had there been space enough and time, she would probably have run herself to death. As she sped wildly along the reed-walled tunnel down towards the water, she brushed against the dead vegetation and, invisibly but thickly, long-legged ticks began to rain down upon her from their hiding places high on the grey stalks.

The air between the thick reeds was absolutely still, no wind could move it though a tempest raged above, and as Ann ran down towards the lake, a tempest was indeed beginning to rage above. Had she been thinking with even a tithe of her usual acuity, she would have realised that the gathering light which was blessedly guiding her down the pathway could be nothing to do with either sun or moon. And had she been at all interested in extraneous sounds, she would have thought beyond the explosions of a phantom military barrage at her back and realised that these were not the shells from Gogol's tanks pursuing her at all, but the sounds of something much more immediately deadly. Had she even paused to look up, she would have seen that the stars had come low and turned red – and that they were rushing westwards like the river itself.

The rain of blazing sparks set the reeds alight as soon as

they began to settle. A hundred little fires sprang up all around Ann, but the magic stillness of the tunnel of air down which she was running kept even the faintest trace of smoke out of her lungs for a few moments more. But this was a situation which could not persist for long. The wind did not die down after the first wild wave of sparks sped west. On the contrary, it gathered strength and the sparks thickened as the blaze intensified so that the fires in the reeds, too, became more and more numerous. The first that Ann knew of her terrible danger was a sudden flash of yellow brightness which she half glimpsed through the stalks as through a bamboo screen. Disorientatingly, she supposed for an instant that she had somehow run full circle and returned to the camp and the fire she had been so proud of lighting. She paused in her panic flight and would have drawn breath to call to Robert but something drove her on – something blessed, for had she stopped for long enough to come to realise what she was doing to her body, to register even the tiniest part of the pain and exhaustion she was inflicting on herself, she would have collapsed and died where she was.

The pause was only the hesitation of the running deer; it lasted less than an instant and she was off again, with every part of her brain closed down except that part where the irresistible urge towards self-preservation lies. The pathway led straight down towards the river which in fact came closer to the parched outthrust of the tall, stately skeletons than it did to the rest of the jungle which had died for lack of it. Beyond the outer edge of the reeds there was scarcely a hundred metres of steep, animal-roughened mud before a sluggish wash of shallow water filled the outer edge of what had been the lake-still bow of a meander. But once the fires caught hold in that band along the outer edge of the wind's capacity to bear substantial sparks, the restless, intensifying breeze spread them sideways as it drove them down towards the water.

Had Ann been able to take an aerial view, as the passengers in the last train to Mawanga that night halfway up the opposite cliff could and as the observer in the police helicopter summoned by the first reports of the conflagration did, she would have seen a whole range of black fans all across the terrain in front of her, each fan topped with a thick arch of flame. Had she been able to see what she was running into, she would have paused for thought and realised the full hopelessness of her situation. And collapsed. And died.

Instead, she hurled herself like a stampeding animal along the final section of the track. Unsuspected, the flames closed in on either hand. Now all she could see between the thin reeds beside her was mocking, dancing brightness and the sky in front of her was filled with bright-bellied billows of smoke. Distantly, she thought of trick or treat and a terrifying night of childhood when she had been pushed irresistibly towards the biggest bonfire she had ever seen. And still she ran on, like a lemming towards a cliff top. The roaring all around her cocooned her, pushed her further into her adrenaline-drugged dream world, hid the added thunder of the helicopter passing just above her. She never knew that it was the down-draught of the machine which upset the almost magic stasis which had kept her safe so far. The whirl of air beneath the machine's great rotors sucked the nearest pincer of fire inwards and as the chopper lifted to turn and speed away downstream, the walls of the passage Ann had been following exploded into flame on either side of her.

And still she ran on, plunging madly through the wild whirl of blazing air, screaming nonstop as the withering caress of the flames moved lovingly over her curves, igniting every little hair on her thighs and flanks into a tiny prick of agony. She beat her hands before her face as though she could knock the deadly flames aside. But some part of her knew that her hands were useless against the heat and her only chance of survival lay in the water of the river. A chance of survival which receded almost unreachably when her thick brown hair caught fire.

Out onto the sloping bank she exploded, the wash of flame pursuing her as she flashed down the rough bank, miraculously keeping her footing, until the cool, healing balm of the River Mau welcomed her and she went under, and stayed there until her lungs threatened to suck in water, leeches and all, if she did not let them breathe.

She put her head above the water, but ducked back under again immediately, with only the beginning of a breath in her lungs, for the inferno she had just escaped was attaining its full fury now and the heat from the bank, worse even than the sun at midday had been, threatened to re-ignite her hair. But her body, coming out of its animal panic, imperiously demanded sustenance and although it had continued to function without food, it refused flatly to work a moment longer without air. Weary unto death, shaking with shock, she rolled onto her back and let her lips and nose break the surface so that they could gulp down great shuddering gulps of hot air. Half fainting, she allowed herself to drift like this as the sluggish current pulled her slowly along the curving shoreline towards the west. She did not think of Robert. She did not think of dangers – not even of crocodiles. She did not really think at all. She drifted slowly in the shallows, with the slick mud brushing along her back, the surface tickling her belly and thighs while the weight of the camera case sat on her chest like a drowning friend and the hot air filled her lungs, alive, and scarcely more.

When the current began to pull her southwards, she didn't notice, nor did she register much when the bank gathered over her like a black wave breaking, fringed with fire. When she slid sleepily into the black mouth of the tunnel, something registered, and she opened her eyes. She sat up at once, shocked out of her torpor. This was not some natural runnel or bore created by an incoming stream. This was manmade – the precise curve of the opening told her that, and the wide steps cut into the wall which mutely invited her to climb them. She rolled onto her hands and knees and crawled across to the steps. Where she found the energy to come up onto her feet she would never know, but come erect she did. There were six square steps up to a walkway which led intriguingly down the tunnel into the cool darkness. What had she to lose? She followed it.

The walkway was at least a metre wide. Along the high curve of the wall on her right was a cool handrail and she used this to guide her, for all too soon her eyes could see nothing in the darkness. Just before this happened, when there was barely enough light for her to see what was ahead of her, she came across a low barrier beside a metal wire grille behind which was trapped a wild mess of detritus. There was a low gate here, with wire-edged holes in it about ten centimetres square.

It almost stopped her, for it was obvious that she would only be able to negotiate it if she climbed over it and she would only be able to do that if she took off her boots and her camera bag. But she could not – would not – stop here, so, wearily, she sat and began to unlace the boots. It took a long time to achieve this, for her hands were stiff and swollen, and her laces were wet and intransigent. But in the end she was able to pull off the sodden footware and place it carefully on the walkway by her side. She placed her camera bag beside it, then she climbed over the gate. It cost her some flesh from her upper chest and shoulders to squeeze past the top of the grille and she whimpered with a combination of discomfort and panic when, uncomfortably astride the top of the gate, she thought that she was stuck. But at last she forced herself through to the other side.

Then she realised that she had left everything precious

to her back on the other side. She collapsed on the spot and sat for an unmeasured time, sobbing brokenly. But eventually the same determination which had brought her this far forced her on. She could not go back, therefore she would go forward. She pulled herself up and placed her feet carefully on the cold concrete ahead.

All along the floor of the tunnel she was following, water trickled and slopped, and had she hoped to be free of the agonising attentions of the massive river mosquitoes, she was unlucky. Only the thickness of the mud on her back gave her some measure of relief. At last, driven almost insane by the whining, burning biting on her face, she took the last piece of cloth she possessed – the wreckage of her underpants – and clutched the cotton over her nose and mouth. As she walked, her mind shrank away from the present. It fled into the past; into fantasy. For a while Robert walked by her side. Then Nico joined him and the two men had a fight. Her father came to have a chat with her and then she really began to be surprised because he had been dead for many years.

She was still talking to him when she walked over the end of the walkway and fell flat on her face into the bottom of an irrigation ditch two metres straight down.

And that was where she was when Nimrod Chala and Valerii Gogol found her. The two men who had been pursuing her for two days were there when she was discovered. She knew this because she heard them speaking. She did not open her eyes or speak herself, but she heard them.

A rough hand woke her by taking her by the left shoulder and rolling her onto her back against the slope of the ditch wall. A voice called something loud in impenetrably Kyoga dialect.

Feet arrived.

There was more conversation which she could not understand at all.

Had she been more alive, she would have been speechless with terror, for what was happening to her now was the most terrible thing she had ever imagined happening to her. As it was, she lay like a doll, loosely in their hands, and pretended to be dead.

'Speak English! I cannot understand these Kyoga grunts and gibbers!' She recognised the Russian accent and the sharp-edged tones all too well.

'He says here is another one.'

'I can see that, Comrade General. Pick her up. I want a closer look.'

She felt strong hands fasten on her limbs and she was hefted into the air. Without the warning of the words, she would have reacted to the casually intimate handling. As it was, she remained flaccid as a rag doll. She was so terrified she really felt that she was dying.

'This is not the woman. This is some native. Can you not see? Look at her face! Her lips and eyes! Her hair. You stupid ape, can you not see that her skin is black? How can this be the right one?'

She was cast down again and fell with stunning force against the rock-solid wall.

'Look at her! A naked, mud-covered savage, ugly as a baboon and probably full of disease. Leave her! She is as good as dead in any case. It isn't even worth playing the game with her, we'd never get her to stand up for long enough! Leave her. We have better things to do!'

Footsteps retreated.

A hand groped speculatively between her legs. A distant voice rapped an order in angry Kyoga. The hand was taken away and the last set of footsteps retreated. A helicopter lifted off and thundered away.

Ann rolled over onto her side and was rackingly sick, then she rolled back onto her back and waited to die.

A long, long time later, the footsteps returned.

Thinking of the rough hand between her legs, she

flinched. She knew it was death to do so, but she could not help herself. 'She's alive,' called a voice. A new voice. A woman's voice speaking in American English. The footsteps came up close and a shadow moved between Ann's bloated, bitten face and the sun. There was a grinding of shoe leather on concrete as the shadow knelt by her side.

'Jesus Christ,' said the American voice, infinitely tenderly. 'How do they come to this? How can we let them come to this?'

Ann tried to open her eyes, but they didn't seem to be working. She tried to speak, but only succeeded in making her body twitch and jump. The soft voice said something soothing in dialect which Ann did not understand, and suddenly cleft by the terrifying realisation that this woman might simply take her to the nearest native village, she forced words into her swollen mouth. English words.

'My name is Ann Cable. I am an American citizen.'

'What? Say that again! Joe, come here! Get over here at once.'

'My name is Ann Cable . . .' It was all she had the strength to say.

It was enough. 'It's OK, honey, just you lie there. You're in safe hands now and we've got just what you need. My name is Emily Karanga and I'm going to take care of you.'

Bight

GUINEA AND BENIN

Beware, beware the Bight of Benin

Chapter Twenty-Five

Richard Mariner pressed the walkie-talkie to his lips, thumbed SEND and talked to four helmsmen at once. Four helmsmen and three other captains, come to that. 'One degree more,' he said. 'One degree further west.'

'That'll be one ninety-one magnetic, Captain,' said his own helmsman helpfully.

'I know. But not for all of us.' He thumbed SEND. 'John?'

'Here, Richard.'

'How is *Niobe* heading?'

'One ninety-eight magnetic on your order.'

'Peter?' he asked Captain Walcott next.

'*Psyche* is at one eighty-six, magnetic.' Peter Walcott's voice was weary and cold. Both he and Gendo Odate were being a little short with Richard at the moment. Asha had yet to diagnose exactly what it was that was causing the skin damage to their crews, though she was treating it with apparent success. It was still spreading, though the incidence of new cases reported was falling off. The first panic seemed to be fading now that everyone knew that the condition was not life-threatening and that it responded to treatment. But where it came from and why it struck remained a mystery which niggled the giant body of Richard's organisation like an itch it could not scratch, and with each new case reported to Gendo or Peter, things took a small step further down a dangerous road. The atmosphere aboard the two ships shackled nearest to the high flanks of Manhattan simmered darkly – and Richard had made things worse by appropriating their helicopter.

He had taken it first to remove the frozen corpse of the murderous eco-terrorist Henri LeFever into *Titan*'s cold storage, but then he had found that he needed to keep it. A new chopper was on its way out to them, he knew, but there was no definite ETA for it yet and in the meantime he simply had to have the facility of going high above or far ahead as he laid his plans.

'Bob?'

'*Achilles* is at one eighty-two, magnetic,' came Bob Stark's cheerful New England tones. There had been no cases of the mystery disease reported on his ship. Yet.

Richard looked down at the diagram on the chart table in front of him, the different headings for all his ships carefully calculated and meticulously plotted, as they needed to be. While Manhattan pursued its own majestic way, the six ships tethered to her each sailed along a slightly different bearing, their corporate objective to influence in the minimum amount of time the course it was actually following.

They had reached the next really critical stage now, for they were preparing to turn the corner as they came past Freetown, Sierra Leone. The Canaries current had carried them safely southwards during the last few days, and its coastal offshoot would combine with the gathering eastward pressure of the equatorial counter current to swing them into the grip of the Guinea current within the next few hours when they would head east along the final leg of their journey. But the Guinea current swept along the shallow, coral-fanged seas off Guinea and Benin before it reached the deep-water anchorages of Mau's tectonic coast. *Titan* and her team were swinging their massive burden out across the water's drift, therefore, in an attempt to place the massive burden on the outer, deep-water edge of the current, far from lee shores and sharp reefs.

Captain Gendo Odate was the only one of them whose course matched the iceberg's, for *Kraken* was too close to the ice to follow anything but a carefully parallel heading. Even Anna Borodin in *Ajax* was angling her course slightly, trying to support the efforts of Bob Stark in *Achilles*.

'Gendo?' Silence. 'Captain Odate?'

'*Hai?*'

'Course and speed, please.'

'We continue to proceed due south, Captain Mariner, at eleven knots precisely. You are a miracle-worker, sir.'

With the passage of time and the increasing stress, Captain Odate had become so much more formal that Richard sometimes wondered whether he was getting at the sake more than was good for him.

'Thank you, Captain Odate. Inform me at once if we deviate from that course at all, please.'

'*Hai!*'

Their course was right, then, and it looked as though they could maintain it – until the full force of the counter current came down on their starboard quarter, at any rate. Their position he could read for himself. He strolled across to the satnav equipment and looked down at the figures which placed his ship accurately to within mere metres on the earth's surface. Yes, there they were, at eight degrees north latitude and ten degrees west longitude, with the berg behind them still scraping over the Sierra Leone rise while the ships out in front were heading hard for the Guinea basin.

Even now, he found he had to doublecheck when he was looking at courses, bearings, and especially location readings and reckonings. He was well enough used to placing vessels more than a quarter of a mile long, but Manhattan was something else. He had to keep reminding himself that his command was at the leading edge of an oblong on

491

the earth's surface one hundred kilometres long and fifteen or more wide. The measurements were increasingly rough, but they included the positions of the ships and the increasing puddle of cold, clear, pure water through which they were sailing. A puddle of water which had registered on the eastern coasts of the Azores, on the western ones of the Canaries and on the eastern side of the Cape Verdes as they had come past the three sets of islands during the last ten days. Now they were preparing to turn east onto the final leg and there was only a week to go – if nothing else went wrong.

But what else could possibly go wrong?

Certainly, during the week since his memory had returned, the situation on the six ships and the berg itself seemed to have been held almost immobile. The wind had abated and the weather had become clear and summery all around them, and it seemed that the worst was over. With the last of the bodies off the ice, even the sand-shrouded Manhattan seemed to be exercising a relatively beneficent air – except, perhaps, in the perceptions of those still closest to it.

By the time he had come to this point in his thoughts, Richard was once again standing by his chart. The pale colours showed all too vividly the shallow waters, the coral reefs, the narrowness of the entrance to the gigantic harbour of Mawanga, the nearness of the city to the final resting place of Manhattan, the all too obvious dangers of moving it into place and stopping that movement in time. There was someone in the United Nations building, he knew, whose sole job was to calculate the effects both locally and globally if one billion tonnes of ice was still moving at any kind of speed when it collided with the African coast. Bracingly, they had already informed him that it was unlikely that the whole continent would shift on its foundations . . .

He dragged his thoughts back to the matter in hand,

492

never one to cross his bridges before he came to them, no matter how carefully or acutely he scouted them first.

'Yves? Any update on the currents?' He had asked about the 'current situation' last time, but the Frenchman on the forecastle head had failed to recognise the pun. Or, more likely, refused to recognise it as he had not made the joke himself.

'Yes. You should go out onto your right bridge wing, Richard. The sea presents an interesting sight this afternoon.'

Richard walked across and looked through the clear-view. Thick glass still tinged with a fine dusting of sand placed a patina on everything. Yves was right: if he wanted to make out any fine detail he would have to go out onto the bridge wing.

The late afternoon was warm, wide and magnificent. Africa lay just below the eastern horizon beyond the bulk of the iceberg and, from Richard's point of view, behind the bridgehouse. In a subtle way, however, the great continent still exercised its influence even though the harmattan was long gone, leaving only the sand and the sorrow. That subtle influence was part of the wider picture, subsumed into the size and colour of the sky, into the scents carried almost subliminally with the high-flying gulls on the soft easterly breeze. And, perhaps most of all, in the waters through which they were sailing. Ahead and all around lay a wonderland of water. Richard was used to wide, unvary-ing waters which remained the same day after day; here there was a kaleidoscope of textures and hues, their vivid contrast breathtaking. It was slightly disorientating, as though he was driving across the rolling patchwork fields of the downland around Ashenden, his home.

But it was not the unusual beauty of the scene or the poignancy of the thought that made him slap the metal safety rail in front of him. For even with its colours, the sea spoke to him. He narrowed his eyes against the late afternoon glare and looked again. Then his walkie-talkie was at his lips.

'You're right, Yves. I'm going up to take a closer look. Want a ride?'

'*D'accord!* I'm on my way.'

Richard strode back onto the bridge and called across to Sally Bell, 'Call the pilot. Tell him I want to go up asap, please.'

'Yes sir.' She crossed to the phone and punched in the pilot's number while Richard ran down the stairs.

With his return of memory had come all his old self-confidence and drive. The weather and the sailing conditions simply added to his new access of energy. He felt on top of the situation, in charge, and certain of success. He was well aware that this was a combination of chemical secretions in his recovering body – and probably some psychological reaction as well. Whatever it was, he was using it to his best advantage. He had been on the phone during the last few days, to Robin at length, soothing her and re-igniting her normal sunny cheeriness of nature; to Charles Lee in Heritage Mariner's executive boardroom in London; to the Mau Club in New York, to whose number had now been added Sir William Heritage, his father-in-law, friend and mentor.

He knew that his children were well and missing him almost as much as his wife, and that the autumn was glorious at Ashenden. He knew that the payments due were being met in full and on demand so that Heritage Mariner was standing tall in the City. The impact of their sterling work was the talk of the business world and Charles was currently being forced to turn down lucrative business deals, knowing that there were bigger ones in the offing – especially if Manhattan reached Mawanga safe and sound. Richard knew that waiting for him in Mawanga city itself was a team of UN experts, diplomats, and workers, all geared up to welcoming his massive cargo and putting it immediately to the best possible use, though the rest of that troubled state, especially upcountry, simmered on the edge of civil war still. He knew that in New York his reputation, and that of his company, stood even higher than it did in London. Even in troubled Moscow, Heritage Mariner's standing was such that the whole of the late Russian Empire was considering making the company sole transporter of all nuclear waste due for disposal or reprocessing. To add weight to this, the only hard currency actually coming out of the Soviet Union was all heading his way. And he knew that also heading his way, as quickly as possible, was a Bell helicopter to replace the little reconnaissance craft which he had lost little more than a week ago.

It did not even occur to him to wonder how radically most of these things would be affected if anything went wrong during the next week.

Wally Gough was at the edge of the helipad talking to the French scientist when Richard arrived. 'What are you up to at the moment?' asked Richard. The cadet was under Sally Bell's tutelage and not likely to be hanging around with both hands idle.

'Just finished clearing this section of the deck, Captain. The last of the sand is gone now, sir, and I've dismissed my work team. The first officer is too busy to check my work at present.' He looked at his watch a little glumly. 'Navigation class after dinner.'

'But nothing until then?'

'No, Captain.'

'Up you go then. All set, Yves?'

'Yes.'

The side of the Westland opened wide and the three of them clambered in. The pilot was already in the seat going through his pre-flight checks. Richard swung the sliding door closed as the other two strapped themselves in. He and Yves would share the co-pilot's seat when the time came to check the detail of the sea and sky ahead. The Westland was not perfectly designed for this kind of observation, but it was a great deal better than nothing – and worth its weight in gold when it came to performing the functions it had been designed for.

'Off!' bellowed the pilot, and the rotors began to turn.

They were airborne a moment or two later, with the two men leaning back lost in their own thoughts while the cadet strained excitedly to see everything there was to see around him, both inside the fuselage and outside.

'Heading?' bellowed the pilot.

Richard stirred himself and went up into the co-pilot's seat. 'Due south,' he answered through the intercom, then he set about strapping himself in place.

The big chopper dropped its nose accommodatingly and ran them rapidly down towards the equator. From here they could almost see it, a fine black horizon-line sitting on the curved edge of the earth.

Richard looked around, narrow-eyed against the afternoon glare, even though the silver-coloured pilot's glasses he wore – a present from his pilot wife – had the darkest of Polaroid lenses. 'More height, please,' he ordered.

Upwards they swooped, the nose still staying low, the fuselage still tilted forward to give him a grandstand view of the sea. With the glasses high on the fine beak of his nose, his vision swept from horizon to horizon, from far Atlantic to the first dark bulge of Africa. Then he took the glasses off and, frowning, looked back, his mind busy. Yves had been right to draw his attention to this, for it was striking. Strange.

The water around the berg was blood-red. He had expected that, it was the sand washing off. The red puddle had absolute edges. It did not fade into the green sea around it like wet watercolours running. It had an edge defined almost with a solid line, as though it was contained in some huge submerged glass. Beyond it, level with the ice itself, away to the west, the sea was deep green. From the heart of the Western Ocean it came in a series of majestic waves. And when the water's motion reached the red outwash from Manhattan, the strangely coloured water took it up, but here the faces of the waves seemed blue, although their foundations were of disturbing ruby. And blue as well were the waters to the south and west. Blue and utterly different in form.

Richard's hair stirred as he was carried back to the last few moments he had spent in the company of Doug Buchanan in the ill-fated Bell. There, too, the sea had behaved in an unusual way, with a band of different form and colour revealing the existence of a major current. As it did here, too. For the strange water formation in the west was the counter current coming in. Away to the east, under the dark swell of Liberia and the pale watery outwash below it, the long blue ribbon of water surged on, gaining depth, darkness and strength. Surging eastwards, as strong as the Stream along the eastern Maritimes, all the way to Mau.

Richard looked back over his shoulder and saw Yves beginning to stir. 'Wally!' he yelled. 'Get up here now!'

The cadet was slim and quick; he was out of his seat far more quickly than the French scientist and rushed unsteadily up the length of the fuselage.

'Steady!' called Richard, and he caught the boy's hand as he came up to the back of the pilot's seat. He guided the cadet's grip to the curve of plastic-covered metal, giving the boy a chance to hold on and steady himself. As he did so, something caught his eye and he took a closer look at the hand he was holding.

The back of Wally Gough's right hand was a mass of small white blisters where the skin was beginning to fall away.

Chapter Twenty-Six

The boy would not stop shaking. He sat at the examination table clad in a hospital gown, still blushing with the thought of having been seen naked by Dr Higgins, and trembled like a leaf in Richard's gentle grip. His arms shook, making his hands almost impossible for Asha to examine. His shoulders shook and his torso jumped. He could not keep his legs still and the sound of his slippers drumming on the lino of the deck almost drowned out the low grumbling of Lamia Lykiardropolous and the rest in the isolation rooms next door. Just as he seemed incapable of keeping his body still, so he seemed incapable of controlling his tongue.

'Is it serious, Doctor?'

'Let's just see, shall we?'

'I don't know how long it's been there. It doesn't hurt. Does that matter? I've heard your hands and feet go numb with some diseases. Like leprosy. It isn't leprosy, is it, Doctor? I mean . . .' He stopped. He could not remember what he meant.

'It's all right,' Richard said quietly, imagining his son William sixteen years older. He held the terrified boy more tightly. Wally was doing all right.

'I mean I can feel my fingers and everything. Know what I mean? I can feel the top of the table here and everything, I just can't feel the blisters. Is that important? Does it mean anything? I mean, I haven't got leprosy, have I?'

499

'No, of course you haven't. Don't you worry.' It was Richard who spoke. Asha was busy.

Then, 'Where have you been?' she asked.

'I've been in the helicopter,' he answered, literally, child-like with shock.

'During the last week or so,' she prompted gently.

'On deck, mostly,' he answered ruefully. 'During the day at least. I've been in charge of one work party after another. Ding-dong likes a clean ship.'

' "Ding-dong"?' asked Richard, though he suspected what the answer would be.

'First Officer Bell.' Wally paused, then fired up in his own defence. 'I don't call her that! Well, not usually. And anyway . . .'

'Anyway?' prompted Richard.

'Anyway, Ding-dong is nothing. Some of them . . . the engineers, I think . . . well, they call her Hells.'

Richard's eyes met Asha's. The corners of each pair crinkled. Hells Bells. She was tall, she was blonde, she was in charge of the sexist so-and-sos. What could you expect?

'In my day,' said Richard, 'they would have called her "Is-a". Times change.'

'And not for the better,' supplied Asha. 'Can you feel that?' She pushed a sterile needle into the tip of the most heavily blistered finger.

'OUCH! Yes, I can.'

'And this?'

'OUCH!'

'It's probably not leprosy, then,' she informed him, bracingly.

'So what is it?'

'The same as the others have got, as far as I can tell. Whatever that is. Now, *where* have you been?'

'On deck during the day, getting that sand cleared away. With First Officer Bell in the evening, learning navigation.'

'Lucky you,' teased Richard, trying to lighten the situation a little.

Wally looked at him, eyes wide with shock. 'Captain!' he breathed. 'She's an *officer*!'

'And a very good one too,' interjected Asha severely, frowning. 'Is that all? I mean, you haven't been upon the ice?'

'No, Doctor.'

'Or in the outwash from the glacier?'

'No. It doesn't come out as far as *Titan*. And—'

'And you haven't been swimming in the sea?'

'Doctor! I mean, there are sharks . . .'

'Right. 'Nuff said. Now, I'm going to spread this ointment onto your hands and bandage them lightly. Then you'll have to stay here for a while, but I don't think it's serious and I don't think you have anything to worry about. OK?'

'Yes . . .'

'Good. Anything you want?'

His wide, defenceless eyes looked up at Richard. 'All my stuff. My book on navigation. The first officer's going to give me a test on it tomorrow . . .'

Richard smiled. 'We'll bring your stuff across. Just write a list, OK? If you can hold a pen with that stuff on your hands. And I promise you, First Officer Bell will definitely *not* give you a test tomorrow. You just get some rest, and try not to worry. That's an order. All right?'

'Yes, Captain. Thank you, Captain.'

In the corridor outside he said at once, 'Well?'

'Impossible to say. He's got the same thing as the others, but he hasn't been in any of the same places. They've all been at least wetted by water from Manhattan, but he hasn't been anywhere near it. They're all convinced that it's to do with the ice or something in it.'

'Something radioactive.'

'Precisely. But Wally's had nothing to do with any of that. And anyway . . .'

'Yes?'

501

'No doctor worth her salt listens to the opinions of a patient. You have to make up your own mind; you're the doctor, after all.'

'Quite. I see.'

'So, we take with a pinch of salt the suggestion that this is in fact anything to do with the iceberg, and we keep looking for an alternative which also fits the facts as we know them.'

'When you have eliminated all the probabilities, the alternative, no matter how improbable, must be true.'

'That sounds like a quote.'

'Sherlock Holmes, I believe. Or Hercule Poirot, perhaps . . .'

'True, nevertheless.'

'As long as you are clear about what the one remaining alternative actually turns out to be.'

'I take your point. But I cannot see, if there is an infection and the iceberg is the source of it, how the cadet caught it if he never went anywhere near the iceberg in the first place.'

'Unless,' said Richard without thinking, 'unless it is contagious.'

'Don't,' begged Asha. 'I've had nightmares about that for a week and I don't want to think about it any more, thank you very much.'

Richard had had no choice but to bring Wally to the ship's hospital but he knew it was doing no good at all to add one more infected soul to the already frightened crew of *Psyche*. Peter Walcott made no secret of the fact that he was finding the situation difficult to control.

As he walked up towards the navigation bridge deep in conversation with Asha, Richard could not help but recall the power of the moment he had pulled the juju doll out of the dead Russian woman's body bag and the unexpectedly fierce reaction from the apparently cool Major Tom Snell.

There was an atmosphere aboard this ship which would have graced the supernatural opening of *Macbeth*. He was well aware that the crew was muttering with superstitious discontent; now it was as though the very shadows were whispering. He realised that he had been a little too dismissive of the Guyanese captain's worries. Well, not dismissive exactly; perhaps he had just been preoccupied. But there was no doubting the power of the atmosphere now that he was aboard.

He decided to stay aboard, at least until Asha gave him some idea of how the cadet was likely to progress. He hoped that someone would prove equally careful with the welfare of his son William or his daughter Mary if they fell into a similar situation in due time. He remembered all too clearly what his father-in-law had told him of a visit to a quiet terraced house in Portsmouth a year or two ago, when the old man had gone to tell a quiet pair of parents called Mr and Mrs Curtis how their only child Jamie, also a Heritage Mariner cadet, had died at the hand of a terrorist on a Heritage Mariner ship. Bill had talked it over time and again with Richard, trying to explain away the hurt he had felt at innocently inflicting so much pain. Richard would always remember that Bill had said he could actually see the joy die out of their life during the minutes he had sat and talked to them. He had destroyed their happiness for ever and they had given him chocolate biscuits and tea. Not long afterwards, Bill had succumbed to a colossal heart attack, and Richard could easily see why.

The murderous terrorist in question had been the associate and lover of the last man found frozen on Manhattan, the dead man lying stiffly in *Titan*'s cold storage, the thrice accursed Henri LeFever, long may he burn in hell.

Wally Gough had two brothers, so if he was infected with anything fatal, at least his poor parents would not have their lives utterly destroyed. In any case, it wouldn't be Sir William bearing the news this time, because he was in New York. No, it would be Robin. She was the senior executive in place. She was den-mother to the Heritage Mariner cadets. She would have been the one to go to Portsmouth last time to break the tidings to Mr and Mrs Curtis, but she had been at sea when the boy was killed. Now, she would not hesitate. She would go and tell the Goughs herself. And Richard could not bear the thought of that.

Peter Walcott was on the bridge, staring moodily out into the sunset – though, to be fair, the sun was in fact going down well aft of his ship. Richard's brief reconnaissance had been enough to tell him the lie of the land, so to speak, and the ships were now swinging round with Manhattan onto the due easterly setting which would bring them into Maui waters within the week, and into Mawanga harbour soon after that, if all went well. And at least *Psyche* had a sunset. *Kraken* on the far side of the ice mountain was well into evening shade already, for the shadow cast by Manhattan must stretch most of the way to the coast of Liberia now. But Richard had to admit once again that his gloomy colleague had good reason to worry. Looking out from the blood-red bridge, the light seemed to shimmer on the air as it reflected and multiplied between the scarlet sky and the blood-streaming flank of the iceberg against which they were moored. And the water all around, of course, thought Richard gloomily. It was as though they were sailing slowly through the handiwork of a giant Jack the Ripper. It would have been bad enough even had their ship not been loaded with dead bodies for a couple of weeks; even had their mess mates not been stricken by a mysterious, nameless, disfiguring disease.

Unconsciously, he began to scratch the back of his neck as though there might be some kind of rash there, spreading down and across his shoulder blades. Still rubbing, he crossed to stand beside Peter Walcott. 'I'm looking forward to meeting your officers again,' he said quietly. 'You have a good mess aboard. And an excellent galley, I think.'

Peter nodded curtly, just on the edge of being rudely dismissive. He was still caught up in directing the passage of his command as the whole mass of Manhattan, and all the ships propelling her, swung onto the new heading. Richard was silent, content to consider how lucky he was to spend most of his time on the bridge of *Titan* where his concentration could come and go depending on the dictates of his greater responsibilities. *Titan* was a forgiving ship and Sally Bell a rock-solid back-up to anything he wanted to achieve. And, of course, his situation in point position also gave him some latitude. How different was the grinding precision required here where one minute of inaccurate heading – one second, let alone one full degree – would ram the all too fragile bows against the unforgiving ice. And, as everyone else had no doubt calculated long ago, damage to the bow would lead to the whole vessel being pushed under by the unhesitating progress of the iceberg towering above them.

It was no wonder that Peter insisted that line watches should be mounted round the clock, no matter what the weather, no matter what the complaints he received as a result. Richard found that the atmosphere on the bridge was making him edgy so he walked out onto the port bridge wing. He chose this one on purpose, knowing it was closest to the ice, wanting to feel the full effect of the forces threatening to pull this particular command apart.

Even before he opened the door, he could hear the constant thundering of the water down onto the inner edge of the bridgehouse. As soon as he walked outside, he found himself in a filthy, clinging mist made of a combination of spray and sand. He remembered at once the efforts to which Sally Bell had gone, restoring *Titan*'s cleanliness and dignity after the ravages of the sand-laden harmattan, and he paused, unconscious of the state he was getting into, while he thought about the effect this filthiness must be having on Peter Walcott's command.

But what to do? He felt the steady, powerful throb of the diesel motor beneath his feet as it drove that one great screw through the eastward-flowing water. The power it was providing was too precious and too well paced; neither *Psyche* nor *Kraken* could be relieved of this duty, no matter how unpleasant it became. But was there any way of making it less unpleasant? Still completely disregarding the freezing, filthy spray, he strode forward to the rail and looked along the drizzle-soiled deck, then up at the cliff of the ice. Ahead, the overhang remained about the same: no relief there. What about behind? He strode back, moving out into the aft of the bridge wing. Yes. The cliff fell back here. If they pulled in the lines until they were as short as possible, all except the forecastle would be pulled free of the waterfall.

And, thinking about that waterfall . . .

Lost in thought, he walked back onto the bridge. Completely unconscious of the figure he presented, of the mess he was making or of the looks he was eliciting, he said, 'Could I use your walkie-talkie, please, Captain Walcott?'

'Well, yes of course, but—'

'Thank you. I'll just take it out here.' He paused in the doorway and grinned. 'Lucky they're waterproof, isn't it?'

'*Hai?*'

'Captain Odate, it's Richard Mariner here. I'm speaking from *Psyche*. Can you hear me all right?'

'Yes, Captain.'

'I'm out on the bridge wing looking aft of the ship. The cliff immediately abaft *Psyche* seems to be free of overhang. It's where the engineers placed the main body of their charges, I think. Have you got a similar clear area immediately aft of you?'

'Please wait a moment, Captain. I am just going out

onto the starboard bridge wing.' The static on the line built up and Richard realised that the sound resembled a waterfall at the far end because that was exactly what it was.

Gendo Odate came back on line, calm and unruffled although he too was obviously standing under a filthy waterfall, like Richard. But Richard was not captain here and had nothing to lose – unlike Captain Odate in every respect. It was the old samurai spirit shining through. 'Yes, Captain Mariner. I see what you mean. There is a section of cliff which does not overhang. It is aft of *Kraken*, immediately above the anchorage points.'

'Good. Do you think you could pull *Kraken* back into position there if you tightened the lines sufficiently?'

'Assuredly, Captain Mariner. But there would be a problem with that course of action. My crew are extremely nervous. There has been an atmosphere aboard, especially as some of our men have contracted the . . . the disease . . .'

'I understand, Captain. But the object of this exercise would be to allay your crew's fears and to dissipate the atmosphere in both commands.'

'But we lengthened the lines in order to give us some freedom from the ice.'

'Yes, I understand that. But it hasn't really worked, has it? Both ships have simply swung into the side of the berg, under the overhang. If we shorten the lines again, it will pull both *Psyche* and *Kraken* out from under the overhang so that the vast majority of the deck will be free of the water. That will help the atmosphere on both vessels, I think.'

'Perhaps. But the good done by the new position will be undone by the short lines. You must understand, Captain, that there is a very real fear aboard these ships. The iceberg is rising more quickly than ever because of the loss of the weight of the sand combined with the water washing off. I know we have the charts you worked out with Ross, which cover the rate of melt and rise and give us to within a centimetre how much line to pay out, but I think you must understand how great is the fear on both ships that Manhattan will simply roll over on top of us one night. The lines are utterly unbreakable, remember.'

'I do appreciate that, Captain Odate, I assure you. And I believe I have the answer. The lines might be unbreakable, but they are not impossible to cut. How would your men feel if, while we were readjusting the lines, we put in place the cutters so that at the slightest sign of trouble you could cut loose and run free?'

There was a silence, emphasised by the slushy hissing of the waterfall under which the intrepid Japanese was standing. Then, 'Yes,' said Gendo Odate. 'Yes, I believe that might work well.'

The next couple of hours were extremely busy for Richard, and for every other able-bodied man aboard *Psyche* and *Kraken*. With Richard in overall charge, they slowly tightened the lines fore and aft, both ships in concert, with careful reference to both John Higgins and Bob Stark who were able to advise on placing and propulsion respectively. But, most important of all as far as the crew of *Psyche* was concerned, after the lines had been tightened and their ship heaved out of the enervating slush-fall from the overhang on high, the huge yellow cutting discs were brought out fore and aft. They sat on tall adjustable legs and were designed to clamp round the black thickness of the space rope. Handles on their sides released laser beams from the circumferences of the big yellow discs to cut inwards, the beams crossing like spokes at the axle of a bicycle wheel. Thin as light, sharp as acetylene flame, the beams were designed to slide in between the parallel molecules of the strands, to part the lines at once.

And, because the crews of *Kraken* and *Psyche* were proud men, like their captains, Richard ordered the other ships under his command also to put the cutters in place. They all knew that he was being almost patronising in his care for their feelings, but they also knew that he was motivated only for their welfare and not at all by any sense of his superiority. He had what used to be called, in old and reactionary days, the common touch. They knew he was simply trying to help them and they loved him for it.

Richard, of course, was blissfully ignorant of their feelings. Once the lines were shortened and the major problem solved, once the cutters were in place on all the ships, he was concerned only with making himself clean and respectable enough to take dinner with Captain Walcott and his crew. He went to the spare cabin beside the owner's cabin on C deck – Asha Higgins was in the owner's cabin – and prepared to take a shower. He was surprised to find on entering his quarters just how much had been provided for his comfort. There was a complete change of clothes – tropical whites which looked as though they would be a perfect fit. There was a range of toiletries, several disposable razors, a choice of aerosol shaving foam and an embarrassment of aftershave. All that was lacking was a bar of bath soap and a flannel.

Until he entered the shower.

In the shower he discovered a plethora of soap outmatched only by the selection of shampoo. He had never been forced to dress from the slop chest before, but if this was anything to go by, Gieves and Hawkes of St James's, London, had better look to their laurels.

With a wry smile he climbed into the cubicle and turned on the hot tap. Full on. As he angled his body, allowing the water to thunder off his left shoulder blade and run tepidly – but promisingly – down his spine, he began to unscrew the top of his preferred shampoo bottle. Soon the water was hot and he was contentedly lathering the thick green liquid into his scalp. After a rinse, a repeat and a rinse, he reached for some soap. He had always been an Imperial

Leather man and he was fortunate in being able to find a bar among all those on offer. He raised his hands to spread the lather under his arms and beyond, and it was then that he saw that his own skin, like Wally's, was peeling off and washing away.

Chapter Twenty-Seven

So Richard, too, became trapped aboard *Psyche*, and, for a time, part of the dark atmosphere which brooded over her. He was in a good position to gauge the effects of his decision to shorten the lines and place the cutters, for, as he soon discovered, the makeshift isolation ward which was home to Lamia and his acolytes was the source of much of the unrest. These men warily observed the shortening of the lines and the way in which the high ice was pulled even closer. They noted the manner in which the great yellow cutting discs were clamped into place. They watched from various ports and windows while the line watches were carefully briefed on the procedure for cutting the lines in an emergency.

'We're all dead,' opined the Greek gloomily, as yet unaware that the man in overall command was now privy to his speculations. 'They have tied us so close to this man-killing monster that even they are afraid! Why else do you think they have at last put the cutters in place?'

The isolation ward was slowly expanding down the A deck corridor as Asha appropriated the rooms nearest to the ship's sickbay. Lamia and his cronies from the main forecastle line watch were in the four-bed ward off the sickbay itself, for they had presented the symptoms first. To these had been added two men from *Psyche*'s second line watch, one a huge black Haitian called Duvalier who was rumoured to have planted the juju doll on the Russian woman's corpse. These had been joined by four men from *Kraken*, also line watch men, a varied sprinkling of GP seamen from *Ajax*, and now from *Titan*. Only *Achilles* and *Niobe* seemed to be clear. Give it time, said the sick men who were, in fact, quite fit apart from the blisters, and idle and bored and restless, give it time.

At its outer edge, the isolation area was little more than a line on the lino flooring which no crew member was allowed to cross. A line which was moving further down the corridor and closer to the crew's day rooms with each new infected arrival. Richard, indeed, moved into the room which would have been the crew's ping-pong room had any of them expressed any interest in the game. He got it because it was big enough to double as an office and he chose to share it with the terrified, isolated Wally Gough, but even so the video room was next and things were looking bleak.

Because one end of the isolation area was so open and none of the windows out onto the weather deck could be locked, Lamia had had no trouble in setting up a lively smuggling route. He now had unrivalled access to medication – always a popular bargaining counter – and he missed his cigarettes and pornography. As the contraband was exchanged either way, so was the mutinous seaman's cynical speculation. The situation was extremely damaging; indeed, it was beginning to turn dangerous.

Richard did not discover all this at once, of course, but he was an extremely acute man and a widely experienced one; it was only a matter of a few days before he had worked out what was going on in the restricted world around him.

Once he had discovered that the skin condition was unsightly and uncomfortable but by no means enervating, he reassumed command and arranged with a more than willing Peter Walcott for the ping-pong room to be turned into a fully functioning office. The walkie-talkie particularly freed him; linked as it was to the main communication of *Psyche*'s powerful radio room, it allowed him to communicate with anyone he wanted to talk to, anywhere.

On his flight across here, when he had known about Wally's condition but not his own, he had completed his discussion with Yves Maille about exactly what it was they could see in the sea and directed the final series of course changes which, when fully executed, swung the convoy round onto its eastern heading. During the next few days they would follow the southern edge of the busy Guinea current, safely away from the shallow shoreline, the outwash of the Niger and the gathering reefs of coral, heading over the deep water of the Guinea basin directly for the wide embrace of Mawanga's tectonic harbour.

Richard reported their progress to the Mau Club, and passed on Asha's description of the symptoms which they were all suffering to be sent out to the United Nations' tropical medicine experts, and to their experts in radiation sickness at UCLA hospital, though no one made specific mention of this fact. He agreed that when the new Bell helicopter arrived, Asha should send samples ashore to the nearest hospital with a research facility and UN affiliation. The nearest were either in Abidjan on the Ivory Coast or Accra in Ghana; the one two days' sailing away, the other three days'.

By the end of his first working day in the isolation unit, Richard was very much back in charge and had impressed everyone around him, except the group of malcontents he was currently trapped with. They soon realised who he was, however, and, with eyes ever on the main chance, they began to make overtures to Wally who was an obvious conduit of influence and information.

As the evening of that first day in the isolation ward gathered around him, Richard stood looking out through the window across the poop deck towards the line watch and the great flank of the berg beyond them. The light was thickening and turning ruby again, though none of the recent sunsets had achieved the spectacular beauty of those behind the high sands of the harmattan. The men of the line watch were in animated conversation, gesturing at the line, the ice and the yellow line cutter. Richard felt he could almost hear what they were saying – but that was impossible in fact because to the constant grumble of generators and throb of engine beneath his feet was added the hum of the air conditioning. Even under the influence of the berg, the air was warm outside. The meltwater would have been running even more intensely down upon these men had they not moved the ship. The thought triggered another in Richard's mind, a lateral leap of association into something which had been niggling him since they turned south in Biscay and the melt rate had begun to climb.

The ships had been running in ballast, but they were tankers, after all, with massive carrying capacity as yet unused. It was time to do some complex calculations, he thought. And that thought brought to mind the best technical ship handler he knew. The one he was married to. It was time to call Robin. Still looking at the aft line watch, Richard brought the walkie-talkie to his lips and called through to the radio officer.

Five minutes later, he heard the ringing sound and closed his eyes, shutting out the garnet cliff which dominated his view and instead imagining the warm intimacy of the sitting room at Ashenden. It was the phone by the sofa which was ringing, he imagined, and she was coming through from the kitchen to answer it. He always phoned at this time if he could and she would know it was probably him. She would be walking through, having left the twins with Janet to finish their supper, ready to curl up on the sofa and talk to him with the gentle, quiet intimacy they both treasured. He always phoned at this time because he knew she would be able to look out through the French windows towards France itself as they talked, and watch the sun set over the Channel.

'Mariner.'

He had been so busy daydreaming he was surprised when she answered.

'Hello, Mariner.'

'Hello, darling. I hoped it would be you.' He heard the familiar sounds she made as she sat on the sofa.

'Sorry I didn't get through last night.'

'Bit of a crisis?'

'You could say that. How are the terrors?'

'Terrible. They miss you. We all do. Even Ashenden gets lonely after a while.'

'I'll be home soon.'

'Do. Or we'll be coming out to Mawanga.'

'Don't do that! It's going to be a circus.'

'No, I was joking. I don't want to put the twins through all those jabs yet. What crisis?'

He began to tell her a little, making light of it, playing mind games with himself as he always did when he was less than honest with her, worrying that he was being over-protective and patronising, suspecting acutely that she could read him so well – even at this distance on a crackly line – that she would go to the other extreme and imagine that his reticence covered things which were much worse than they actually were.

'But you're in safe hands.'

'Yes. I'm with Asha and she's got every expert the UN can contact to advise her over the phone.'

'But they don't know what it is.'

'Not yet.'

'And the skin is coming off your hands and face.'

'Not all of it; it's just as though I'm peeling a bit after sunburn. That's all.'

'Off your hands and face.'

'Well, not so much my face as my neck, you know . . .' His voice trailed off.

Silence.

'Maybe I'll come out after all,' she said.

'Oh darling! There's nothing you could do!'

'I could take over your command for a start. I hope you're paying poor Sally Bell captain's rates because she's been in command of that ship for longer than you have, by the sound of things.'

'Talking of that . . .'

'Talking of Sally?'

'Talking of taking command, I've got a bit of a conundrum, and I'd like your advice, as the most gifted ship handler in the family . . .'

Next morning's captains' conference was held on the walkie-talkies – on the 'party line', as Bob Stark insisted on calling it. This was by no means an unusual procedure. Since the loss of one helicopter and the difficulty, and time wasted, of hopping from one ship to another, the conference had often been held this way. But this one Richard would have preferred to hold face to face. Even though he could and did fax all the calculations and the sheets of lading schedules to everybody as they discussed what he and Robin had worked on until late last night, he would have preferred to see their faces as he talked. But he was able to tell a good deal from their tone of voice and had to satisfy himself with that.

'We'll have to completely rebrief the line watches,' Peter Walcott began. Richard was beginning to understand what strain Peter was under and why he was always automatically negative on first knockings.

'All on the schedules going round on the fax,' answered Richard.

'Obviously we'll have to check and recalculate them for ourselves,' said Gendo Odate, under similar pressure to Peter; also negative, first off.

'Yes, you will, Gendo. If we're going to make much of a go of it, we'll have to be fast, but yes, you'll need to recalculate.'

'Hard work for first officers all round,' mused Bob Stark.

'Yes.'

'Still, that's what first officers are for. What are you going to do about Sally Bell, though? She's lading officer and acting captain all rolled into one.'

'Let her talk for herself, Bob. Sally?'

'I don't know, Richard. I could sleep less, I guess.'

'I could lend you Steve Bollom,' interposed John Higgins. 'He could work for you and I'll sort out my end myself.'

Richard chuckled to himself. He had known in his bones that John would find it hard to let anyone else look after something as complex as this.

'OK, John, but I'll need you to recheck some of the figures anyway, especially the figures on line pay-out. Don't over-tax yourself.'

'No. I won't.'

'Because you've got another set of calculations to make in any case.'

'When we start to slow Manhattan down so that she doesn't shove Africa a couple of hundred metres east when she hits? Yes, I know. I get faxes from the Mau Club all the time.'

'Any use?'

'Might make decent toilet paper, I suppose.'

'They've got mathematicians, not ship handlers,' soothed Richard.

'No, they've got ship handlers. The best ship handlers in the world. But we're all out here,' said Bob Stark.

'Very funny,' said John.

'No,' said Bob. 'I mean it.'

'Is this relevant?' demanded Katya Borodin stiffly. 'Captain Higgins will do the relevant calculations for slowing Manhattan's progress at the relevant time. What we have to worry about now are the figures we have in front of us. Why is this so urgent that we have to work all night?'

'If my figures are correct, and Dr Ross's melt and runoff figures as updated yesterday are accurate—'

'They are, Richard,' interposed Colin Ross gruffly.

'And the most interesting discussion I had with Dr Maille on the way south in the Westland holds water, then the runoff is simply a big discrete pool of fresh water marked clearly for us by the sand it contains. It will not have mixed with the sea water around it because of the difference in specific gravity and temperature, and it should all be available for use if we can get it all aboard. The runoff so far should come to about two full loads for all of us.'

'Yes, I see that but where . . .' Katya Borodin, unimaginatively for her, asked the obvious question.

'That's the rub, Katya. I'll have to call Mawanga city and see if there are any coastal tankers we can offload into.'

'It seems quite likely that there would be.' Her mind was obviously hotting up. 'After all, they are clearing all shipping out of the inner harbour in anticipation of our arrival. And if there are?'

'Then it would be possible to load fully within the next twenty-four hours.'

'Yes, indeed,' she agreed.

'And unload in two days' time.'

'*Da!* I see!'

'And reload so that we come into Mawanga fully laden again.'

There was a slight silence, then careful John summed it up, nominally to clear his own mind, actually to ensure that the others understood exactly what Richard was proposing. 'So,' he said slowly, 'we pump the clear water aboard out of the ocean around us on the assumption it has not been contaminated with brine and that the sand will settle out of it. We try to drum up enough coastal tankers to offload one and a half million tonnes of water in a couple of days' time, then we fill up again on the way down to Mawanga.'

'That should save about all the runoff it's possible to save, yes . . .'

'But it does require some interesting mathematics, doesn't it?' said Peter Walcott drily. 'Especially for those of us who'll be bobbing up and down in relation to the iceberg which is continuing to bob up and down in relation to us – at a different rate!'

'We'll go through the figures again, of course, Peter. I think, if you look, you'll see that you and Gendo have two complete schedules each. One for the bow line and one for the stern; and they vary depending on your preferred sequence of lading.'

'Yes, I see that.' Peter Walcott was mollified by the amount of careful calculation that had already been done on his behalf. 'You've thought this through pretty carefully.'

'I had help.' Richard let it rest at that, looking down at the sheets of figures in front of him, waiting for the final reaction to his scheme. It came from Peter Walcott, the hardest to convince of all of them.

'If you get this amount of work done when you're sick,' said the Guyanese captain, giving in with a dry laugh, 'I'd hate to have you aboard when you're one hundred per cent fit!'

The harbour master at Mawanga port was a Kyoga of the old school, rude and officious. And he was not particularly enamoured of Richard, or of the United Nations, for between them they had turned a restful sinecure into the most demanding job on the west coast of Africa. He soon made it absolutely clear that he had no intention of giving Richard any of the information he needed. He had not time, he stated stiffly, in thickly accented English, to give callers on the telephone the registered owners of shipping of any kind in his harbour, let alone to discover which of the tankers nearby had no cargo and the capacity to carry water. No, he certainly would not pass on the names of their commanding officers. Or even the names and ports of registration of any ships of more than ten thousand deadweight tonnes. Captain Mariner had best contact some of the United Nations officials with which his port was currently being overrun and ask them!

Captain Mariner tried. It was still the morning where he was, though it was early afternoon in Mau. More importantly, it was not yet breakfast time in New York, so he could get the names of no UN personnel on the ground, let alone their telephone numbers.

But then, at the end of his tether and out of patience, he remembered. He already had the name of a United Nations officer in Mawanga. With a smile of relief, he called the radio officer. 'Get me Mawanga Directory Enquiries, please,' he ordered.

It came through at once: one of the new breed of Kyogas, a woman speaking in English. 'Directory Enquiries. What name, please?'

'Can you tell me the number for the Mawanga Hilton, please?'

'Is that Reception at the Mawanga Hilton, sir?'

'Yes, please.'

'I can connect you directly from here, caller.'

'Please do so . . .' He was cut off at once.

'Hello? Mawanga Hilton Reception.' A woman again. Perhaps not a Kyoga this time. Speaking in English with a slight American accent.

'Good afternoon. My name is Richard Mariner. Can you put me in contact with Emily Karanga, please?'

'Can you hold for a moment, Mr Mariner? I will see if I can find Ms Karanga for you . . .' The line went dead.

Richard was long past feeling surprise at the ease and

precision with which it was possible to communicate across the world these days. His call to Bill Heritage at the United Nations had been no more complex than a call home, necessitating only a multiple-number dialling code. The old man had picked up the phone himself. It was fantastic.

'. . . Karanga here. Is that you, Richard?'

'Hello, Emily? Yes, it's Richard here. I wonder if I might ask a favour?'

'Yes, of course. Name it.'

'There's a crusty old harbour master down at the port I need to have charmed out of his tree.'

'Well . . .' Emily didn't sound all that impressed.

'Look. This is more important than it sounds. We've come up with a scheme for bringing meltwater aboard here. We need some small coastal tankers to put it onto. We can offload one and a half million tonnes of fresh water. If we can do that, then we can bring in the same again – an extra three million tonnes in all. That's a good-sized lake, for crying out loud! But I can't get the harbour master to tell me the names of any tankers. Not their captains or their owners. And he's got all the information I need.'

There was a brief silence while Emily assimilated the information and thought about how best to deal with it. Then she said, 'Right. Is there any special sort or size of tanker you need to know about?'

'Yes, indeed there is . . .'

As he began to explain, he felt the weight of a certain amount of responsibility lift off his shoulders. And he was relieved.

While the afternoon rolled by and the convoy with Manhattan at its heart came past Harper, Liberia, past Cape Palmas, and then past Tabou, Ivory Coast, Richard went through with Asha his current condition and applied ointment under her direction, then worked at arranging the final details of his office. When everything was exactly as he wanted it to be, he sent up to the bridge for the Admiralty chart of the west coast of Africa and, together with the Admiralty Pilot, began to go through the fine detail of what exactly would be involved in delivering Manhattan safely into the interior anchorage of Mawanga harbour.

At four, he phoned round all his captains again and checked up on how their calculations from this morning's meeting were going. After the others had rung off, Colin Ross stayed on the party line, but it was clear that he was trying to ensure that no one else could overhear what he was saying. 'You know, Richard,' he began, and Richard knew him well enough now to recognise that slight Scottish burr as a sign of worry, 'the melt rate figures I gave you have a wider relevance than simply the tonnage of fresh water you can pick up.'

'Yes, I know that, Colin.'

'I mean to say, I don't think we're going to make it as we are. I can't be absolutely accurate of course, and not even Kate, who's as experienced in this area as I am myself, can give me any guidance.'

'It's in the lap of the gods, Colin.'

'Aye, you can put it like that if you want, but it will affect all of your calculations about the depth and width of the harbour entrance. It will have to affect your sailing orders – everything. Will we need to warn the coastal areas? I mean, God knows what will happen.'

'As I understand it, that will depend on whether it rolls to the north or to the south.'

'That it will!'

'Well, the best I can offer is this. When Manhattan is sitting so high that it looks from your figures that she's going to roll, I'll ask the ships to cut themselves free in a carefully calculated sequence.'

'*Psyche* last.'

'*Psyche* and *Niobe* last.'

There was a short silence, then Colin observed, 'That would be dangerous.'

'Yes. But it comes with the territory. I'll have to call the odds between two ships and eighty lives, and the probable damage to the whole of the coast north of us if it rolls the other way.'

'But you recognise that it will roll. Before we get to Mawanga. All my figures point to it.'

'I know that, Colin. We all knew it was a probability right from the outset. Now it's just something else I have to try and include in my calculations.'

'Talking of calculations, I have another set of schedules which allow for a wide range of melt rates.'

'Fax them over to me here. I'll go through them and see if I can calculate the critical point. I'm the one responsible, after all. I have to warn the captains – give them an accurate countdown if I can.'

'Rather you than me!'

'What can I say? It's what I get paid for.'

'You don't get paid enough. Believe me!'

Richard looked at his left hand – his right was holding the walkie-talkie to his ear – and saw through the light gauze of the bandage that the skin was still soft and full of blisters. His blood ran cold and he shivered with revulsion. 'I believe you,' he said feelingly.

He was holding the walkie-talkie, getting ready to phone Robin, when Emily Karanga came back through.

'Hello, Emily?' he said, his spirits lightening just to be talking to her. She was such a dynamo that it was possible to soak up energy from the simple idea of her.

'Hi, Richard. That information you wanted is on its way over by fax. He wasn't such a bad old guy. He just needed someone to appreciate what an outstanding job he was doing, and in extremely difficult circumstances, too.'

Richard wasn't sure whether she was joking or not. 'Oh, yes?' he said noncommittally.

'Certainly. We Kyoga are a badly underrated tribe. We've always done all the work here and never received any of the recognition due to us. It is most upsetting. Even the United Nations is really only interested in saving the lives and property of thousands of worthless, feckless N'Kuru peasants who have never been anything but a drain on the state. If we Kyoga had our way, they would all be used for what they are best suited for – manure.'

'Oh Emily! I'm sorry!'

'Never mind. I got what you wanted and I hope it's useful. Hey! I've got a message from an old friend for you!'

'Oh? Who?'

'Ann Cable. She's been in the biggest private hospital we have here for a week now and she only came round this afternoon. I was the one who brought her in, so they called me at once and I went straight over.'

'How is she? What happened to her?'

'She's surprisingly well. She seemed in a pretty bad way when I found her in an irrigation ditch upcountry. But they say she's pretty good. Pulling through nicely now. When I told her I knew you, she brightened up a lot. All the nice girls love a sailor, I guess.'

'She does, but not this sailor. I'll give the right man a call later. What on earth was she doing in an irrigation ditch?'

Emily explained what little she knew.

'Sounds grim,' he said when she had finished.

'It is. I haven't been right into the interior, but there are all sorts of stories coming out of there. You don't want to know!'

'Horrific.'

'Do tell! Well, you just get that ice cube of yours over here before we run out of Martini.'

'I'll do my best.'

'Hey! That's not too impressive, Richard! *I'll do my best!*

524

Where's that old Mariner spirit? Are you all right? You sound pretty beat to me. As a matter of fact, Ann sounded a good deal brighter. What's the matter?'

'Well, now that you ask . . .'

And, against his nature, breaking the rule of a lifetime, too exhausted to maintain his usual façade of granite, he told her exactly what the matter was.

Which, as it turned out, was the best thing he could possibly have done.

'Only on the hands and face?'

'That's right.'

'OK, let's be clear about this. None of you is missing skin from under their clothing? It's just, like, faces, hands and legs?'

'That's right. Why so exact, Emily? You sound as though you know what's happening.'

'Maybe I do. Let me take it from here for a while, though. You just stop me if I'm wrong, OK?'

'OK. Fire away.'

'You've been sailing through a sandstorm, right?'

'Yes.'

'Strong southerly wind, full of sand. Head on, unrelenting. No gusting.'

'Yes, that's right.'

'And the men who have been affected are all people who've been out in it for a while.'

'Yes. They've all been doing deck work. Line watches, deck officers . . . Yes!'

'And the people who are worst affected have been out in the most exposed sections.'

'Yes. *Yes!* My God, you're right! How did you know?'

'Anyone down here would know. Anyone from Mau, Cameroon, any of the countries with a Saharan border. It's the harmattan.'

'That's right. We've had a harmattan blowing! It blew for days!'

'Then anyone who was out in it for any length of time must expect to lose a little skin. That's what the harmattan does. It skins you. It's a vicious wind.'

'And that's all? I mean, there are no other side effects?'

'Never heard of any. I'll check in the hospital if you like, there'll be someone there who will know for sure.'

'No, that's all right, Emily. I'll do it from here. You've done enough. Thank you. Thank you very much!'

He switched off his walkie-talkie and looked at his hand. Already the blisters looked less repulsive. He knew what had caused them. He knew that they were nothing to worry about. He raised the walkie-talkie again, but now there was a song in his heart and the unbounded cheeriness he had felt a couple of days ago which had only taken a bit of a knock from this affair returned tenfold.

Even as he asked for Directory Enquiries in Mawanga, he pulled himself to his feet, too excited to sit down any longer, too full of energy to try.

This was the last setback, it had to be. And it had turned out to be nothing important at all.

They were only a few days out of Mawanga harbour and he suddenly felt certain that everything was going to go smoothly to plan. They would get Manhattan there and save most of her meltwater on the way. In spite of Colin Ross's figures, the berg would remain stable. The area of radioactive contamination seemed to be relatively limited after all, if the readings collected on the day they found LeFever's corpse were correct. Once the ice island was safe in harbour it could be inspected in more detail and the contaminated sections cut off and disposed of. His company, in actual fact, were expert in the transport of such waste and it suddenly seemed entirely possible that even the existence of radioactive debris in the ice could work out, like everything else so far, to the advantage of Heritage Mariner. He closed his eyes and thought as hard as he could, but in his euphoric state he simply could not imagine anything going awry which they had not allowed for, which they could not handle easily.

Chapter Twenty-Eight

Valerii Gogol had brought eight Hind-D attack helicopters with him to support the division of tanks he was engaged in selling to the power-hungry government of Congo Libre. The Congo Librens were on the point of agreeing the purchase of the whole package, but a certain amount of jealousy and infighting had slowed things down. Which had allowed him to join the men across the border fomenting trouble in Mau, preparing to place Nimrod Chala in undisputed control of the country – which would then become a docile satellite of Congo Libre and a guaranteed soul-mate of Russia. He had also found the atrocities of the vicious little bush war very much to his taste and, for the first time in many years, he had found he was actually enjoying himself.

Which is what he had been doing when the game warden, the UN man and the American reporter had stumbled across him and his putative N'Kuru Lion commando. He had been fortunate that the delay had continued long enough to allow him to hunt them down to death. He had been over the grasslands upcountry with a fine-tooth comb and had seen detailed reports from Nimrod Chala's ubiquitous paramilitary police patrols. He had no doubt that they were all dead. It was a pity, though, that he had seen only one of them die.

The delay also allowed him time to take five of his Hind-Ds, arm the big helicopters with all the air-to-surface rocketry he could lay his hands on, and go, as General Bovary had ordered, to destroy this iceberg called Manhattan.

The five Hinds came over the Blood River and past the lake on the late Harry Parkinson's game reserve at zero feet, tearing the tops off the last green trees between here and the coast as they went. Then there was just the endless red dust bowl which had once been the great rolling grasslands of Mau. Gogol looked down on the dead land, smiling slightly. He knew it well; he had been flying over it regularly for more than a month now, usually in one of Nimrod Chala's police helicopters. The Russian's cold eyes swept from side to side as he considered Chala's helicopters. They were going to be a problem sooner or later and the question was, should he destroy them on the way in or on the way back out?

He had omitted to inform Chala of his current plans – the General of Police had made no secret of the fact that he very much wanted the iceberg to arrive. Chala didn't mind fomenting a small civil war and assisting several million people to starve to death, but he had no intention of becoming the political leader of a permanent economic ruin. And now that the United Nations had declared its intention of delivering a great deal of aid to support the good work begun by the water which the iceberg represented, the possibilities of infinite power had been gilded by the possibilities of infinite pilferage. Oh yes, Nimrod Chala desperately wanted to see Manhattan come safely to Mau. Once he knew what Gogol and his helicopters were up to, he would use any power at his command to stop them – or destroy them in revenge.

'What kind of resistance can we expect when we register on their radar?' asked Captain Illych Kizel anxiously.

Gogol regarded him. He was young for a squadron commander. He worried too much. He was a genius with helicopters, an inspired pilot and an excellent, decisive leader with his peers and juniors but he was too easily over-awed and he worried too much. 'There will be no resistance worth worrying about, Illych,' grated the general. 'Either in the air or on the ground.' He winced as he talked, hating the pain it cost him to utter sound and hating the ugliness of the sound. Once upon a time, he had been the proud possessor of a fine bass voice. When he sang – and he sang often in the days before Chernobyl – people who knew about music had compared him to the great Fyodor Chaliapin.

He sang no more and spoke as little as possible. He reached into the breast pocket of his blouson and pulled out another painkiller. He had learned to function with massive dosages of morphine in his system. It was the only way he could function at all, nowadays.

But he wanted Captain Kizel calm, at least until Manhattan came into view, so he enlarged. 'They have no air force, Illych. Their army has no airborne wing worth the name. The paramilitary police have five secondhand Sikorsky Black Hawks. They're all fifteen years old, basically equipped and badly maintained. They're there to make a jumped-up little policeman called Nimrod Chala look good. They're no match for us. But they will, of course, be bringing us a nice present, one way or another.'

Captain Kizel looked across at the general with a great deal of surprise. That was the longest speech he had ever heard the senior officer give. And it had taken its toll. What he could see of Gogol's face was white with strain. He looked back at his display and, beyond, down to the ground. They were sweeping northwards as well as westwards because they proposed to use the River Mau as their primary navigational aid. And the tectonic basalt cliff above it would work as extremely effective protection against radar. They were going out fast and low in the early morning with the rising sun at their backs and, all things being equal, would be coming back the same way in the late afternoon with the setting sun exactly behind them.

This was important, of course; they were most at risk in Maui airspace, and on Maui sovereign territory, in spite of what the general said.

'There it is,' said Kizel as the cliff came up over the northern horizon. He looked down briefly. They were moving at more than 250 kph through the low, still, heavy morning air. They would be there in a few moments. He glanced at his watch and checked his time-plan. Bang on time. He looked at the green read-out which gave him the position of the four aircraft flying in close formation behind him. He glanced up at the mirror above his head which allowed him to check on the disposition of the six heavily armed men occupying the seats in the body of the fuselage behind him. His eyes flicked back. The cliff was coming up fast. He pressed the button on his throat mike. 'Here we are,' he said. 'Execute manoeuvre number one on my mark . . . *Now*.'

Kizel swung the head of his chopper hard west and the others behind him fell into line astern. They were so low, their down-draught disturbed the cinder bed under the track of the Mawanga railway, so that as they sped past they were followed by a rain of pebbles and grit which spilled over the edge into the withered water below. Within a very few minutes they were hurtling over a labouring train and the smoke from its stack exploded around them and leaped into delicate whirls in their wake. A disused lift and some ruined buildings flashed past, ancient corrugated tin reverberating to the sound of their engines.

Such was the power of their passing that the first police guard hut was torn apart as though by a hurricane – but the dazed policeman managed to get through to Mawanga city with a report of what had happened.

Gogol looked down idly, recognising landmarks. There was the pulpit where he and Chala had questioned the man and woman from the train. Their bones lay scattered on that tongue of red mud below. He glanced back without thinking, and the uncontrolled movement tore his cancerous neck with such acute pain that nausea welled in his throat. But he had eaten nothing for two days; there was nothing to come up. He was never hungry nowadays. He thought that the huge tumour which they told him was growing in his stomach probably filled it well enough, and he only ate when he needed to stoke up his strength, and when he was tempted. The foul concoction called *achu* which the Congo Librens subsisted on did not tempt him at all. He saw his body as a machine now, it was the only way he could hang on to his sanity. A machine which was beginning to malfunction because of what had happened to it at Chernobyl.

Captain Kizel jumped and turned towards Gogol, then reached across to switch on the radio's cockpit speaker. A woman's anxious voice filled the cockpit at once, speaking in English. '. . . I say again, please identify yourselves. This is air traffic control at Mawanga airport calling the five aircraft closing with Mawanga city from the east at zero feet. You have no registered authorisation to cross Maui airspace, please identify yourselves at once . . .'

The captain looked at Gogol. The general shook his head once, carefully. Kizel pressed his throat mike. 'Maintain radio silence,' he ordered and switched his own radio off.

Below, a great area of grey ash overlapped the first straight pattern of irrigation ditches spreading out in geometric designs from the edge of a dry lake. Idly, Gogol wondered if the naked Kyoga woman was still down there, dead in the ditch where he had left her. No. That had been a week ago, before General Bovary's orders had come in. The scavengers would have had her long ago. He found himself shaking his head almost with sorrow.

He was the man who had invented the shooting competition which used native girls as targets and sorted out the men from the boys. How could he be concerned over one savage woman? No. He was not concerned; he simply speculated. She remained in his memory only because she had not been the American woman who had been their quarry but some tick-ridden, fuzzy-haired, fat-faced native. Thoughtlessly, he sucked his teeth and his mouth at once filled with blood. He choked, body rigid, refusing to cough or vomit, willing himself to maintain the massive dignity which had to be associated with his rank. They had warned him about this at the institute when they had advised him to have all his teeth out. It would be better for him in the long run, they had said. They would only perish like the rest of his bones, and his gums were shot to hell in any case. And, like his hair, they would fall out in no time at all. He had been bald as an egg for six years and was mildly surprised that his teeth had lasted so long. They were another reason he ate so little nowadays; when he chewed anything even faintly solid, he could hear the roots of his molars stirring in his head.

Vodka was out of the question too, given the state of his liver.

Really and truly, now he came to look at it, there was only one thing left worth living for: killing.

The Sikorsky Black Hawk came down over the top of the cliff above them and skipped along just in front of their nose, moving at full speed – the better part of 300 kph.

'He's trying to make contact,' said Captain Kizel urgently. 'Shall I answer?'

'Yes. With that.' The general pointed to the weapons system control. The helicopter was equipped not only with the AS–7 Kerry air-to-surface missiles they proposed to use against the iceberg – and the ships controlling it if necessary – but also several AA–2 A-toll air-to-air missiles as well. The Sikorsky, Gogol knew, was armed with a 30 millimetre cannon. But it probably wasn't loaded and even if it was, it would jam. And none of Chala's police pilots would ever open fire without direct orders from their beloved leader, signed, in triplicate. The General of Police did not approve of independence of thought, least of all among such dashing characters as his helicopter pilots.

Gogol's pilot, however, did not hesitate. Kizel launched the missile on his commander's word. The A–22 A-toll was old, but still effective. It was one of a range of Russian designs based on the American Sidewinder. This one was armed with a high-explosive warhead and controlled by a heat-seeking guidance system. The Sikorsky had no sooner settled like a black dragon fly to race along beside the Hinds than it exploded into a dazzling blossom of red and yellow flame. Pieces of wreckage sped out and down, trailing smoke like failed fireworks. The last two helicopters in the line astern dipped and jumped over the shock wave of the explosion and that was all.

I hope Chala was in that one, thought Gogol. But he doubted it.

They raced on, unmolested for ten minutes until, far below, beyond the dry river bed at the foot of the basalt cliff, the first reception camps appeared. These had been set up by Chala's police to look after the starving millions from the interior as they tried to get into Mawanga city itself – and, more importantly, to relieve them of anything of worth that they still possessed.

Five more minutes of thunderous flight brought them to the first shantytown outskirts of the city, hardly distinguishable from the refugee camps. A great six-lane highway sprang into existence apparently out of nowhere. Immediately, the black slope on their right fell away and the rest of the city became clearly visible ahead as it rolled down to the sea, all laid out in squares and blocks of city districts. Only the great red scar of the dry river bed, widening out into the sea-sparkling grey of the massive port, gave an impression of a design beyond the square designs of men. Gogol sat up stiffly, his eyes busy down among the desolate encampments of the destitute. 'There!' he said.

Captain Kizel nodded once. He touched his throat mike again. 'Execute manoeuvre number two on my mark . . . *Now!*'

The helicopters reformed into a diamond with Gogol's machine at its head and swung down to their left. Below, at the line of convergence between the camps and the shanties a great square of open ground suddenly appeared. The sounds from Kizel's headphones reached a piercing shrillness. The words 'illegal use of air-space', 'invasion' and 'act of war' could be heard as the officials in the control tower immediately below suddenly realised where the unidentified invaders on their radar were heading for. But the occupants of the control tower need not have worried. The diamond of Hinds swept across the buildings, over the hangars and across to the far side of the field where they settled into a high-wired compound. Here the aviation fuel reserved for the exclusive use of Nimrod Chala's Black Hawks was stored. It was usually kept under guard, but the guards had run away as soon as it seemed likely to them that the helicopters would attack.

No sooner were the Hinds on the ground than their occupants were out and forming two groups, both busy. One group ran out to set up a defensive perimeter. The other group broke into the storage facility and began loading fuel into the Hinds, filling main tanks and long-range auxiliary tanks to overflowing as quickly as they could.

As soon as Illych Kizel had calculated a realistic work rate he crossed to General Gogol. 'It will take twenty minutes, just as we calculated.'

'Is there enough?'

'Yes, General. It is just as you said – he sent the extra fuel from the bush landing strip back here before he burned it. Well, all he could load into the trucks he had with him, at any rate.'

'All except the petrol that the man Parkinson had hidden away. That was such a good trap. I could have had them all then. If only . . .'

He stopped abruptly. The morphine was making him talk too much. The morphine mixed with the adrenaline being pumped out by those few glands in his irradiated body which still worked adequately.

'General!' One of the perimeter guards was hurrying across towards him.

'Yes?'

The man handed him a pair of field glasses and gestured across at the main gate.

Gogol pressed the binoculars to his eyes and adjusted the focus. 'Ah, there he is. Right on time.'

In through the main gate came Nimrod Chala's armoured command reconnaissance vehicle. It was the latest of the series, adapted to carry the new generation 14.5mm KPVT turret and the coaxial 7.62mm PKT machine-gun. Gogol knew it well; it was the type of vehicle that had been his headquarters in every tank battle he had commanded. He knew this particular vehicle well, too, for Chala had showed him over it more than once and he had noted all the details he could. Such details as the command radio frequency, for instance.

Gogol lowered the binoculars and walked across to his helicopter. He switched the radio to the correct frequency, put the earphones to his ear and pressed SEND on the handset.

'Chala?' he barked. 'Please put General Chala on.' He spoke English.

'Who is this?' The voice of the ACRV's radio operator answered in the same language.

'This is General Valerii Gogol. Put General Chala on now.'

There was the sound of whispering, the movement of large bodies in a constricted place, the passage of a radio handset from hand to hand.

'Gogol! What is going on?' General Chala was a man of bulk and significant physical impact, but he had a high, child-like voice.

'Just a little misunderstanding, my friend.' Gogol lifted his thumb and said to Captain Kizel, 'Illych, tell me what the vehicle's movements are.'

'Gogol? What was that?'

'Why did your Black Hawk helicopter attack us without warning, Nimrod?'

'*The vehicle is still approaching, General.*'

'It did not! It had orders simply to investigate—'

'It launched something at us. Looked like a Hellfire missile to me.'

'But that's impossible . . .'

'*It's still coming in, General, less than fifteen hundred metres now.*'

'That's what it looked like, Nimrod. I'm sorry but I guess we might have overreacted a little . . .'

'But what are you doing here, Gogol? Stop the vehicle. Do you hear me, driver? I do not understand what you are doing here, Gogol.'

'*He's stopped now, General. Sideways on, a thousand metres out.*'

'Fool,' said Gogol, wearily.

He dropped the handset and reached into the belly of the helicopter.

'Gogol?' came Nimrod Chala's voice from the radio, rising from a treble to a petulant whine. 'Can you hear me?'

Gogol walked to the perimeter and looked across the flat airfield to the vehicle. As Kizel had said, it was sitting sideways on. The turret was pointing straight ahead, covering the southern edge of the field as though the real danger lay in the withered palm trees there. It was in the middle of the roadway connecting the compound with the main gate and thus Gogol was able to look at it over the low barrier which crossed the black tarmac at the perimeter line.

'Valerii?' whined Chala, 'I don't understand . . . What . . .'

With a little movement climaxing in a guttural grunt, Gogol swung the SA–7 Grail anti-tank missile onto his shoulder. It was the latest version, brought in with the T–80 main battle tanks. It had a 2.5 kg high-explosive head in a smooth fragmentation armour-piercing warhead with both graze and impact fuses. It had an accurate range of five thousand metres and it moved faster than sound. With the apparently casual fluidity of total, long practised control, Gogol swung the missile onto target and pressed the firing mechanism.

'What . . .' screamed Nimrod Chala at the moment the missile was launched. The word was only half out of the Hind's radio when the command vehicle erupted in a ball of shocking yellow flame, its iron sides seeming to stretch out and burst like an over-filled balloon. The turret spun lazily up into the air and turned on its axis, still pointing the wrong way. The thunder of Chala's passing rolled over the compound, then there was only the hissing of the vacant channel on the radio and the slurp of fuel gushing into thirsty tanks.

The sound of helicopters jerked Ann Cable out of a nightmare and out of her hospital bed both at once. Although she was still swollen, stiff and sore and her long body was bound up in the tangle of sheets and hospital gown which resulted from her nightmare, she was standing at her window before she was properly awake. The window was wide and right in the middle of the topmost floor of the tallest tower in downtown Mawanga. It looked westwards across the last of the city before the sea began. It had been modelled on St Thomas's, the great teaching hospital in London, and was built upon the bank of the river. But where the Thames was a couple of hundred metres wide, the Mau was a couple of kilometres. And where the Thames was full, the Mau was dry.

As Ann looked down on the desolation of dry mud which split the dying city apart, she saw a diamond-shaped formation of helicopters sweep past. They were large machines, but they were flying low, following the river bed at zero metres. They were so low, in fact, that the stunned woman could look down on them as they hurled past the hospital tower. So fast were they moving, any glimpse she might have caught of General Gogol in the front of the lead helicopter must surely have been subliminal. Helicopters were associated with such disturbing events in her still shaken mind that she watched the desert-coloured diamond as though it was some kind of repulsive thing, the head of a rattlesnake.

As the machines vanished behind the billowing smoke of their exhausts into the silver-grey shimmer which joined the sky to the sea and the thudding rumbling of their engines faded, her eyes refocused on the faint reflection of her face in the double-glazing of the window. It had white skin now, for the black colour of smoke, soot and mud had been gently washed away during the last week. But her nose was still slightly misshapen from her fall, and her lips and eyes still swollen from the bites of the mosquitoes and all the other nameless blood suckers of the bush. Her hair clustered round the unnatural moon-shape of her face in dark, fire-curled ringlets. If her parents had still been alive, they would never have recognised her, even now. In another week or so she would either be well enough to get on with her life or she would be deep in the grip of tick fever. At the moment she didn't really care which alternative turned out to be true.

The door behind her opened and she shifted her desolate gaze to see the reflection of Emily Karanga standing there. 'How are you feeling?'

Ann took a deep breath and turned stiffly but with a

smile. 'Much better, thanks,' she lied heroically.

Gogol looked lazily down. He was not a sailor and had never much liked the sea, but he found the simple scale of Mawanga harbour impressive. The dry river split the seaward side of the city like the wound from a giant axe. A great ridge of mud-covered rock kept the sea out of the dry bed, but the silt from a million and more years of flow still stretched out like a pair of bull's horns seventy-five kilometres long and five wide astride the almost bottomless, fault-floored bay of the anchorage. Only where the horns of land all but joined again, at their tips far out in the Gulf of Guinea, did the sea bed begin to rise once more, into another ridge which broke the force of the waves and made the fifteen-kilometre width of water as calm as a pond.

Down the middle of each horn ran a busy roadway and dotted along these were warehouses, storage facilities and factories. On either side of the pair of horns were docks but only on the outside were there ships. The whole great bay of the anchorage was empty, still, waiting. Along the horns, crouching on the insides above the still surface of the water between the docks and the buildings was a series of massive free-standing pumps capable of moving millions of litres an hour. They were in place but untended. For most of their length, the great low ridges of land were deserted. At the very tips of the horns, however, was a bustle of men and machines so active that Captain Kizel automatically jerked his stick back so that the formation of Hind helicopters jumped bodily over the entrance to the empty, expectant anchorage.

General Warren Cord, US Army (Rtd), explosives expert and UN representative, looked up as the helicopters roared overhead and frowned. Now just what in hell's name were five big Soviet gunships doing racing around at zero metres out here? Automatically, he checked around himself, but there was nothing else to see in the sky. There wasn't all that much to see in the sea, either, come to that. Certainly not since all the local tankers had pulled out and sailed west to offload the first consignment of water. There was a lot to see on the land around him, however, for he and his men were busily involved in the most dangerous part of the reception being prepared for the iceberg. The plan looked simple enough on paper, but getting it to work in practice was going to be something else again. Thank the Lord they still had a good few days to get everything in place and properly primed. He turned back to the engineers and the other explosives experts and forgot about the helicopters.

Out over the Gulf of Guinea, the Hinds went to a heading a couple of degrees north of due west and swung into line-abreast formation. With their noses low and their throttles wide, they roared out over the wavetops at 250 kph. After ninety minutes they hopped over a flotilla of heavy-laden freighters. 'We're on the right heading,' observed Kizel. 'That's encouraging.'

Gogol leaned back into the depths of the helicopter's seat. It was not comfortable as such things go and would never have been given space on a Western passenger plane, but it was the most comfortable seat Gogol had occupied in his life. He relaxed, and let exhaustion wash over him. Nothing could go wrong now until they reached the iceberg itself. 'Wake me in two hours, Illych,' he ordered and surrendered to the Greek god whose name was shared with the drug he used so much.

An instant later, he was blinking himself awake, his body one long agonising ache. Only the intensity of the pain told him that he had been asleep for hours and needed another morphine pill at once. Even before he orientated himself properly, he had reached into his breast pocket and pulled the pill box out. He crunched the unutterably bitter pill into powder and swallowed convulsively, knowing that this was the quickest way to get it into his system and disrupt the all too efficient communication between the pain centres in his brain and the nerve filaments reaching into the excruciating carcinomas with which his body was filled. Unusually, he took a second, even before the soothing warmth of the first had spread through him. Then he counted to a hundred, slowly, and opened his eyes.

The iceberg was coming up over the horizon now. They were approaching it low and bow on. He had expected it to be white but it was dirty, almost the same colour as his desert-camouflaged helicopters. He had expected it to tower magnificently like an alp. Even from this angle, it seemed to be squat and low. It was only when he registered that the long black water beetles around it were in fact laden supertankers that he really got to grips with the scale of the thing. And it made him catch his breath. He thought back to the anchorage at Mawanga harbour, all that grey area of still water between the bull's horns of land. This would just fit inside there; just and no more, like a key into a lock. He began to get a sense of its size then, of its weight and latent power. It had taken nearly twenty minutes to cross the harbour even at full speed.

Richard Mariner was on the bridge of *Psyche* beside Peter Walcott, overseeing the final grudging loosening of the lines to let the fully laden ship settle into her new relationship with the iceberg. Everyone aboard was tense – some of them were terrified, if the truth be known – for it was becoming increasingly obvious that Manhattan was growing unstable.

'It's going to be a close-run thing,' Colin Ross had said last night, and Richard had been forced to agree with him. But their options were severely limited: There was no action they could take which would cause the berg to roll

safely. Or to stop it rolling once it began to move. Sometimes it seemed that all that was holding it upright was the
speed at which it was moving forward, as though it was
some kind of gargantuan bicycle. They couldn't just cut
and run, for they had a responsibility at the very least to
try and influence the direction of the roll and direct the
resulting waves away from the nearest coasts. They
couldn't just stand by and allow the iceberg to flood the
nearest land to the north and east. They had held it up and
kept it under their sway, more or less, for twenty-eight days
so far. They had moved it further and faster than anyone
had ever believed possible – except the men and women
whose vision had started the experiment in the first place.
They were mere days out from their destination and they
could not let it all slip away now.

But they were going to have to cut themselves free soon,
reverse their courses, re-anchor themselves to the rear section, and sail west as hard as they could for as long as their
ships would stand the strain, trying to slow the giant down.
And, according to Colin's figures, even if the berg
remained stable now, it would almost certainly tip over as
it slowed. That was the backbone of their contingency
plan. They proposed to slow the berg and test its stability
over the next thirty-six hours. Then they were due to swing
it round onto a more southerly heading, in preparation for
running it directly into the mouth of Mawanga harbour.
They reckoned – he and Colin and the mathematicians in
the United Nations – that this would be the best time to tip
it over if they could, rolling it south-westwards so that the
waves it caused would run away harmlessly out to sea.

Well, that was out of their control at the moment. Right
now Richard was like the skipper of a small ship watching
for the arrival of a storm. There were limits as to what he
could do other than to batten down, head for a safe haven,
and prepare to ride it out if it hit. They had made all the
preparations they could. They knew what their objectives

were, short term, medium term and long term. They all had a clear set of orders which would cover everything that could conceivably go wrong. They would just have to get on with things and hope for the best.

'Right,' he said to Peter Walcott. 'That's it, I think. The line watches fore and aft can tie off on that.' He raised the walkie-talkie to his lips and issued the orders. It was as though they could all feel *Psyche* begin to settle contentedly and take up the full strain once more.

'Well done, all of you,' said Richard, for this had been a long, complex, stressful job. He looked around the bridge. All the watch officers were nodding to themselves; he hoped it was with approval. 'I'll go back down to the isolation ward now,' he continued a little ruefully. 'The doctor wants me to keep reporting in for observation for a while. Apparently she's preparing a paper on the effects of the harmattan.' He paused. A chuckle ran round the bridge. Good, he thought. Things aboard *Psyche* were getting lighter at last. He turned back to Peter. The late morning light caught the ointment with which his hands and face were still covered and made them gleam. Unconsciously he rubbed a still itchy area of his wrist against his leg, leaving a smear of yellow on the white cotton of the boiler suit he was wearing. On his way out through the door, he turned back and added, 'When everything has settled down, we'll start to reduce speed. See what happens then.'

He had no sooner left the bridge than the radio officer stuck his head out of the radio room. '*Titan*'s just been on,' he reported to his captain. 'There's a small squadron of helicopters coming over fast and low from the south-east.'

The others in the isolation ward had settled into a relaxed routine now that they knew there was no immediate danger. They looked upon it as a week's welcome if unexpected holiday. To a man they were very pleased to be off duty and out of their watch responsibilities. It was really only Richard who found the place so irritatingly restrictive, but he was not the sort of leader who insisted on special treatment and although he was quite capable of exerting a great deal of pressure on Asha whenever it seemed to him that she was keeping them under observation for too long, he was in the end prepared to remain in her charge until she declared that he was fully fit for duty. There was, as he observed with some bitterness, no sense in keeping a doctor and diagnosing yourself. Just the way he said it put his listeners in mind of dogs and barking.

He came into his makeshift command headquarters cum ping-pong room almost at a run. He wanted to get through to Colin first and discuss his thoughts about the solidity of the iceberg. He also wanted to go through the records which John had made of their Geiger counter readings on their last visit to the berg, on the day he had found Henri LeFever and regained his memory. He was still worrying at a half-formed plan to try and use the movement of the berg when it rolled somehow to break off the irradiated section of the ice, if that was possible. Lost in thought, he crossed to his desk and began to sort through the papers there, looking for the pages full of John's neat script and careful drawings.

Behind him, outside and away towards the bow of Manhattan, a small section of ice cliff broke free and slid into the roaring sea. The noise it made covered the sound of five helicopters touching down on the high ice three hundred metres up and five kilometres west.

Thank God the ships had moved out from under the overhangs, Richard thought, pausing in his search and listening to the thunder of ice and water in conflict. The constant rain of meltwater was being more regularly supplemented by chunks of sheer cliff face now. They would really have been in trouble if the large sections of ice had started to collapse directly onto the decks, or, heaven forfend, the bridgehouses themselves. It would have been as dangerous as being hit by high-powered missiles.

They touched down in diamond formation and all the men were out in moments, lined up and ready for final briefing. Gogol walked slowly to the front and looked over the expectant ranks. 'What these people in their gigantic ships are being asked to do is very dangerous and almost impossible,' he began. The dreamlike state which excitement, the promise of action and the massive dose of morphine engendered held him firmly in its grip. 'The iceberg they are towing is too large for adequate control. Their ships are too puny to dictate its course by more than a degree or so. The waters through which they are sailing are shallow and fanged with coral; the channel they have chosen is deep but narrow and hard to follow. The slightest error or deviation will completely upset their pathetic plans. How easy it would be for an accident to happen. How almost inevitably must disaster strike!'

He looked at them, remembering how his voice used to boom and rumble like sonorous thunder at a time like this. He almost imagined that it could do so again; that it was doing so again.

'We are that disaster! We are the force of the storm which will turn them one degree to the north. We are the wind and the waves which will drive the ice onto the reefs and wedge it there to melt and run away.'

He listened, imagining he could hear his ringing words echo away westwards on the wind. That it should have come to this, he thought. That it should have come to this for him of all men.

'What we will do is this,' he said. 'The four helicopters detailed will place themselves where their armaments can cover the ships either individually or in pairs. The fifth, my command helicopter, will deposit on each ship a commando of half a dozen men who will seize the bridge and take the captain hostage. Then we will take over the engine rooms and hold the engineers so that we can dictate both course and propulsion. There will be no resistance under the guns of the Hinds. We will not even need to round up the crews. They will be helpless without their officers to guide them. And, once we are in place, we will order the change in course required. Before the end of the day, the iceberg will be wedged immovably on the coral reefs which reach out south and west from the shores close by here. When the iceberg is thus disposed of, we will return to our helicopters and vanish. No one will ever know who we are or why we did what we did. But I know, and I will tell you.'

He leaned forward, narrow-eyed, intense. 'It is for Russia we do this! Make no mistake, our orders come directly from Moscow and we cannot hesitate. This iceberg which they call Manhattan must never arrive in Mau. If it does, the damage to our beloved country will be incalculable. There may even be a civil war! Imagine it: Moscow itself reduced to another Sarajevo! Our parents, brothers, wives and children reduced to destitution. Starvation. Death. It will happen if this iceberg comes safely to Mawanga harbour. It must be destroyed, and it is we who will destroy it, for the glory of our country and no matter what the cost!'

John Higgins was actually on the bridge of *Niobe* when it happened, close beside the helmsman looking forward down the deck. And so he got perhaps the best view of all. He never knew exactly where the helicopter appeared from. It was just there, suddenly, its cockpit windows dead level with his eyes, a matter of metres in front of him, its rotors beating the air apparently only millimetres up. The shock – the sound – was overpowering.

Ropes cascaded out of the side and men slid down them. Men in uniform, armed to the teeth. 'My God,' he whispered, and drew in his breath to order a general distress signal. Then he saw how many air-to-surface missiles were pointing directly at him. And, for the first time in his life, he felt faint. Every bullet-shaped warhead etched itself indelibly on his consciousness and he heard someone swearing very loudly and extremely obscenely. It could well have been himself.

The helicopter jerked up and away abruptly, as though it had been hooked like a fish, and John swung round and tensed to sprint across to the radio room, just as the three-man commando came in through the door.

Silence.

Stillness.

Then, 'Good afternoon, gentlemen,' said a deep voice in slow, heavily accented English. 'May I introduce you to our weapons? This is what is called in the West the 5.45mm AKS–74 assault rifle. It can fire its full magazine of bullets in very much less than a tenth of a second with a muzzle velocity in excess of 870 metres per second over a range of about 500 metres. My colleague over there who has just incapacitated your communications equipment is holding the 7.62mm SVD rifle which is deadly at more than 1500 metres. And this is the RGD–5 hand grenade. For your further information, the men in the engine room with the engineering officers are similarly armed. Now, are there any questions so far?'

With very slight variations, this was what happened to all of them. Hardly surprisingly, the abrupt appearance of a heavily armed Hind–D helicopter hovering within scant metres of the bridge clearview while soldiers abseiled out of it onto the deck stopped everyone dead in their tracks. No one managed to contact any of the others and within a very short time each ship had had its main radio equipment destroyed and was cut off from the rest of the convoy, with a group of heavily armed, quietly courteous soldiers on the bridge and in the engine room only too ready to explain both their own arms and those on the helicopters currently aimed unerringly at each bridgehouse. Only with Katya Borodin and her crew was there any threat of trouble at first for they reacted particularly violently to being pirated by their own compatriots, but it was obvious that the invading soldiers knew that they were going to be dealing with Russian officers and crew and after a while they calmed things down. So all the soldiers were in their allotted places and all the messages of confirmation had been radioed up to the command helicopter on the ice, and the next stage of the iceberg's destruction could begin.

Gogol had positioned his helicopter in the logical place: exactly in the middle of Manhattan, equidistant from the four other helicopters which were stationed on the cliff edges closest to the ships they were threatening, available to back any one of them up. The communications were clear, and it was easy enough to pass out orders either individually on the prearranged closed channels or generally on the open frequency. But between giving the orders, hearing that they were being obeyed, and seeing the result, there was a long wait. And during that time, with the tension sending adrenaline fizzing through his system, adding its weight to the morphine overdose, the general began to talk.

To the stunned young Captain Illych Kizel he described that night at Chernobyl and its aftermath. How, still ignorant of what the radiation was doing to him, he oversaw the digging up and crating of the black glass he had created. He relived the long train ride north to the coast and the loading of the *Leonid Brezhnev*. He described the horror with which the loss of that good ship had been welcomed in some rarefied political circles and his own feelings of sadness as his body had finally begun to show him what must have happened to the men and women on the freighter far out in the Arctic Ocean. He described, for the first time in his life and the last, exactly what was wrong with him and what the doctors at the institute had done to try and control it. How he had entered periods of remission for long enough to give evidence at the inquiry, then been forced to take early retirement, with nothing left to do but count the days of his consumption from within.

Then came the chance of coming to Africa and getting back into the swing of things, working with his beloved tanks again. And the sudden shock, the horror, of discovering that, entombed in the iceberg on its way to Mau, the irradiated contents of the lost ship were returning to haunt him. That Chernobyl was forcing its way back into his life.

'It is here,' he said. 'Somewhere below us. They are certain of it. They have found evidence. They have found pieces of the glass, the glass which no one in the world outside Russia must ever know about. The black glass which even now could destroy our international standing and bring us to the edge of the abyss. The glass I made, on that terrible, terrible night.'

He pulled himself up, surprised to discover that the weight of the story had bowed him down until he was almost on his knees beside the open side of the helicopter. The act of straightening brought sweat to his white lips and he crunched up another morphine tablet before he raised the helicopter's handset to his lips and said on the open channel, 'We are not moving off line quickly enough. Tell the two lead ships to steer north as hard as they can.'

It was Wally Gough who first alerted Richard, coming into the ping-pong room at a dead run, his face alive with excitement, yelling, 'Have you seen that helicopter, sir? My God, I've never seen anything like it in all my life! I think it's actually flying backwards in front of the bridge.'

Richard had been deep in concentrated calculations and, because his room was closer to the cliff than to the sea, he had not even heard the helicopter. As soon as he realised that the excited boy was not engaged in some kind

551

of joke he was on his feet and following him out into the corridor. They arrived just in time to see six heavily armed soldiers pounding up the stairs towards the navigation bridge. Richard ran back to his makeshift office and grabbed his walkie-talkie. By the grace of God he had it on channel twelve, an open channel to the radio room, and he knew exactly what it meant when the signal suddenly went silent.

He swung round, stunned by the speed of events, just as Wally came back in through the door behind him. All the boy's excited elation had been replaced by sick fear. 'They've destroyed the main radio,' said Richard without thinking. 'My God, they've cut us off!'

Wally stopped dead, as though he had been hit. He sank into a nearby chair and it was a mark of his shock that he did not ask permission first. 'What is it?' he asked faintly. 'What do you think is going on, sir?'

'We're being hijacked! Well, I'm damned.'

'But why?'

'Well, offhand I'd say that either someone doesn't want Manhattan to arrive at Mawanga, or they want it to arrive somewhere else.'

'But there's nowhere else on the west coast of Africa that could take anything this big.'

'Quite right, my boy. It makes you think, doesn't it?' As he was speaking, Richard was punching in the contact number for the engine room, but the number just rang and rang without answer. 'Damn! They've beaten me to it,' he said. He took in a deep breath. 'So, they control the bridge and the engine room on *Psyche* . . .'

A matter of moments proved that they controlled the bridge and engine room on each of the other ships too, and Richard, with the enormity of the situation suddenly breaking through even his massive self-control, hurled the useless walkie-talkie across the room. No sooner had he done so than it began to whine with an incoming signal. Wally scuttled across the room and snatched it up, handing it back to Richard at once, behaving exactly as though it was alive and repulsive. He was too scared even to press RECEIVE and answer it.

Richard had no such qualms. 'Yes?'

'Is that you, Captain Mariner?'

'Yes.'

'Thank God. It's the forecastle head line watch here, sir. The bridge is full of soldiers, sir. Came out of that bloody great helicopter, down onto the deck on ropes like the Royal Tournament. They seem to have the captain and everyone up there under armed guard. What do you want us to do?'

'Wait!' said Richard, his voice suddenly full of hope. 'Wait and I'll get back to you.'

It took a little longer to establish that while he could not communicate with any of his captains or chief engineers, he could communicate with all of his line watches, for the line watch on each ship had been equipped with a wide-band high-powered walkie-talkie to accompany the bright yellow line-cutters.

His eyes went narrow with thought as he tried to calculate the likelihood that the invaders, whoever they were, understood about the lines up onto the ice or the manner in which they could be cut. Whether they had considered that they could be cut at all. It seemed most unlikely to him.

And so, while Gogol told Captain Illych Kizel the story of what they were here to do, Richard discussed with the men on the forecastles and the poops how he would go about foiling whatever might be planned by their paramilitary invaders.

'Right!' said Richard, with mounting satisfaction when he had completed the first briefing. 'I still don't know who these pirate bastards are, but if they've got me by the nose, then I've got them by the balls. And I can cut them off if I have to!'

'But surely we need to know who they are and what they

have in mind before we can do anything!'

'Right you are, Wally. But how can we find it out?'

'Scan all the channels on your walkie-talkie?'

'It's pre-set. Switched from channel to channel by buttons. I'd be lucky to switch in to any waveband they're communicating on. No, we'll have to come up with something better.'

He switched through all the channels available on his walkie-talkie handset, listing them as he did so: 'Radio room – dead; engine room – dead; line watches, *Titan*; line watches, *Niobe* . . .' and so on. There were twelve channels available, and after ten his voice was growing bored. But on channel eleven, the radio hissed and he stopped his litany. 'That's the bridge,' he half whispered. 'The channel to the bridge is still functioning.' He fell silent, thinking rapidly.

Then, 'Look, do you remember the layout of the bridge? I'm thinking particularly of the panel immediately beneath the clearview, just to the left of the helm.'

'Yes. There's a microphone on a stalk there.'

'That's right! Now, just at the base of that there's a button. Remember it?'

'Yup!' Caught up in the excitement of passing this strange test, Wally really wasn't thinking this through or he would have been much less enthusiastic much earlier on.

'Well, if I could get you onto the bridge, could you switch that button without being noticed? Could you open that channel so that I can hear what is happening on the bridge?'

'*What?*' Wally paled again.

'Look. It won't be dangerous if you're careful. I'll work out a way to get you up there without making the guards suspicious. All you need to do is stand beside the helmsman, then turn round clumsily and it's done!'

'Well . . .'

'If I can get you onto the bridge with no danger at all?'

'Well . . .'

There was nothing more that Richard could think of to say.

'Well, all right.'

Richard nodded once and went through into the sickbay. Lamia and his cronies were sitting watching a video as though nothing going on aboard the ship was anything to do with any of them. Richard strode across and snapped the set off. 'Right,' he said. 'I want a fight. A big fight. A noisy fight. I don't care what gets broken and I will enhance the pay of anyone who joins in.'

The men looked at him in stunned disbelief.

Asha came rushing out of her office, making it plain that she had heard every word he had said. 'Richard! Have you taken leave of your senses?'

'Sorry, Asha. Needs must when the Devil drives. Come on, you lot. I want it big and noisy and destructive. A bottle of Scotch to the man who throws the first punch! *Move!*'

They pulled themselves to their feet, looking around, dazed with surprise.

'Two bottles. Any liquor of your choice. A crate of spirits to the last man standing!'

'Are you serious?' asked the giant Haitian Duvalier.

'Yes, I am. You play your cards right, you can end up with fourteen bottles of your favourite drink!'

'I'm a rum-drinking man.'

'Of course you are. Appleton Gold?'

The punch Duvalier threw chucked one of his slower-thinking colleagues right across the room.

'You get me Gold,' yelled the massive Haitian over the sudden pandemonium, 'and you can call me Doc.'

He ducked as a chair tumbled past his bullet head and exploded through the screen of the video. The whole lot went backwards noisily and landed on Lamia's foot. The Greek howled and Richard winced. It looked as though he would be responsible for some medical bills as well as for the mess bill.

'Go!' he yelled at Wally. 'Big fight in the sickbay! Go and report to the captain at once!'

By the time Peter Walcott and a paramilitary guard arrived, the fight had been resolved, Duvalier was due to receive an awful lot of Appleton Gold, the medical bill was not going to be as high as feared and the isolation ward looked like a bomb had hit it. The soldier's eyes swept coldly over the wreckage and Peter looked about in complete confusion, then they both left.

Richard went back into the ping-pong room and switched his walkie-talkie to channel eleven. His hair stirring with tension as though he was watching a procession of ghosts, he listened to the handset hissing quietly.

'*Hssssssssssss* . . . over there? I thought I saw something over by the iceberg. Oh. It's a section of the cliff collapsing.' The voice belonged to Wally.

Richard took a deep breath. He really expected to hear a word of rage or accusation and a single shot. But there was nothing.

'What are we heading, Captain?' came the innocent, almost childlike question. Typical of a youthful, over-anxious cadet. They had them in every army and navy. No matter what nationality the invaders were, they would recognise the type.

Wally had pulled it off.

Richard drew a pad of blank paper towards him and started making detailed notes of the conversation on the bridge. As he did this, picking up the answers to Wally's pointed questions then recording the information being fed out by the rest of the watch as the penny began to drop, and even picking up unconscious hints from the occasional words of the taciturn pirates in control, so he began to see the grand design. Began to realise precisely what was involved here. And he laid his plans accordingly.

He did not move into action, however, until he heard that *Titan* and *Niobe* had been ordered hard north. Then he began to call the line watches, saying in a low voice, 'Now listen. It looks as though we're out of time. Here's what I want you to do first . . .'

Ten minutes later Richard went back into the sickbay. There was an atmosphere of ill-controlled surliness as the men grudgingly worked through the room, tidying the mess they had just made under the eye of Asha Higgins. He paused on the threshold for an instant. Then, 'Doc,' he said quietly, 'you want to earn another crate of Appleton Gold?'

The big man straightened up and a slow grin spread across his battered face. 'Who've I got to kill?' he asked.

All the way up the stairs, Asha held Richard in animated, enraged discussion but on the C deck landing, one deck below the bridge, he stopped her. 'Look,' he said. 'I know it's dangerous. It may be irresponsible, juvenile, stupid and everything else. I know you and John have been through this before and were lucky not to be killed. But look at the alternative. These people are going to run Manhattan at full speed up onto the coral reefs off Nigeria. The damage will be incalculable, both to the wildlife and the coast. The coral will just crush back like polystyrene until the berg hits solid rock. Then there will be floods. Earthquakes, probably. You can probably kiss the islands goodbye – Sao Tome, Ferdinand Po; to Cameroon, to Guinea. And all those millions of poor souls in Mau won't get their water either. Except that they won't need it because they'll all be dead. The impact of that mass of ice moving north-east at thirteen knots is going to smash the black cliff back a good ten centimetres, open up the tectonic fault line and tear their whole country apart!'

While he talked, the men accompanying them had

levered the lift doors open and they all stepped into the little car. The doors slid silently shut again.

'Will you do it?' he asked hoarsely.

She hesitated for an instant. But she knew what he said was probably right. 'Yes, all right,' she said gracelessly. 'I'll do it.'

Asha's anger was still evident when she walked onto the bridge and the fact served her well. The four guards all glanced over towards her, but none moved to cover her for she was obviously alone. She strode across to Peter Walcott, spitting with obvious anger. 'Well, you can take care of it this time. They're all at it now and the whole isolation area is a total mess. I don't want anything else to do with them and if I were you I'd put the whole lot of them under some kind of restraint!'

Peter reacted with rage, as any captain would in the face of such a report, and was halfway to the door when he remembered the situation. He stopped and looked at the paramilitary leader. The soldier spat a couple of words of Russian and two of the guards began to move.

'I'll show you,' snapped Asha. 'I don't want you getting any bullshit excuses from the ringleaders!' and she led the little group out.

She was so obviously in charge, lent authority by her rage, that they all followed quite meekly as she crossed to the lift and punched the button. When the lift came she stepped in and the others followed without a second thought.

There was just enough room in the car for a man to stand behind each door panel and be invisible even when the door was wide. Asha and Peter stepped through to the back of the lift and the guards followed them in. By the time they had turned, Lamia and Doc Duvalier had grabbed the unsuspecting guards and wrestled them silently to the floor. The doors closed and the lift departed with no one any the wiser.

By the time the doors opened on A deck to reveal the anxious faces of Richard and the men who had been waiting in the stairwell just in case, both the guards were unconscious and both the crewmen were armed.

'Right,' said Richard. 'We go back up at once.'

This time he went up, with Lamia and Doc Duvalier. 'Can you use those things?' he asked tensely, his mind racing, recoiling from the logic of the situation but unable to see any way out other than immediate confrontation.

'I've done a bit,' said Lamia cryptically. 'Used these Kalashnikovs before.'

'Trained with the Tonton Macaute,' admitted Duvalier. 'Used the AK–47, but never the 74.'

'Well, put them on automatic and shoot to kill,' said Richard. 'Don't give them any chance at all.'

'Right,' they both said at once. And Richard realised he would only have got an argument if he had ordered anything else.

The three of them went in through the bridge door together. 'DOWN!' screamed Richard at the top of his voice.

But his order was lost in the gunfire as his two henchmen opened up at once. Neither soldier even managed to turn, let alone bring his weapon to bear. Neither stood a chance. They were dead even before the watch on the bridge hit the floor, their chests and heads simply blown open. Richard stood for a moment, sickened. He had forgotten about the noise, the stench. The gut-deep, soul-deep revulsion.

What was left of the two men was something from his worst nightmares and he could hardly bring himself to look at the wreckage as he wrestled the guns and grenades free. He had forgotten that blood and brains each have an individual smell when violently released from bodies. He had forgotten how vividly white teeth could be when blown free of their sockets in a mess of red slush; that eyes could still watch you even when they were white marbles blown free of ruptured sockets. He had forgotten that fists remain clenched while sphincters and anuses relax immediately after death. He had forgotten that the stress, the responsibility, the waste would make him immediately enraged.

'Get down to the engine room now!' he yelled. 'That noise will have sent them insane down there!'

But no. The two men in the engine room had simply assumed that some member of the crew had irritated one of the guards. They were absolutely stunned when four fully armed crew members appeared, their leader fearsomely badged with blood. They were tank men, brought over to run and maintain the big T–80s. They were engineers, not infantry. They had managed to win the trust of their mad general by shooting a few naked African girls, but facing up to guns in the hands of desperate men and certain death no matter what else transpired was something else again.

'Right,' said Richard, breathing deeply with some relief and then regretting it because of the sickening stench on the bridge. Even though they had removed the bodies and made some attempt to clear up the blood during the last quarter of an hour, the whole place still reeked disgustingly. 'We have some kind of control here. The first thing we need to do is to check with the others and see how things are going with them. How long until you are supposed to report in?'

The soldier to whom that final question was addressed stood with his trousers down and the full pouch of his scrotum resting on the eighteen inches of honed steel blade belonging to Doc Duvalier's antique bowie knife. He was being very accurate indeed. 'Fifteen minutes.'

'OK.' Richard breathed deeply twice and pressed the first channel button on his walkie-talkie. 'Line watch on *Titan*, can you hear me?'

'Captain Mariner? Line watch *Titan* here, sir. Captain Bell in command on the bridge, sir. All clear.'

'Something's wrong,' snarled General Gogol looking at his watch. '*Kraken* is ninety seconds late.'

The ships were supposed to report in to their leader once every half-hour. There were six ships, so Gogol should have been receiving one message every five minutes; a delay of even ninety seconds was significant. He began to beat his fist against the side of the command helicopter, one beat per second. But this did not summon the message he required from the tanker, and he was just about to dispatch *Kraken*'s guard helicopter to see what was going on when the radio leaped into life.

'Yes?' he snarled.

The radio began to babble at him in breathless Russian. 'Sergeant Suslov on *Psyche* here, General. The code word is Tomsk. We've just heard from *Kraken*. There's something wrong with the communications, General. They can get us but they can't get through to you. Can you check you radio, General? Things seem to be going . . .' The transmission ended abruptly.

Gogol looked down at the hissing radio. His gaunt face folded slowly into a frown. 'Now what was that all about?'

The tone in which the question was asked made Illych Kizel's blood run cold. He could feel it all beginning to slip out of control. Starting with Gogol's sanity. 'That was not the correct procedure at all!'

And even though the code word was correct, it didn't sound at all like Sergeant Suslov either, thought Kizel; but he said nothing, fearing Gogol's reaction.

'Send the helicopters out,' ordered the general at once. 'I want things checked.'

'Excuse me, but if we send them out now, General,' countered Kizel gently, trying to disguise his desperation, 'we may not have enough fuel to get back to base again. Even with the extra we picked up in Mawanga, things will be very tight.'

Gogol paused. Thought. Took a morphine tablet. 'Very well,' he said. 'We'll wait for the next set of reports to come in.'

'The bridge is a mess,' reported *Kraken*'s first officer. 'Captain Odate is dead. He threw himself on a grenade. Saved most of the rest of us, though. The soldiers are all dead but everything is shot to pieces. I don't know whether or not we have control.'

Richard was not a trained battle commander but he had been in war situations and tight spots. He knew that the horror threatening to overcome him must be forced down at all costs or it would incapacitate him. But he could not remember whether or not the Japanese captain was married. Would he have to write to the man's family? Had he been a Heritage Mariner captain, it would have merited a personal visit to break the news, even to Japan.

His face when he swung round to his captive reflected all of his frustrated rage. The young man's scrotum clenched automatically with fear and only Duvalier's quick reactions saved him from castration. 'When should *Kraken* be reporting in?' snarled Richard, and the young soldier told him. Everything.

'He suspects something,' said Richard after the terrified boy had pretended to be the dead sergeant. 'He has to. We'd better cut and run.'

He meant it literally.

He gave the order directly to the line watches. He could check what was happening on the bridges later – though quite frankly he did not want to at all. On his command, they each pulled down the handle on the side of the bright yellow disc which clasped the massive, unbreakable hawser attaching them to the ice.

As soon as the red handles were pulled, bright laser beams, invisible within the bright casing, began to force themselves irresistibly and rapidly between the molecules of the black carbon fibre. The ropes fell back, pulling the cutters with them. The ropes connected to the iceberg had little elasticity, only that lent to them by the fact that the strands had been plaited round each other, and so they could hardly be said to have sprung back.

At one moment the iceberg called Manhattan was tethered to six supertankers. The next it was free, running at thirteen knots, a little north of due east, while the tankers began to sail away.

Kraken's guardian helicopter, alerted by Gogol's request for extra vigilance, noticed first. Such was the slowness of the whole proceeding, however, that it was not until the ship was pulling quite appreciably clear of the iceberg that they really believed their eyes. And by then it was too late. The situation was this. General Gogol's last order had caused the two lead ships to turn north. The force exerted by these vessels was enough to swing the head of the iceberg round by four degrees, pulling it across the northern flow of the Guinea current and up out of the northernmost deep of the Guinea trench. Just as the ships cut themselves loose and the Hind guarding *Kraken* began to report in, the northernmost flank of Manhattan grazed the southernmost edge of the outwash of the River Niger.

Far beneath the water, a cliff of solid ice swept up against a desert of submarine dunes. At first the soft silt yielded to the hard ice but all too soon Manhattan grazed up against the rock-solid lip of the trench edge. The iceberg's impetus was all to the north and east. The edge of the rock curved to the south. The sound of the glancing impact was overwhelming. The submarine cliff was smashed back and shattered. Cracks like bolts of lightning split the rock, racing northwards at the speed of sound.

The iceberg rocked, tipping its flat top towards Nigeria. While the pilot was still talking into the handset of his radio, reporting to his general that *Kraken* seemed to be sailing away, a sort of earthquake overtook him and the whole surface of the ice seemed to heave beneath him. While he was still looking around in confusion, the helicopter simply tipped up and toppled slowly over the edge of the cliff. And, halfway through the report, screaming wordlessly as he fell, the soldier went with it.

All the other helicopters stayed on the surface of the ice. They slid for a metre or two while the ice inclined northwards, but then they slowed to a stand. The incapacitating cacophony of sound began to echo sluggishly towards a kind of silence. The men picked themselves up, slowly dusted themselves off, and looked uncomprehendingly around. Then, one and all, with the exception of Illych Kizel, they reached for their handsets and began to report in.

'Get in the helicopter, General,' Kizel was yelling.

The Hind stood still but was rocking on its suspension at the end of the little trenches carved by its undercarriage. Gogol sat beside it, looking upwards. The Hind had been facing eastwards along the length of the iceberg towards its forecastle head. The helicopter had slid sideways and the general had been fortunate not to be crushed beneath it as it moved. The handset of his radio dangled out of the open side and the radio itself shrilled with incoming messages.

'Get in the helicopter, General. We have to lift off at once!'

Gogol looked across at Kizel and his lip curled. 'There is no need to panic, Illych, the movement has stopped!'

Kizel almost danced with impatience. 'No it has not, General. Think! If the iceberg tilts one way and stops, then that is only a pause before it tilts the other way! It is obvious. It is a simple law of physics.'

The general looked up, uncomprehendingly.

'Did you never play with boats in your bath? What goes one way rocks back the other way too!' Kizel's throat tore as he yelled. And as he yelled, he realised that the sounds he was making were vanishing. Being eaten. Swallowed. Swept under. Drowned beyond rescue in the rising tide of thunder which could mean only one thing.

He ran forward, surprised – horrified – to realise that he was already running up a slight slope.

Slight, but steepening.

The Hind hesitated on the very edge of motion, trembling at the top of the little trenches, ready to slide back down.

Illych Kizel caught up the body of his general officer and, too preoccupied to be surprised by the lightness of his burden, climbed into the helicopter with Gogol in his arms. No sooner were they inside the square space of the fuselage than he felt the Hind begin to slide away under him. He dropped the general at once and began to fight his way up the bucking length of the helicopter. He was vaguely aware that Gogol was following him but at some distance. Then he forgot about his commanding officer and threw himself into his seat. The horizon was already looking seriously out of true to his eyes, but that was nothing to the way it looked on the instruments in front of him. And it continued to tilt further and further over in a slow, majestic surge as he fought to get the engine started.

Gogol arrived, dumping himself in the co-pilot's seat and raising a long, clumsy tube into plain sight. 'Another Grail missile,' he said. 'Like the one we used on Chala. Get me to one of those bastard tankers and I'll light a big enough fire to call down all of your heat-seeking missiles!'

Kizel nodded, but he wasn't really paying much attention. He was going through the shortest pre-flight of his flying life. The tanks were half empty and the gas was not too keen on pushing itself up into tubes at this odd angle. The engine coughed and snarled. The rotors surged into motion then slowed as the motor failed to catch. The Hind reached the end of its little trenches and hesitated, apparently unwilling to go up over the rough, sandy snow.

The sound of the rolling iceberg was of a thunderstorm in an echo chamber with a recording of a military barrage at full volume behind it on the biggest speakers in the world. Kizel was crying because of the pain in his ears. And yet even that seemed secondary to the agony in his chest. The very air that he breathed was vibrating so hard it threatened to tear his lung linings loose. His heart was actually being massaged by the throbbing in the shaking air. He could feel his brain trembling in his skull and his sight began to fail as the smallest blood vessels behind his eyes ruptured and began to spray threads of blood across his vision.

A fully-laden Hind-D helicopter weighs in excess of 25,000 kilograms. There were four left on the upper surface of Manhattan, and so 100,000 kilos, nearly a quarter of a million pounds, was sliding down the slope adding weight and inertia to the slow, inexorable tilt of the ice. Compared with the mass of the whole thing, of course, this weight was less than nothing. But the balance of the iceberg was so questionable, its reaction to brushing the lip of the submarine cliff so intense, the destabilising effect of being cut loose and slowing down suddenly so cataclysmic that the extra weight of the helicopters was more than enough to turn it over.

With a kind of languorous majesty, it heaved and tipped, throwing its sand-marked upper surfaces southwards and pulling its submarine foundations up into the heaving air. It was so massive that the physics of its movement caused enormous disturbance of the sea which heaved up into great waves speeding south. Only the quick-thinking and desperate orders of Richard Mariner turned the ships in time so that at least they were riding stern on to the swell.

Psyche was nearly drowned by spray and her whole bridge-house was discovered, later, to have moved one clear metre forward down her deck. Nevertheless, she survived.

Titan and *Niobe*, running away to the east, were battered but unbowed. *Ajax* and *Achilles* in harness to the west likewise escaped.

Exactly what happened to *Kraken*, however, no one ever knew.

As the iceberg rolled, it rose up in the water as though the sideways motion was causing it to leap into the air for joy. It hurled itself upwards far faster than the slow ocean could ever move to fill in the unutterable, abysmal vacancies it left behind it. For the instants of its unimaginable arousal, it literally tore a hole in nature. And the tanker was simply gulped down. Running north and east for safety though she was, she never stood a chance, for the movement of something as gigantic as Manhattan caused even the winds to move, and the same forces that piled up the sea on one side into great waves and made a Grand Canyon in the ocean on the other acted on the air as well. The hurricane storm to the south which threw the spray so hard at *Psyche*'s upper works that her funnel was hurled over her forecastle head and away across the sea in front of her, simply, on the northern side of the rolling berg, sucked *Kraken* like a feather into the hole in the Gulf of Guinea made by a billion tonnes of solid water in violent motion, and swallowed a quarter of a million ton super-tanker as easily as it had swallowed the Hind helicopter a little earlier.

Only the instruments told Kizel that the engine had caught. By the time it came to life, its sound was as nothing in the storm. He engaged the rotors once again and actually began to pray as the great span of the blades began to swing into its accustomed circle. He was extremely fortunate that *Kraken*'s guardian had already fallen off, for by the time he had his own craft under some kind of control it was plain that everything else on the surface was in violent motion down the slope which was all too rapidly steepening into a cliff. Even as he lifted off, he kept looking up that dirty white slope, expecting to see *Kraken*'s helicopter come tumbling down on top of him.

The lurch as the cabin swung back down to a horizontal setting threatened to throw both men out of their seats, for neither was strapped in. Whereas it nearly knocked Kizel out, it served to wake Gogol up. By this time he had consumed so many of his morphine tablets that he was far removed from reality. The drug's painkilling properties cocooned him from the agonies of noise and concussion which were threatening to incapacitate his pilot. He pulled himself up and looked around. If he was beyond pain, he was by no means beyond the reach of shock, and what he saw smashed into his consciousness like a right hook from a heavyweight champion. He had lost his command. That much seemed certain. And, for the first time in his life, he had failed in a mission. Increasingly wildly, he looked around the swinging cabin of the Hind as Kizel fought to bring it dancing out from under the rearing avalanche of the spinning iceberg.

The same deft hands and feet which had made the Hind seem to fly backwards before *Psyche*'s bridgehouse and had jerked the craft away like a fish on a line fought to carry the bucking helicopter through the increasingly wild winds piling up under the lip of solid ice which was breaking down over them like a big surf. At last, the helicopter was indeed flying backwards and Kizel, a pilot of real genius, perhaps the greatest helicopter pilot in the Russian armed services, was bringing his craft back out of the jaws of hell to the first heart-stopping promise of safety.

'Yes!' He tore his throat, screaming with the wild, ecstatic combination of hope and elation, feeling his labouring craft beginning to come to life.

He hauled her nose up as though he was a weightlifter at the outer edge of his strength. His eyes began to clear, for he had been flying by touch up until now, and he began to see, rising out of the billowing clouds of spray on which he seemed to be floating, more and more and more of the eternal iceberg rising up to meet him. The glass in front of him split across and began to leak inward at once. He screamed. The Hind screamed. Neither could be heard. He gained another gramme or two of strength. The metal of the control column began to twist out of shape in the force of his grip. His foot slid another millimetre down the slowly warping pedal. And by main force, the Hind continued to climb on the back of the hurricane wind, skipping backwards all the time and away from that massive leap of the ice which, far back behind the rising, rolling mountain, was gulping *Kraken* down and creating massive waves in the southern edge of the Bight.

Kizel's eyes were clouding up and out of focus; he was flying by touch again and just succumbing to the blessed belief that he was pulling free after all when he felt the fist of his commanding officer come pounding on his shoulder. His eyes leaped wide and he risked a quick, startled glance to his left.

Gogol had gone utterly insane. His face was twisted with a wild, terrifying combination of stress and agony. He was yelling as loudly as he could through a throat no longer designed to accept volume, forcing air up out of lungs which no longer should have known how to breathe. He was doing to his cancer-corrupted body what Kizel was doing to the buckling frame of the Hind. He was screaming at the top of his voice and he was pounding on the pilot's shoulder and gesturing wildly dead ahead and upwards.

At first, still believing the man was mad with fear, Kizel thought Gogol was ordering him to get the helicopter up and away. He shook his head, frowned, shrugged the importunate man away. But Gogol would not be dismissed. He screamed until blood came boltering from his gaping mouth. He battered the pilot and gestured.

At last Kizel looked upwards towards where the general was pointing. He never really believed what he saw but he saw it so clearly that he carried the sight to his grave. The crest of the frozen wave was etched against the bright blue sky so absolutely that the ice itself seemed dark. And, frozen into the line of that crest, was the forecastle of a ship. The steel sides were twisted; blast-damaged, burned, half-melted out of shape, but they were there. And they were unmistakable. There was part of a ship frozen into the ice.

Abruptly, as though a spike of ice had been pushed down his throat, Kizel froze. He knew what ship this was. There could only be one. He glanced back across at Gogol. The general was slumped back in his seat now and he seemed to have grown a bright red beard.

From that moment on, Illych Kizel saw things only in still pictures, as though the sun had become a massive strobe light. He saw the bows of the ship *Leonid Brezhnev* rear in silhouette against the sky. He saw the general leaning back in his seat coughing up more blood. He saw the cliff falling as the helicopter continued to rise at his implacable command. He saw the ship topple forward beneath the nose of the Hind. He saw Gogol, gesturing wildly, jerk forward as the frozen ship fell, and he understood. He saw the open front of the ship, its metal spread wide open by the force of some unimaginable explosion, its name still readable. Its identity and nationality still all too obvious. He saw Gogol jerking as his lifeblood burst out to run away down his chest and onto the heaving floor. But still the man would not give in. He should have been dead eight years earlier; he was not going to lie down now.

The hand he laid on Illych Kizel's shoulder was the merest feather now, but it had more force and command than all the battering which had rained down earlier. Both men were permanently deaf and yet the pointing of that quaking finger spoke more eloquently than the words of Chekov himself.

The nose of the Hind dropped back down as Kizel aimed the whole machine at the tumbling bow of the ship. His face swung towards Gogol, stunned with confusion. All of their air-to-surface missiles were heat-seeking and he was pointing them at ice! But even as he looked at the general, so he saw him smashing the Grail anti-tank missile through the cracked windscreen in front of him. A hail of glass shards burst in over the pair of them. The wind grasped Kizel and tried to chuck him bodily out into the sea. The Hind's head dropped, but not before Gogol had pulled the trigger on the Grail. The rocket fumes filled the cockpit, only to be snatched away again by the rabid wind. A section of the ice immediately below the frozen bows erupted and Kizel launched the first series of missiles.

The whole side of the iceberg burst asunder. The shock wave hit the helicopter, causing it to fall the better part of fifty metres into the top of the mist.

Kizel knew that his choice was very simple now. He could wrestle the dancing Hind up out of the mist again and fly away, leaving the job half done, or he could obey the last order of his general.

He glanced across into the co-pilot's seat. Gogol seemed to be asleep now, nursing the empty tube of the Grail's launcher, but Kizel wasn't fooled for a second. The decision was his and, thinking of the prediction at the end of the general's story of civil war for Russia if the ship was ever discovered, he made it. The wall of white in front of him might have been made entirely of mist except that part of it was unnaturally bright. That was where his missiles were exploding in the solid ice. He pressed the button which launched the next flight and pushed the controls forward.

The Hind came up just sufficiently to maintain level flight through the shock wave caused by the second wave of missiles. It would have fallen from the sky upon the impact of the third wave, but instead it flew directly into the cliff and blew the last signs of *Leonid Brezhnev* away into the heaving sea.

Haven

MAU

*I have desired to go
Where springs not fail
To fields where flies no sharp and sided hail
And a few lilies blow.
And I have asked to be
Where no storms come,
Where the green swell is in the havens dumb
And out of the swing of the sea*

Gerard Manley Hopkins, *Heaven-Haven*

Chapter Twenty-Nine

Psyche joined *Ajax* and *Achilles* at the westernmost end of the iceberg which could no longer really be called Manhattan. *Titan* and *Niobe* continued to take the lead at the eastern end, but where they had been anchored to an island with coastal cliffs three hundred metres high, the new tabular configuration of the berg meant that the cliffs now were little more than one hundred metres tall at their highest point and sloped back down to almost nothing at their lowest.

Richard was back on *Titan* and fully in charge. He had been on *Psyche* for a while, up on the ice with the engineers re-establishing the line, on *Ajax* with Katya Borodin, trying to discover whether her crew had noticed anything in particular about the pirates. Everyone was now agreed that the helicopters had been Russian and the accents of even the English-speakers has been Russian, and that they had talked to each other in Russian. Their one, taciturn, prisoner was certainly Russian. He had prepared a preliminary report of the tragedy to send to the United Nations and faxed it out from *Ajax*. Then he had returned to *Titan* and started making the plans he was discussing now. No one had seen him sleep since the attack, and that had been over for seventy-two hours now – to the extent that it would ever be over for any of them.

He was driving himself and his command as hard as he could as the days ticked by and Mawanga harbour came closer and closer. By mid-afternoon, more than three days after the iceberg had rolled over, the ships were re-anchored in their new positions and back up to full power, though they were now moving forward at the five knots of the Guinea current, effectively idling in still water only just in control, while Richard held his captains' conference in the big office aboard *Titan*. His first objective was to establish clearly the new position; then he needed to confirm the complex series of manoeuvres they would be performing during the next few days to bring the iceberg safely to port.

'The whole thing has rolled right over and settled upside down,' he was saying, referring to a carefully drawn scale diagram pinned to the wall behind him. 'The top is flat and the bottom, deep below the surface of the ocean, is now uneven, with two keels which used to be the islands we could see above the surface. The forward keel, about fifty kilometres long, reaches nearly one thousand metres straight down. It combines the three hundred metres of cliff which stood above the waves with the nine hundred which reached down below. The rear keel is much smaller and represents the inverted remains of the little island at the back of the berg to which *Ajax* and *Achilles* have been tethered for the last month.'

'It's a hell of a way to wash the sand off,' observed Bob Stark grimly, and his dark attempt at a little humour failed to ignite any response from the others. They were all exhausted. They were shocked and depressed by the loss of *Kraken* and her complement. They were still in clinical shock from the unexpected, violent nature of the mysterious attempt to wreck their mission. They were all still looking over their shoulders all the time, expecting another gang of armed men to drop out of the sky. Even the iceberg, now obviously in an utterly stable position, remained a source of wonderment and terror. All the ships were on the longest possible lines, and Richard was quite content that they should stay that way.

'The keels are important,' Richard persisted. 'They give the berg even more stability than it had before . . .'

'Which was not one hell of a lot, as it turned out. Be fair—'

Richard's hand slammed down onto the table. 'Bob! I will *not* be held responsible because I couldn't dictate the exact movements of a billion-tonne iceberg in the middle of an airborne invasion by armed soldiers! Now for Christ's sake, let it rest.'

The American looked stunned. He literally gaped at his old friend, then he swept the cow's lick of gold hair out of his bright eyes. 'God, Richard, I didn't mean . . . Jesus . . . I'm sorry.'

Richard took a great, racking breath. 'No,' he said more quietly. '*I'm* sorry. I know you didn't mean anything. It's just that . . . Well, let's get on.'

He turned back to the diagram on the wall.

All his friends exchanged glances. They all tended to regard him as a man of steel, especially those who knew him best and longest, and his outburst had shocked them. Not so much the outburst, perhaps, but the depth of the strain it revealed. This was Richard at his grimmest, with all of his cheery self-confidence gone and all his breezy self-assurance buried under the dogged, joyless need to get a dirty job done. The joy had gone out of the work for all of them, but they still had their contract to fulfil, and a difficult job to do with absolute precision; for each of the forty men and women dead in this venture so far, one hundred thousand more stood to die.

'The keels will keep the berg stable and ensure that it continues to move in an absolutely straight line. It is our job, of course, to ensure that the straight line it is following takes it in through the opening of Mawanga harbour. Also, and this is equally important, we have to ensure she is still moving fast enough to reach all the way down the full length of the anchorage but that the way comes off her completely before she smashes into the mouth of the River Mau and rides up into the middle of the city itself. I understand there are hundreds of thousands of insurance claims ready to go if there is the slightest evidence of any property damage at all.'

'And almost all of the residents of Mawanga city have taken to the hills,' supplied John, who had been listening to Mawanga Radio earlier that morning. 'Except for reporters and disaster freaks.'

'Welcome to Mawanga!' said Bob, with bitter irony. And this time Richard at least gave a grunt of wry laughter.

'Welcome to Mawanga!' said a distant but familiar voice not quite lost among the babble of official greeting. Indira Dyal looked past the welcoming faces of the reception committee and caught the eye of Emily Karanga. She raised her hand and swept forward, leaving Mohammed Aziz to deal with polite officialdom.

Emily and Warren Cord were standing on the tarmac apron, just off the wide red carpet laid out to conduct the Executive Assistant and the Chef de Cabinet from their aeroplane to their official car. There was some talk that the Secretary General himself would be here tomorrow in order to welcome the iceberg on its arrival in two days' time, but in the meantime the leaders of the Mau Club were getting the full treatment.

'I'll rely on Mohammed to represent us at as many official functions as possible,' said the elegant Indian woman decisively. 'I want you two to show me what's really going on here.'

That was all she had time to say before she was swept back into the line of minor government dignitaries desperate to get their faces in the papers and on the television screen.

Emily and Warren walked back towards the car they were sharing. 'That's our Indira,' observed the American.

'You decided what you're going to show her?'

'Everything I can. And what she can't see for herself I'll get witnesses to describe to her.'

'Ann Cable?'

'If she's well enough. I'm just on my way over to see her now. Can I drop you?'

'Yeah. Shoot on past the hospital for a kilometre. Drop me at the docks. We've still got to get the harbour mouth fixed up.'

'Is it being particularly difficult?'

'I don't know. No one's ever tried to make a door that will open wide enough to let in a billion tonne iceberg and then close it right up behind it.'

'I see your problem.'

'No matter how you look at it, the problem will be time,' said Warren Cord to the chief engineer.

The tall black man nodded in agreement, his eyes narrow as he checked across the opening of the anchorage again. He was a man who placed absolute reliance on accurate drawings – then came out to check them at the site as often as he could. The two of them were standing on the westernmost edge of the northern arm of land. A slight wind gusted over the bull's horns of the anchorage mouth, carrying the United Nations man's words away southwards across the twenty kilometres of restless water.

'I mean,' persisted the American, 'you're dealing with an opening here which is almost as wide as the Straits of Gibraltar. It's only just going to be wide enough to let the sucker in, but once it *is* in, then you've got to close it off. Build a barrage, or a dam or something like that before the iceberg melts and starts leaking fresh water back out again.'

'I've looked into all that very carefully and—'

'You don't have a shallow base to build up from because the iceberg is a thousand metres deep and that's at least how deep the harbour mouth has to be.'

'And is. We know all this, Warren.'

'I know! I'm just thinking out loud, for heaven's sake.'

The black civil engineer gave a bark of laughter as he realised what Warren was really up to. 'You are practising for press interviews! Are you going to be seen around town with the devastating Dr Dyal, then, my friend? You will need to move fast to get her away from Aziz!'

Wearing an outfit of khaki bush gear instead of her usual stately sari, Dr Indira Dyal was almost impossible to recognise. Those heads which turned, and there were a good few, were turned not by fame but by the sight of two such striking women riding together in an open-topped jeep out through the shantytown towards the reception camps. Only the small truck of armed guards behind them gave any hint of their true political importance. But the guards were tense and watchful – it was little more than a week since their leader General of Police Nimrod Chala had been assassinated. The country still simmered on the edge of civil war, but the dead leader had left a power vacuum. Many of the men who so smilingly greeted Dr Dyal at the airport were scheming to fill the vacuum themselves, but General Moses M'Diid was best placed to take advantage, for the army stood behind him as firmly as the police had stood behind their leader. Moses was especially well placed now because his younger brother Aaron was currently acting head of state. As soon as the matter of the water was sorted out, there would be elections. And Nimrod Chala was no longer there to fight them or disrupt them or seize power and make them redundant.

Emily was one of those drivers who liked to divide their concentration between control and conversation. With her right hand on the wheel, she gestured extravagantly with her left. With her eyes firmly on the road ahead – which was coming towards them at more than thirty miles an hour – her tongue was in animated overdrive.

'You will see. Millions of them, helpless and hopeless. Only now is the true horror of what has been happening upcountry beginning to emerge. Ann Cable has agreed to see you tomorrow if she feels strong enough and she will give you a taste of the overall picture. But I can show you a thousand – a million – examples of individual suffering. In a way it is fortunate that they are all here. At least when the iceberg arrives we will only have to get the water a couple of kilometres up here to them. And, when they are stronger, they can help us move more and more of it. The food aid has been tremendous, but it is the water which will set us free. Even if it only gets these people back on their feet, it will have been worthwhile, but I'm sure there will be enough to get the irrigation system working again.' Her shining eyes left the road and swung across to look at the Indian woman. The hope they contained was so intense, Indira seemed to feel it on her skin like sunlight.

'There's almost as much water there as in Lake Nasser behind the Aswan Dam! All fresh and clear! It will bring my country back to life, I know it!'

On the last day before the serious ship-handling began, they split the new area of exposed ice into sections and scanned them as fully as they could for radioactivity. The process was as laborious and difficult to achieve as had been the sweep across the now submerged island which John had organised. But Richard was willing to use all the crews he had, a team which was effectively 150 strong. And they found nothing. Insofar as they were able, they examined the surface of the ice in detail from the new wide shoreline at the back to the low cliffs at the front, which still formed a rough forecastle head. The new Bell had arrived and all that day the helicopter plied back and forth transporting, checking, guarding and carrying back. It was little enough cause for celebration, but it would serve. Richard asked his captains to give their crews a 'well done' party and he himself joined in the swing of things in *Titan*'s wardroom, playing the genial host overseeing a breathtaking feast with a range of courses carefully selected to guarantee that everyone enjoyed themselves to the full. And he led the festivities at the dance afterwards, though women were in short supply and they had to rely on the ship's ancient audio-tape collection.

'I don't know how he does it,' said Sally Bell to Wally Gough as he ran breathlessly up to her just before she broke up the party by going up onto her watch. 'He's not what you'd call mercurial, but he was so down yesterday and he's on such good form tonight.'

Wally looked at his captain with some speculation. It had never occurred to the youthful cadet that there was more under the surface than appeared at first glance. With childlike simplicity, he had assumed that if the captain seemed cheerful then he must be so. And most of the crew seemed to share his thoughts, for as the night wore on, so the morale aboard *Titan* – and aboard the other ships too – began to rise back up to its usual level.

Richard felt it; he was hoping for it and looking out for it. The sacrifice of one fine ship and so many men was worthwhile only if the whole enterprise was worthwhile. And independently of the intrinsic worth of what they were trying to do, it would only be fully worthwhile if the next two days passed off without a hitch.

Oh, how he was tempted to go to his charts again and look through the figures ready for the morning. But he would not dream of doing so. Here came young Wally Gough, tipsy with excitement from having talked Sally Bell into dancing with him on her way up to the bridge.

'Wow!' said the cadet breathlessly. 'That was better than navigation lessons!'

It was as though they were standing side by side, looking out through the same clearview into the first glimmer of dawn together, but in fact Richard and John were ten kilometres apart, with their ships on parallel courses, swinging the head of the iceberg round onto the due easterly straight line which would take them over the bar and into Mawanga harbour in thirty-six hours' time. Each had a walkie-talkie and as they dictated the increasingly minute course changes to their helmsmen, they kept in contact with each other, checking, discussing, adapting. Both were using the satnav system to place themselves exactly on the surface of the earth and each was checking the other's readings.

As the sun came up over the horizon, Sally Bell hurried out onto the bridge wing with her sextant and Richard briefly found himself talking to Steve Bollom as John did the same. The reading they achieved agreed exactly with the readings from the satnavs and the commanders felt more relaxed about placing absolute reliance on the machines as they charted, almost metre by metre, the progress of the ships towards their destination.

As soon as it was light, Yves Maille appeared on *Titan*'s bridge, and Richard nodded at once, knowing what the Frenchman wanted and happy to let him take it. Ten minutes after that silent nod, the Bell helicopter lifted off the main deck and skimmed away at wavetop level.

All day it plied back and forth, covering and re-covering the increasingly narrow band of water between the lead ship and their destination. It hovered low, dropping markers and watching them drift. Colleagues from the shore came out in boats and fed the Frenchman readings of temperature, salinity, current.

Especially current.

The weather was calm. Noon and afternoon ticked by without the slightest stir of wind. The waves swept in from behind the iceberg and, as its guardians moved it more slowly and more slowly still, the waves swept past it in majestic green series, moving shorewards and showing it the way. Until, just at the point where Yves hovered most anxiously and his colleagues bobbed and puttered in their boats, little more than fifty metres out from the tips of the bull's horns, the waves began to break up unaccountably and what had been a regular corrugation became instead a restless, cross-hatched mess of sharp-sided, triangular waves.

'Of course, we never even considered actually closing the outer end of the anchorage after we got the iceberg into it. That would have been like building the Aswan Dam, under water, in a matter of days. A little difficult, even for the United Nations, I think you'll agree!'

Warren Cord had got his press conference and he was enjoying it. All of the UN personnel in place had assembled for an early evening reception at the residence of the President. Present were the senior staff like Indira and Mohammed Aziz; the Mau Club representatives like Emily and Warren himself; aid workers, diplomatic staff, UNICEF reps, Save the Children men and women. During the last month more than a hundred people had arrived and there were many more on the way. The Secretary General was due tomorrow; but so was the iceberg itself and it seemed more sensible to hold the reception now. And, with a view to the proposed elections, acting President Aaron M'Diid had allowed the proceedings to begin with a press call. It was a little unexpected and the others were unprepared and not too happy about it, but Warren was ready for this and he was not a man to pass up such a heaven-sent opportunity.

'Now I don't want to bore the good folks out there, but the idea is this. As you know, there's quite a current flowing in the ocean off Mau. It's the southern end of the Guinea current and it runs south along the coast here, down towards the Congo. The flow is fast, it doesn't vary much, and it comes right in along the coast. And, most especially, it comes across the mouth of Mawanga harbour.

'Now, if you're careful and make allowances, you can get a ship in and out easily, and we reckon the same will be true of the iceberg. We'll wedge the whole thing in the harbour and be ready to pump out any salt water it displaces. The berg is so big that to begin with, it will block the entrance itself, like a great frozen cork. What will happen next of course is that the iceberg will begin to melt. I'm speculating here, but what we think will occur under these circumstances is this: as the clear water flows back along the anchorage, filling it with a lake of fresh water, it will come up against what is effectively a wall of salt water flowing south. The temperatures and specific gravities will be very different. The two sorts of water won't mix too readily, and we reckon that, as long as we control the level of the meltwater in the anchorage carefully, the good old Guinea current will keep most of it bottled up for us. And, just in case there's any miscalculation here, we'll have our biggest pumps positioned up that end to pump the fresh water free.'

'In fact,' enlarged Emily Karanga later that night, 'we're hoping that most of the pure water will be transported over the ridge of rock at the mouth of the River Mau. The ridge that keeps the sea water from flowing further up into the dry valley. In fact, it is the first of a series of ridges which has created a sequence of dried-up lakes along the course of the river itself. If we can use the fresh water to fill these lakes, we will have the equivalent of a series of small dams, each holding back a self-contained reservoir of more than a million tonnes of water and refilling the irrigation system my father put in place shortly before his assassination. And we can continue to refill each reservoir as it goes dry until all the ice has gone. Even to melt it all into water will take some time! And I mean, while the ice is hard, we can cut it up and carry it up there in trucks! Think of it!

'Political ambitions? Oh no. I couldn't say. Yes, I know my father is remembered ... revered ... But, well, let's just get the water back into the land and the first seed corn planted. Let's just get every refugee back to his own home farm. Let's just get all these poor, sick people strong and well again. Then it will be time to talk about politics!'

Ann Cable spent most of that evening standing at her hospital window staring away to the west. The iceberg was still below the horizon but even so, it was making its presence felt in the western sky. The sun bled down behind it, sinking through shades of ruby and garnet to burnt red, magenta and damask. But, just as it settled out of her sight, the sun seemed to rise again, its light flooding up in a dazzling display across the undersides of those high clouds. Bands of burning brightness seemed to come rolling in towards the land as though some Biblical curse was being worked out. After she recovered from her first shiver of unreasoning dread, she stood entranced, watching the searchlight beams of crimson light leaping up from behind the horizon as though some huge volcano were active there and the western waves were all afire, not freezing under the influence of the island of ice which was causing the beautiful show.

It had begun abruptly, but it faded slowly. Ann watched every second of it, her face running with tears for the first time since Emily found her. It was as though she found some kind of healing catharsis in the extravagant, overwhelming beauty she was witnessing. As though she found strength in the knowledge that the cause of all this beauty was coming here to heal this broken land.

She did not remember sleeping at all that night. The light show seemed to carry on almost to midnight, when it was augmented by a real firework display from the President's residence. Perhaps she slept but she did not remember even sitting down. She was back at that window watching when the first light of dawn began to glimmer like the ash of pink roses on the air. There was hardly any light at all, just that exquisite, almost mauve mist and shadows pointing out to sea. And, out to sea, there the iceberg was. The long light ran like water down Mau's dry valley; it spilled across the anchorage and ran away into the distance until it thundered silently up against a cliff of utter, absolute, heartstopping whiteness.

Ann caught her breath and stood until she was faint with want of breath, simply stunned by the beauty.

'I have to get this down on paper,' she said aloud. She ran her hands down her face and they came away wet with tears. 'Then I've got to find my camera bag and get those photographs processed. There's some kind of prize somewhere in this, Ann, old girl . . .'

During the next thirty-six hours as the iceberg was painstakingly pulled in across the south-running Guinea current and bedded infinitely carefully into the waiting arms of the anchorage, Ann Cable saw more than anyone else involved. With the kind of energy granted to very few people, she managed to put herself in every location where something important was going on. She had money, contacts, influence. She had a clear view of where she wanted to be and what – whom – she wanted to see. She had the drive of a door-to-door Bible salesman. She had the timing of a prima ballerina with the Bolshoi. She had the sort of luck Napoleon required in his generals. She was simply unstoppable.

It was Ann who was in the reception camps as day broke properly, discussing with the dying what this solid water meant; exploring with villagers who had never in all their lives seen ice outside a freezer what one billion metric tonnes of the stuff would mean to them. It was Ann who rode with Emily to pick up Indira and who interviewed her in the bouncing jeep as they went out to the airport to await the Secretary General's plane. It was she who took the opportunity of a slight delay to interview the acting President in a waiting room, both of them caught between relief and surprise to discover that the rest of the press corps were out at the mouth of the anchorage looking at the sight which Ann, hundreds of feet higher, had seen a couple of hours earlier. Of all the things she learned in the interview with the urbane, charming, acting President M'Diid, the most important of all was how irreplaceable was the view from her sickroom window.

But, inevitably, as the Secretary General's plane at last arrived, the rest of the pack arrived too and Ann swapped places with them. She stepped out onto the furthest point of the northern arm of the anchorage and discussed with Warren Cord the manner in which the lead tankers would sail along the outside of the harbour until they could hand down their unbreakable lines. How these would then be attached to whole series of the largest earthbound vehicles Ann had ever seen, and how these incredible earth movers would grind down the roads, replacing the power of the supertankers as best they could. *Titan*, she knew, would remain at the harbour mouth, acting as go-between for the drivers of the massive vehicles and the captains of the three ships nearly a hundred kilometres away, whose ships by that time would be working in full reverse, trying to slow the stately progress of the massive inertia of one billion tonnes of ice as it was grudgingly ameliorated from two knots to dead stop in the seventy-five kilometres of the anchorage itself.

She was just about to go and interview the men waiting to start the massive pumps further down, which were designed to get rid of the overflow which would be trapped in the anchorage by the forward motion of the iceberg, when a Bell helicopter came thudding in from the west to settle beside Warren's men. Yves Maille climbed out and Ann was in motion again. Even this early in the day the

Frenchman was susceptible to charm. He never stood a chance. The helicopter was soon airborne again and heading back the way it had come.

And that brought the only really bad shock she had in all that magical time: the sight of her dear friend Richard Mariner. She had seen him in a wide range of circumstances and few of them had been pleasant but she had never seen him like this. He was drained, depressed, almost desperate. She could feel the burden of responsibility weighing about him like a cowl of lead. She arrived on *Titan* quite blithe, looking forward to seeing him, but at once she realised that he was all too close to the state she had been in herself during the last two weeks. Moved by sympathy and empathy, she waded in at once, describing what she had found ashore. Wisely, she did not mention the range of dignitaries waiting to greet him and the abundance of dignities they were preparing to confer upon him. Instead she told him about the millions of desperate people she had seen in the reception camps. She regaled him, not with her adventures, but with the ruination of the land that she had crossed and how the water which he was bringing would restore so much for so many. Little by little as she lingered through the afternoon, she saw the magnesium spark rekindle in the eyes which reminded her so much of circles of sapphire. When Yves bustled up, concerned that the bow of the berg was sweeping into the rush of the southbound current, she surrendered, gave Richard the sort of kiss she normally reserved for Nico Niccolo, and left, pleased with the obvious good she had done. At the door to the lift she was stopped by a tall blonde woman who spoke with an Irish accent. 'I don't know how you did it,' she said, 'but thanks. Thanks a lot!'

Ann charmed Yves into dropping her back at the city end of the anchorage and picked up a taxi easily. She was back at the hospital within minutes. She went up to her room and into the province of her less than happy doctors.

Still fizzing with energy, she reluctantly agreed to remain in their care for another thirty-six hours but refused to remain in hospital for all that time. She had a variety of plans – but they had lingering fears about tick fever.

They met halfway. She spent a quiet evening turning her impressions of the day into prose, pausing every now and then to take a look out of the window, all too vividly aware that the bow of the iceberg was moving ever closer to the outer markers of the harbour. At midnight her resolve broke; she crept out into the streets. The same taxi driver took her right down to the tip of the northern harbour wall, a round trip of a hundred and fifty kilometres and very expensive at that time of night. But worth it.

Why had so few other people, so few so-called reporters, placed themselves here to watch, as a white cliff of ice came sailing into the harbour? There was a gentle, reverberating thunder as the keel a thousand metres below grazed the ridge which separated the tectonic basin from the Gulf of Guinea. The earth trembled – it did not quite shake. Ann knew that her hospital bed would have been disturbed by this same vibration and she would have tossed in her sleep, scared that the roof was coming in upon her. How much more satisfying it was to be out here, watching a wall of ice many times higher than the fabled White Cliffs of Dover which Richard had described and eventually shown to her. How glorious to stand on this balmy, moonlit evening watching history in the making. How simply good it was to be alive!

Twenty-four hours later, Ann stood in her hospital room looking out of her window thinking the same thing, but this time she was not alone. She had described the view from her room to Warren Cord, but he could not be here: he was in charge of the gigantic tractors pulling the unbreakable lines in place of the supertankers *Titan* and *Niobe*. She had mentioned it to Indira Dyal and Mohammed Aziz but both of them were in the tight grip of social and political requirements. There was another reception, and this one included the Secretary General. They could not refuse. She had mentioned it also to Emily Karanga and she at least was here. Emily, ever practical, had brought a thermos full of strong black coffee and they stood at the window with fragrant cups of Blue Mountain steaming on the sill in front of them. Further away, seemingly just beyond the double-glazing, the sharp-edged cliff of ice was pushing itself inexorably into the heart of the city. It overhung the inner harbour wall by more than half a kilometre, sloping back through its hundred-metre height. It continued to move forward into place, though its movement was only appreciable if one looked away for ten minutes or so and then looked back.

Side by side, awed by the achievement of the man they both knew and respected so well, they watched as the iceberg slid into place as slowly, as absolutely, as inevitably as the sunrise. They were on the twentieth floor, in the penthouse of the hospital, and so were just able to look down upon the flat surface – but only as a child on tiptoe may look across a tabletop. The broad span of the berg threatened to overfill the triangle of the estuary and crush the very buildings aside. But no. At five minutes past midnight, a bass note seemed to sound throughout the city as the bow cut through the red mud of the dry River Mau and ground to a halt against the slope of black, basalt rock. For the first time since the *Leonid Brezhnev* blew it free of the Greenland glacier that gave it birth, the iceberg had come to rest in a safe haven.

Gleaming in the moonlight, like a picture on a Christmas card, a fine dusting of ice crystals fell forward like snow into the broad cup of the first dry lake. The coffee in the cups upon the windowsill stirred slightly and rippled darkly as the women watched, entranced. The coffee stirred again, in a kind of gentle aftershock, and then there was utter, blissful silence. Ann reached forward impulsively. Unusually for a building in a tropical country, the windows in the hospital had adjustable double-glazing. She took the handles and slid back the inner sheet of glass. Then she loosened the outer casement and opened it wide. The air that flowed in was cold, and smelt of cucumbers.

It gave both of the women who smelt it so much energy that they embraced in uncontrollable excitement.

'Now,' said Ann, bubbling over with energy, 'I want you to take me back to where you found me in that irrigation ditch in the bush. In the morning will do, but you must take me soon. Or, at the very least, you must promise to tell me exactly where it is. I've got a bag hidden there with a camera and some pictures which are going to win me the Pulitzer Prize!'

At four o'clock that morning, a tall man in a light trench coat came down the gangplank from *Titan* onto the dock of Mawanga harbour. There was only the most dilatory immigration check and no customs check at all. Even at this time in the morning, there was a taxi waiting.

'Where to?' asked the driver cheerily in English, correctly guessing the most likely nationality of his passenger.

'To the airport,' his fare ordered.

'You're choosing a bad time to leave,' the driver said, still cheery.

'No, there's a flight at six to Paris and London,' the fare corrected wearily.

The battered old Mercedes eased itself along the townbound road. The harbour lights reflected off the side of the iceberg so brightly that it might almost have been day, all the way back to the eastern outskirts of the city and the first reception camp for refugees. There it was still dark, and would stay dark for a while yet.

'That's not what I mean!' said the driver with a laugh, settling into the easy drive along the deserted highway east.

'It's party time in Mawanga! The Secretary General of the United Nations is here. There are all sorts of important people here! Why, there's going to be a festival nonstop until the first thousand tons of that iceberg are carried into the refugee camps. They say the men on board your ships are all going to get rewards. They say your captain is going to get the Medal of Honour! Don't you want to be here to see that?'

'See what?' asked the passenger, who must have dozed a little during the driver's impassioned speech.

'Don't you want to see your captain being awarded the Medal of Honour?'

'No,' answered the fare, 'I don't think I do.'

'Well, hell,' said the cabby, very surprised, 'what do you want to do?'

'I just want,' said the fare, 'to go home.'

Authorities

'Much has been written in recent years about the possibility of using icebergs as a freshwater source. (Small cubes of ice from the Greenland ice-sheet are already being sold to discerning Americans who like their Scotch to be diluted with pre-industrial ice!) On a vastly greater scale there are plans for towing tabular icebergs from the Ross Sea and other parts of the Antarctic pack-ice belt to areas where there is a desperate water shortage. There are plans to irrigate deserts of western Australia, Peru, Mexico, California and even the Middle East with water from giant bergs towed by tugs.'

Brian John, *The World of Ice*, 1979

'Plans to tow icebergs from the Arctic to solve Britain's desperate water shortage have been rejected in a discussion document by the National Rivers Authority . . . "Towing icebergs to warmer waters should be feasible in other parched areas of the world but would be uneconomic and unworkable here," Mr Jerry-Sherriff, the authority's head of water resources, said yesterday. "Even after moving an iceberg, we would have to find somewhere to berth it, a way to control the rate of melting and collect the water. The environmental impact of a huge iceberg moored off the South Coast would be unimaginable." '

News story by Robert Bedlow,

Daily Telegraph, summer 1992

'*HARMATTAN* – a very dry wind blowing from the interior of Africa to the Atlantic in December, January and February that is said to cause human skin to peel off.'

Robert Hendrickson, *The Ocean Almanac*, 1992

Source Books

John and Julie Batchelor, *In Stanley's Footsteps* (Blandford 1990)

Charles Berlitz, *The Bermuda Triangle* (Grafton 1975)

Ray Bonds, *The Illustrated Dictionary of MODERN AMERICAN WEAPONS* and *The Illustrated Dictionary of MODERN SOVIET WEAPONS* (Salamander Books 1986)

Chris Bonington and Robin Knox-Johnston, *Sea, Ice and Rock* (Hodder and Stoughton 1992)

Richard Brown, *Voyage of the Iceberg* (Bodley Head 1983)

de Marenches and Ockrent, *The Evil Empire* (Sidgwick and Jackson 1988)

Frank Dodman, *Observers SHIPS* (Bloomsbury 1992)

Gale and Hauser, *CHERNOBYL The Final Warning* (Hamish Hamilton 1988)

Haynes and Bojkun, *The Chernobyl Disaster* (Hogarth Press 1988)

Robert Hendrickson, *The Ocean Almanac* (BCA/Helicon 1992)

Brian John, *The World of Ice* (Orbis 1979)

Nicholas Luard, *The Last Wilderness* (Elm Tree 1981)

Eileen MacDonald, *Shoot the Women First* (Fourth Estate 1991)

William H. MacLeish, *The Gulf Stream* (Abacus 1989)

Peter Matthiessen, *African Silences* (HarperCollins 1991)

William Millinship, *FRONTLINE – The Women of the New Russia* (Methuen 1993)

Dervla Murphy, *Cameroon with Egbert* (John Murray 1989)

Shiva Naipaul, *North of South* (André Deutsch 1978)

Conor Cruise O'Brien, *To Katanga And Back* (Hutchinson 1962)

Douglas Phillips-Birt, *Reflections in the Sea* (Nautical Publishing Company 1968)

Piers Paul Read, *ABLAZE – The Story of Chernobyl* (Secker & Warburg 1993)

Reader's Digest 'Discovery' series: *The Frozen World; The Challenge of Africa; Secrets of the Sea* (Aldus 1979)

John Ridgway, *Storm Passage* (Hodder and Stoughton 1975)

Rosenblum and Williamson, *Squandering Eden* (Bodley Head 1987)

Ray Sanderson, *Meteorology at Sea* (Stanford Maritime 1984)

J. M. Scott, *Icebound* (Gordon and Cremonesi 1977)

Richard Snailham, *A Giant among Rivers* (Hutchinson 1976)

Gerry Spiess, *Alone against the Atlantic* (Souvenir Press 1981)

D. A. Taylor, *Introduction to Marine Engineering* (Butterworths 1985)

Jenny Wood, *Icebergs* (Two-Can 1990)

Acknowledgements

As usual, it has been the people who helped who have been the real inspiration, beyond even the authors of the books I have listed. Amongst the people who have helped during the year and more in which I have been at work on this story, I must thank first my colleagues at The Wildernesse School who have given of their time and advice in spite of the challenges of new Grant Maintained status, recent re-designation as a Comprehensive school, and the extremely heavy burdens heaped upon us all by the politicians in the Department of Education and beyond. I would like to thank Chris Prickett and Denise Sheridan of the maths department, whose advice about scales and volumes has been fundamental. Secondly, I must thank Steve Sawyer and Roger Hood for their support, especially in the areas of research amongst CD Roms. Paul Clarke and John Wright of the geography department advised invaluably on the birth and life of icebergs and upon the likely environmental impact of their movement. As always, Barry Wheeler has given freely both advice and anecdote based upon his broad maritime experience.

For an armchair adventurer who has never ventured deeper into Africa than Ceuta on the north coast, I have been fortunate indeed to have the unstinted advice of four men who know the continent better than most. These men, each one a retired big-game hunter, have filled the African sections with touches of vividness springing from

599

their freely offered experience and from equally freely given advice. They are Alan North and Trevor Trennery, and, most especially, Charles Hodgson and Emile Lenferna de la Motte. Without the help of the latter two, and, indeed, the further help of their wives Vera Hodgson and Judy Lenferna de la Motte, *The Iceberg* might well have been a very different – considerably shorter – book. I thank all of these extremely kind advisers most sincerely.

The bulk of the book was written, however, on the Isle of Man. I am very pleased to pay a debt of thanks to Peter Waugh, as promised, for the use of his sitting room as a study, for the advice he offered and the stories he told.

Finally, I must register a different, deeper debt to Debra Jane Curran, and I know I am speaking for many friends and colleagues when I record deep sadness at her untimely death. It amused her a little that she was so much a part of the character of Robin Mariner, and it is slightly ironic that Debbie who was so active and decisive should be commemorated, even in this small way, in a book where Robin does so little. The irony wouldn't have worried Debbie, however; and I must thank Dan Curran for his permission to add these few, inadequate thoughts here.

Peter Tonkin, Sevenoaks and the Isle of Man, 1993/4